Patricia Roenbeck's Futurist
tales of timeless love and fi

Futuristic Romance

Love in another time, another place.

"Is it Rakkad?"

Kolt's head swung toward Aylyn. "You think to find him here, on Annan?"

"Yes. How else would he have known to place me in supposedly unreachable caverns?"

Aylyn watched Kolt's changing expression. She had hoped her information would help him locate Laaryc's life-ender. "You are frowning. What I said didn't help?"

"Yes, it helped. Now I know where to confine my search."

"Then you've believed all along that he is Annanite?"

"Yes."

"Why didn't you tell me? He is *my* enemy, Kolt! *My* enemy! He robbed my best friend of his life." She stormed away and then whirled back to him. "And what of your vow to help me seek vengeance? Does your word mean nothing?"

Cover photograph posed by professional models.

Other *Leisure Books* by Patricia Roenbeck:
GOLDEN TEMPTRESS

PATRICIA ROENBECK

LEISURE BOOKS   **NEW YORK CITY**

A LEISURE BOOK®

October 1992

Published by

Dorchester Publishing Co., Inc.
276 Fifth Avenue
New York, NY 10001

If you purchased this book without a cover you should be aware that this book is stolen property. It was reported as "unsold and destroyed" to the publisher and neither the author nor the publisher has received any payment for this "stripped book."

Copyright © 1992 by Patricia Roenbeck

All rights reserved. No part of this book may be reproduced or transmitted in any form or by any electronic or mechanical means, including photocopying, recording or by any information storage and retrieval system, without the written permission of the Publisher, except where permitted by law.

The name "Leisure Books" and the stylized "L" with design are trademarks of Dorchester Publishing Co., Inc.

Printed in the United States of America.

To David, for your love and belief.

To Jude, Diane, Maryanne, and Peg, for always being there with an ear or a hand—especially in those last frantic days.

Thank you

Chapter One

"You want me to what?"

The Sulian ambassador's party who were taking advantage of a lull in the formalities to stretch their legs stopped and stared at the obviously overwrought Laaryc. Aylyn smiled at them, grabbed Laaryc's arm and led him away from the crowd.

"Life bond with me," she repeated in a husky whisper. "And please keep your voice down."

"Keep my voice down!" Turbulent blue sparks flashed across eyes that, till now, had never been anything but serene. "Out of nowhere you ask me to bond with you for life and you want me to be *quiet*? I think not."

Aylyn grabbed Laaryc's hand and attempted to pull him into the Garden of Colors, but he refused to budge. He seemed not to care that they risked creating a scene in the middle of welcoming ceremonies for the Yrianot envoy. "Laaryc—"

"Don't!" The slender Dianthian put his hands up. "You've said enough." He turned and strode away, only to stop after three steps and face her once again. "This goes beyond any scheme you have ever concocted!" He reached up and yanked an orange leaf from the low-growing vumta tree.

Aylyn sighed. She had expected a reaction from him, but not to this extreme.

"Aylyn. Laaryc." The short, squat, blue-skinned ambassador from Quille drew up next to them. "I just toured the Garden of Colors again." He gestured to the lush and vibrant garden, running along one side of the grounds of the lord director's keep, filled with exotic flowers and trees from various worlds and transplanted on Rhianon.

"Wonderful. Absolutely wonderful. And to think, Aylyn, your father commissioned it just to please your mother. Touching. Absolutely touching." He rubbed his rotund abdomen. "Think I should make my way back to the nourishment tables. Wonderful selection. Just wonderful. Your mother outdid herself, young Aylyn. As always." He squinted his lone green eye. "You think there might be more squizzal left?" he asked hopefully, referring to a favorite Quilleian delicacy.

"Why, yes, Ambassador. Mother set some aside knowing how much you enjoyed them. I'll show you where she hid them."

The ambassador chuckled, a deep gargly sound, and patted her hand. "No need, my dear. No need. You and young Laaryc enjoy the moonlight and the magnificent view. I'll grab one of the servers. She should be able to help me." He chuckled again and shook his bald head. "Of course, Lady Eirriel has more. Always has everything her guests want. Or think they want. Before they want it. Best thing your father did, young Aylyn. Bonding with her. Yes, it was." He rolled his shoulders. "But what else would you expect? Even as a cub, Aubin had an eye for the best. Just because he's Rhianon's lord director, wouldn't expect that to change. Opposite really. Could have chosen one like Purgr of Fargra did."

Aylyn sighed as the ambassador rambled on about the fiasco caused by Purgr's mate at the last function he had attended, nodded her head, and smiled. As daughter of the lord director, Aylyn had grown up among the envoys, ambassadors and councilors who, for one reason or another, sought help or advice from the powerful ruler of the Rhianonian Alliance. Diplomacy was, after all, a necessity to those who would rule. And, since she intended to become the primary councilor to the lord director, she had learned at an

Golden Conquest

early age to smile at the appropriate time, to comment as the need arose and usually she didn't mind observing these formalities.

However, tonight her mind was not on the ceremonies, but on her personal crisis. One that would not be solved as long as the Quilleian ambassador kept her occupied. She spied a server leading a hovering nourishment tray among those who strolled in and around the Garden of Colors. She raised her hand and motioned her over.

"Ambassador," Aylyn said when he took a breath. "Leyl will lead you to the—"

"Ah. Just as efficient as your mother. Indeed you are." He turned to Laaryc who was pacing off to the side. "You, young Laaryc. Hold onto this one. Won't find one like her on your Dianthia. No, indeed."

Laaryc gritted his teeth, smiled, and gave the ambassador a polite bow. "How right you are, Ambassador. As always."

Aylyn noted Laaryc's rising impatience and nodded to Leyl.

"Come with me, Ambassador," the dark-skinned Hemalite purred. "I will see to all your needs."

The ambassador's eye lit up. "All my needs, you say?"

Leyl giggled, took his hand, and led him away.

"I thought he'd never leave," Aylyn said, turning to face Laaryc.

"You may wish he hadn't," Laaryc growled ominously.

"You might be right." She turned toward the keep. "My mother may need me."

His arm shot out and he grabbed her wrist. "You're not going anywhere until I have some answers." He led her into the garden.

"Laaryc, slow down!"

"Slow down. Well, that's a first."

"If you were dressed like this, you'd be forced to take smaller steps, too!"

Laaryc's gaze raked down Aylyn's tall, slender form, and he had to admit that the floor-length, strapless black sheath clung tightly to her ample curves and allowed little room for large steps. "I apologize," he said as he slowed his gait. "I hadn't realized." A moment later, they drew close to the falls and he released her.

For the first time Aylyn felt unable to judge Laaryc's mood and decided that keeping a slight distance, between them would serve her better. She moved to the water's edge and waited.

"Do you realize what you ask of me?" Laaryc began. "Your father would feed me to the kriekors," he exclaimed, referring to the small but deadly creatures found in the dank caves of Mont Kriek, "and watch calmly as they drained my life's energy!" He blanched. "And Lady Eirriel! By all the gods, I think I would rather face the kriekors!"

Aylyn kicked at the tiny rounded prism crystals that surrounded the pool. She had been so certain Laaryc would do as she asked. He always had ever since his arrival on Rhianon shortly before her tenth life cycle and after his fifteenth. A freak Dianthian storm had thrown the water vessel carrying Laaryc's parents against some rocks, and both had died instantly. Timos, chief concile of Dianthia, noticed that the quiet and reserved youth seemed to slip deeper within himself and decided a change of venue might help. He begged assistance from his childhood companion, Eirriel, and her lifebond, Aubin who readily agreed to foster Laaryc, thinking he would be a companion to their son, Alaran.

But, although Laaryc and Alaran did become friends, it was the precociously independent Aylyn who had formed the deeper friendship with the grave and reticent Dianthian. She had walked up to the frightened boy, slipped her hand into his, and demanded that he take her to the falls to see the zliwers who swam in the cool water. He had, and then searchers were sent to find them and return them to the keep. And it continued over the years. Wherever one was, so was the other, and Laaryc's studious hesitancy was the perfect foil for Aylyn's adventurous spontaneity.

Golden Conquest

Until now.

Aylyn's golden eyes darkened, and she kicked again, this time with a force fed by frustration. A spray of crystals thunked into the pond, sending the zliwers that rested on the smooth bottom swimming for calmer waters. Laaryc had to help her. She couldn't bear it if he failed her.

She turned to study the man who had become her closest friend and confidant. Of equal height to her, she knew his slight stature was considered tall for a Dianthian and small for a Rhianonian. His build had never bothered her, though she often wondered if it played a part in his unwillingness to seek friendship other than her and her brother's. She saw him run a shaky hand through his collar-length light brown hair and smiled, struck as always by the beauty of his pale fragility so typically Dianthian and so at odds with the strikingly rugged and bronzed handsomeness of Rhianonian males. She heard his ragged sigh and knew he was searching for a solution to her dilemma. She realized then that it had been unfair of her to beg such a heavy and binding boon of him without explanation.

She drew up next to him, and in a small voice confessed, "I'm afraid, Laaryc."

Chapter Two

Laaryc pulled her to him. His arms circled her back, and he held her close, offering her comfort and protection. His slender hands rubbed the back of her neck.

"Afraid? You, the girl who took on a kilgra to save a lost child?"

"I would gladly face twenty kilgras," she said fiercely. "They can only kill me." She paused, then continued, "It's changed, Laaryc. The dream. He's closer. He almost caught me last night."

He. So that was what was behind all of this. Her mind-toucher. Laaryc didn't know whether to be relieved or further distressed.

Since Aylyn's life cycle of thirteen, a mysterious force had reached out through the night to touch her mind as she slept. Laaryc remembered her telling him about it the day after the first incident, and her insistence that it was more than a dream. "A warm gentle touch. One of friendship. Deep friendship," she had said. He had asked her if she was afraid, and she had laughed and said no. "He won't harm me. Not ever," had been her fierce reply. And he had felt jealous that someone beside himself had laid claim to *his* Aylyn. Over the years as they discussed her mind-toucher, of whom they told no one except Alaran who had quickly dismissed it as an adolescent fantasy, Laaryc had come to the grim realization that *his* Aylyn was not his, but the mind-toucher's. He had known by seeing her face or hearing her voice as she attempted to describe someone she had never seen or heard but only felt.

Laaryc gently tipped her chin up until their eyes met. "All those years ago, when you first shared knowledge of him with me, you assured me he would never harm you. You knew it then, yet now you fear him. Why? What has changed?"

She stepped away from him, and Laaryc fought against viewing her action as a portent of things to come.

"I've always felt his touch as a gentle caress without substance. Like a whisper. Or a puff of air against my cheek. But last night . . . last night was different."

"Different how?" Laaryc asked, then regretted it as he watched her eyes soften with awed remembrance and her fingers brush against her lips.

"I felt him as surely as if he were standing in my chamber with me. The strength of his hands. The hardness of his chest. The heat of his mouth. He . . ."

Laaryc's heart contracted painfully. Gods, he did not want to hear more!

"He means to have me, Laaryc."

Laaryc felt her words like a physical blow to his stomach. That he had known all along did nothing to stop the pain that smote his heart. But his voice revealed none of his torment as he said, "You have said he is goodness and strength. Nobility and courage. If he is all you have described, he is someone worth having."

Aylyn wrung her hands together. "Gods, don't you understand? He could be standing in a chamber with me and I would not know him unless he called my name."

Laaryc frowned. "Are you worried that he may be unfit to look upon?"

"I'm worried that he *knows* me! With that knowledge, he can control me."

"You think he would use his gifts against you?" Laaryc asked, stunned. It was something he had not considered.

Aylyn shook her head. "His honor would not allow it."

"Then how can he control you? I know you. Your parents and brother know you, and none of us can control you."

"He has touched my soul, Laaryc. He knows all that I am. All that I want to be. I fear that if I go to him, I'll never be free again."

"Free? An odd choice of word."

"Odd, yes. But perfect. His feelings are too strong, too intense. He'll consume me and I'll be lost." She stretched out her hands in a gesture of helpless frustration. "I know it doesn't make sense, but it is what I fear. And it is why I asked that you life bond with me. I sought safety in your embrace."

"Here now, what's this?"

The two spun around to see Aylyn's brother approaching, his green eyes narrowed in speculation. "She didn't take it well, did she, my friend?"

Laaryc groaned. Just what he needed. Alaran tweaking him about his return to Dianthia. Something he had been unable to mention to Aylyn, especially now. She would look at his leaving as a deliberate desertion. He scuffed at the prism crystals. Life was very complicated at times.

Alaran stood with his hands on his lean hips, his feet spread apart, and a look of expectation on his chiseled face. When Laaryc just continued to look as if he were facing a sonulator's deadly beam, Alaran turned to his sister. "Surely you're not holding it against him. He has, after all, devoted nigh on ten years of his life to you. It is only fair that he return home."

Aylyn blanched as the import of Alaran's words struck her. She whirled on Laaryc. "Return home? To Dianthia?"

Alarmed by his sister's reaction, Alaran looked at the smaller man. "Gods! You haven't told her."

"No, he has not," Aylyn ground out between clenched teeth, then stormed a short distance away.

"But I thought—"

Golden Conquest

Laaryc interrupted him. "We had other things to discuss."

Alaran started to back away. "Er, formal nourishment is about to be served. It's why I searched for you." He glanced over at Aylyn. "Mother noticed her absence." Then back at Laaryc. "You two talk, I'll make excuses."

"Coward," Laaryc said softly.

Alaran touched his hand to his head. "When it comes to Aylyn's temper, always." His full mouth twisted in a sheepish smile. "It was not my intention to make your telling her difficult. I ask your pardon."

Laaryc shook his head. "None is needed. My departure has been known to all but Aylyn for the past eightnight. Gods, but I wish I didn't have to go. Especially now."

"Then don't. You know you will always be welcome in our home. Father has already spoken of a post for you."

"Lord Aubin offered it to me last evening. I turned him down."

"How did he take that? Not many turn down a request by Rhianon's lord director."

"He understood my need to return to Dianthia. It is after all my home."

Alaran placed his hand on Laaryc's slim shoulder. "You will be missed, my friend." His green eyes darkened as his gaze swung to his sister. "By Aylyn most of all." Alaran dropped his hand. "I will see you inside."

Laaryc nodded and turned to study Aylyn. He could not help but smile at the picture she presented. Garbed in a formal gown, her long golden hair pulled back from her face by two combs of black crystal shot through with silver, she was ferociously tossing prism crystals into the water. Her outward appearance of a perfect lady was enhanced by her violent actions of an outraged child. It was a sight he would carry in his memory forever. He sighed and moved toward her. He had best get on with his explanation.

Patricia Roenbeck

Aylyn threw another crystal into the water, wishing it were at Laaryc's head instead. How dare he hold back news of such import? Had he not called her his dearest friend? Was it all a farce? If he cared for her, he would have shared his thoughts with her, as she had shared hers. Suddenly it struck her. She stared down at the remaining crystals in her hand and let them fall through her fingers. Gods, he was leaving her! How would she bear it?

"I'm sorry I didn't tell you."

"Were you even going to?" she asked, her eyes not leaving her now empty hand.

"Yes, of course." His mouth turned up in a chiding curve. "If you remember, I asked you to meet me here."

At once, the anger fled her eyes replaced by chagrin. "And I didn't give you a chance. I'm sorry. Once again, I put my problems before yours."

"I was glad for the reprieve"—his eyes twinkled—"until I heard what you wanted."

"Must you go?"

"I must." He held her close, his hand tangling in her waist-length hair. "Your parents know and agree. It is time."

Aylyn pulled her head back so that she could study his face. Her heart lurched at the bleakness in his eyes. "You are so unhappy here?"

"Never believe that I've been unhappy. From the first, your family and you, most especially you, have done all to make me feel I belonged here. But I don't. I am Dianthian. My place is on Dianthia. And now I will bring the knowledge I have garnered from my time on Rhianon to my people, as your mother, Lady Eirriel, did with what she learned from her time aboard the *Celestial*."

Aylyn had often heard the story of her mother's capture twenty-four years ago, by the Blagdenian commodore, Kedar, who had landed on Dianthia with his invasion force, bringing death to all who opposed him. Eirriel's father, the primary olden of Dianthia, had

Golden Conquest

been executed, and when Eirriel refused Kedar's suit, he sent her to his world, thinking to offer her to his Blagdenian ruler.

But she had never reached Blagden as Aubin, then captain of the Empyreal Protectorate's finest fleetship, the *Celestial*, had rescued her. Eirriel stayed with him until Kedar reentered her life, and she exchanged her life for Aubin's. She had made that decision without hesitation, for she had come to love the fierce Rhianonian with an all-consuming passion. Eventually, Kedar was destroyed, and Eirriel, using the knowledge she had gained during her time on the *Celestial*, helped improved the lot of Dianthia and her people.

"Chief Concile Timos has asked that I come. He is my leader. And I must go," Laaryc finished quietly.

"Is it so easy to leave us then?"

"Easy?" Laaryc looked into Aylyn's loving eyes and his breath caught in his throat. "No, my Aylyn, it is not easy." He touched his mouth to hers, gently, tenderly, quickly. "It is perhaps the most difficult task I will ever be called upon to do."

"Oh, Laaryc . . ." Aylyn threw her arms around his slim shoulders and buried her face in his neck. "I cannot bear it. I cannot."

Laaryc rested his head on hers. "But you will. As will I." After a moment, he took her hand. "Now come, your parents wait for you."

"You won't leave me to face the rest of the ceremonies alone?"

Laaryc heard the underlying edge in her voice and fought against changing his plans and remaining on Rhianon. If he thought her fear of the mind-toucher anything other than the normal dread of an independent young woman faced with sharing her needs and wants with a yet unknown man, he would have. But once she conquered her fear, as Laaryc knew she would, he believed she would once again see her mind-toucher as the familiar reassuring presence he had always been.

"Leave you when you need me most?" Laaryc teased. "Never."

Patricia Roenbeck

But that is just what you are doing, she replied silently, then thrust the thought from her mind. Laaryc needed her now, and she would be there for him as he had always been there for her. As for the mind-toucher. She was safe from him for now. But she knew her safety was fragile at best, for when he wanted her, he would find her.

Chapter Three

Kolt, laedan of Annan, stood in the darkened antechamber, looking down on the garden he had ordered created. He saw Aylyn there as she would one day be: blond hair, thick and straight to the middle of her back, with wisp bangs; eyes, oval and brilliant as golden golithium crystal beneath finely arched brows; high cheekbones; pert nose; and full sensuously curved lips turned up in a welcoming smile as she walked toward him. The off-the-shoulder gown flowed over the inviting swell of her bosom to a tiny waist and concealed the long, slender legs he was certain she possessed. As was his wont, when he thought of Aylyn his mind reached out, searching for her.

Ah, there she was. Carefully, he slipped into her dreams. He saw her turn and then he saw her run.

He sighed and gave chase, his touch following her. Slowly. Persistently. Until he reached her. He felt her fear then of what he offered, of who he was. He was saddened by it, but not concerned. He knew it would not last, and deny it though she would, she knew it, too.

"Laedan, this just arrived!"

The hand touching his shoulder commanded his attention, and yanked him from her. Kolt turned and faced the intruder, his blue eyes dark with anger.

"Yes, what is so important that it could not wait until I was in the council chambers?"

Patricia Roenbeck

The young Annanite who had been Kolt's personal server for seven years took a step back. "I beg forgiveness, Kolt. I—I thought you would want to see this."

Kolt took a deep breath and calmed himself. "Forgive me, Dakkar. I had my mind on another matter and—"

"Ah." Dakkar's responsibilities made him privy to almost all portions of the laedan's life, and there was very little that Dakkar did not know. "You were thinking of Aylyn again?"

Kolt smiled. "Yes, my friend, I was thinking of her again. Now, what do you have for me."

The slight, dark-haired Annanite handed his leader the message. "It's from the Protectorate." He paused, then the question came out in a rush of hope, "Do you think they agreed this time? Are we accepted as a member?"

Kolt winced at Dakkar's innocent enthusiasm. Entrance into the Empyreal Protectorate's hallowed ranks was not easily gained.

Four centuries ago, representatives of six powerful worlds had met on the planet Hakon, sharing one common denominator—overpopulation. To protect native populations of different planets from elimination by unscrupulous invaders searching for new worlds to inhabit, it was decided that the six would unite and form an alliance of explorers. Under the standard of the newly formed Empyreal Protectorate, they traversed the galaxy, searching for new worlds to colonize, offering peaceful co-existence or inclusion in their membership to those planets already populated.

Over time, the purpose of the Protectorate changed, and it became the governing force of the galaxy. Laws, proposed, voted on, and passed on Hakon, the main terminal of the Empyreal Protectorate, were universally accepted. Though each member planet maintained its own language, laws, and customs, it was agreed that Hakonese would be the official language. Each newly

Golden Conquest

accepted planet would be expected to master Hakonese and adapt Hakonese time measurements and customs at the time of their joining the Protectorate.

Colony status placed a world under the aegis of the Protectorate. For this privilege, an annual percentage of all the colony's revenues and first choice of all the colony's minerals, ores, and goods were given to the Protectorate. Once a colony attained member status, the percentage was reduced to a mere token payment, and the Protectorate, like every other buyer, had to bid for its former colony's products.

To enjoy all the privileges, benefits, and respect due to the now 150 members of the Empyreal Protectorate, more than fifty colonies, Annan among them, sought to be recognized. A feat not readily accomplished, as Kolt had learned many times.

The Protectorate's reasons for refusing Annan membership were varied, and, to Kolt's way of thinking, unfair. To them, Annan was an upstart mining colony, with no real claim to member status. After all, they argued, the occupants of Annan who called themselves Annanites were nothing more than descendants of the original harvesters who came from other worlds to harvest the mines. Over the years some harvesters left, and others stayed and intermingled with newcomers to the planet. This phenomenon reoccurred down through the generations until no one feature, no one color, no one belief could identify someone as an Annanite. Yet those factors alone, labeled one Annanite. Therefore, Annan was a true colony by the Protectorate's own definition. The denial that they were was only an excuse.

Kolt knew the true reason for their refusal was because of the Protectorate's first claim policy and the enormous percentage they received from the ores and crystal Annan harvested and sold.

Kolt looked at Dakkar's outstretched hand, holding the message that contained the answer to his people's dreams. He took it and moved away. Breaking the seal, he unrolled it and glanced at it, quick to note that it

Patricia Roenbeck

had been sent coded, an indication there was more to it than the expected denial. He looked at it once more, then closed his eyes.

In the blackness behind his lowered lids the words formed, a bright glaring white. He thought once, and the harsh color muted. The words danced in and out of the shadows of his mind, fading to nothing and reappearing as they should be. Within moments he had decoded the letter.

Kolt opened his eyes. "Another rejection." *And another missing shipment of Khrystallyn*, he added silently. Gods curse whoever was behind the hijackings of Annan's ships!

Dakkar gaped at him. "You know what it said? Already? I wish I could do that. It is a miracle this gift you possess."

Kolt was an extraordinarily powerful mind-toucher. Tasks such as decoding messages were mere child's play to him. He had practiced many simple chores as a youth to help hone and refine the skills he had been born with. Skills he had always known to keep hidden until the time was right.

That time had arrived, as Kolt had known it would, when his life cycle was but twelve and his name was still Boruk.

It was then that Kedar, the hated commodore of the Blagdenian invasion force, calling himself Lamd, arrived on Annan not to conquer, but to destroy. Within an eight-night, Kedar, having wrested control from the ailing laedan, Tiala, had appointed himself laedan. Mercilessly, Kedar increased the tithe paid to the laedan. Those who refused to pay he publicly and violently executed. Their crops burned, their mines bombed, and their tithe continually increased, the Annanites soon succumbed to despair.

The lone exceptions were a common hawker of goods, Koltrax, and his young brother, Boruk. Together they formed a force of resisters. Aided by Boruk's ability to touch the minds of Kedar-Lamd's men, they were able to thwart many an arrest and execution.

Golden Conquest

But it was not enough. Annan and her people were dying.

Two months after Kedar-Lamd's arrival, Aubin, captain of the E.P.F. *Celestial*, was sent by the Protectorate to investigate rumors of Blagdenian involvement on Annan. Expecting to meet secretly with Tiala, Aubin was instead greeted by Kedar-Lamd's men and captured. Koltrax, believing the Protectorate to be Annan's only hope, set out to rescue Aubin and was himself seized and executed.

Aubin, wounded and near death, was released when Eirriel, Aubin's lifebond and Kedar's former Dianthian captive, offered herself to her enemy in exchange for her beloved Aubin's life. Unwilling to risk losing Eirriel, an unexpected bonus in his conquest of Annan, Kedar departed a ravished and depleted Annan for Dianthia.

The Protectorate ordered Aubin and his crew to assist the Annanites in restoring their ruined world, but the order proved unnecessary. For Boruk, despite his young age, used his mind-touching skills to reopen blocked mines, uncover hidden nourishment stores, and locate missing people with a mere thought. Boruk, knowing that Aubin offered direction and not control, only turned to him for guidance in the matter of governing. A quick and lasting friendship formed between Boruk, the child who chose to become a leader, and Aubin, the man who had no choice but to rule.

Now, twenty-three years later, Boruk was called Kolt as tribute to the love he had for his brother, and he was laedan of a prosperous and thriving Annan, and of a proud and energetic people. He was wise enough to know it had been his gifts that had made it so.

"And so it is a miracle, this power that I have, though ofttimes it seems anything but." Kolt sighed. "Please tell my councilors I will be delayed. There are matters in this missive that I must address at once."

"Oh?" Dakkar's brows arched. "What matters?"

Kolt laughed. "Your thirst for knowledge is unceasing, Dakkar, and much to be admired. But I fear in this it must go unquenched. It *was* coded."

Dakkar slapped his forehead. "Of course. And that means none save you can know. I will go and deliver your message. Shall I return?"

Kolt shook his head. "It is not necessary. I believe I can find my council chambers by myself."

"I did not mean that you could not." At once Dakkar looked apologetic. "I meant no offense."

"None taken. I was teasing. You must learn to laugh, my young friend."

"I will try, Laedan," Dakkar said fervently, then laughed. "See."

Kolt just shook his head as Dakkar bowed and left, his attempt at laughter following him. When the door closed behind the shorter man, Kolt gave in to the rage that had been building inside him since he had read the message.

Khrystallyn! The Protectorate now claimed *all* of Annan's Khrystallyn! Free! Kolt swept his desk clear. It was their due they claimed! Arrogant, thieving bastards! Did they think it came to Kolt free? Did they care not at all that harvesters lost their lives braving the treacherous peaks of Quixtallyn Heights in search of the rare mirror crystals? Or that grinders who, despite the best precautions, breathed in deadly amounts of minute slivers that sliced up their lungs as they ground the rough crystal into powder? He snorted. No. All they wanted, all they cared about, was Khrystallyn!

Fifteen years ago during a trek beneath Quixtallyn Heights, Nnels, a cave walker and part-time alchemist, discovered a vein of unusually brilliant silver-colored crystal. To his dismay, the crystal he dubbed Khrystallyn was too fragile to be used as construction material. Undaunted, he persisted in his attempts to prove the Khrystallyn useful. He soon found that when ground into a powder and combined with common minerals, ores, or herbs, the Khrystallyn underwent a startling metamorphosis. Immediately, he had petitioned Kolt for the rights to harvest Quixtallyn Heights.

Golden Conquest

"When mixed with oralianinon," Nnels had explained excitedly, "it will cure the Zxyon plague."

"You are certain?" Kolt asked. Zxyon plague was always fatal and had been known to wipe out entire populations. Galaxy-wide, healers, medics, and scientists had been futilely seeking a cure for it for years.

Nnels was atwitter. "Yes. Yes. I'm most certain. And, Laedan, the best is yet to come."

The thin drawn alchemist, his green eyes alight with a fanatical gleam, reached into his pocket and withdrew a neutralizer. Kolt, seeing the weapon, cursed. He had been so engrossed in Nnels' presentation that he had let his guard down. Unable to believe the old one would actually fire, Kolt was nonetheless prepared to throw up a physical opaque shield around himself within the space of a breath should it prove necessary. Warily, Kolt watched Nnels approach.

"Now, hold this." Nnels absently shoved the weapon at Kolt, who felt alternately relieved and foolish.

Nnels continued across the chamber and proceeded to assemble a target. "Fire the weapon here," Nnels said, pointing to a center circle.

Kolt, noting the weapon's setting on maximum, started to slide the control down.

"No! No!" Nnels shouted. "Just as it is!"

Kolt quirked a brow. "Just as it is?"

"Yes. Yes. Just as it is."

"If you are sure," Kolt muttered skeptically. He raised the weapon, gave a quick mind-touch to assure that no one was within range when the beam went through the target on the wall and into the next chamber, and fired.

The target absorbed the beam!

Kolt's mouth gaped. He knew it was an inappropriate response, but couldn't help it. Nnels' remarkable discovery would give Annan the bargaining power it needed to attain membership in the Protectorate!

Nnels, his eyes still on the target, chattered feverishly, "Does that every time. Don't know how yet, but it does. I mixed the Khrystallyn with all the alloys and ores used in the construction of the fleetships and this is what happened. Every time! Works the same with a sonulator blast." He looked at Kolt. "Can't be made anywhere but here."

Kolt rushed to Nnels and pounded him on the back. "Well done, Nnels! Annan, and you, of course, will be rich."

"Rich? Hmm. Thought to give it away."

"Give it away!" Kolt choked. "That would be your right, of course."

"Just can't see charging a fee to save lines. Lost my lifebond to the plague. Offspring, too."

Kolt, who had seen a bright future for Annan purchased with his share of the profits, groaned. As laedan, he could insist Nnels sell the Khrystallyn, as twenty-five percent of the profits would, by his position as laedan, be Kolt's. But Kolt had never abused his power or his gifts, and he would not start now.

He nodded. "As you will, Nnels. The Khrystallyn is yours."

"Course"—Nnels chewed on his lower lip—"can't see what's wrong with charging for the metal enhancer, can you?"

Kolt laughed and granted an immediate and exclusive charter that made Nnels the sole owner of the Khrystallyn formula, mines, and processing plants. A charter that could only be passed on to his heirs and could never be sold or given away to anyone but his heirs.

The Protectorate, as Kolt had known they would, claimed a right to all of it, but Kolt had refused. By their own law, all they were entitled to was thirty percent, an amount too little for them and too much for Kolt.

And now, after more than twelve years of perfect service, the Protectorate invoked a little-known noncompliance clause to demand the production formula and grinding plants be turned over to them. Kolt, they insisted, had invalidated their agreement

Golden Conquest

when the contracted shipments of Khrystallyn had not arrived. The hijackings, the Protectorate said, were his problem. The only way Kolt had been able to prevent the Protectorate from enforcing their supposed right was by promising them double the original percentages.

A promise that would cut greatly into the profits Kolt received and in turn used for the betterment of his people. A promise he was having difficulty meeting because there had been a sudden and unforeseen change in management. Noble and honest Nnels had fallen victim to a fatal accident shortly after life-bonding with Iilde, a much younger woman. Since neither Kolt nor his councilors could prove Iilde responsible for Nnels' life-ending, all rights to the Khrystallyn were now in the hands of the grasping and avaricious woman.

Kolt's long powerful legs carried him quickly across the room. A brief thought and the doors swept open, and he stepped out onto the terrace. How did the Protectorate expect him to purchase needed nourishment supplies if not with profit from the sale of the powder? Did they think he could nourish his people on the crystal they harvested? Or did they believe he had the power to make crystal into nourishment? Kolt's full lips turned up in a bittersweet smile. Not that he hadn't tried.

He scanned the horizon, taking in the sights and sounds of the bustling city and the majestic Quixtallyn Heights. The gods knew he was constantly trying to improve the straits of his people. The giant dome had helped—a dome patterned after those of Rhianon, Aubin's homeworld.

During Annan's reconstruction, Aubin had suggested expanding Inner Sumal's boundaries to include the barren wasteland at the foot of the mountains. With the domed environment artificially controlled, the dry earth became fertile, and for the first time in generations, the people of Annan were not forced to barter their goods for nourishment.

Patricia Roenbeck

A claim that would not be true for long, Kolt thought bitterly, raking his hand through his thick dark hair which reached well below his shoulders. Annan's population had flourished along with its people and the nourishment yield had fallen to just above adequate. Unless Kolt could expand the domes, time would see his people once again begging to eat. And to expand the domes, he needed supplies purchased from the sale of Khrystallyn.

A shout below drew him from his thoughts, and he waved to the crowd gathered in the courtyard of the keep. His gaze turned skyward for a brief moment. Ah, it was almost time. Again he waved to those below, his frown replaced, like theirs, by a smile of childish expectation.

When Aubin had first mentioned the dome, Kolt had quickly recognized that it would serve a dual purpose—the feeding of the populace in body and in spirit. Like Aubin's city of Loridan, Inner Sumal had been mapped out so that it lay directly below the path of the sun, and like Rhianon, Annan had an abundance of crystal. Since Kedar-Lamd's sanctuary had been destroyed, a new home for the laedan of Annan, under Aubin's guidance, was constructed out of the purest prism crystal. The dome over the keep was a blend of grounded prism crystal and transparent deurronn.

And so now, when the sun reached its highest point, Inner Sumal became ablaze with a rainbow of color that radiated outward from the Crystal Keep. Even as Kolt was remembering the city's origins, the sun reached its zenith, and he gasped, a gasp magnified a hundredfold by the Annanites who watched.

The sky suddenly lit up with colors, their shades and brilliance unsurpassed by anything Kolt could have imagined. The play of colors swirled across the sky and danced up to the dome where they were reflected groundwards once again in a brilliant and dazzling choreography of light. It lasted less than a moment, as the angle of the sun's beams no longer produced the desired affect. But to all who viewed it, the briefness of the display only created within them an eagerness for the morrow. And that had been Kolt's true motive for constructing the dome.

"Laedan! Laedan! Laedan!"

The chant rose to greet him as the people paid homage to the man who had never disappointed them, not even as a child. Kolt waved and smiled in recognition of their tribute, at once pleased and discomfitted by the tremendous love they had for him. Only the gods knew if he was truly worthy of it and, as disloyal as it might be, he couldn't help but wonder if they would still love him when their nourishment became scarce.

He stepped back within his antechamber and closed the doors. His councilors would be waiting for the news. News he had hoped he would not have had to impart. As he crossed the chamber, he saw the mess his anger had caused. With one thought, papers, writing instruments, a miniature version of the keep sculpted by a young Annanite and given to him on his life celebration, rose from the ground and returned to their appropriate places on the desk.

That done, he closed his eyes again and vanished.

Chapter Four

Kolt reappeared in his sleeping chamber. He looked over his shoulder at the door leading to the antechamber he had just left and counted the steps his *actualizing* had saved him. Twenty. Maybe twenty-five. He shook his head. He should have walked. Crossing to the large black crystal wardrobe that stood against the far wall, he gave thanks to all the gods that Naydir had not been around to witness his little hop. His friend would have teased him unmercifully.

Thoughts of Naydir turned Kolt's attention back to the Khrystallyn, since Naydir was away seeking clues to the hijackings, and then to the upcoming council meeting. His mind on what he would say, on his councilors' reactions to another denial as well as his own little surprise, he paid little attention to the apparel he withdrew from the wardrobe.

Not that it mattered. All his garments were of a quality and cut that enhanced his broad shoulders, lean waist, and sinewy thighs. Quickly and efficiently, he pulled on the dark blue leggings and matching long-sleeved, blousy shirt, then slipped his arms through the sleeveless, waisted jerkin of matching oogala hide. A few tugs at the thongs at the side molded it to his shape, but as always, he opted to only loosely secure the ones that crisscrossed up the front. He was just bending down to lace up the knee-high hide boots when he realized he was not alone.

He straightened.

"You value your life so little, my friend?" a deep husky voice taunted from the shadows.

At once Kolt smiled. "Naydir! You return at last."

The tall, slender man stepped from the shadows and met Kolt halfway. They embraced, the two men similar in height and demeanor yet opposite in coloring and in form. Kolt was dark, his skin the color of honey, his eyes the brilliant blue of safirium; while Naydir was fair, his shoulder-length wavy hair a burnished gold, his eyes the color of amber and his skin the color of cream. Kolt's broad muscles were well evidenced whether garbed or not, while Naydir's lean, wiry strength went unremarked until encountered. They clapped each other heartily on the back.

"Well come, my friend. Your journey was fair?"

"The winds were mild and of no consequence," Naydir replied.

Kolt arched a dark brow. "The *winds* were mild?"

Naydir met Kolt's inquiring gaze. "All else was not."

Kolt sighed and ran a hand across his neatly trimmed beard. He had expected disheartening news from Naydir, and, fate plague him, it would seem his expectations were to be met. Seeking to delay the inevitable dismal report, Kolt turned the conversation to a safer subject. Or so he thought.

"How long were you skulking about my chambers?"

"Since before you *actualized*," came the quiet reply.

Kolt started. More than twenty minutes had passed since he had teleported into his chambers. More than enough time for him to have been taken or killed.

"You did not hear me?" Naydir asked, raising one fair brow.

"No," Kolt replied grimly.

Not feeling the touch of Naydir's mind was not the reason for Kolt's grimace. Since Naydir's shipwreck on Annan five years ago and Kolt's pulling him from the burning wreckage, Kolt had never once been able to read him. He was, however, privy to what he called "common chattering ground," the place where immediate thoughts and reactions occurred, and in time of great need he could and did touch Naydir there. But beyond that, Naydir's mind was blocked behind an unfamiliar and impenetrable mental barrier.

In the beginning, it had been the source of much discussion between the two men who discovered they were but four life cycles apart and who had quickly become fast friends. All memory of his life before the crash lost to him, Naydir had desperately wanted Kolt to unlock the secret of his past. But the few times Kolt had tried to break through the mental barrier, Naydir experienced great pain, and Kolt withdrew, leaving the barrier intact. Forced to rely on his instinct and the man Naydir had proven himself to be over the years, Kolt had long since given up wondering why even Naydir's present-day memories were shielded from him and he accepted that he was mind-blind when it came to his friend. Naydir still longed for the day when his shield would dissolve and he would know of his life before Annan.

No, it was not that Kolt had been unable to touch Naydir that troubled him; it was that he had not heard him, either. Not his breath, not the rustle of his clothes. Nothing. And that could have meant his death had it been anyone else.

Naydir watched the play of emotions over Kolt's features and knew that further words were unnecessary. From the moment of his awakening after the crash, Naydir had felt it his duty to teach the ruler of Annan that he must never rely on his mind-touching abilities alone. He must listen with his ears as well. Luckily, the unknown assailant who had thrice in as many eight-nights, attempted to assassinate Kolt had been far from silent. The reason for the attacks were unknown, although Naydir suspected they were connected with the missing Khrystallyn shipments and was conducting his own private investigation. But until he found the assassin, Kolt had to remain on his guard. Silence could

Golden Conquest

be learned, if one was skilled enough. Naydir was proof of that.

The lesson taught, Naydir now sought to rid his friend of his scowl.

"Were you too tired to walk to your chambers?" Naydir gave Kolt's firmly muscled shoulder a solid punch. "You'll become as weak as a newly birthed yiichi cub from lack of exercise."

As Naydir had planned, Kolt responded to the taunt. But his response was more than Naydir had expected as Kolt spun quickly on the balls of his feet, grabbed Naydir's arm and with a brilliantly executed move, sent him flying across the room to land gently on Kolt's sleeper.

"At least this newly birthed yiichi has good aim."

"I will thank the gods daily," came the muffled reply as Naydir struggled to untangle himself from the coverings and protective screening that had fallen over him. "Damn you for a comfort-loving zifra! Kolt, curse you! Help me out of here!"

Kolt, barely able to contain his laughter, quickly complied, and soon Naydir was on his feet. The older man yanked at his twisted jerkin, then glared at Kolt as he gave another shout of laughter. When Naydir had righted his apparel, he crossed to the table and poured two goblets of sylva, the blood-red juice of the axsta tree fermented and mixed with the potent gyps ale, and aged. He handed one to Kolt.

"You were going to tell me why you were too tired to walk."

At once Kolt sobered. "Not too tired, Naydir. Rather too angered. I received word that we were denied membership in the Protectorate yet again."

"And what excuse did they give this time?"

"The same. None."

Naydir knew Kolt well enough to know that the rejection alone had not caused him to be so distracted that he had dropped his guard. "There is more?"

A muscle ticked in Kolt's lean cheek, and his eyes darkened as he ground out, "Yes, there is more. The last shipment of Khrystallyn never reached them. They question that it was sent at all."

"They accuse us of thievery?" Naydir was stunned. Kolt's reputation as a man of honor was above reproach.

Kolt nodded curtly. "The shipments disappeared without a trace, ship and all. They have scanned the routes and can detect no sign of debris. And now, they will allow us to prove our honor by giving them double the Khrystallyn. When it is ready, they will provide an escort."

"Do they think us so ignorant that we did not send an escort?"

"They think the escort escorted it elsewhere," Kolt replied dryly.

"It is a possibility."

"Yes, and your investigation of the missing shipments?"

"Turned up nothing," Naydir reported gravely. "This recent shipment is not the only item to turn up missing."

Kolt looked up in question.

"The man I assigned to work at the harvesting plant has failed to report to his duty station for three days."

"About the time the shipment left." Kolt paused. "We have an informant close to us. Possibly within the keep."

Naydir nodded. "So I have concluded."

"We must solve this. Our very economy depends on our Khrystallyn trade."

"And if we give the Protectorate their Khrystallyn, will that insure Annan's acceptance the next time you petition for entrance?"

"No."

"What will you do?"

Kolt took a long swallow of the icy brew. "I will ask Iilde. Again."

Naydir sighed. "It will do no good. My other news is that her position remains firm. You want the Khrystallyn. She wants you."

Golden Conquest

"Arrugh!" Kolt hurled the goblet across the room and watched it shatter against the black crystal wall. "I will not bond with Iilde. I will not!"

Naydir studied his friend over the brim of his goblet. "You still believe Aylyn will come?"

"Yes, but even if I am wrong, I cannot bring myself to commit the rest of my life to Iilde."

"Not even for Annan?"

"Not even for Annan."

Chapter Five

The councilors were in an uproar which could be heard through the heavy chamber doors and halfway down the long corridor. Kolt grimaced. Naydir scowled.

"Dakkar has broken the news."

"So it would seem."

Naydir's eyes darkened. "You trust him too well."

"He is young and the news distressed him. As his life cycle increases . . ."

"It has already reached twenty-two, Kolt. He is frail of body, not mind. He should have learned discretion by now."

Kolt held up his hand. "Cease, my friend. I agree and I will have words with him but after the chamber is free of my councilors. Dakkar is easily crushed."

"And if his free-flowing tongue aids the assassin, it will be you who will be crushed. Your lifeblood which will be spilt. Not Dakkar's."

"With these two"—Kolt gestured to the large powerfully built guards who followed a few feet behind him—"the chances of that happening are slim." He stopped walking a moment, turned, and studied them. "They are new. How many have you now?"

"Not enough," Naydir growled. And to his way of thinking it did not matter that the elite force he had assembled to protect Kolt were some of the finest mercenaries in the galaxy or were champions of hand-to-hand combat and highly skilled in all forms of weaponry. Though they had readily pledged their lifelong loyalty to Kolt, they still weren't enough to protect him.

But he had to admit, the sight of them in uniform was daunting, as he had planned. The black boots, leggings, and long-sleeved shirt were cut in such a fashion that none would doubt the steely muscles that lay beneath them. And lest anyone question to whom they owed their allegiance, on the back of their white sleeveless jerkin was emblazoned a black kilgra caught in mid-leap, its razor-sharp white teeth bared, its claws extended. The four-legged, uni-horned Rhianonian feline was Kolt's symbol. It was chosen during the time of reconstruction of Annan when Aubin had said that Kolt reminded him of a young male kilgra trying to prove itself and not letting anything stop it. It was on the banners that flew over the Crystal Keep, the window coverings in the Great Hall and now, on the backs of those who would fight to the death for the Annanite leader.

Kolt arched a brow at Naydir. "How many is not enough?"

"Twenty."

"Um, twenty. Who pays for them?" Kolt asked, lights dancing in his eyes. "The uniform looks costly. Their weapons as well." When Naydir's eyebrows grew together, Kolt knew he should cease his teasing. After all, it was his life Naydir was seeking to protect, but he couldn't control the urge to needle Naydir. "Pleasing to the eye, though. How think you I would look in them?"

"Kolt," Naydir began darkly.

"Peace, my friend," Kolt said, putting up his hand. "You are too serious of late. I found I could not resist teasing you. It was unfair and I beg your forgiveness."

Naydir smiled. "And I yours. If I appear overly serious, it is that I cannot rid my mind of this assassin."

He paused. "As I cannot help but wish he would plague your mind more than he does."

"He does, Naydir. But I cannot dwell on him all the time. Not when there are other more serious matters to attend to."

"More serious than your life?"

Kolt had no response to that. After a moment they reached the council chamber, and Kolt nodded to the keeper of the chamber, who pushed open the doors. The silence was instantaneous as ten pairs of eyes turned.

"The Laedan of Annan and Councilor of Inner Sumal," the keeper of the chamber announced.

Those councilors not already standing did so as Kolt and Naydir entered.

"Day's passing to all of you. If you would." Kolt gestured to the seats at the semicircular table.

The five women and five men representing six of the seven major sektors and the work forces of hawkers, users, growers, and harvesters took their seats. They waited expectantly as Kolt and Naydir settled themselves at the small table situated, at the open end of the large *U*. Kolt's two guards remained standing at readiness, one on either side of the doors.

Before Kolt could speak, a knock came and Dakkar entered, the large and heavily stocked serving tray hovering at his side. Quietly, he made his way to the back of the room to await the councilors' requests for nourishment.

"You all are aware," Kolt began, "of the result of our latest bid to the Protectorate. I ask that you not despair. Should the gods smile kindly on us, our next one will be accepted."

Luthias, the portly councilor of the sektor of Mayrald, got to his feet, his anger made obvious by the deepening green flush creeping over his normally pale complexion. "It will not and well you know it."

Kolt turned his intense gaze on the irate councilor. "I *know* nothing. The whims of the Protectorate are known only to those who govern it."

Golden Conquest

"That was the same gibberish you spouted the last time. And the time before that. And before that. Know you this, Ladean, I will accept it no longer. I demand that you—"

Kolt stood. His hands spread on the table before him, he leaned toward Luthias. "You demand? You who cringed in your keep while Lamd tortured and tithed your people into poverty? Ah, yes." Kolt straightened. "I had forgotten. You were restrained during that time, were you not?" When an answer was not readily given, Kolt demanded one. "Were you not?"

"Yes, Laedan," came the sputtering and damning reply. "It was as you said."

"I ask you once again, Luthias, that all may bear witness. You were detained within your keep and unable to come to the aid of those you had sworn to protect?"

"I have already given my answer."

"I would hear it again."

"Yes, damn you! I was detained within my keep and unable to see to my people's protection. There. I have answered you twice. Now *I* want an answer. What purpose is there in bringing up the past?"

"An answer you want?" Kolt moved away from his table. "An answer I'll give." He stopped in front of the older man. In a schooled and chilling voice that gave no hint to the pleasure he felt, Kolt said, "Luthias of Mayrald, I formally charge that you have twice forsworn the most sacred oath of councilor."

"Forsworn my oath? Bah, what foolishness is this?"

Kolt arched a brow at the councilor. "Foolishness? Those whom you did not protect, think you they—"

"I have ever protected my people!"

"Except when you were detained by Lamd's men," Kolt qualified in a bland voice that belied the importance of his reply.

"It is as I have said, Laedan. I was imprisoned and unable to fulfill my oath to my people. Would you fault me for what I could do naught about?"

"Ah, but good Luthias, there is the rub. That you were a helpless captive has been challenged."

Luthias shoved back his caftan's sleeves to reveal well-healed marks around each wrist. "How think you I came by these?" he demanded shrilly.

Kolt's lips curled in disdain. "It is common knowledge that your preference within your sleeping chamber runs to the bizarre. Think not to fool me with marks your lover gave to you."

The green color drained from Luthias's face, leaving it a pasty yellow, and he dropped his hands. Before he could give voice to further lies, Kolt turned to Naydir. "Bring young Cal in."

Naydir rose and gracefully moved to the door. He knocked once. The door opened. Cal, whose slanted yellow eyes, light golden fur, and long tawny mane proclaimed him more his Xerthian mother's son than Luthias's, entered.

He bowed to Kolt. "Ladean."

Kolt gripped his furred hand firmly. "Well come, Cal of Mayrald. Well come, indeed. Your patience and mine have at last paid off."

"He has forsworn then?"

"Yes, he has forsworn. This day will see you as councilor of Mayrald."

Luthias jumped to his feet, his face blotchy with rage, his voice shrill. "You cannot replace me unless you have proof that I have purposely harmed those in my care."

Kolt's gaze once again rested on Luthias, as he said softly, "Oh, there is proof."

"By your own rule, you cannot speak of what your touch has read."

"I did not touch you."

Confusion revealed itself on Luthias's craggy face for a moment. Then he drew himself up, and demanded in an outraged voice, "Then I would see my accuser!"

Cal stepped to his father, his yellow eyes burning with a hatred long suppressed. "My dam is your accuser, Sire."

"But she is dead!"

"By your hand."

Golden Conquest

"Ladean!" Luthias turned to Kolt. "Surely you cannot believe this—this drivel. He is as mad as his dam!"

With a roar, Cal lunged across the table. His long powerful fingers linked behind his father's meaty neck. "If she was mad, old man," he snarled as he slowly depressed his thumbs, "it was you who made her so."

Naydir, his eyes glinting darkly, watched as Luthias clawed futilely at his son's hand. Until now, all had gone as Kolt had planned, but, as much as Naydir would have it otherwise, Kolt did not wish Luthias dead. Nor would he want Cal charged with life-ending. He moved to the young man's side and placed a firm hand on his shoulder. "Do not destroy what was so hard won."

Cal swung his head toward Naydir. "You are right, as always." He withdrew his hands and forcibly shoved the gasping man away. He watched dispassionately as the man who had sired him tripped over his long robes and fell, his head striking the wall with a solid thunk.

"Here is my proof." Cal drew a small cube from the pocket of his jerkin and tossed it on the table. "Before my dam succumbed to the potion you gave her, she called me to her side and gave me a recording she had made. It details all of your dealings with Lamd. You were not a victim, a prisoner of Lamd, but his loyal man! He did not steal our people's nourishment, but was given it by you. He had but to ask and you willingly life-ended those within Mayrald who opposed him. And there is more. Including your collusion with Lamd that ended the life of Ruler Tiala!"

Luthias's shoulders slumped in defeat. He was well and truly snared by his own words. And by the words of a woman he had life-ended to keep silent.

The occupants of the room had seemed too taken aback by the suddenness of the events to react, but Cal's final accusation brought them all to their feet. Annan's late ruler, Tiala, had been much loved. That one of their own had a hand in his death was not to be borne. Their shouts for retribution rang out in a deafening din.

Patricia Roenbeck

"Silence!" Kolt reinforced his bellow with an insistent mind-touch.

All mouths closed. All eyes turned to Kolt.

"I have seen the recordings, as you all shall before the sun passes the horizon twice. Then and only then, will your recommendations for Luthias's punishment be heard and justice meted out. But for now"—Kolt gestured Cal forward—"Cal of Mayrald, do you swear to protect those who look to you for protection?"

"Yes."

"Do you swear to dispense justice fairly and swiftly?"

"Yes."

"Do you swear to speak honestly in all matters that concern the sektor of Mayrald?"

"Yes."

"Then take your seat, Councilor of Mayrald."

As Cal strode proudly to his appointed place within the ranks of councilors, Kolt glanced around the room certain that the day's events had earned him further enemies, but well pleased nonetheless. Cal was strong and fair. He would see Mayrald's people well, their pockets and bellies full.

Once Cal was seated, Kolt turned to Naydir. "Luthias seems to have a fondness for detainment. See to it."

Naydir grabbed the older man by his arm and dragged him to his feet. "I would very much like to save Kolt the trouble of dealing further with you, old man, so please protest."

Wisely, Luthias said nothing.

His promise to Naydir to speak to Dakkar of his loose tongue set aside for the moment, Kolt nodded to the assemblage, closed his eyes, and *actualized*.

Chapter Six

Kolt opened his eyes. After the noise of the council chamber, he basked in the insulating silence of the memory cubiculum.

Many had thought him mad when he had commissioned this chamber. But to Kolt, it mattered not that Koltrax's manner of death had rendered his body nonexistent. His brother would have his cubiculum and Kolt would design it.

Chasl, the master-shaper, had done well in bringing his leader's vision to life. Circular flooring of black crystal extended upward, unseamed, to four high, rounded walls and a ceiling shot through with glittering golithium crystal. It was lit always with hundreds of tiny flame lights, their muted yet fiery flickering the only life in a chamber dedicated to the dead.

Kolt's long strides brought him swiftly to his destination. And in this, too, Chasl had not disappointed him, for the pedestal flowed upward, unbroken by seam or joint—a great frozen fountain of black crystal. Atop it rested a long ovoid sarcophagus of green verdanthium crystal.

Kolt touched his hand to his head, his heart, and to the face of Koltrax meticulously engraved on the sarcophagus in a gesture of love and respect. Then he closed his eyes, pressed his palms against each other, and slowly extended his arms outward. As he did, he drew from deep within his memories of Koltrax's form, features, his very soul, and sent them coursing from his mind, down his arms to his hands.

His eyes opened, as did his palms, and there, hovering inches above his hands was an image formed of mental energy and love. Koltrax.

Kolt studied the apparition his gift had given life to, pleased by the accuracy and detail. The small figure turning in his hands was amazed that it could be done.

Koltrax, my brother.

Koltrax raised his eyes and smiled up at Kolt. His hand touched his head in a carefree salute, and Kolt felt the jolt of that familiar gesture throughout his whole body. He wanted, no needed, more.

Once again, he closed his eyes and reached back through the years for the rich vibrant laughter and deep teasing tones of Koltrax's voice. There. Faint, but, yes, it was what he searched for. Kolt concentrated and heard the words again. This time a little louder and then a little louder. And louder still. Until now they were a shout within his mind, and he threw the essence of that sound toward the image.

He opened his eyes and laughed as he watched Koltrax's mouth struggle to form the words. Then suddenly, Koltrax smiled, an infectious triumphant smile.

"Day's passing to you, little brother."

Suddenly, Kolt shuddered and gasped for breath. His concentration faltered and flew, taking the illusion of Koltrax with it. From deep within Kolt, his soul cried out in protest over the loss of his brother's image, even as he threw up shields against the cloying suffocating presence of the intruder. Without turning, he spoke her name.

"Iilde."

She laughed, an overbearingly smug sound that rankled. "Is it not telling that you knew it was I?"

The want, desire, and need that flowed from her like a great tidal wave struck him again, and the sensation of drowning was so strong that he would have fallen

Golden Conquest

had it not been for the sarcophagus. As his hands felt the cool firmness of the crystal, he reinforced his barriers and slowly turned.

"I am a mind-toucher, Iilde, it is part of who I am to sense the presence of those who intrude."

Iilde's slanted pink eyes turned to ice. "Intrude. Not I. You sent for me."

Kolt's knowing gaze swept the tall, statuesque beauty. As always she was garbed in a way that dared men to ignore her, dramatically in a vivid red that matched the tint of her full lips and contrasted with the starkness of her closely cropped white hair. Much of her long slender legs, though covered in skin-tight leggings, were revealed by a skirt cut well above midthigh in the front and mid-knee in the back that swung provocatively with each movement of her nicely rounded hips. A long-sleeved, body-hugging shirt dipped precariously low over her voluptuously full bosom. Simple, dyed-to-match, oogala hide slippers with handhigh heels added to her already impressive height and forced most men to raise their head to meet her eyes. From her ears dangled clusters of dazzling bloodstones and around her neck a matching choker.

"Sent for you? I think not."

"Then you would have."

Kolt arched a brow. "Oh?"

"I have heard that your need is great. And that only I can fulfill it."

Kolt gritted his teeth against the influx of her naked lust and again strengthened his shields. By all the gods, if he did not take himself from her presence soon, he would never feel clean again! He forced himself to smile, to step forward, to press his lips to her hand.

"Yes, my need is great, as you have heard." He paused, then added, in a voice as cold as the peak of Quixtallyn Mount, "But never so great that I must have it from you."

Iilde yanked her hand from his. "But the demand for Khrystallyn—"

"Will be met."

"Not from my mines!"

Kolt placed his hand on his heart. "No? I find myself crushed."

"Spawn of Schargaz! Mock me if you will, but this I swear, until I give them leave, my harvesters will not harvest!" Iilde ground out fiercely as she turned to sweep from the cubiculum.

Kolt watched her progress, and when her hand flicked across the opening light, he said softly, "I would be much careful of what I swear, my beautiful Iilde. This day has already marked the replacement of one who has forsworn."

Her head jerked around, her eyes questioning, but Kolt was in no mood to enlighten her and merely smiled. "As you have heard of my great need, you will hear his name. A day's passing to you."

Kolt gave her a gentle push, and she found herself in the corridor, the door closed and secured behind her.

Kolt drew in a ragged breath and lowered his shields. By all the gods, so strong was her hunger for him that his head ached from the effort to block it. Not for the first time he wondered how it was so. Though he was skilled in dealing with women, none had assailed his senses with such longing as Iilde did. And this from a woman he had never had! He shuddered. Would never have, thank the gods.

With a nod to Koltrax's symbolic coffin, he sent an arc of light flashing toward a sensor in the rear wall, then stepped through the opening. He had no desire to meet Iilde in the passageway. Once had been enough. As the wall slid shut, he sped down the hidden corridor that led to his sleeping chamber. He desperately needed to rid himself of Iilde and there was only one place, and one person who could do that.

Kolt tore off the last of his clothes. Before his feet touched the purple-and-pink sand surrounding the pond at the base of the Rainbow Falls, he was at full run. He arched into the air, then sliced the water, letting the force of his motion carry him

Golden Conquest

to the cooling depths of the basin. He sat on the bottom, watching the dance of the sun's light across the surface, until his lungs could stand no more, then shot upward. A few kicks of his powerful legs and he surfaced. He rolled onto his back, his eyes closed, his ears listening to the sound of the rushing falls. He let his mind drift free to seek out and touch the one who was for now and all eternity his own mind's love.

Iilde stood in the corridor outside the cubiculum and shrieked in frustration.

"Well done, my sweet."

She spun on her heels and met the mocking gaze of her lover. "You—you—you slimy son of a—" Iilde caught herself. She had learned long ago to control her caustic tongue from remarking about his heritage. She continued sullenly, "He did not ask for my help."

"He will."

"You are so sure?"

"Yes. When all other options are taken from him." He laughed. "And we will do our best to see that all other options are taken from him, won't we? But for this passing, you have given us so much more than his request."

Iilde arched a brow in question.

"You angered him, my wonderful sparkra, and well we know where he goes to cool his temper. As we know that he goes alone. He will be vulnerable."

"And you will seek him out again?"

"Yes, but this time I will not miss."

She pressed her hand to his cheek and her eyes searched his face. "What if he should touch you? He would know you then, and it will be you who are life-ended."

He laughed again, a strong firm sound of confidence. "He cannot touch me. Of that I am most certain." He shook his head. "No. I need have no fear of him. In truth, it is he who should fear me." He ran a hand up her waist to her breast and squeezed. "There is time to spare before I must act." He took her hand. "Come. For you, I will be Kolt, and for me, you will be Aylyn."

Chapter Seven

Garbed in blousy teal pants, a matching long-sleeved, knee-length tunic, and heelless black slippers, Aylyn stood by the casement and looked down at her mother and father as they walked in the courtyard. As always, they were close together, heads touching, hands touching, bodies touching.

Normally, she would expect nothing less from her parents, but the feelings evoked by her mind-toucher made her hypersensitive to all aspects of their relationship. What she had previously viewed as routine, she now saw as suspect. Eirriel had suddenly cancelled a long-awaited visit with an old friend to stay at Aubin's side, and Aylyn mistakenly saw her mother's decision, not as a concern over a potential problem to her lifebond, but as an inability to enjoy life anywhere but at his side. The love they had for each other was powerful, everybody said as much. Aylyn now believed it too powerful. The kind that controls.

A knock drew her attention from the lord director and his consort. She turned to see Alaran entering and grimaced. Since making her decision, she had done her best to avoid her brother. Alaran had an uncanny knack of knowing when she was planning something that would not meet with their parent's approval. With a life cycle of twenty-one, one more than hers, she knew he felt it his place to counsel her on the possible ramifications of her impulsive actions.

Of course, once he had, he believed his duty dispelled and willingly joined her in any act of mischief she conceived. But leaving Rhianon would be too much, even for him. He would most certainly tell Laaryc, and, if that didn't stop her, their parents.

"I would like to be alone," she said in what she hoped was a sufficiently haughty voice.

Alaran dropped onto the sleeper and crossed his arms behind his head, an expectant look on his handsome face. "So?"

"So what?"

"So what are you planning?"

Aylyn turned back to the casement. Curse him and his instincts! "What makes you think I'm planning anything?"

Alaran just laughed, but when she refused to tell him, he grew serious. "Whatever it is, it isn't your usual harmless prank."

"Why do you say that?" she asked. Anything to keep him talking long enough for her to come up with some excuse for her odd behavior.

"From the way you've been hiding in your chambers. Laaryc thinks you're mad at him because he's leaving. Are you? Is that what this is all about?"

Aylyn could have kissed her brother. She schooled her features into acute distress and turned to face him. Wringing her hands, she hesitated and then nodded. "Yes. I—I don't want him to leave. I—I'll miss him terribly." At least that was no lie.

"And?"

"And what?"

"Give it up, Aylyn. I know you're upset by Laaryc's sudden decision. Just as I know there's more." He paused. "Much more."

Aylyn blinked. Not only was Alaran looking more and more like their father, now he was starting to sound like him.

"Are you going to tell Mother?" Aylyn asked.

"I wouldn't have to if she wasn't so worried about Father's mission."

Golden Conquest

Aylyn frowned. Several days ago the Yrianot envoy had arrived to beg her father's help in a mission of utmost importance. Or so he had said. And little else. That same night, Eirriel had awakened screaming Aubin's name and begging him not to go. Aubin had assured her that he could take care of himself, but her fears had not diminished. "She still thinks something will happen when he leaves."

"Yes. She doesn't know what it is. Just a sense, a very strong sense, of danger. I think that's what upsets her the most. That as strong as her mind-touching skills have become over the years, they still aren't enough. She still can't see, can't get anything other than vague impressions."

Aylyn crossed to the sleeper and sat down next to her brother. "Is it because it is so sudden? Or because it involves the Yrianots?"

"I wonder if it has anything to do with Father at all," Alaran said quietly.

"What do you mean? Mother's first concern has always been Father."

"You really believe that, don't you?" Alaran sat up. "Why? Because they enjoy being with each other? Touching each other? Why shouldn't they? They are life-bonded."

"And that means they should ignore everyone else?" In the past, her mother had always sensed when Aylyn was distressed and come to her. Now, when she needed her mother the most, Eirriel had not come. In her confusion, Aylyn never questioned why she did not go to her mother.

Alaran's green eyes, his only physical link to their mother, narrowed. "Is that what's got you so out of sorts? Mother's concern for Father?" Alaran hopped off the sleeper and crossed to the door. "I didn't think you were so self-absorbed."

Aylyn flinched as he slammed the door. She hadn't meant it the way it sounded. But how could she explain to Alaran what she didn't understand herself? She moved back to the casement. Her father was kissing her mother now, neither one of them caring that people were watching them or worried about what others might think. They were totally lost in themselves. In their love. She shuddered. To be so controlled by one person.

That is it, is it not?

Aylyn gasped. No! It couldn't be.

Love does not control.

Aylyn pressed her hands to her head. She was awake. He never *touched* her when she was awake.

And should it be that love does control, mine will not.

Get out of my mind! You have no right!

I alone have the right.

You have the power you mean.

He laughed. *That too.*

I do not want you! I will not have you!

Ah, but you will. You are my mind's love. You have always been such.

Aylyn struggled for control. She had to do something. Fight him some way. *I am not yours. I am Laaryc's.*

No!

Aylyn's knees buckled under the force of his pained cry, and she grabbed onto the casement ledge.

You are mine now as you have always been. As you will always be.

You shall see. You shall see. Aylyn thought of Laaryc then. *This is Laaryc, the lifebond of my choice.*

The image of Laaryc vanished, pushed from her mind as if by a mighty wind. She concentrated harder, and pictured Laaryc standing before her, his eyes intense, burning with passion. His hands reaching for her, pulling her to him. His head lowering, his mouth pressing hers. Again, the image lasted but moments.

I know what you are about and it will not work. For now and for always, you are mine!

No, I am Laaryc's. When Laaryc leaves for Dianthia this night, I leave with him. You cannot stop me!

If thoughts of Laaryc wouldn't work, she thought desperately, let him combat this. Aylyn ran across the

Golden Conquest

chamber and yanked open the door. Laaryc would be in his chambers, preparing for his trip. She reached his door. Without knocking, she pushed it open.

Laaryc startled, spun around as Aylyn burst into his chamber. "Aylyn? What is it?"

She stopped in front of him, her eyes round and wild. "Kiss me."

"What?"

She raised her arms to his neck and forced his head to hers. "Kiss me now."

Never a fool, despite his bookish ways, Laaryc pressed his lips to Aylyn's.

Nooo!

Aylyn flinched and raised her head. "He is here. Now." Her eyes grew luminous. "Help me, Laaryc. Please, help me."

"He will know what we do?"

Aylyn nodded.

"Then, yes, I will help you," Laaryc growled, and slanted his mouth across hers.

Nooo! You cannot!

Aylyn did not answer, choosing instead to concentrate on Laaryc and his kiss. It was pleasant, as it had been the few times he had kissed her. And as always, Laaryc started to pull away after the first brief touch. But this time she would not let the kiss end. She had felt the mind-toucher withdraw his touch and feared he would return the moment Laaryc stepped away. So she followed Laaryc as he raised his head and kept her lips pressed to his.

Emboldened by her unspoken request, Laaryc tightened his grip about her waist and opened his mouth, flicking her closed lips with his tongue. Aylyn's eyes shot open. *This is interesting*, she thought. *Much nic* . . . Suddenly, a suffocating wave of loathing washed over her. She yanked her mouth from Laaryc's, her eyes dark with confusion.

"Aylyn?"

"I—something—by all the gods!" Aylyn gasped, and shoved herself from him.

"What is it? What's wrong?"

She jerked at the sudden breath-stealing pain that tore through her back and drove her to her knees.

"Aylyn!"

She heard Laaryc's muffled cry and tried to reach for him, but she couldn't move. She felt momentary relief from the icy numbness that was spreading across her back, then doubled over as another fiercer pain drilled through her, robbing her of her breath. And then she knew, somehow, that her mind-toucher was in trouble and that what she was feeling was in actuality happening to him.

Aylyn! I am sorry!

Gods! But his touch was so faint! "No! Do not die!" *Come back! Do not leave me! Come back!*

She screamed once more then pitched forward.

Chapter Eight

Kolt watched as Laaryc's mouth lowered to Aylyn's.

Nooo! You cannot! Feelings of betrayal swept over him, and he jerked his mind from Aylyn's. "You are mine! Mine!" The last was emphasized by a fierce splash as his arm slammed down on the water. He rolled onto his belly and sliced through the water. His rage fed his strength, and he was within a few short strokes up the water's edge. Blindly, he snatched up his clothes and threw them on.

Life bond with another! His Aylyn! It could not be. She was to come to him in just a few days. Whatever plan she had in mind he would stop it. Somehow. There had to be a way.

Kolt was so lost in his mental anguish that he did not hear the sound of approaching footsteps or feel the malevolent touch of the assassin's mind. Nor did he see the pulsating whiteness of the energy dagger that hovered just above his back until it was too late.

He went rigid as a wave of intense and unrelenting hatred struck him an instant before he felt an icy heat slice through the skin and muscle in his back. In that moment Kolt knew that Naydir's warnings had been well given. Kolt's obsession with Aylyn had made him vulnerable to the assassin's attack.

He tried to turn to catch a glimpse of his life-ender, but his body refused to obey his command. Instead, he focused on Naydir and called to him. He gritted his teeth as the blade seemed to be yanked from his back. The next blow would see the end of him. His heart was already slowing, and he was finding it more and more difficult to breathe. Ignoring the fiery pain that was rapidly consuming him, he called on all his skill and threw up a shield.

He felt the weapon bump the luminous blue-white barrier once, twice, and heard his assailant's frustration as the murderous hand was once more brought down, this time easily passing through the weakened shield and burying itself forcefully into his back.

Kolt fought the blackness that threatened to consume him, combating it with a rage that he would never hold Aylyn, never see her face as he buried himself inside her and branded her his, and the knowledge that Naydir would never forgive him for allowing this to happen. He reached out to Naydir one last time.

And then he knew no more.

Naydir's yellow eyes glowed as he positioned himself between his mistress's lovely thighs. "I have missed you, my sweet. We have much—."

Naydir!

Naydir's head shot up as Kolt's shout rang through his head. In an instant, Naydir was on his feet. "Kolt! Damn you!" Not taking the time to dress, he snatched up his gauntlet and neutralizer from the table near the sleeper and ran from the chamber, the blistering curses of his irate mistress and a carafe of ale following him.

Startling a passing group of servers, Naydir burst into the passageway and roared for his captain of the guards. "Morald!" Strapping the fingerless gauntlet onto his left hand, Naydir activated its translucent energy shield with a quick jerk of his wrist, even as he rushed down the passageway.

Kolt, my friend, hold on. Though he did not feel it, Naydir hoped Kolt's touch was still with him and kept his mind open to receive it. His bare feet slapped at the crystal flooring as he rounded the corner and reached the staircase.

Nay–dir–the–pond.

The flash of hope that Kolt's answering touch gave Naydir was quickly destroyed by its weakness. *Gods spare him*, he prayed, taking the winding stairs three steps at a time.

Morald and three guards met him at the bottom. Kolt's name on Naydir's lips was enough of an order, and the three men activated their shields, checked that their neutralizers were primed and ready, and followed Naydir.

At last he reached the entrance to the courtyard and was out in the blinding sunlight. He gestured to the guards to spread out, leaving the center section to him, and his long strides quickly ate up the ground between the keep and the garden.

Naydir's frantic mental shout jerked the assassin's head around. Curse the interfering bastard! He hadn't finished. The usurper still lived. Well, he smiled cruelly, he could still see to it that Kolt suffered. Viciously, he twisted the Zorbian tri-blade into Kolt. Though the glowing thought-dagger had initially rendered Kolt almost defenseless, and it would have been safer to continue the attack from a distance with more thought-daggers or a neutralizer, neither one could give him the extreme pleasure of seeing and feeling Kolt's unconscious body twitch and shudder from the pain of the three serrated blades. And if the wounds didn't life-end Kolt, the deadly Zorbian taint that coated the blades would. His eyes glinting with pleasure, he gave the weapon one final twist, then yanked it free.

He turned his thoughts on the weapon and it vanished. He looked down, pleased by the sight of the lifeblood that pooled around Kolt's unconscious body. Perhaps the fates had not deserted him, but had merely stayed his hand for a more perfect moment. It was better that the usurper still lived, he thought as he drifted into the shadows. The pain of his body would be as nothing to the pain in his soul when he next tried to touch his beloved.

"Curse you, Kolt! Why so many paths?" Naydir raged as he was forced to double back once more and seek yet another way into the garden. He cursed again, this time at himself. Why hadn't he paid more attention to Kolt's habits?

"Naydir!"

Naydir spun around to see Dakkar running from one of the outer buildings.

"What is it? What's wrong?" Dakkar stopped in front of Naydir, then stepped back as the sun reflected off Naydir's ever-present golden amulet and momentarily blinded Dakkar. "Why are you unclothed?"

"I've no time for questions, Dakkar," Naydir snapped impatiently. "Kolt's been injured."

"Mother of the universe, no! How is he?"

"Gods save me from fools!" Naydir shoved Dakkar out of the way and continued into the garden. He had only taken a few steps when he spied Kolt's inert form. His heart thudded in his chest as his eyes took in all the blood.

"Morald!" he shouted, and then he was kneeling at his friend's side, unaware that he had even moved.

Morald and the guards arrived and surrounded Naydir and their fallen leader, their gauntleted arms crossed in front of them so that the transparent shields formed a perfect circle of protection around the two men. Naydir jerked his wrist, deactivating his gauntlet, then searched Kolt's neck for a pulse. Thready though it might be, it was enough to reassure Naydir that his leader and his friend still lived.

"Kolt, my friend," Naydir called gently. "Can you hear me?"

"Oh, gods!" Dakkar cried as he moved through the opening Morald made and halted near Naydir. "I think I will be ill."

"Be ill if you must," Naydir growled. "But first take off your shirt."

Golden Conquest

"My shirt?" Dakkar blinked. "Just because you are unclothed, I—"

The sentence ended in a squawk as Naydir's large hand yanked the cloth from Dakkar's body.

"Now move!" Naydir snapped.

His eyes glued to Kolt's gaping back, Dakkar remained motionless as Naydir pressed the silky material into one of the large gaping wounds. "I am truly going to be ill, Naydir. Truly."

"Choke on it for all I care, but get out of my light!" The last was a roar and seemed to do the trick as Dakkar stumbled away.

Naydir had finished packing the second wound when four other guards arrived and spoke to Morald, who ordered the shields dropped.

"No sign of anyone, Councilor," Morald reported.

Naydir nodded grimly. He had expected nothing else. He stood as a petite and fragile-looking female approached and knelt at Kolt's side.

"I see you have saved him again, Councilor."

"Have I, Healer?"

Eadoine pressed a few knobs on the mediscan and ran it across Kolt's body. She frowned, made an adjustment, and her frown deepened. She looked up at Naydir. "There is much damage."

Naydir felt her words like a blow to his midsection. "Then he will die?"

"It will be close, but, no, Kolt will not die." She looked up at him and smiled. "Next time you might want to get to him a little sooner."

Naydir took more comfort in her attempt to tease him then he did in her prediction that Kolt would live. His face lit up. "I will try, Healer. I will try."

"Good. He is lucky to have you to watch over him." Eadoine beckoned to two young aides and instructed them to move their leader carefully onto the transporter. Once Kolt was secure, she pressed a button, and the transporter rose to hip level. She gently drew one of the insulcovers over Kolt and handed the other to Naydir.

Patricia Roenbeck

"As nice a view as it is, young man, you might want this."

Aware of the heated color creeping into his cheek, Naydir cursed under his breath as he wrapped the covering around his waist, then turned his steely gaze on the chuckling guards who fell silent immediately.

"Morald!"

The captain of the guards stepped forward. "Yes, Councilor."

"I want a detailed search of this area. Every bush, every tree, every piece of crystal. The would-be assassin was here long enough to ambush Kolt. There's got to be a clue. Find it!"

Naydir strode off as Morald began to dispatch the teams.

Chapter Nine

Laaryc caught Aylyn before she hit the floor. Holding her limp body close, he carried her to the sleeper and gently lay her down.

"Aylyn!" His voice was hoarse with worry. "Aylyn, my love, can you hear me?"

He ran to the door to seek help and was about to jerk it open when he heard her.

"Laaryc?" Her voice was weak.

He turned to see her trying to sit up. He moved to her side and placed a hand on her shoulder. "Lie still."

"I'm all right. It has passed."

"You are sure? I was about to get your mother."

"There is no need. I am fine." She gave him a slight smile. "I'm sorry I worried you."

"Worried me?" He sat on the bed next to her. "Worried me! You damn near ended my life! One moment you're kissing me, the next, screaming in pain." He looked her over. She appeared pale, but otherwise well. "Are you sure you don't want your mother?"

"She has enough on her mind."

Laaryc nodded. "Do you know what happened?"

Aylyn's eyes darkened. "It was a knife, I think."

Laaryc jumped to his feet. "A knife! Gods, where—" He looked at her again, his eyes running down her. He frowned. "I don't see any lifeblood."

"You won't. It wasn't me." Her voice caught in her throat and she gasped. "As it entered and tore through his back, I felt it. And it was as strong and as real as if it had happened to me. But it hadn't. It was his back the dagger pierced. Not once, but twice." She shuddered. "Oh, gods, he is wounded, Laaryc! Gravely so!"

Laaryc sat down heavily. He shook his head. "You mean all of this was because of him? Your mind-toucher? I can't believe it."

"Believe it," she replied quietly.

"I don't really have a choice. I saw the end result."

She shook her head. "Not the end. Someone was trying to kill him."

"And this . . . troubles you?"

"Only as it would if any living creature were in danger," she lied.

"Of course," he mocked, and Aylyn knew at once that he had heard the lie in her voice. "Did you see the attacker?"

"No."

"And him? Did you at last see him?"

"No."

"Then what drove you into my arms?"

"We . . . communicated."

"You what?"

"Communicated. Mother said full-blooded mind-touchers can do that." She searched for words to explain. "As I told you before, he's only touched me while I slept. And it's never been more than a feeling, a sensing of his presence in my mind. This time I was awake, and his voice filled my mind. I heard him as clearly as if he were in my chamber talking to me. His touch was as rich and firm and as passionate as any voice would have been when saying what he said."

"And what was that?" Laaryc asked, not knowing if he really wanted her to answer.

Aylyn lowered her gaze to her hands. "He told me I was his. That I always have been and always would be." She paused, then added softly, "He called me his mind's love." Suddenly, she sat up and took Laaryc's

Golden Conquest

hand. She looked at him, her eyes intense, her voice urgent. "Please, Laaryc, if you have any love at all for me, please take me with you."

If he had any love for her at all! Laaryc's heart contracted violently in his chest, and his eyes darkened with pain. He turned from her, unwilling for her to witness the anguish her words caused him. Gods, with every breath, with every thought, he loved her! He had from the first. And she had loved him, too. Until him. Her mind-toucher.

"Laaryc?"

"You said he is wounded. Perhaps he did not survive and you flee for no purpose."

"He is alive. I would feel it were he not."

Laaryc groaned. She would feel it. Gods, but the link between them was strong! Too strong. Maybe she was right to want to sever the connection now, while there was still time. He nodded grimly. "If distance will break this bond, then yes, you should try."

"Distance will not, that I go with you will."

"And your parents?"

"They will refuse permission unless I can explain, and I cannot. I will contact them from Dianthia."

"I do not like this."

"There is no other way. You will not tell them?"

Reluctantly, Laaryc shook his head and received a blinding smile as his reward.

"You are, and always will be, my dearest love," Aylyn said softly.

"As you are mine," Laaryc replied fervently.

"When does our adventure begin?" she asked, getting to her feet.

"The *Star Jumper* departs when the moon reaches its zenith."

"I will be ready," she promised, and left.

"I can't believe we did it." Aylyn was leaning over Laaryc, who was seated at the command console of the *Star Jumper*, staring at the large viewer in front of them and watching Rhianon disappear.

"I still do not like it," Laaryc growled as he programmed the navacomputer. "Lady Eirriel will be frantic when she discovers you gone."

"No, she won't," Aylyn said as she crossed to the recreation cubicle that adjoined the control center.

Laaryc looked over his shoulder. "You seem certain."

Aylyn punched in an order at the nourishment dispenser. "I left a message in Alaran's cubicle. He will see that my parents receive it when the time is right."

When she turned with the two trays, Laaryc was standing in front of her. "Do I want to know what it said?"

She handed Laaryc one tray and sat down at the table that extended from the rear wall. "No."

Laaryc groaned. "What did you do?"

"I—I told them I left with you."

"There is more," he said as he took the seat across from her.

"Yes." She took a breath and the words came out in a rush. "I told them I wanted to life bond with you."

"And when we arrive on Dianthia? What will we tell Chief Concile Timos? He will insist that we life bond."

"Would that be so very terrible?"

Laaryc cursed fiercely and loudly and threw himself from the table. "It would."

Aylyn gasped. "You—you do not want me?"

"I told you on Rhianon that I would not life bond with you. Why didn't you listen?"

"I—I don't understand. I thought you were afraid to face my father."

"I may prefer learning to fighting, but I would fight to the death for you."

"I know. I did not mean to imply that you would not. But it *is* because of my parents, isn't it?"

Laaryc nodded as he reclaimed his seat. "In part, yes. From my conversations with Alaran, I have always believed that Lord Aubin wished you to bond with his friend, Kolt."

Golden Conquest

"But I do not know him!"

"You refused even to meet him."

"He's a harvester!" Aylyn said, seeking any excuse, no matter how foolish or untrue to counter Laaryc's attack.

"And when we return to Dianthia, I will be a simple ryland worker, tilling the land, reaping the crop, and feeding the people."

"It does not matter."

"To you perhaps, but to me it does. Lord Aubin's Kolt rules Annan."

"A piece of rock in the middle of nowhere."

"Your father seems to believe it is much more."

"Well, I do not want him," Aylyn said emphatically.

"As you do not want me," Laaryc said softly.

"Do not want—"

Laaryc put up his hand, and Aylyn fell silent. He looked at her. Her heart twisted at what she saw revealed in his eyes. Love, yes, but an underlying and unbelievably deep sadness. Why had she never seen it before? "Laaryc?"

"How is it that it can be so very clear to me, Aylyn, and not to you at all?" He got up and moved to the small viewer and stared out on the stars as they rushed passed them. "From the first, I knew. Your destiny lies not with me, my love, but with him."

Aylyn's eyes widened. "You can't possibly mean . . ."

"Gods help me, Aylyn, I do." He took a deep shuddering breath. "And I would give all I own to make it otherwise."

Chapter Ten

Aubin, lord director of Rhianon, raised his head from the reports he had been studying and glared at his son with eyes that glinted like golden steel. "She what?"

"Went with Laaryc," Alaran repeated as he handed Aylyn's note to Aubin, unfazed as always by his father's formidable anger.

Alaran had anticipated it and therefore had waited until they were alone before delivering his sister's too-brief message. He had not wanted Aubin's rage to spilling over onto an innocent server or guest. And when his father finished reading it, he knew his move had been correct, for Aubin's hands were clenched into fists and his chiseled features suddenly seemed cut from stone.

"I'll offer his life's energy to the kriekors," Aubin ground out. "And when they're through with him I'll . . . Why are you laughing?"

"Because that is precisely what Laaryc said you would do when Aylyn asked to life bond with him."

"She what?"

"You're repeating yourself."

Aubin chuckled. "So I am." He stood and placed a hand on his son's shoulder, noticing, not for the first time, that his son had already equaled his 6'2" height. And Rhianonians did not stop growing until well after their twenty-fifth year. "Thank you."

"For what?"

Golden Conquest

"For diffusing my anger. You have your mother's gift in that."

"I wish I had all of her gifts," Alaran replied fervently.

"Wishing doesn't help, I'm afraid," Aubin remarked. "If it did, I would be a great and powerful mind-toucher."

"Instead you are merely a great and powerful lord director. The envy of many."

"Enough flattery. Come"—he gestured to the relaxers in the corner of the chamber—"tell me what you know about all of this."

Alaran followed his father, stopping first in front of the nourishment dispenser. He punched in an order for two Melonnian sweet and sours. "You'll need this," he said, handing one to his father.

Aubin took the cruet. "That bad."

"I'm afraid so." Alaran lowered himself into the relaxer across from Aubin and took a long swallow of the brew. "Laaryc turned her down."

"Why? He's been in love with her for years."

"Because he didn't feel worthy of her."

"That's ridiculous," Aubin muttered.

"Yes, and I think in time he would have realized that. If . . ." Alaran paused, took another sip, and then continued, "he didn't believe her in love with another."

Aubin's brows shot up. "Who?"

Alaran shrugged. "He wouldn't say. Or couldn't."

Aubin shot to his feet. "Gods! What is wrong with the boy—"

"Man, Father. His life cycle is greater than mine."

"Yes, I know. It's just that he is so . . . so . . ."

"Dianthian," Alaran supplied.

"Dianthian," Aubin admitted, and sighed as he shoved back the persistent lock of hair that had fallen across his forehead. Although he respected all Dianthians, Aubin could not help but view their gentle passive beliefs as a weakness. His lifebond was the lone exception. Never could he see Eirriel as weak. "If truly loves her, he should have fought for her."

"He would die for her, Father. Never doubt that. As for fighting, I don't think he felt he had a chance."

"This other man? Is he the reason she left Rhianon?"

"I am sure of it."

Aubin started to pace. "Your mother doesn't need this latest trouble. My trip has her worried enough."

"But what if Aylyn's leaving is what has Mother so upset? I've been thinking. Aylyn started acting strangely the same time the Yrianot envoy arrived. The same night Mother sensed danger." A movement caught Alaran's eyes and he turned his head. "It appears our private conversation is about to come to an end."

Aubin spun around to see Eirriel standing in the entrance to his work chamber, and he cursed under his breath. The emerald-green jumpsuit that clung to her shapely curves and the disarray of her long golden hair told him she had been participating in her favorite pastime. Her paleness beneath the windblown redness of her cheeks and her green eyes dark with worry led him to conclude she had been standing there overly long. He quickly moved to her side.

"Welcome back, little one." He drew her to him and kissed her deeply. "I missed you."

Eirriel laughed and, as always, Aubin felt the sound of it caress his soul. "I was only riding Onyx." The laughter fled, replaced again by concern. "Now tell me what this is all about."

"You've been eavesdropping, my love."

"You had barriers up, my lord. I *heard* them all the way out into the passageway."

Barriers. Aubin sighed. After all the years spent together, he had still to figure out how his mind-touching lifebond knew he, who had not a drop of Kiiryan blood, had barriers up. *He* didn't even know he had them up. Ah, well. He would probably go to his grave not knowing. Aubin looked at his son. "Send word to Timos."

"At once," Alaran said, then nodded to his mother and left.

Golden Conquest

Aubin led Eirriel to the relaxer and, leaving nothing unsaid, relayed all he knew of Aylyn, Laaryc, and Aylyn's unknown suitor. "Alaran wonders if your sense of unease is not because of me."

"And you agree? You think it is Aylyn who is in jeopardy and not you?"

"I don't honestly know, my love, but I can't help but believe the Yrianots the least likeliest threat."

"But the menace is real," Eirriel insisted.

"That you sense danger is not the question," Aubin explained gravely, "but the interpretation of that danger is."

Eirriel nodded, then stood. Aubin watched her as she crossed to the casement and stared out at the night sky visible through the dome.

Not for the first time, Eirriel cursed the limits her mixed blood forced upon her. Her mother, one of the elusive Kiiryans, a people of extraordinarily advanced parapsychic ability who were believed to exist only in legends, would have known immediately who and what was the cause of the danger she sensed. But the blood of Eirriel's Dianthian father narrowed the scope of her Kiiryan mind-touching abilities.

She could not see into minds, only sense strong emotions. She could not predict the future, only sense great danger. She could not move objects by thought, only part from her body and move about as mental energy. There was one other skill she possessed, a terrible power and ironically the only one not affected by her mixed heritage. She had used it once to rid Dianthia of the hated invader Kedar and since then had done her utmost to forget it ever existed. And she had, until today. Suddenly chilled, Eirriel hugged herself, abstractedly rubbing her upper arms. Kedar! Why, after all these years, was she suddenly thinking of him?

"My love."

Aubin's hand on her shoulder startled her out of her thoughts, and she jerked around. It was a sign of his distraction that he did not take notice of her reaction.

"I want you to share with me."

Eirriel looked at Aubin in surprise. It wasn't that he never asked; it was the grimness she heard in his voice and the bleakness she saw in his eyes. Her heart leapt in her chest. "You really believe it is Aylyn?"

"Show me."

Eirriel nodded and closed her eyes. She called upon the memory of her dream and, fixing it firmly in her mind, reached out to Aubin.

Aubin felt her touch and her fear. Then he saw it. A sleek black mini-cruiser with a double-sun crest. It was all he needed. He knew the ship. Gods, he knew the ship! He was about to pull away when Aubin knew the cause of Eirriel's terror. The air around the ship, the air around himself changed. Aubin felt it closing in on him. Cold. Dark. Airless. He gasped for breath and wrenched his mind free.

Wild-eyed, he stared at his lifebond, not at all surprised to see she looked no better than he imagined himself to look. He shook his head in an attempt to be rid of the deep, soul-robbing foreboding that remained even now. He could not.

"That's not the *Ceallach*, Eirriel. It's the *Star Jumper*."

"Gods! You are certain?"

Aubin looked at her. "I know my ships."

Eirriel wrung her hands and her eyes grew luminous. "I'm sorry, I did not mean . . ."

Aubin pulled her to him. "Sh, my love. I know."

"Oh, Aubin." Her voice caught in her throat. "I want to talk to my daughter."

Aubin nodded. Silently, they made their way to the communications center down the passageway from his work chambers.

The on-duty tech looked up as they entered, then jumped to his feet. "Lord Director! Consort!" The flustered tech suddenly remembered protocol and touched his forehead in obeisance.

"Get me the *Star Jumper*."

Concern robbed Aubin of his usual courtesy, and when the tech did not move fast enough for Aubin's

Golden Conquest

liking, he shoved him out of the way and punched in the numbers, unaware that Eirriel had taken the bemused tech aside and in a few softly spoken words explained Aubin's actions.

The computer was just signaling that the com-system was open when Alaran walked in. He took one look at his father and shook his head. "He won't answer. I tried."

"He'll answer me," Aubin growled. "Or he'll live to regret it."

"Lord Director." Laaryc's nervous voice filled the chamber.

"I want to talk to my daughter, you young fool."

"She . . . is resting."

Alaran laughed. "Resting. Laaryc, she is sitting at your side."

Laaryc's only reply was a groan.

"Aylyn, I demand—"

The rest was cut off as Eirriel put her hand over her lifebond's mouth and shook her head. "Do you forget who you are speaking to? Demand anything of Aylyn . . ." Aubin's short nod told Eirriel he understood and she removed her hand.

"My daughter is well?"

"Yes, my lord."

"Good. Her mother senses danger and is worried."

Alaran rolled his eyes. His *mother* was worried? Did his father think his words fooled anyone? Alaran looked at Aubin and realized that he knew he fooled no one, least of all himself.

"Please beg Lady Eirriel's pardon for me, my lord. I am sorry to have caused her concern. As for the message your daughter left, please disregard it. Aylyn was just . . . being Aylyn," Laaryc finished helplessly.

"No pardon is needed, good Laaryc," Eirriel said softly. "I understand."

"Thank you, my lady," Laaryc replied in obvious relief.

"You will contact me when you reach Dianthia."

"Yes, my lord."

Patricia Roenbeck

"And, Laaryc."
"Yes, my lord."
"Guard my daughter well."
"With my life."

Aubin reached up to sever communications, but his hand froze when he heard his daughter gasp, followed immediately by Laaryc's frantic hoarse demand.

"By all the gods, who are you?"

Chapter Eleven

Aylyn's eyes widened as she stared at the man hovering in the center of the recreation area several hand-spans above the flooring.

He was garbed as a Guberian from the long-sleeved full shirt and blousy pants worn tucked into calf-high boots to the open flowing caftan and two lengths of material, one wrapped loosely around his lower face, the other turban-style around his head. He even had the multicolored iridescent eye patches. Aylyn, well-schooled in protocol, knew Guberians never wore blue. It was a color reserved for their dead, and it would bring dishonor to anyone who wore it.

The intruder wore blue.

No, he was no Guberian, merely a common villain capitalizing on the traditional concealment of the Guberians' apparel and too stupid to know the color gave him away.

On the contrary, my dear. I chose with great care.

Aylyn's hand flew to her mouth. Gods! He was a mind-toucher!

Laaryc, unaware of the silent communication, pulled Aylyn behind him as he repeated his demand, "Who are you?"

The intruder continued to ignore Laaryc and nodded to Aylyn. *Greetings, Aylyn of Rhianon.*

"How do you know me?" Aylyn asked in Hakonese, the language the mind-toucher had addressed her in.

Patricia Roenbeck

Laaryc twisted around. "Know you? He said noth..." His voice faded as he realized the intruder had indeed said nothing. That could only mean... Laaryc's head swung back, and he stared at the man he believed was his competition, trying to penetrate the disguise. "You are he?" Like Aylyn, Laaryc spoke in Hakonese.

"No."

Aylyn's answer was softly spoken but without question, and Laaryc sighed in relief. As foolish as it might prove to be, he would much rather deal with a stranger than with the man Aylyn loved. Still, he needed clarification.

"He did touch you?"

Yes, fool, I touched her.

Laaryc raised a hand to his temple. So this intrusion was what it was like to be *touched*. Laaryc frowned. How could Aylyn think it pleasant? But then, he quickly surmised, the tone of her mind-toucher's thoughts would not be as abrasive.

"And I will touch her again," the intruder continued. "But I am not he. Never him."

Laaryc had dedicated his life to learning. He studied and observed everything. As he listened to the muffled sound of the stranger's voice, he heard much more than was said. As powerful as this man might be, there was one who was more so. And the stranger knew it. Laaryc did not doubt it for a moment. He smiled. "So, Aylyn's mind-toucher is familiar to you." Laaryc stroked his chin. "Interesting."

The intruder cocked his head. "Interesting?"

"Yes. Aylyn fears him. And now I see she is not the only one."

Laaryc waited. He shook his head as it took their unwanted visitor a little longer to get the point. His arrogance was strong. Laaryc smirked. It would prove to be his undoing.

"Fear him!" the man scoffed. "I fear no one, little Dianthian, least of all him."

"Yes, you do. I—"

"Laaryc, don't!" Aylyn cried, not understanding what

Golden Conquest

Laaryc was doing, only knowing that whatever it was, he would be made to pay for challenging the mind-toucher.

But Laaryc was not about to be put off and continued as if Aylyn hadn't spoken. "I can hear the fear in your voice."

"Silence!" The command was reinforced by a mental shout that drove Laaryc to his knees. *You should have listened to her.*

"Laaryc!"

Laaryc's hands tore at the collar of his tunic. "Can't . . . breathe."

"Stop!" Aylyn cried as she moved to help Laaryc. "You're killing him!"

"He deserves to die for his words."

Laaryc was turning blue, and Aylyn knew he had little time left. Desperate, she sneered her contempt. "Are you so weak mere comments from a 'little Dianthian' can strike a mortal blow?"

"Weak? I? You speak as foolishly as your companion."

She glared at him. "And will you kill me as well?"

"Never."

The vehemence of his reply stunned Aylyn, but it also gave her the answer. "If he dies, I die. We are linked."

"You lie."

Aylyn raised her head and stared at him with eyes that dared. "Do I?"

The Guberian impostor smiled behind his mask. She lied. He was certain of it. And since it served his purpose to let her think him swayed by her statement, he released the Dianthian.

Aylyn held Laaryc as he took a great gasping breath, sucking in air.

"As amusing as all this is, I would be away from here."

"Don't let us stop you!" Aylyn spat.

"Until the game has been played out, I cannot take my leave."

"What game?" Laaryc rasped.

"This one." He nodded at the communications console.

Aubin's frantic shout suddenly filled the air. "Aylyn! Laaryc!"

Aylyn's face lit up with hope. She had forgotten Laaryc was speaking with her father when the intruder arrived. "Father!"

"Aylyn! What's happening? Aylyn! Curse you, why isn't this working?"

"Father, it is. Father!"

The stranger's laugh filled the air. "No, in truth, it is not. Though we cannot hear them, from the first they could hear us. How great your father's frustration must be, to know his child is in trouble and yet to be unable to communicate with her." The villain's voice was heavy with amusement. "Now we can hear them and they can hear us."

"This is Aubin, Lord Direc—"

The intruder cut in. "Think you I know not who you are, *Captain*?"

"Captain? I haven't been—"

"But you were. And so you shall pay. Both of you."

"If you harm my daughter, I'll see you in Nithrach!"

"You need not fear for your daughter. She belongs to me now!"

"No!" Laaryc lunged at him, and the intruder flicked his hand at him.

Aylyn screamed as Laaryc hurtled backwards, his head striking the console. He slipped to the floor, unconscious.

"You son of Schargaz!" Aylyn dropped to Laaryc and gathered him to her. She looked at the man with eyes dark with hatred. "You will pay for this, I swear to you! You will pay!"

"Aylyn! Don't do anything!"

"Ahh, the beautiful Eirriel. At last. My greetings to the one who has brought me here."

"I?"

"Yes, Eirriel of Dianthia, now Lady of Rhianon. You."

Golden Conquest

There was a moment of stunned silence followed by Eirriel's soft chiding laugh. "If it is I you want, I find your sense of direction greatly lacking."

"Mind-witch!" he hissed. "You would do well to guard your tongue!" He paused, then continued almost apologetically, "You misunderstand, my sweet Eirriel. It is not you I want, merely you who brought me here."

"Damn you!" Aubin bit out, his frustration obvious. "What do you want?"

"Patience, Captain. All will be revealed in time."

"Do you tell us who you are or are we to guess?" Eirriel asked.

"You wish to know who I am, beautiful lady? Do you not know? Can you not guess, Lady Eirriel, mind-toucher? Do you need a hint, Lady Eirriel, life-ender?"

"Life-ender? What?" The confusion suddenly fled Eirriel's voice, replaced by shocked disbelief. "Oh, gods! You cannot mean him!"

"Ah, but I can. See"—the tormentor flung his hand to the communications board—"see and know!" A white light arced from his hand to the console.

Eirriel's cry of pain mingled with Aubin's crazed roar. "Eirriel! Release her, you son of Schargaz!"

Aylyn had not been idle as she watched and listened to the intruder bait her mother. She had managed to slip Laaryc's dagger, a gift from his father that he was never without, from his belt and was gripping it tightly, waiting for an opportunity to use it. The instant the light flashed outward, Aylyn stood, took aim, and let the weapon fly.

It froze in midair a finger's breath from the intruder's chest.

Panic clawed at Aylyn's stomach. She had taken a gamble and lost. But as her mother's soft sobs and her father's gentle reassurances reached her ears, she knew she had succeeded in turning the stranger's mind from her mother and that made her attempt worth whatever punishment he would mete out. Satisfied that she had at least tried to kill him before he focused his malevolent power on her, she straightened her back, tossed

77

back her head, and glowered at him.

The man's pleased laugh made Aylyn blink. He was insane, she decided quickly, more than she had believed him to be. And when he spoke, his words chilled her to her very soul.

"Excellent, my sweet. You show much fire. That pleases me greatly." He opened his hand and extended it to her. "Come to me."

"No!"

"Come!" He flexed his arm to emphasize his order.

Aylyn took a step back and repeated, "No!"

"As you wish." The intruder relaxed his pose a moment, then extended his hand once again. *Now come*.

Aylyn felt his touch and his silent command. And though she would refuse it, she found she could not. Slowly, she closed the distance and placed her hand in his. He raised her to him, and, as they hovered side by side, he pressed a muffled kiss on her hand.

"Very good, my sweet. Please excuse the lack in my gesture of affection. Necessity decrees this disguise. But when you and I are together, nothing will come between us."

"Gods, no!" Aylyn gasped. "You cannot mean . . ."

The intruder's answer was a brief nod and to fit her closely to his side.

"Now, my Lord and Lady of Rhianon, know this. I am Rakkad, son of Kedar, and I claim a life for a life."

"Aylyn!" Aubin's enraged roar was greeted by silence.

His daughter and his enemy had vanished.

Chapter Twelve

Naydir looked down on his friend, lying pale and motionless on his back, pleased to note no sign of his wounds. "He is out of danger, Healer?"

Eadoine nodded. "The procedure repaired all that was injured. He needs to be watched, but I do not expect trouble."

A knock drew Naydir's gaze from Kolt. "Come."

Cal entered. "You sent for me, Councilor?"

"Yes."

"There are others in need, brave Naydir." Eadoine completed packing her supplies. "If he burns, send word and I will come."

Naydir nodded and escorted her to the door. "You have my gratitude. Whatever you ask, it shall be yours."

She laughed, and Naydir was struck by the youthful quality of the sound. "I have done only my duty to my leader and to my skills. Your gratitude is appreciated, your reward unneeded."

"As you will."

The healer stepped out into the passageway and then turned to Naydir once again, a twinkle in her blue and red eyes. "You will see to yourself now? You look chilled."

Naydir, still garbed in the covering, flushed and with a curt nod, shut the door. At Kolt's side, Cal bit his lip to keep from laughing. The action, however, did nothing for the amused glimmer in his eyes. Naydir scowled.

"It is the laedan who needs your attention, Cal of Mayrald, not me."

The reminder was enough to drive the amusement from Cal's yellow eyes. "What would you have of me?"

"I have received word of a man in Mayrald who brags that he has brought down a man of worth."

"Mayrald?" This brought a worried frown to Cal's leonine face. "Surely you don't think that I—"

"Be at peace, young Cal of Mayrald. I hold your honor as I hold my own. I but mention the city so you will know of whence this Goron hails."

"His details are correct?"

Naydir nodded. "To the twisting exit wound."

A knock and a voice bidding permission to enter brought both men to silence. Naydir's dresser garbed him, and the server laid out nourishment on a small corner table. The men broke their silence when they were alone once again.

"Surely someone sly enough to penetrate the keep without detection would be beyond such petty bragging," Cal commented as he helped himself to a generous portion of the tasty fare.

"Such is my thought," Naydir agreed as he reached for a platter. "I'll know for a certainty when I have spoken with Goron."

"Since he is of Mayrald, would I not be the better choice to go? My presence in Mayrald would not be suspect."

"None but Goron will know I am there."

"But why must you leave now? Kolt is vulnerable and must be guarded."

Naydir said nothing, content merely to eat and wait. If Cal was to be all Kolt hoped him to be, he would need to see beyond the evident. Naydir's patience was rewarded when the younger man suddenly lowered his flagon and smiled.

"You think the deed was done by another and Goron naught but a purchased tongue."

Golden Conquest

Naydir nodded.

"And if he refuses to speak the name of his employer?"

"Then I shall have to convince him otherwise," Naydir said quietly, the feral lights that burned deep within Naydir's amber eyes boding ill for Goron. "Though I hold little hope that Goron yet lives, I cannot assume that he is dead." Naydir drained his flagon, then poured himself another one which he likewise drained. Placing the empty flagon down on the table, he leaned toward Cal, his eyes dark with warning. "Listen well, young Cal, I know not how long I will be away, but while I am, Kolt's safety lays in your hands. Trust no one."

"What about Dakkar?"

"He has yet to recover from his glimpse of Kolt's wounds," Naydir spat in disgust. "And should he, keep him away as well."

Cal nodded. "We agree on him then."

"Yes, it is Kolt who is yet to be persuaded." Naydir slipped a vicious-looking knife into the sheath he wore inside his boot. The six-inch Zandrian blade with inch-long razor-sharp notches that ran down the length of one side was his weapon of choice when it came to convincing the unconvincible.

"When do you leave?" Cal asked as Naydir pulled on his gauntlet and checked the power supply on his neutralizer.

"This moment." Naydir made to put words to action, but paused when Cal called his name.

"I am well aware of the honor you have given me, Councilor," he said fervently. "I will not fail you."

Naydir nodded and left.

Naydir had been gone a short time when Kolt's restless thrashings began. Cal dropped the reports he had been studying and rushed to the laedan's side. He was stunned to see the red flush of his skin. Murmuring a prayer, he placed his hand on Kolt's brow, then jerked it back. Gods! He was burning with fever!

At Cal's touch, Kolt's eyes opened. He swung his

head, and Cal felt a deep fear at the sight of Kolt's bright glassy eyes.

"Aylyn?" Kolt's voice was a hoarse whisper.

"No, Laedan, it is..."

Kolt's hand shot up and he grabbed Cal, his fingers slipping into the long hair of Cal's mane and yanking him close to his face. "Where is she?"

Cal locked his hand around Kolt's wrist. "Hear me, Laedan! It's Cal!" he rasped. "Cal!"

If Kolt heard, it did not register, for his grip tightened. "What have you done with her?"

"Nothing," Cal said, then cried out as he felt the full force of Kolt's probing mind.

As quickly as it began, it ended. As did Kolt's grip on him. For a moment, Kolt's eyes opened, and he looked at the younger man. "Cal."

Cal's relief that Kolt had known him fled as Kolt suddenly went very still. Rubbing his much-abused neck, Cal ran to the door and yanked it open.

"Get Eadoine!" he barked.

He saw the guard move off and then returned to Kolt who was again struggling to sit up. Cal pushed against Kolt's shoulders. Kolt reacted swiftly and forcibly. Cal flew backwards, hurled by unseen hands, and slammed into the wall, the breath knocked from him.

"What happens here?" the healer asked as she entered.

"He burns," Cal gasped.

"Father of Creation! It cannot be!" The healer started toward Kolt.

"Go with care!" Cal, who was on his feet, grabbed for her arm. "He calls for someone named Aylyn. He thinks her harmed. When I tried to hold him down, he flung me here. He used his gift," Cal added quietly, and not without a little shock. Kolt was well-known for not misusing his powers.

Eadoine nodded grimly. She readjusted the mediscan and aimed it at Kolt. A short burst of blue light struck his temple, and he lay still.

Golden Conquest

"He is not the first patient I have had to restrain in this manner. Although, it is usually not at such a distance."

"Aylyn." His muted cry drew two pairs of eyes, and it was obvious to both that he was fighting against the sedative and winning.

"I like this not at all." Eadoine frowned. "He should be asleep and remain so for several hours. And he should be without fever."

"Could the blade have been tainted?"

"It can be nothing else." She drew a long, thin, clear tubing from the mediscan and positioned it against Kolt's wrist. "The taint must be rare for it to have gone undetected in the earlier scan." She depressed a button on the mediscan. As she studied the readout, the red in her eyes crept over the blue, a sign that her concern was deep. "Nothing." She pressed another set of buttons and waited. "Curse him! Nothing still."

"Aylyn." Kolt's voice was a hoarse, pained whisper.

"Could his concern for her cause this sickness?"

"It does not help. Hold him still," she ordered as Kolt began thrashing again. When Cal made no attempt to move, she scowled. "You need not fear his gift, the sedative has—"

"You misread my hesitation, Eadoine," Cal cut in. "I fear my strength, not his gift. I have no wish to harm my leader."

Eadoine nodded. "I ask your pardon. I had not considered that. Where's Naydir? Kolt may listen to him, and if he does not, Naydir can hold him still."

"He is gone in search of the one behind this crime."

"Then send for Dakkar."

Cal shook his head. "I cannot. Naydir has forbidden it."

"I care not what Naydir forbids. Dakkar has been raised within the keep at Kolt's behest and long been a favorite of his. Dakkar's voice may calm him."

Reluctantly, Cal agreed, and a guard was dispatched only to return alone.

"Dakkar is too ill to leave his sleeper."

83

The healer's head shot up. "Ill? Both of them?"

"Ill with cowardice," Cal growled.

Eadoine's brows arched in question.

"He saw Kolt as he lay wounded, his lifeblood pooling around him."

"Ah. He has always been delicate."

"Weak, you mean."

She smiled. "As you say."

Cal turned back to the guard. "You spoke with Dakkar himself?"

"No, Councilor. His dam."

"Go back and drag him here. If his voice will help Kolt, then—"

"There is no need!" Eadoine's eyes were once again red and blue. "I have my answer." She pressed a knob on the mediscan and the tube retracted. "I must go to my chamber and prepare the anti-taint."

Cal dismissed the guard, then asked, "How long?"

"A third of an hour at most." Her gaze slid to Kolt who was once again mumbling under his breath. "I think I will also retrieve the sfliox." Cal looked at her. "When I return, you will have an explanation." Cal nodded.

True to her word, Eadoine was gone and back before Kolt did more than just toss restlessly. Within moments of administering the injection, Kolt calmed. An hour later the fever had abated.

Eadoine withdrew the monitoring device and stretched, rolling her neck from side to side to relieve the kinks. She raked her hands through her short orange curls and smiled. "He is safe." Her belly rumbled and she laughed. "My belly seeks to remind me that I have neglected it overlong."

"I will send for some nourishment, if you would partake of it with me?"

"That will help this old woman greatly."

Cal's intense gaze swept over the petite healer. He saw a delicately structured face, fragile hands that moved with grace and certainty, eyes that burned with knowledge and caring, and a body that flowed and

Golden Conquest

curved most pleasantly beneath the full gray gown. He did not see great age, and he said as much.

The healer laughed. "I have been on Annan for ten generations, my young Councilor. And on Tragoy for many before that. The gods have blessed me and mine with a longer span in which to do our work."

Cal was so stunned he blurted out, "How long?"

"Long enough," came the quiet reply.

And from the set of her head, Cal knew that was all that would be forthcoming. He heard a noise in Kolt's antechamber and saw that the server had appeared with their nourishment. Knowing Eadoine would want to keep Kolt in sight, he gestured to the corner table in Kolt's sleeping chamber. The server set up quickly and silently, then was gone.

"Shall we?" he asked, extending his arm.

She linked her arm through his, and he led her to a chair. Cal then sat down and ate heartily. When he had filled his belly to his satisfaction, he sat back and waited for the healer, who had finished long before him and was once again checking Kolt, to rejoin him at the table. When she did, he poured her another beaker of the hot and tangy brew she favored, and leaned back in his chair.

"You promised me an explanation," he reminded her. "Of the sfliox you gave him."

"So I did." She took a sip of the brew. "When Kolt was five, he caught one of the usual childhood ailments and as is the case with most, he burned. But unlike most, he took to throwing things in his fevered state." Her eyes crinkled as she smiled. "His brother, Koltrax, was one of the things he most liked to throw. Much as happened here, happened then. I entered to find Koltrax picking himself up from the floor, none too happy. It was then that I remembered a package that had been left in my care three years earlier.

"It had been brought to me by Iseabal, a very beautiful woman with hair as golden as golithium and eyes as blue as safirium." The healer's eyes grew distant, and Cal knew that she was seeing Iseabal standing before her. "Sad eyes they were. So very sad. She placed the package in my hand and told me it was special. 'It is sfliox,' she said. 'He will need it one day to neutralize what makes him different.' The day Koltrax sent word requesting my help I knew. Iseabal had been Kolt's dam."

Cal started and he leaned forward. Kolt's dam! It was common knowledge that the two brothers were of different dams. Koltrax's dam was Tayr, the daughter of a wealthy grower, who had succumbed to an illness when Koltrax was ten. Of Iseabal naught was ever spoken. "What happened to her?"

"She went home."

"Home?" Cal frowned. He had thought her dead since Kolt had never spoken of her. And now to find that she had merely gone home and deserted him! "What manner of dam was Iseabal that she left her young son?"

"One without choice, so do not judge what you cannot know," Eadoine rebuked him sharply. "She just appeared one day and offered herself to Bhaltair, Kolt's sire, for however long she could stay. He took her in, cared for her, and grew to love her. And she loved him. I have heard that to see them together was to see love. And she loved her sons, the one of her body as equally as the one of another's. An eight-night after she came to me, Iseabal disappeared. The choice she made was no easy one, Cal of Mayrald. She was rent in two. You had only to look into her speaking eyes to know that. None know of her life before she came. Or after."

"Where did she go?"

"The gods alone can answer that, but far from Annan I think. Bhaltair never looked for her. His gift from the gods, as he called her, was gone. He had always known he would have her for only a short time. As it was, I think her love for him and his sons kept her overlong. Bhaltair was never the same. Never. And when Kolt was eleven, he died. A year later Koltrax was life-ended."

"Who saw to Kolt?"

Golden Conquest

"He saw to himself. And to us."

"Does Kolt know of all this?"

She nodded. "He asked to probe my mind and I agreed. But he learned no more than he had already known."

Cal's eyes drifted to his leader. "I have often wondered . . ."

"As have we all. Koltrax and Kolt have the look of Bhaltair, but the eyes of their dams. And Kolt's dam gave him more. She gave him his gift. It was, I believe, the reason she came."

Chapter Thirteen

Rakkad stood at the base of the opalescent circular platform and extended his hand. Reluctantly, Aylyn took it. She had considered ignoring it, but she was certain that would give him a reason to force her to his will, and the thought of him touching her again sent her stomach roiling. As Rakkad led her from the small cubicle, she made careful note of all she saw. That she was aboard a ship, there was no doubt. If—no, she corrected firmly, not if, when. When the opportunity came for her to make her escape, she had no desire to be floundering helplessly. However, she risked a quick side-glance at Rakkad; it might well serve her purpose if he thought her the image of a useless Blagdenian female. Instantly, she schooled her expression into one of witless terror. And to keep him from discerning her plan should he touch her, she focused all her thoughts on her fear.

Aylyn's plan did not keep her from filing away the shadowy presence of the tech who had worked the teleport, or any of the others she encountered as her captor led her through his ship. Nor did she fail to note that all, like Rakkad, were garbed as Guberians.

A conveyor portal opened in front of them, and Rakkad stepped aside, gesturing for Aylyn to enter. She did and when she saw him stand facing her, she thought a few tears called for, and maybe a little quaking question.

Golden Conquest

"Wh–what a–are y–your pl–plans?" she asked, pleased at the tremble she managed and the tears that trickled down her cheeks.

"Do not trouble yourself, my lovely one." Rakkad's hand came up to brush away her tears.

Aylyn jerked her head back, repulsed also by his physical touch. Quickly, realizing her mistake, she begged, "Please don't hurt me," and swallowed back the bile that rose in her throat at her cowering tone.

"You wound me. Surely you must know I would never harm you. You are mine."

Aylyn's gasp and the color draining from her face were no ruse. "No, I cannot. I belong to another."

"Belonged, my Aylyn. Belonged. As I will show you."

The portal swooshed open, and they stepped into the ship's com-center. Two "Guberians" sat before a long control panel in front of a wide screen.

Rakkad took his seat in the lone chair behind the men. Aylyn noticed it was raised several hand-spans above the floor. She thought perhaps he needed to tower over his companions—a supposition which she had no way of proving, as the guise they all affected hid their heights. When he gestured for her to stand at his feet, she couldn't stem her slight show of spirit as she stepped onto the platform and stood next to him. If Rakkad noticed, he gave no indication as he barked an order to his crew.

"Show me the ship."

The *Star Jumper* appeared on the viewer.

"You spoke of another, Aylyn." He nodded to one of his men. "As of this moment there is no other."

"No! You cannot!" Gone was the ruse of cowering fear. In its place was a terror she had never known before as Aylyn realized what Rakkad intended. "Laaryc! Laaryc!" she screamed his name as the *Star Jumper* was struck by a fiery green ball and exploded.

Aylyn launched herself at Rakkad. "You spawn of—"

The rest of her shrieked curse was cut off by her throat rapidly closing. Aylyn tore at the neckline of her tunic, her mouth working to drag in a few breaths of air. Rakkad's smiling image turned to swirling black dots, then her knees gave out, and she sank to the floor, unconscious.

Aylyn slowly roused. Even before she opened her eyes, she remembered the *Star Jumper*. Gods, Laaryc! A knot formed in the center of her chest and her throat closed, this time not from the ungentle mind's touch but from a mind's pain. Tears burned against her lids. *Laaryc, my friend, my gentle love, I vow to you I will make him pay!*

And the only way to do that was do find a way to defend herself. She opened her eyes to discover herself in a small cubicle. She sat up and looked around, searching for something to use as a weapon. Then she laughed, a harsh rasping sound that sent a sharp pain shooting through her abused throat, a painful reminder of the strength of her enemy.

Her hand rubbed her aching throat, and she sank back in defeat. Nothing she could find would aid her against a mind-toucher. Nothing! She was well and truly lost. And her vow of vengeance! How had she thought to see it fulfilled? She was a fool. A thrice damned one, for her impetuous mad flight from Rhianon had brought harm to those she loved.

She swiped at the tears that rushed unbidden to her eyes. Now was not the time to sink into a haze of self-pity, she told herself firmly. It would only feed his ego. Faking tears was one thing. . . .

"Did she teach you that?"

Aylyn's head shot around, and she saw Rakkad standing in the darkened corner of the cubicle. "She? Teach me?" she asked, her voice strained and roughened by its recent trauma. "I don't understand."

"That mind-witch who spawned you. Did she teach you to shield your thoughts?" Rakkad moved next to her as he spoke.

"If you cannot read my thoughts, you are as incompetent as you are mad," Aylyn spat, not caring if he turned his power on her again.

Golden Conquest

Rakkad laughed. "So you say, but this"—he tipped her chin up—"is not the face you arrived with. It is the face of a kilgra, teeth bared and prepared to rend me in two should I venture too closely." He laughed as she jerked her face from his hand. "You please me greatly."

"That was not my intention."

"No, I would think not, but you have nonetheless."

He punched an order into the nourishment dispenser in the wall near her sleeper. A beaker of steaming liquid slid into the opening. Rakkad retrieved it and handed it to Aylyn, who eyed it suspiciously. "It will help your throat." When she made no move to take it, he snapped, "It is not my aim to cause you harm!"

"Really?" Her brows arched, and she raised her hand to her throat. "Your touch was that of a friend?"

"It was a reaction to the suddenness of your attack. I am on my guard now. It will not happen again. You have my word."

"And your word is something I should trust?"

"I would have it so. Yes." He thrust the beaker toward her. "Take it."

I would sooner trust the dark God of Nithrach! Aylyn thought, but she reached for the beaker. Hesitantly, she sipped the blue liquid and was surprised that it did as he had said. The burning sting in her throat eased, and it was then that she decided. Foolish though she may be, she would not accept this coil she was in. Somehow she would escape. Somehow she would see her thirst for vengeance slaked. And in order to see it done, she would need to know all she could of him. She looked at him. Would he unwittingly aid her in her search for a weapon that would bring him down?

"You are truly Kedar's son?" she asked in a voice returned to normal.

Rakkad waited for the chair to complete its extension from the wall, and twisted around to turn his concealed gaze on her. "Yes, of a ruler's daughter on a conquered planet."

"Blagdenians are not mind-touchers." *They are scum*, she added silently, then continued, "You are. Your mother was Kiiryan?"

Rakkad laughed as he lowered himself into the chair. "My dam, unlike yours, is useless. She brought to me nothing. What I am, I am not from birth, but from knowledge and wealth. What I have, I was forced to earn after your mother caused my sire to be stripped of his power and standing on Blagden."

"And for this you call her life-ender?"

"I call her life-ender because she wished him life-ended and so he was."

"He was an invader. Many of her people died horribly and by his orders. That she wanted him dead should surprise no one."

"I did not say she wanted him dead, Aylyn. I said she life-ended him herself."

"My mother could never—"

"Your mother possesses the power to kill with a thought. You doubt me, do you not? Well, my Aylyn, doubt this."

Aylyn drew back against the pillows as Rakkad touched her. She closed her eyes against the image of a slim, darkly handsome man in black and her mother, tall, slender, and naked. She saw the man's eyes darken with rage as he turned his weapon on her mother. Saw her mother slam against the wall. Saw her mother crying and the man fly across the room. And then she heard her mother's voice. "You will die for what you have done. You are burning. Blistering. Your lifeblood is no more. In its place is rock. Flowing molten rock." The man screamed and dropped to the floor, writhing. "Scalding. Scorching. Molten rock." The man tore at his skin. "A life for a life." Then Aylyn felt the silence and saw only darkness as Rakkad's touch ceased.

Tears streamed from Aylyn's eyes. Tears not for Kedar, but for what he had done to her mother. Gods, but she never knew! Her parents' reluctance to talk about that time of their life, saying only that

Golden Conquest

the invader had been killed and Dianthia restored, now seemed painfully clear. Gods! How had her mother stood it? But . . . what if it wasn't real?

Aylyn opened her eyes to see Rakkad sitting, waiting. She swiped at the tears defiantly, then drew her lips back in a sneer. "You are a mind-toucher. You can touch me with any image you want. Your manipulation only proves you are lying, you vicious father's lying, vicious son."

Rakkad jumped to his feet and loomed over Aylyn. "You would be wise, Aylyn, to guard that tongue." He stormed away, then whirled to face her again. "You think I lie? I tell you I do not. I am the heir to the House of Keda. All the power, the riches, the honor of that house should have been mine! And yet I have nothing save what I have purchased for myself because of one person. When I asked that fool who gave birth to me who it was, she gave me a name. Eirriel. And I have searched long and hard for a reason why I am naught to any Blagdenian. And what I have learned has made me what I am today. All that I am." He laughed. "I need not touch you to know that you think me mad. But as I do not lie of what I showed you, I do not lie about this. My sire's obsession for your dam cost me my birthright. What, I wondered, was there about her to bring down so powerful a leader? My quest brought me another name. Balthasar. Know him?"

Another name her parents had preferred not to discuss. "Yes, he was the chief safeguard officer aboard my father's ship."

"He was that. And he was more. He was a mind-toucher."

Aylyn frowned. Another fact never mentioned by her parents. By chance or by purpose? The answer, she knew, would lie in Rakkad's tale. A tale she suddenly believed to be true. "Was he Kiiryan?"

"No. He was from Tri-III."

"I have heard they had outlawed scientific practices on Tri-III."

"Yes, but not soon enough to save poor Balthasar's mind. The mind-touching skills they gave him through their experiments left him with an uncontrollable need to rule the galaxy. When he met Eirriel and felt her power, he thought to make your dam help him. She and your sire thought otherwise. He didn't survive the final encounter with your sire, I'm afraid.

"When I learned of Balthasar, I had to go to Tri-III. I was mind-blind, like you and all others that are not born of Kiiryans, when I arrived there." He laughed. "With a little convincing and a lot of crystal, the scientists agreed to help me and so I am as you see me, a mind-toucher."

"And your father's life-ending? How did you learn . . ."

"That your dam did it and how? Why, from the old Dianthian, Moriah."

Aylyn frowned. "The woman who raised my mother?"

Rakkad nodded. "She didn't wish to tell me anything, but I . . . insisted. Apparently, she had heard shouting in Eirriel's chamber and thinking her lady was dreaming went to wake her. She opened the door to witness what I showed you. She fled to search for Timos after hearing your dam's final vow."

"A life for a life. That's what you said to my father before you took me here."

"And so it will be." Rakkad stood and crossed to her. Aylyn cringed as he ran a finger down the side of her face and across her lips. "Your life is mine now and forever."

"No! You cannot mean to keep me. You cannot! My father—"

"Your sire's life will be forfeit if he attempts to take you from me."

Aylyn's face blanched. He would do as he promised, of that she had no doubt. She had seen what he had done through the communication linkage aboard the *Star Jumper*. If her father tried to use a weapon, he would find it turned upon him before he could react.

Golden Conquest

Gods! She was lost! None could fight a mind-toucher—except another mind-toucher! Aylyn closed her eyes and concentrated. She hadn't felt the other's touch since he was wounded, but if the gods were with her, they were still linked and he would hear her now.

I think not, my Aylyn.

Aylyn shuddered as Rakkad touched her, and she opened her eyes. She cried out when she saw him leaning over her, a sharp tubular instrument in his hand.

"No! Please!" She tried to back away, but she was trapped against a wall. He grabbed her chin with his free hand. Her arms came up to push at his chest, and when that didn't work, she used them to pound and slash at him. A quick touch of blinding pain brought an end to her struggles.

"That's better. You will learn that to fight me is to cause you pain."

"You lying, son-of-a-Blagdenian whore, you—."

Anything more Aylyn would have shrieked was cut off by her shrill scream as Rakkad touched her once again. This time when the pain ceased, she said nothing and just stared at him with eyes that spoke of her hatred. And her fear.

Rakkad forced her head up and away so that her long slender neck was exposed. Aylyn felt the icy metal against her skin and resolved not to cry out, but she could not hold back the whimper of terror at the prick of its sharp point.

"My mind-touching was not the only result of my trip to Tri-III, sweet Aylyn. There was also this."

Aylyn screamed once again. Not from Rakkad's touch, but from the metal as it pierced her neck deeply and the liquid, at once fire and ice, that forced its way into her bloodstream.

"You do not like the caress of vxanza, my love?" Rakkad asked, as he removed the needle and straightened. "A pity for it brings the deep sleep of forgetfulness. Ah, I see you are surprised. Did you not question that I spoke so freely of who and what I am? Powdered vxanza was also added to your brew."

"Is that how you treat my trust, by adding a drug to my drink?" Aylyn demanded.

"Trust? You did not give me your trust, Aylyn. You but sought to trick me. I am no fool, as you will learn."

"What I have learned is your word is as useless as your father's."

"When you at last awaken, you will be in a place far from here and you will pay for your unwise remark. I did warn you, did I not? And then I will make you mine."

"Never will I be yours."

"You will be unable to stop me," Rakkad promised darkly.

Aylyn fought against the seductive darkness that beckoned to her and called her mind-toucher's strong gentle caress to mind. She focused on it and begged the gods to lend their assistance and let him hear her cry of help.

Rakkad's gloating laugh replaced the warm tenderness of her remembrance. Aylyn shook her head. She tried to force her mind to concentrate, but it would not. Instead, Rakkad's laugh grew louder and his voice said, *Should he hear your cry, sweet love, it will be the last he will hear of you. Vxanza now mixes with your lifeblood to create a shield. The next time he reaches out to you, he will touch emptiness.*

Help me. Please help me, Aylyn called to him once more before she could resist no more and lost herself to the power of vxanza.

Chapter Fourteen

Kolt ran through the thick murky fog that surrounded him. He saw nothing. Not his feet striking the ground. Not his hands held out in front of him. And he heard nothing. Just the insulating silence of the mist.

But he *had* heard something, of that he was certain.

It had been the faint cry of protest, of help, that had drawn him here—wherever *here* was. He had heard it only once. But it had been enough.

Aylyn needed him.

She was distressed. Gravely so. And afraid. He had gotten that much in the brief touch. And now, try though he would to touch her, he could not.

"Aylyn? Answer me. Aylyn!"

Nothing. Just more silence. Gods, let her be safe! Let him be in time!

He tripped and fell to the ground. He struggled to his feet, combating the sudden strength-robbing fatigue that had settled over him. Each step he took was a fight. But he continued on. One foot in front of the other. He tried for speed, but could summon none. He recoiled as his next step carried him into a furnace of heat. He stumbled backwards under the onslaught, the heat followed, enveloping him, robbing him of his breath. But still he pressed on.

Aylyn needed him. He would not let her down. And if his feet would not carry him. . . .

"Aylyn, my love." Kolt closed his eyes. "I am coming."

"Aylyn!"

The weak cry roused Cal who had taken advantage of Kolt's seemingly peaceful sleep to grab some of his own. He turned his head and saw Kolt struggling to sit up. Leaping from the temporary sleeper he'd been using during the three days since the assassination attempt, Cal prayed to all the gods he could think of that Kolt's fever had not returned. Eadoine had reassured him that it wouldn't, adding gravely that if it did, Kolt did not have the strength to fight it. His hand on Kolt's forehead laid that fear to rest. But brought another.

If the fever was not causing this unrelenting agitation, what was?

"Laedan," Cal called gruffly as Kolt swung his legs over the sleeper's side. "You must not."

Ever careful of his strength, Cal pressed Kolt's unresisting shoulders back and pulled his legs back onto the sleeper. Cal's frown increased as Kolt took a few deep breaths and then fought to sit up again. Once again, Cal pushed him back, this time tucking his legs under the covers and pulling them tightly as Eadoine had commanded. Perhaps the constriction would keep him still. Cal stepped away when he saw that it worked. For a moment.

Then Kolt tried to pull back and away. He gasped and grabbed at his throat. "Aylyn. I am coming."

He was trying to *actualize*, Cal realized in horror as Kolt began to fade. Fearing the consequence of his attempt under the influence of sfliox, Cal roared Kolt's name, thinking to jar him back. Whether it had worked, Cal did not know, but Kolt was suddenly whole and complete. And deathly still.

Cal's panicked bellow brought in Morald, who had personally taken charge of guarding Kolt's chambers.

"Fetch Eadoine! And be quick about it!" Cal barked as he moved to Kolt's side. He pressed his large hand

Golden Conquest

to Kolt's neck and was relieved to feel his pulse under his fingers. Thus reassured, he stood helplessly and waited.

Eadoine rushed into the chamber. "What happens here?"

"He calls for her again. But this time when she did not answer, he thought to go to her."

Cal's grim tone turned Eadoine's eyes all red. "Surely you can't mean he attempted to *actualize*?"

Cal nodded. "He almost succeeded."

"Gods, but he should not have been able! Who is this Aylyn that she has such a hold on him?"

"The one he has chosen as his lifebond," Morald said.

Healer and councilor turned to Morald standing just inside the chamber. "Naydir felt I should know should she arrive while he was away," Morald explained.

"Arrive? On Annan? When?" Eadoine demanded. "If she speaks to him, it may set his soul at peace and he can rest."

"She is to come this night Naydir said. But as to where or when or even how, not even the laedan knew." Morald's frown deepened until his dark brows were nearly one. "Naydir said the laedan had been touching her. If they are linked in some manner and she were troubled, would not the laedan sense that?"

"If it is as you say and she is in danger, he may be trying to reach her," Cal surmised.

"Mother of the Universe!" Eadoine's eyes turned red. "From the first, their link has been great enough to penetrate the haze created by the drug. Why did I not realize the danger of the sfliox?"

"What danger?" Cal demanded.

"The strength of the laedan's will has never been weak. It is his body that has betrayed him. If he should succeed in *actualizing*, the sfliox may so confuse him psychically that he may not be able to complete the re-materialization."

"What does all this mean?" Cal demanded. The understanding of how and why Kolt could do what he could do had always been an impossible concept for him to

99

grasp. "Are you saying that he cannot *actualize*?"

Eadoine shook her head grimly. "I am saying that if he does, he may very well succeed where the assassin failed. He may life-end himself."

"Can you not flush the sfliox from his body?"

"Gods, but I wish I could! It mixes with the lifeblood, Councilor. Nothing will rid him of it. It must wear off by itself."

"And until it does?"

"You will watch and wait. And should he seek to leave, you must hold him here."

Kolt opened his eyes, then groaned as the bright sun streaming in from the casement seemed to burn through to his soul. He slammed his lids closed and raised a hand to his throbbing head. Gods! But it ached!

"Dakkar!" He struggled to push himself up, confused by the unusual fatigue that had sapped his arms of their strength. "Curse you, why have you not lowered the casement coverings? Dakkar!" he yelled, then winced as his voice magnified a hundredfold within his head.

Not again, Cal groaned. There had been no sign of the fever, no sign of anything but restful sleep since the last episode, for which Cal heartily thanked the gods. And now, to have been roused suddenly from his sleep by Kolt's feverish thrashings! Eadoine's warning made Cal a little afraid. He quickly got to his feet, his yellow eyes darkening as he saw Kolt leaning against the wall, his eyes squeezed shut, and his hands pressed against his head. How much more could the laedan take?

"Dakkar," Kolt called again, but softly, when he heard the movement. "Lower the drapes. The glare of the sun tears at my eyes."

Cal quickly did as he bid, but he was worried. The laedan had not complained of pain before. Had not said anything except Aylyn's name since his wounding. He liked it not. He would send for Eadoine at once.

Kolt heard the sound of the coverings being lowered and risked a peek. When he saw the light dimmed, he

Golden Conquest

opened his eyes fully. Better, not perfect, but tolerable. He lowered his hands and turned to Dakkar to thank him.

"Cal?" He was surprised to see the large Mayraldan apporaching him.

The sound of his name halted Cal's steps. "Laedan?"

"Who else would it be, Cal of Mayrald?" Despite the insistent thumping within his head, Kolt smiled cheerfully and gestured to his surroundings. "These are my chambers, are they not?"

"Gods be praised!" Cal rushed to his leader's side and stared down at him. "How do you fare?"

"Fare?" Kolt frowned. "Except for a head that holds all of Inner Sumal within it, well enough."

Cal nodded. "Eadoine warned you would awaken with a fierce ache in your head. It is from the sfliox."

"Sfliox?"

Cal nodded. "You have been gravely ill."

It was then that Kolt remembered the icy fire that had torn through his back not once but twice. The terrible twisting of the knife as it had been removed. Kolt rolled his shoulders. "Eadoine has done well. It pains me naught at all. But what is sfliox?"

"You were fevered."

Kolt scowled. "Did I toss you?" Cal nodded. "I beg forgiveness. It is beyond my control and I like it not."

Cal smiled. "I suffered no ill affects from my flight, so there is nothing to forgive. And Eadoine saw to it that I would take no more." When Kolt did not appear to understand, he explained, "Sfliox neutralizes your gifts and leaves you as the rest of us."

"Ah. But how came I to be fevered?"

"The blade was tainted."

"Tainted?" A sudden dread filled Kolt. "How long have I been ill?"

"The sun has reached its zenith five times since—"

"Five times!" Kolt jumped out of the sleeper. Ignoring the weakness in his knees, he took a step toward Cal. "The day? What is the day?"

"Why it is twenty-seventh day of—"

Patricia Roenbeck

"The twenty-seventh! Gods! Aylyn was to have arrived on the twenty-fifth!" Kolt moved to his wardrobe, his concern for Aylyn overcoming the lingering fatigue.

"Laedan! You cannot mean to clothe yourself!"

Kolt turned and cast such a dark dangerous look at Cal that the councilor stepped back. Kolt returned to his dressing.

"You've been ill."

"Yes. And while I have been cosseted and cared for, Aylyn has been alone. In darkness." Even as he drew on his shirt, he reached out for her. And touched nothing.

Kolt staggered against the wardrobe. He had always been able to touch her, even when she was young and did not know. And now, when she was here on Annan, he could not! Why?

"The sfliox? Would it keep me from touching?" Kolt demanded, praying to all the gods that was the answer.

Cal, not understanding the full import of the question, nodded. "Yes. Eadoine said it mixes with your lifeblood and neutralizes your abilities."

Relief shot through Kolt until he realized that he was hearing Cal's concern and without trying. He sent a quick purposeful touch toward him and easily saw all Cal had gone through the last few days. And he read Cal's confusion and concern for Aylyn. He yanked away from Cal swiftly. Gods! Why could he not touch her now when he had been able to even when drugged? He gnashed his teeth. If she needed him and that accursed drug kept him from finding her. . . .

Cal, thinking to take advantage of Kolt's distraction and force him back to the sleeper, moved toward Kolt.

"Do not." Kolt's voice was deadly soft. "I give you warning. If you would see tomorrow, do not stop me."

Cal knew the laedan's mood made reasoning with him impossible and started from the chamber. He would send Morald for Eadoine. Perhaps the healer could accomplish what he could not. When he returned, Kolt was seated in the chair drawing on his boots.

Golden Conquest

"Where do you go?"

"Where she is." *If she is there. If she is alive. Gods, but if she is not* . . . Kolt's heart twisted in his chest. How could he even consider life without the woman he had been waiting for since he was twelve. Since the time he had met Aubin and a face formed in his mind. One of beauty and grace. Of strength and courage. Of laughter and the promise of a love worth dying for.

"Can you not wait?"

"Wait? You would have me wait when I am already late by two days." He drew in a ragged breath and looked up at Cal, his blue eyes haunted. "I cannot touch her, Cal. I have tried and I cannot. Why?"

Cal could only shake his head. "I do not know."

Kolt stood. "Neither do I. But I will."

Kolt closed his eyes and *actualized*.

Chapter Fifteen

Bone-weary, Naydir trudged up the stairs that led to Kolt's chambers.

In the five days he had been away, his loyalties had constantly been torn between his need to find the assassin and his need to watch over Kolt. Confident though he was that Kolt would be well guarded by Morald, he couldn't escape the niggling doubt. He alone of all challengers had been able to defeat Morald and his presence had not kept Kolt safe.

His scowl deepened as he thought of the accursed assassin and his recent effort to find him. As he had expected, Goron had been silenced. Five witnesses reported that a man swathed in blue appeared suddenly, sent an arc of dazzling blue light toward Goron, and disappeared even before his victim had ceased to exist. Had Naydir not thought it an impossibility, he would have believed him a mind-toucher rather than the owner of some new weaponry. But mind-touchers were extremely uncommon and that two of them should be found on Annan was inconceivable. Still, Naydir did not like it, for it made him question the assassin's choice of weapon for his latest attack against Kolt.

Why a blade? Why not the neutralizer that had been used previously? Or the new weapon he had used to dispatch Goron or any number of weapons that could be fired from a safe distance? That the attempts had failed or been foiled hardly seemed a reason the assassin should suddenly risk his own life with a hand-held weapon.

Naydir dragged a hand through his hair. If the Mother of the Universe granted him her favor, he would find the assassin before another attempt. The use of a blade indicated that the would-be murderer was becoming desperate. Would he become reckless enough to succeed?

"Greetings, Councilor."

Naydir glared at his captain who stood guard outside Kolt's chambers. "Why are you here, Morald, and not Hbrueck? I thought I assigned him to the laedan's chambers?"

"He is on the terrace outside the laedan's sleeping chambers. I thought to stand watch here myself."

"Has there been another attack?" Naydir demanded. It was unlike Morald to countermand his orders.

Morald shook his head. "Eadoine found the blade tainted," Morald reported grimly, "but . . . No! He is recovering," he quickly reassured Naydir when he saw the color drain from the councilor's face. "Forgive the manner of my telling. My mind is but a little fogged."

"When did you last sleep?" Naydir asked, studying his captain's face and seeing the intense fatigue shadowing his purple eyes.

"I dared not, Councilor. Kolt was gravely ill, and I feared him most vulnerable."

"I understand. You have done well, Captain."

Morald glowed at the praise but shrugged it off. "I but did my duty."

A sudden shout from within drew the men's attention. In less than a breath, both had their shield activated, neutralizers at ready, and were inside.

"Kolt! No!"

Cal's frantic cry led them to Kolt's sleeping chamber. Naydir rush forward and ground to a halt as he saw Kolt vanish.

"What happens here, Cal of Mayrald?" Naydir demanded, his rage evident in the flash of his eyes and the whiteness around his tightly drawn mouth. In his anger, he threw Cal's own words back at him. "Is this how you see to the honor I have bestowed on you?"

Not liking his honor questioned, Cal drew himself up to his full height, a full foot more than Naydir. "He has gone to his Aylyn, Councilor," he bit out curtly. "And I have not the means to stay him. Nor have you," he added, his pride stung greatly by Naydir's callous accusation.

"Then Aylyn has arrived."

"It would seem so."

Naydir remembered Kolt's knowledge of her and the day of her arrival. And that he had refused to share with him the place he would meet her. "Did Kolt say where she is?"

Cal shook his head, his bleak eyes settling on the empty sleeper. "No."

A persistent gnawing in her stomach and an absence of sound drew Aylyn from the depths of her dreamless sleep. Slowly opening her eyes, she glanced around and saw, by the eerie light of a flame light placed near her pallet, that she was no longer on Rakkad's ship, the *Vartex*. She was in what appeared to be a cave. How had she arrived there? She frowned. Her mind held no answer, merely a hazy fog of mixed impressions. Curiosity made her ignore her belly's demand for nourishment.

She picked up the flame light and held it to the wall next to her. Black crystal? She ran her hand down it, feeling the cool smooth texture that affirmed her guess. The inner depths of Mont Kriek were of black crystal. Could Rakkad have been cagey enough to place her within her father's reach? She quickly found her feet. If that were so, then she would soon be safe. If—and it was a very large if—she could find her way out of the cave.

Golden Conquest

The flame light raised high above her head, she scanned the darkness, seeking some indication of a break in the wall, of a way out. And she could see none. Did she dare risk getting lost by stumbling around in the obsidian depths? A sudden terrifying thought hit her. If she was within Mont Kriek, as she believed, she could very well fall victim to the kriekors. She laughed at the bitter irony of it. Had not Laaryc feared her flight with him would have *him* facing the kriekors? Gods, but she wished he were. At least then he would be still be alive.

Despair, as thick and unpenetrable as the ebony that lay beyond the flame light's muted glow, rushed over her as she thought of what her mad flight had cost Laaryc. She dropped back onto the pallet as she pictured the intensity that had burned within his eyes as he spoke of returning to Dianthia, of the knowledge he would impart to his fellow Diathians. She heard his lighthearted laughter, so rare and so much treasured because of its rarity, saw him sitting in the grass, studying, when others were running around at some form of play. Pain and loss ripped at her heart. Would the gods ever forgive her for causing Laaryc's death? And should they? Could she ever forgive herself? She thought not.

She sat there, unmoving, lost in self-hatred, until the grumbling of her hollow belly caused her to question when last she ate. She saw a bundle at the foot of her pallet and opened it. Her brows rose as she dumped its contents onto the ground. There was enough nourishment and water to last her many days as well as several pieces of clothing. Had Rakkad not thought to return? Gods, but if she could only remember!

Opening up a packet of what appeared to be dried meat, she gingerly tasted it. It was not bad, though it was strong and gritty. Could that mean the meat was real? That it had not come from a replicator? She dropped it quickly, not at all surprised that Rakkad was uncivilized enough to insure his survival at the expense of a defenseless animal.

Patricia Roenbeck

She pushed through the many containers until she found one that held some kind of fruit. Sinking her teeth in it, she smiled. It was sweet and tasty. A further shuffle found five such packages. Good. If she rationed them carefully, they would hold her for a time. Hopefully until she found a means of escape. Frugally, she sipped water from one of the ten water holders. Her schooling had taught her that she could exist longer without nourishment than without water.

Her belly satisfied, if not full, and her thirst sufficiently quenched, she tossed the receptacles back into the bundle. The air within the cave was cool, something she had not taken notice of till then. So she slipped on a lined, long-sleeved tunic before adding the other articles of clothing to the nourishment supplies and sealing the bundle.

While she was eating, she had come to the unhappy conclusion that she was not on Rhianon. How could she be, when the only black crystal on Rhianon was located in Mont Kriek and in Mont Kriek were the kriekors? Since none had attacked, which they *always* did, none were around. Therefore, she must be on some other world that boasted of black crystal. *Now what?* she wondered as she twisted her hair into a knot at the back of her neck, then bent her knees, placed her elbows on them, and leaned her chin on her hands. Did she just sit and wait for Rakkad to return for her, or did she chance getting lost somewhere within the depths of this unknown mountain? If she did not try, if she merely waited meekly for Rakkad, she would have another crime to lay on her conscience when he used her to exact his vengeance on her parents. That sobering thought was enough to drive Aylyn to action.

She would try to find her way out. But how to mark the trail? She looked over what she had available, then smiled. The pallet's heavy outer covering was woven! She picked at the thread and was happy to see it unravel in one complete thread. Working diligently, she wound the thread round and round until she had a

Golden Conquest

large ball of thread in her hand. If she let it trail behind her, she would be able to retrace her steps if the terrain was impossible to travel. Though Rakkad could use the same method to track her, she thought that if the gods were with her, she would be beyond his reach by then. If they were not, he would find her and she would have to take satisfaction in that she had made his task more difficult.

She took one of the meat containers, dumped out its contents, and placed the ball of thread inside. Checking to see that it spun freely, she placed the ball and its container into her bundle, holding the free end in her hand. She glanced around. How was she to secure the thread to her point of departure? Perhaps if she placed the extra meat containers in the middle of the pallet and rolled the holder around them, then wrapped the thread it and knotted it tightly, the containers' weight would immobilize the pallet so that it would withstand the pull of the thread as she walked. Quickly, she put her plan in motion and was pleased to see that it did indeed work.

She slipped her arms through two straps along the back of the bundle, and checked that the thread still rolled easily. Then, the flame light in one hand, the other against the crystal wall, she slowly began to make her way out—or so she prayed—of the cave.

She had been walking for quite some time when the ground started sloping upward. At first the rise was gentle, but as she pressed on, it grew steeper. Several times she stumbled and fell forward. The first time it had happened, her heart had plunged to her belly as the flame light crashed to the ground. She had breathed a sigh of relief that it had remained lit and unbroken. Without the light, she doubted she possessed the courage to continue on blindly. When she fell again, she decided that as long as she was down she might as well stay down, nourish herself, and rest.

How long she slept, she did not know, but she woke suddenly with a sense of disquiet. She sat up and listened, and a distant rumbling reached her ears. She strained to identify it, but could not. Repacking her supplies, and rechecking the thread, she grabbed the flame light and slowly made her way toward the sound. As she approached, she finally recognized the sound of a great deal of water thundering over falls. She picked up her pace. Perhaps the water would lead to a path out. Soon she was jogging, and within another few steps she felt the wall turn once, twice, and entered a great cavern.

She gasped to find the ground sloped downward to form the catch basin for a huge and powerful waterfall. The rainbow mist created by the force of the water as it plunged over the falls clung to her face. Gods, but it was beautiful! She looked around at the walls and saw they were not black crystal, but prism crystal. And how they sparkled! It was then she realized she was seeing much more than she should have been able to see with her little flame light. She raised her eyes.

High above the falls there was an opening. Sunlight spilled in, bathing the cavern in its warm glow. Her eyes on the opening, she began to run. Until she realized that her feet were getting wet.

She had been so intent on reaching the opening that she had failed to note the considerable expanse of the lake at the bottom of the falls. It extended as far as she could see, in all directions except the one she had just come from. She raised her eyes again to the opening—an opening she now knew she could never reach.

Chapter Sixteen

What was she to do? To be so close, if a hole in a ceiling far above one's head could even be considered close? She fought against the hopelessness that threatened to pervade her very being and turned and made her way back to her bundle. She needed to change. Already, a numbness was settling in her bones, a result of her headlong flight into the icy water. How could she have been so foolish? To run into the lake without looking? What if the bottom of the lake suddenly fell away? What if it was inhabited by fierce life-stealing creatures? She shivered at the thought and the cold.

Rifling through her bundle, she pulled out a pair of pants, then groaned when she realized there was nothing dry to put on her feet. Gods, but she was freezing! She drew out a shirt and wrapped her feet in it, but it was thin and of little protection against the chill rising from the crystal floor. She thought of the flame light, but a quick touch dissuaded her from the thought. It gave off light not heat.

She knew she should draw back into the shelter of the original chamber and away from the mist that was slowly permeating her clothes, but until she knew beyond any doubt that she could not reach the hole, she was not leaving. That made her laugh. Did she think it would move?

So she sat, curled into a ball, growing colder with each passing moment, bleakly staring at a hole her rational mind told her she could not reach. As she listened to the sound of the falls, she realized that it had been the only sound she had heard since she had awakened to find herself in the dark cavern. It was strange that she heard no animal skittering, though the gods knew she was grateful for that, since she could not imagine any creature she came across that spent its life locked within the darkness of the cave as friendly. And it was stranger still that she heard no sound within her mind.

That was what had awakened her, she realized suddenly. Not the gnawing of her stomach or the sound of the distant falls, but the silence in her head. Her mind-toucher had not touched her while she slept.

She remembered that he had been injured and felt a brief flash of fear that he had not survived the wounding, but quickly dismissed it. She would have known if that had happened. As she lay listening, she grew aware of an emptiness within her that had not been there in years. She had thought his touch reached out to her only when she slept, but now she realized that he had been there all the time. Always. Like a gentle whisper in her mind. And now he was gone.

Why? Was it the gods' punishment for her causing Laaryc's death? Selfishly, she couldn't help but wish the price a little less dear. She cringed. Had not Laaryc's price been equally as dear? But gods! How was she to go on? Without Laaryc? Without her mind-toucher? With Rakkad returning at any time and tracking her?

Overwhelmed by all she had caused, by all she had lost, she lay on the cool crystal ground and cried.

Kolt *actualized* in the cave in total darkness. He extended his arm, his palm upward, concentrated on forming a bright tongue of flame in front of him, then beckoned it toward his hand. He caught it in his upraised fingers and held it. He moved his hand around the cave until the light fell on a rolled bundle of material. He moved to it quickly and recognized it

Golden Conquest

as a pallet used by Annan's force of migrating growers. He saw the string attached to it and smiled. He had always known Aylyn was smart and strong, but to have not given in to panic, to have attempted to find a way out only after leaving a clearly marked trail was remarkable. Father of Creation, but she was a woman worth having!

But she should not have had to rely on herself. He should have been there when she arrived, to greet her and to see her to safety. And he would have been if not for the assassin's deadly taint or his friends' well-meant machinations. He felt the anger build within him and took a deep cleansing breath. His anger would not help, but only hinder him. He needed to focus all his energy on finding her, not on cursing what should have been.

He glanced around the area for a clue to how she had come to be there and found none. He remembered a vague image of a ship exploding and that her witnessing the explosion had pained her greatly and her anger and fear had been directed at one person. Ra . . . Rak . . . He cursed. The name would not come. Had it been his ship she was on? Had she left Rhianon on it?

His glance returned to the pallet. No, the ship and its master had been Annanite, it was the one thing in this befuddling mess he knew for certain. But Annan's fleet was limited and, according to his roster, all accounted for. With the exception of the hijacked vessels. Could she be in the hands of the hijackers? Gods, but all he had were questions! At least he knew she was alive and as well as could be expected.

Catching sight of the thread, he smiled. Better than he had expected. But caverns held such perils. That she arrived safely was known, that she was still safe was not. If he could but touch her, his anxiety would lessen. The flame light glinted off the black crystal. Had he lost touch with her when she arrived here in this cavern? Could there be something in the composition of the crystal walls, something that combined with the sfliox and rendered him mind-blind? If that was true, then could he touch her now that he was within the cavern?

As quick as thought, he put words to action. And found the results the same. Nothing. Not a touch. Not a whisper. Nothing. Why? He bit back his roar of frustration certain that if it reached her out of the blackness it would terrify her.

Instead, he thought the flame he held in his hand into a large flaming ball, drew back his hand, and hurled it across the cave. The fiery missile burst against the crystal wall and splattered into a shower of sparkling pinpoints of light that sputtered and went out. Again and again and again, he created and hurled a fireball. One after another. Without variation. Without pause. Until his mind, still combating the residual effects of sfliox and his illness, could form no more, and he sank to his knees gasping for breath and holding his hands to his spinning head. His anger if not gone but at least under control, he sat and waited for the cave to stop whirling and the spirals of flashing lights behind his closed lids to vanish.

When he felt his mental strength return, he picked up the thread and held it lightly across his hand, then concentrated. A phosphorescent pulse of light leapt from his hand, caught the thread, and ran the length of it into the darkness. He gave a moment's pause to how Aylyn might react to this sudden pulse of light shooting out of seemingly nowhere, and called it back a few yards. It was the best he could do.

Then, the thread still in his hand, he sat down, leaned back against the cool crystal wall, closed his eyes and *parted*, separating his essence from his body. Hovering in the air a few feet, he gave his lifeless shell a reassuring glance and then sped away, following the pulsing sliver of light. In no more time than a breath, Kolt reached the end of the glistening strand. He moved toward the ground, then reunited his body and his essence, steadying himself as he felt the steepness of the incline beneath his feet. He cocked his head at the roaring

Golden Conquest

sound that reached him and quickly identified it as the rushing thunder of an underground waterfall.

He had only taken the thread into his hand when a wave of dizziness washed over him. Cursing, he grabbed for the wall, pressing his forehead against the cool crystal. Eadoine should be very grateful that she was nowhere within his reach, he thought ominously. Then he felt unworthy. She had saved his life, and for that he owed her his thanks and not his constant recriminations. The dizzy spell gone as suddenly as it had come, Kolt began to walk, his hand sliding along the thread, pushing the phosphorescence in front of him.

He had moved no more than a few feet when the thread seemed to vanish into an area of muted light. Thinking it the light Aylyn had used to guide her way, he started to run. Then ground to a halt as he entered the cavern that housed the falls. He saw the hole in the ceiling, then glanced below it to the underground lake. His heart thudded in his chest. Surely she hadn't tried to brazen the murky water! He was about to yell her name, when a whimper off to the side drew his attention. He turned and smiled.

He had found Aylyn.

He found himself at her side, unaware that he had even put thought to action and had *actualized*. He rekindled the flame and held his hand high so that he could drink in the sight of the woman who had been so much a part of him for so long. A woman he knew intimately, yet knew not at all.

She was here!

She was lying on her side, her hands pressed together holding her face from the heat-stealing chill of the crystal floor, her knees drawn up to her chest, her feet wrapped in a shirt. He knelt beside her and gently pushed the hair from her eyes. And his breath caught in his throat. He had always known she would be beautiful, for the face in his vision had been. But, Mother of the Universe, had any beheld such beauty! His lips curled up as he remembered the first time he had said those words. He had just seen Eirriel when she arrived in the open-air market of Inner Sumal searching for Aubin. But Aylyn gave new meaning to the words. She was Eirriel and more. Enhanced by her father's Rhianonian features, Aylyn's beauty surpassed even Eirriel's.

His eyes ran across her face, seeking signs of ill use and found none save the darkened rings beneath her eyes that spoke of fatigue.

She was here! The phrase ran over and over in his mind like the chorus of a child's song. She was here!

He could admit it now. Admit that deep down in the darkest depth of his very being he had feared she would not come. That the vision of her face had been naught but the fantasy creation of a child forced by circumstance, by the very nature of what he was, to be a man; the trick of a mind stronger than his ability to control it.

But it wasn't. She was here!

She shuddered and drew her knees closer to her chest, drawing a frown from Kolt. While he knelt there gaping like a lovesick fool, she shivered from the cold wet mist. He cursed. Gods only knew how long she had been lying in it. He gently lifted Aylyn into his arms. When she stirred, he held his breath. He had hoped to have her in a safe place, where the light was bright and would put to rest all her fears before she woke. But she merely rolled her head toward him and snuggled against his chest. A sign, he felt, of her acceptance of him.

He stood, liking the feel of her in his arms. She was his gift from the gods. He started. His father had called his mother such, and less than three years later, she was gone. His gripped tightened around Aylyn. He was no Bhaltair. He would never willingly give her up. Should the gods or anyone else seek to retrieve this Iseabal, he would fight them to the death.

Aylyn shuddered again. Kolt knew he had to get her warm or she would take ill. He thought of his sleeping chambers and was about to *actualize* there,

Golden Conquest

but remembrance of Cal's distraught look and Naydir's roar of rage held him back. While Cal might have taken himself elsewhere, Naydir of certainty would not have. No privacy there. Kolt frowned. Then where? He needed to take her someplace she would be safe. Someplace none knew of. His frown turned quickly to a smile. His hideaway! Naydir alone knew of it, and he would not disturb them unless his need was great. Yes, that would do nicely.

He searched within himself, testing the strength of his skills. Strong enough, he quickly ascertained, to do what needed to be done. But he would have to do it quickly, for he was beginning to feel a heaviness in his limbs, a sign that his body needed rest. And that would make it just as dangerous as if his skills were still hindered by the sfliox. So, holding Aylyn pressed against his chest, he *actualized*.

The first thing Kolt noticed upon their arrival in the small chamber was the cold and dark. A thought and that was remedied as a fire flared in the corner fire holder and the flame lights near the sleeper and hanging from the ceiling sprang to life. He looked toward the sleeper, decided the coverings were too dusty and thought again. The coverings from his chamber in the Crystal Keep appeared and folded around the sleeper. Much better. He placed Aylyn down on the thick softness of the sleeper. Gods, but she must be tired, he thought since her lone reaction to the move was to turn her head into the pillow. He gently pulled the coverings over her.

With a last look at her, he quietly pulled the door closed and set about preparing the hideaway for their stay. His mind ran down all that they would need. Water they had aplenty, but the nourishment supplies had been depleted after his last stay and he had forgotten to order them restocked. Clothing for himself and Aylyn. Extra coverings. Each item appeared as he thought it, and another thought set them in their assigned places. He stretched as the fatigue that nudged at him earlier

Patricia Roenbeck

now attacked with all its strength. He could give in to it now.

Not wanting Aylyn to awaken alone, he made his way to her chamber and lowered himself into the large, sumptuous relaxer that stood against the side wall. Thinking all the flame lights out except for the one on the table near Aylyn's sleeper which he muted, he propped his feet up on the little footrest in front of the relaxer, laid his head back, and pulled up the covering. Just before his eyes closed, he thought once more, and when he fell asleep, he did so with a smile.

Back in the cavern a burst of white light appeared, whirled around, hurled itself to the ground just to the right of Aylyn's discarded bundle and vanished.

Kolt's message to Aylyn's would-be captor had been delivered.

Chapter Seventeen

Naydir shook his head and sighed. Would he ever see Kolt act with care for himself? He thought not. He looked over at Cal, who was seated in the chair next to Kolt's empty sleeper, and Morald who stood next to him, their faces bearing the evidence that they believed they had failed both the laedan and the councilor of Inner Sumal. Naydir knew, in spite of his unthinking words of a moment ago, that the young Mayraldan had discharged his duty in a manner not to cause shame. He crossed to him and placed his hand on Cal's shoulder.

"Do not berate yourself, young Cal of Mayrald. I but spoke in anger. I doubt not your honor or that you did all you could have done. Kolt is ever Kolt. If he thought his Aylyn in danger, the gods themselves would not have been able to stop him."

"You think him in danger?" This from Morald.

"No. In all his talk of Aylyn and her arrival, he never connected it to danger. I can but hope his vision did not lead him astray." Naydir stretched. "I have had but little sleep over the last five days, and from what I have seen, neither have you. Find your sleepers. Kolt will return when he is ready." Naydir pulled his shirt over his head. "I will sleep here. When Kolt returns, I mean to have answers."

"Should he arrive and catch you sleeping and think

to sneak out through the antechamber, I will make up my sleeper there," Cal offered.

"And I in the passageway." Morald grinned. "I would miss his arrival should I take myself elsewhere."

"The laedan would be honored to know he has such loyal friends," Naydir said solemnly. "In his place, I thank you."

"It is but my duty," Morald replied.

"And my honor," Cal finished.

"No, it is much more. Do not think to make light of it." To himself, Naydir vowed to see them well rewarded. "Now, my gallant Annanites, to sleep with you. I vow my eyes will close ere I am fully prone."

Nodding their agreement, Cal and Morald left to seek their own sleepers.

Naydir had just given into the strength-stealing fatigue when his head thunked down against the bedding. He jerked awake and twisted around to find his head cushion gone. Before he had time to register that astonishing fact, the coverings were gone, too. A thump and clatterings followed by a loud curse from the antechamber drew Naydir to his feet. He ran to the outer chamber and Morald rushed from the passageway to find Cal, who had thought to take nourishment before he slept, sitting on the floor, scowling, the nourishment platter and flagon scattered around him. Within moments, the passageway was filled with startled shrieks and frantic shouts. Naydir started to laugh.

Cal took Morald's outstretched hand and got to his feet, his hand rubbing his abused buttocks. Both men jumped in startlement as the casement coverings vanished.

"What in Nithrach happens here?" Cal demanded in such puzzled outrage that Naydir, who had just started to compose himself, began laughing again.

Between gulping gasps of breath, Naydir managed one word. "Kolt."

Cal's bark of laughter and Morald's deep chuckle joined Naydir's as another round of frustrated shrieks

Golden Conquest

drifted up from the open casement. Wherever Kolt was, he apparently was in need of furnishings.

Rakkad materialized in the cavern, eager to see how Aylyn fared. When his flame light spilled onto the rolled pallet, his first thought was that he had grievously underjudged the sedative power of the vxanza. She should have just been rousing. His next was the realization that she was gone and he cursed. He had not considered that should she awaken, she would venture away from the pallet and seek a way out of the cavern. She was a female and she was alone. She should have been weeping and anxious for his return. That was one of the reasons he had chosen this dark cavern within the depths of the Quixtallyn Heights. The other had been the knowledge that every time Kolt looked out his casement—as he was apt to do when he was plagued—he would be unaware that he was staring at the very thing he was missing.

He cursed. He should have realized she would be unpredictable. She had that accursed mind-witch for a mother, he reminded himself. *She* would not have remained here patiently waiting, and it seemed her daughter was more like her than he had thought. She had even been clever enough to mark a path. He smiled. She was proving to be a challenge, and there was little he loved more than a challenge.

He held the flame light up, placed the thread between his fingers, and began to walk. As he did, he planned ways to make her pay for the inconvenience of having to search for her. When he reached the incline and stumbled, he swore and doubled the punishment. Each time he fell, his anger increased, as did the severity of the penance he would mete out to her, until by the time he reached the cavern of the falls, he decided her life-ending would be the only suitable retaliation for his ragged knees and scraped palms.

His rage swiftly changed to confusion when he saw no sign of her and then to frustration as he saw the sign he had been meant to see. Carved into the crystal flooring next to her bundle were the words "SHE IS MINE!" and Rakkad knew, without doubt, that somehow Kolt had found her.

But how? The vxanza should have prevented it. Had prevented it, he knew. Not foolish enough to chance that the vxanza did not work, he had prodded Kolt's mind with the thought of Aylyn's danger and had witnessed Kolt's reaction when his touch had failed. No, he had not touched Aylyn. Yet he had found her. How? His bellowed curses rang through the cavern long after his men, responding to his barked order, snatched him out of the cave and deposited him safely within the one place that held his answers. The Crystal Keep.

It was the heat that woke Aylyn. She kicked off the covers even before she opened her eyes. And when she did, she was stunned to find herself not on the floor of the cold damp cavern, but in a sleeper in a nicely warmed chamber. Obviously, Rakkad had returned and traced her, as she had feared he might, by the thread. That she had no memory of being carried or moved she could not account for. The last thing she remembered was being overwhelmed by fatigue. Had she merely been so tired that she slept through the journey here—wherever here was? Stealthily, she rose and crept to the casement next to the sleeper.

From the glow of the rising sun, she could see that she was in a lodge in the middle of some woods. She smiled. Rakkad had made a serious error in judgement if he thought to keep her here. This would be easier to escape from than some cave or a ship hurtling through space. She pressed her face against the transparent crystal casement shielding and saw what appeared to be a path wending its way into an exceptionally thick growth of brush. Could that be a way out?

A sound off to the side of the chamber drew her attention and made her realize she was not alone. She spun and peered into the shadowed corners. She cocked her head and listened. Someone was there and from the sound of it asleep. Whether it was Rakkad or

Golden Conquest

one of his cronies, she was not staying to find out. She turned and pushed against the casement and breathed a sigh of relief when it gently eased open to reveal a drop of about four hand-spans to the ground. She sat on the ledge and was just about to swing her legs over when a rich, gravelly voice, husky from recent sleep, startled her.

Aware of her confusion and fearful she would recognize his voice from their last touch, Kolt addressed her in Hakonese.

"You've no need to run."

Aylyn's head jerked around. She watched in panic as a tall shape rose from the relaxer and moved toward her. The breadth of his shoulders and his long length told her it was not Rakkad. But who?

"I won't harm you. You can trust me."

"Trust you?" she sneered, in the language of the Protectorate. "I cannot trust your leader, yet I should trust you? My life means more to me than that."

Aylyn quickly dropped from the casement's ledge to the soft springy ground, then took off at run toward the path. She entered and had run no more than a few steps when the brush became so overgrown she was forced to crawl. She heard him calling her and looked over her shoulder to see if he followed. As a result she did not see that the path vanished in a thick intertwining mess of twigs and leaves until she swung her head back around, and right into it. *Now what?* she asked herself, as she wrenched her hair free from the grasping branches. Did he know she had foolishly taken this path? His shout gave her answer. He knew.

Kolt chuckled. "It goes no where, sweeting. Why not come out?"

Curse him! And curse his life-ending, interfering leader! May they rot in Nithrach!

"Please. You mistake me for someone else," the man called.

Mistake him? Was it possible?

"I have no leader. Come out. On my honor, I vow you can trust me with your life."

123

Aylyn listened carefully to his voice. There was something in it, something familiar, yet she was certain she had never heard it before. Suddenly she was just as certain she could trust him. And that scared her more than if he was Rakkad himself.

Kolt cursed. Nothing was going as he had foreseen! Not her arrival. Not his delay. And of a certainty not this! He squatted down and peered into the brushy tunnel. He'd try one more time, and then if she still refused, he'd take her out of there so fast. . . .

"On your honor, then."

Kolt pulled back, startled by the smoky voice that spoke to him from the darkened shrubbery. He smiled as he stood and stepped back. "It would seem we are even now. One startle apiece is all one is allowed on Annan."

"Is that where I am?" Aylyn asked as she stepped out into the open. "Annan? Oh my!" She gasped as she saw the ruggedly handsome man in front of her clearly revealed by the first rays of the sun.

In the darkened chamber he had appeared large, but face to face he was at least two hand-spans taller than she. Though not garbed as such, she knew he was a warrior, for no amount of clothing could disguise his thick powerful legs, broad shoulders, and lean waist. Slowly, she raised her eyes and her breath lodged in her throat as she saw his full, sensuously curved lips curled in a dazzling smile of welcome and his strong chiseled features were accentuated by his closely cropped beard. And his eyes! Gods, but she had never seen ones so blue or so alive!

"Yes, this is Annan." Kolt swore at the rough edge he heard in his voice. The sight of her brilliant eyes studying him approvingly had sent a hot rush of lust straight to his groin. "You know of Annan?"

"Yes." Heat flooded her face as she realized she had been staring, and she lowered her eyes to her hands.

Kolt stepped forward. "Do not," he said as he tipped her head up to meet his eyes. "Do not hide from me. It pleases me that you like what you see," he teased. "I

Golden Conquest

like what I see as well." Father of Creation, was "like" ever a misstatement!

Aylyn took instant umbrage at his arrogant, if truthful, assessment of her slack-jawed gaze. She jerked her face from his hand and stalked away. Kolt reached out, easily capturing her arm.

"This way. We have much to discuss and it would be more comfortable within."

Reluctantly, Aylyn allowed him to lead her through the rear door and into the front sitting chamber. She pulled away and moved to a large and solitary chair in the corner of the chamber. Kolt noted that she kept the chamber's full distance between them, but refrained from chiding her about it. The gods knew that she had a right to be wary.

"Would you care for nourishment?" Kolt offered even as he touched the mind of the chief server in the keep and learned the location of a tray that was to have been brought to Naydir and Cal. "From your meager rations I can but think you undernourished."

"Yes, thank you." Aylyn frowned. "My rations? Then you found me in the cavern?"

Kolt crossed to the nourishment chamber and fetched the tray he had *actualized* from the startled server's hands a moment before she placed it in front of the two councilors. He used the time to come up with a reason other than the truth, which would cause him to explain that he was the mind-toucher she had fled Rhianon to avoid. Already a plan was formulating in his mind. He would take advantage of this time they had and let her get to know him.

"Yes. I am a searcher." He placed the tray on the table in the center of the chamber and pulled out a chair for her. "I explore the caverns of Quixtallyn Heights, seeking veins of crystal to harvest."

Aylyn sat down and Kolt pushed in her chair. "But I saw no way in."

Kolt took the seat across from her. "I use the transmaterialization units from the main harvesting station to transport me to a particular spot. Then I progress on foot until I reach an untraversable terrain or I tire or need supplies. Then I signal and the T-M unit retrieves me. The next time I start where I left off, if possible, or where I began. You were where I last searched."

"I must have been something of a surprise," Aylyn commented as she looked skeptically at the steaming platter.

"That you were." When she made no move to serve herself, Kolt poked a piece of red meat and started to place it on her plate.

"I'll not eat fresh-killed animal."

Kolt's face screwed up in disgust. "Who would? This is replicated."

Aylyn smiled. "Then, yes, please."

Kolt placed the simulated meat and two spoonfuls of the vegetables on her dish, then filled his own. Aylyn reached for the carafe. "It's Melonnian sweet and sour," Kolt explained.

She looked up, startled. "That's my father's favorite drink."

"Then your sire and I have much in common. It is my favorite as well." He took a sip. "Does your sire have a name?" he asked, though he well knew the answer.

"Aubin, Lord Director of Rhianon."

"It is a name well known on Annan. Then you must be Aylyn. You are well come, Aylyn of Rhianon."

Warmth crept up Aylyn's face as she realized she had failed to obey the first rule of protocol—introducing oneself. She smiled sheepishly. "Please excuse my lack of manners. I find my circumstances unsettling, but that should not lead to rudeness. I thank you for your greeting. May I now have your name?"

Had Aubin told her that the laedan of Annan's name was Kolt? That Kolt was a mind-toucher? Praying to the gods that he had not, Kolt gave Aylyn his name.

"I am Kolt."

Chapter Eighteen

"Annan and Kolt?" Aylyn laughed at the irony of it. "Only I could flee my home and land up on the one planet that would most please my father and get rescued by the one man that bears the name I am least comfortable with."

Kolt frowned. "What is it about my name that causes you displeasure?"

"It's the same name as your laedan. My father has long had hopes that I would life bond with him."

Kolt's eyes darkened, and he quickly lowered them, not wishing Aylyn to witness his irritation. Aubin had vowed to keep his wishes between them. How was it that she knew of them? And what had Aubin said that had set her so against him? That she mistrusted the strength of his passion for her as Kolt the mind-toucher, he well understood, but that she would have naught to do with Kolt, the laedan, when she knew him not at all, he could not fathom. With seeming nonchalance, Kolt asked, "That would be so bad?"

Aylyn looked at Kolt. "When I am ready to life bond, it will be with a man of my choosing, not my father's. It is my life, after all."

"You know the laedan so well you care naught for him? Most on Annan speak highly of him."

"As does my father. I don't know him at all."

"Then how can you—."

"I have no desire to spend the rest of my life on a

piece of rock with that—that paragon."

Kolt choked. "Paragon?"

"Yes. To hear my father tell it, the laedan can do no wrong."

"I see." Kolt vowed to thank Aubin in like manner for his too kind words. "Would you now tell me why you call Annan a piece of rock?"

"Father said Annan is a small, underdeveloped harvesting colony. The Protectorate won't even grant them membership."

Kolt bristled. "Perhaps we do not care what the great and powerful Protectorate thinks. Perhaps we believe we are worth something as we are."

Aylyn flushed. "I'm sorry. I spoke of a conversation that took place years ago." She raked her hand through her hair. "I'm usually not so tactless. The mention of your laedan sets me on edge."

"Why?"

"Because, as I have said, I want no one chosen for me."

Kolt had nothing to say to that. "If I promise not to mention the laedan, will you forgive me my name?"

Expecting to find mockery in his eyes, Aylyn looked up to see teasing lights instead and sought to match them. She sighed heavily. "Unless you can change it, I have no choice."

"Good." He held the flagon up. "To new beginnings?"

Aylyn touched her flagon to his. "To new beginnings."

Kolt drained his flagon, and Aylyn followed suit. She set the flagon down, and he offered her more. She shook her head and sat back. Kolt realized that he had given her enough time to relax. He needed answers and now he would have them.

"I've some questions of my own," he said seriously.

"I would imagine that you do." She smiled.

"How came you to be in a cave deep within Quixtallyn Heights, alone and poorly supplied?"

Amusement vanished from Aylyn's eyes. "I don't know. Our ship was attacked and—"

"Our?"

Golden Conquest

"Well, it was actually Laaryc's ship. My friend was on his way back to his home, Dianthia, and I—"

Kolt's eyes darkened. Laaryc! The man she would chose over him. "And where is this Laaryc that he would leave you alone and vulnerable?" he demanded harshly.

"He . . . he is . . . I life-ended him!" Aylyn choked, and buried her head in her hands.

Kolt was stunned! His Aylyn could life-end no one, especially not one who meant to her what he knew this Laaryc did. He knelt by her side and lifted her chin. "Did he harm you that you held him in weapon's sight and fired?"

"Harmed me!" She gave a choked laugh of self-derision. "Laaryc loved me! He would not harm me."

"Then how came you to this conclusion, Aylyn?"

Frantically, she sought a reason for her certainty that she had caused Laaryc's life-ending. "I—I—" Her eyes wild and wide, she shook her head. "I can't remember!"

"Tell me what your memory serves you up." Kolt's voice was gentle, coaxing. "What comes freely into your mind? We will work from there. You made mention of fleeing Rhianon," he prodded. "Why?"

She stared past Kolt, not seeing the concern that darkened his blue eyes or drew his lips into a tight line. "Someone wanted me. I was frightened." Kolt, knowing full well that she referred to him, said nothing and waited. "Laaryc was going home. To Dianthia. I thought if I went with him I would be safe. And because I was there on the ship, Rakkad came."

Kolt's brows shot together. Rakkad? Yes! That was the name he had snatched from her mind when she had cried out to him. He was the hijacker. Every sense he possessed screamed to him that he was but he had no proof. And she had seen him. He could see it in her eyes, hear it in her voice, as she struggled with the memory. Instinctively, desperately, he tried to touch her to take her memory of Rakkad, then swore in frustration when he failed. Again. Gnashing his teeth at a fate that had robbed him of his link with her now when she held locked within her mind what he needed, he had no choice but to wait for her to speak.

"He—he was dressed as a Guberian, but he was not one. He claims to be Kedar's son."

"Kedar's son!" Gods! But can it be?

"He came after me. A life for a life, he said. And then he ordered me to him and I could not prevent it! He held me within his thrall." Panicked golden eyes slashed to Kolt. "He is a mind-toucher!"

"Mind-toucher!" Kolt knew he was repeating her words like a fool, but, in all truth, her words rocked him to his very soul. Kedar's son and a mind-toucher? Could it be? Was this why he could no longer touch her? Had this Rakkad shielded her? It would explain much. Aylyn had begun to speak again, and Kolt forced his attention back to her.

"He—he ordered our ship, the *Star Jumper*, destroyed." A sob caught in her throat. "Laaryc was still on the ship!" Tears streamed from the eyes she raised to him. "Why, Kolt? Why would Kedar's son harm Laaryc? He had nothing to do with Kedar."

Kolt gathered her to him and held her close. No, Laaryc did naught to cause harm to Kedar. He was merely an innocent in a deadly game of revenge. But he could not say as much to Aylyn, for it would confirm her belief that she unwittingly caused Laaryc's life-ending. Nor could Kolt tell her that he knew why Kedar's son sought vengeance. Eirriel had felt it necessary to prove to Kolt that she had avenged his brother's life-ending. She had offered him the memory and he had taken it willingly. Aylyn's gentle sobbing gouged a path through his heart.

He pressed a tender kiss to her forehead, swept her into his arms, and carried her to the relaxer. He sat there, holding her on his lap, enjoying the warmth of her head buried against his shoulder and the feel of her breath against his neck. He ignored the reason that she was in his arms because she was crying over a man she thought she loved.

Golden Conquest

"It is madness that drives Rakkad, Aylyn. It is his essence that bears the guilt and must answer to the god of life, not yours." He gently rubbed her tears from her cheeks. "Come, dry your tears. Your friend would not have you so distraught. He would have you remember the times you spent and the love . . ." The words pierced his heart as a swiftly and as lethally as a dagger, but then he remembered that Laaryc was no more and he could afford to be magnanimous. After all, he had her for now and for all eternity. " . . . you shared."

Comforted by his tender understanding, Aylyn raised her tear-streaked face to him. "You are right. Laaryc was the most unselfish person I have ever known. He would not want me to lose myself in this gloom." Suddenly she realized she was sitting on the lap of a man she hardly knew. It mattered not that he had rescued her and was kind and sympathetic. She drew away and was glad when his hands did not hold her back as she stood. "Thank you for your kindness. I will do as you say and keep Laaryc close to my heart."

Close to her heart! Kolt groaned, and he leaned his head back against the wall. That was not where he wanted Laaryc at all.

Aylyn walked away and then turned, her eyes bright with determination, her hands clenched at her sides. "And one day I will see this Rakkad dispatched to Nithrach for all eternity! Even if it means I must ask help from your laedan."

Kolt's head shot up, thinking to order such foolish plans from her head, but thought better of it. She would not listen. Her heart was too sore. Instead, he questioned, "My laedan?"

"Yes. As much as I wish to avoid him, he owes my father. Rakkad is very powerful. Only someone like your laedan can hold him off til my father arrives."

"You are certain your father is coming?"

"I will ask your laedan to send word to him. Laaryc was fostered within our household. My father will see it as his duty to seek and destroy his life-ender. And that Rakkad threatened my mother! Yes, my father will come."

Kolt arched a brow. It rankled that she said Aubin would come because of Laaryc and Eirriel and not because of her. "Think you your father will not come just for you?"

Aylyn was startled by Kolt's question. "Yes, of course, he would, but now his honor and his love have been touched. It will just make him deadlier. He will demand explanations of your laedan. And your laedan will be wise to have them."

Kolt had known he would have to answer to Aubin's fury when he learned of Aylyn's experience, but it irked him to hear her say it. "The laedan has much to contend with, Aylyn. I know not how much help he will be."

"Oh," she said, defeated. How was she to avenge Laaryc on a strange world and alone?

The bleak hopelessness in Aylyn's golden eyes drew Kolt to his feet. He took her hands in his, and swore, "With all that I am, Aylyn of Rhianon, I will see your vow kept."

"You would do this for me?"

You know not what I would do to keep you safe, my love, he thought, but to Aylyn, he merely said, "Yes."

"Thank you."

The smile she gave him made him ache to taste her lips. But he knew it was too soon and stepped back. "What say you to a brisk walk? Lywl is not far. From there, you can have word sent to your parents that you are safe. The message will take several days to reach Rhianon and more for your father to come. Give me those days, Aylyn, to show you Annan. Its beauty. Its mystery. Its people." *Its laedan*, he finished silently.

Stay on Annan! She had never considered it. But if Rakkad were connected with Annan, as she suspected, remaining on Annan would be the only way to get to him and make him pay for destroying Laaryc and threatening her parents. Kolt had vowed to help

Golden Conquest

her, but it was her battle. She alone would confront Rakkad. If she kept her hatred and grief in obeyance, Kolt would never know the reason she agreed to stay.

"Yes, Kolt. I'll give you those days." And as she gave him his answer and saw the soft lights dance in his eyes and watched the corners of his mouth sweep up into a tender smile, she realized that it was more than vengeance that made her agree. Kolt's deep voice had been rich with his love of his people and world. And, suddenly, she wanted to stay, wanted to see what it was about Annan that made him love it so.

Kolt saw the changing emotions on Aylyn's face and did not need to touch her to know revenge played a part in her agreeing to stay on Annan. But he also saw a softening and hope swept over him. "Perhaps you will grow to love Annan enough to stay," Kolt said softly.

When she opened her mouth to deny the possibility, he placed a finger against her lips. "I'd have you hold your answer." Aylyn nodded. "Good. Now, would you like to make use of the cleanser before our little jaunt?"

Aylyn looked down at her clothing and groaned. "It will take more than cleansing to repair this mess. Your people may take one look at me and run for the Heights."

"My people will see what I see. A beautiful young woman."

Unable to face what she heard in Kolt's voice, Aylyn screwed her face up in a grimace and laughed. "With a deplorable taste in clothing."

Kolt pointed to a small door between the two sleeping chambers. "Make use of the cleanser. When you are done, you will find clothing not so deplorable laid out on your sleeper."

Aylyn thanked him. She entered the small cleansing chamber and gasped at the sight of her in the floor-to-ceiling reflector. The man said *this* was beautiful? Instantly, heat rushed over her. Gods! But he had a way of making her believe it! Turning the water valves on, she snatched up the brush from the crystalline table and attempted to rid her hair of the tangles while she waited for the large oval-shaped water basin to fill.

Her hand froze in mid-stroke as she suddenly realized what his having women's clothing meant. Fool, she told herself when the thought of him lying lovingly in a woman's arms sent her heart plunging to her belly; a man who looked like he did obviously had a lover. She remembered his passion when he spoke of his world and his people. No, she quickly amended, more than one love. Stepping out of her clothes and into the hot swirling waters of the cleansing basin, she couldn't help but wonder how it would feel to have him hold her with something more than compassion.

Kolt waited until the door was closed and then began to pace. Clothes. The ones he had ordered and were waiting for her in the Crystal Keep were no longer appropriate. Perhaps Jupl would help. Kolt cocked his head and listened to the sounds from the cleansing chamber. When he heard her outraged gasp, he knew she had seen herself. She would be occupied for quite some time, he thought smiling. More than enough time to visit Jupl.

His orange-and-purple caftan dragging on the floor, the tiny yellow-skinned man paced back and forth among the mountain of fabrics, his mouth moving rapidly and silently, his head bobbing with each step. Every so often he would stop suddenly, gesture frantically, then start to pace again.

Kolt watched the frenetic motions of Jupl, the master clothesmaker of Inner Sumal, from the corner of the well-lit chamber. When Jupl passed for the tenth time without noticing him, Kolt decided action was called for. He took two steps forward and waited. Jupl would either see him or walk through him.

"Father of Creation, Laedan! You startled me!" Jupl's bushy red eyebrows rose to above his hairline, then lowered to knit together in a frown. "I did not hear you come in."

Golden Conquest

Struggling to hold in his laughter, Kolt shook his head.

Jupl shook his head in time with Kolt. "What? Oh. Oh!" He smiled and snapped his fingers. "You *popped* in, did you?"

Kolt nodded. "I have need of haste and discretion."

"As always, Laedan." He bowed, his long, wispy beard hitting the floor as he did. He straightened suddenly, his orange eyes glowing. "She's arrived!"

"Yes. She's arrived."

"Did they fit? Did she like them? Tell me! Tell me!"

Kolt laughed at Jupl's childlike enthusiasm, understandable since the old man had worked three eight-nights straight to make the lovely gowns and other necessities that waited for Aylyn in the chamber adjoining Kolt's in the Crystal Keep. Rather than tell him she hadn't seen his beautiful creations, nor would she any time soon, Kolt merely said, "She has need of more."

Jupl raked his hand through his scraggly, shoulder-length crimson hair. "More?" His hand slammed against his chest, and he gasped. "Never say she is greedy!"

"No, my good Jupl, you misunderstand. Circumstances have changed. We will be riding and walking. The others are—"

"Ah, I understand." Jupl's hands came together and opened. "You wish her to be merely Aylyn and not the laedan's consort."

"Exactly."

"So. How long do I have this time? One eight-night?"

"One-twentieth of the day."

"Very good, Laedan, I should have no problem . . . What! One-twentieth of a day! Surely you jest?" He looked at Kolt's determined expression. "No, you do not. Of course, you do not. Hmmm." He tugged at his beard with one hand, twisted an eyebrow with the other, and paced.

And paced.

And paced.

135

Patricia Roenbeck

Kolt's patience was about at an end when Jupl stopped suddenly and swung toward him, his face flushed with excitement. "Wait here, Laedan!" He patted Kolt on the chest. "Yes. Yes." His hands fluttered together. "This will be perfect. Perfect." He bustled from the chamber, murmuring, "You jimpnit! Making the laedan wait when all the time . . ."

Whatever Jupl was saying was lost behind the slamming of a rear chamber door. Kolt allowed himself to relax. From experience he knew Jupl would return in a short time and he would have precisely what Kolt required.

"Here, Laedan." Jupl rejoined Kolt and placed a bundle of dark blue material in his hands. "Everything your Aylyn will need for your outing."

"All will fit? No, do not answer," Kolt quickly said when he saw the flash of outrage in Jupl's eyes. "I know they will."

"There's more, but it will take me a little time to wrap them up."

"Where did you get them?"

Jupl frowned, puzzled. "Don't know. They were just there, you see." He flung his hands out. "I never question how, Laedan. I see a need and it's just suddenly there. And it waits and waits until one day someone in need walks in and . . . Well, it's just there. You see."

Kolt didn't, but was certainly not one to question mysterious abilities. "I'll return before the day ends."

"If you're of a mind, Laedan, I'll have it all bundled and ready in the rear chamber. You can just *snatch* them up. You don't have to come."

Kolt smiled. "My thanks, Jupl. I will do just that. Send to the keep for remuneration."

"Won't hear of it, Laedan. You go on now. Dress your lady. And if you need more, I'll have it."

"I've no doubt you will."

Kolt started to clap the master clothesmaker on the back in appreciation, but the old man had already resumed his pacing. Shaking his head, Kolt *actualized*, anxious to see Aylyn's reaction to the clothes.

Chapter Nineteen

"Well, what do you think?"

Kolt looked up from the entertainment transmission he had been scanning and felt his heart slam in his chest.

Aylyn stood in the doorway to the sitting chamber, a hesitant smile on her face. He had always pictured her in the long, elaborately designed formal gowns, but the simplicity of the high-necked tapered dress enhanced her beauty, the whiteness of it accentuating the bronzed hue of her skin.

She tossed her head, and the single, intricately woven braid flipped over her shoulder. "Will I do?"

Gods, but she would do! Clearing his throat, he nodded and said, "I'd not expect the villagers to run away in fright."

When she walked toward him, the cut of the midthigh skirt set it to swaying with her every step, and he ground his teeth. More likely than not, the men of Lywl would do just the opposite!

"There's just one problem." She raised a long slender leg encased in matching skintight leggings onto the table in front of him.

For Kolt, it was fighting the urge to run his hands up her leg and slip his fingers under the lacy undergarment he knew she wore beneath her dress. Her being fully dressed was definitely a problem.

"Notice anything missing?" she persisted, wiggling her toes.

"Missing?" he repeated dully.

"Shoes. Boots. Foot coverings." She laughed. "Kolt, where are you?"

Buried inside you, he thought longingly, then shook his head. Gods! But he needed to get control.

"Kolt!"

His head shot up at her shout, then down at her foot. He smiled sheepishly. "Oh."

She nodded. "Oh." She waited and when he made no move, she asked, "Do you have them?"

He got to his feet. "They are probably within," he said as he swiftly retrieved them and the other clothing Jupl had waiting for him and placed them on his sleeper. He opened the door to his chamber. "Ah, here they are. With the rest."

Aylyn followed him, and he handed her a pair of white, heelless, oogala-hide slouch boots. When she thanked him and sat to slip them on, he snatched up the pile of garments. He was having enough trouble handling his lust, he did not need to see her on his sleeper, no matter how innocently.

"I'll place these in your chamber," he said as he hurried from the chamber. "You can look at them when we return."

His emotions under control, he reentered the sitting chamber, carrying an embroidered shawl of deep crimson which he draped around her shoulders. He offered her his arm. "Shall we?"

Aylyn slipped her arm through his arm. "Kolt?"

"Hmm?"

"You'll do, too."

"My pardon, I don't . . ."

Aylyn's free hand gestured to his clothing. Kolt flushed. He had forgotten he'd quickly changed when he returned from Jupl's. Though his outfit varied little from what he had on earlier, the shirt was white and the leggings and sleeveless jerkin black.

"My thanks," he rasped.

Golden Conquest

Aylyn, delighting in his rising color and his growing discomfiture, couldn't resist slowly sweeping her eyes down his long hard length, and replying, "My pleasure."

The lust he thought he had firmly under control roared to life, and he growled, "Behave." Though he honestly did not know to whom he addressed the word—to Aylyn or to his betraying body.

Aylyn giggled, nodded her head, and let him lead her outside. The sun was at its zenith, and Aylyn gasped at the stark beauty of the woods surrounding the lodge. Spiny and leafless black brush, the kind she had been trapped in earlier, grew in patches beneath tall barren trees of ebony that stretched skyward at odd angles, their long thin branches interweaving, and the ground was sprinkled with what appeared to be silver dust.

"Why does the ground sparkle?"

"We'll return from our jaunt before the sun sets, and you will witness for yourself one of Annan's unique wonders," Kolt said cryptically. "This way."

Kolt led her down a path, which unlike the one she had chosen for her ill-fated flight to freedom, wended its way through the woods. As they walked, Kolt pointed out the various trees, flowers, and creatures in Bwyndyne Woods, the large section of forest that enveloped most of Lywl and its surrounding countryside. He explained that the villagers were mostly growers who tended the tall Bwynd trees. The juice of the black trees was used as a natural sweetener and much in demand.

A warm breeze tugged at the hem of her dress, lifting it. Laughing, Aylyn grabbed at it and held it down. The incident turned the conversation to Annan's weather which she learned varied greatly from region to region. Inner Sumal, the city that housed Annan's government, Kolt said, was domed because of the intense heat that made growing nourishment difficult.

"Here, we are a goodly distance from Inner Sumal and the conditions are usually fair, but flash storms can appear suddenly bringing pounding rain and violent gusts of wind. Lywlians who possess any sense seek shelter during the storms, for though they are brief, the howling winds that accompany them are most fierce."

He spoke on, and by the time they approached the village, Aylyn had learned much about Annan and her companion's pride in his world. She continued to be amazed by the depth of his passion for his land. When she said as much, he turned to her, his confusion obvious.

"Don't you love Rhianon?"

"Yes, but I am from the line of lord directors. It is in our blood to love our world."

"Annan pervades the blood of all our people, from the youngest to the eldest. Rank and wealth have naught to do with it. For centuries, since the Protectorate first decided to use it for a mining colony, Annan has served as a place to live for those who have no place. Annan has much to offer anyone willing to work hard. In return, home worlds long overcrowded, with little space and no work opportunity, have willingly and most times permanently been forfeited."

"And did you forfeit your home world?"

"Annan is my home world. Those of my blood who came before me were among the first to take advantage of all Annan had to offer."

They came to a rushing river, and Aylyn exclaimed over the beauty of the rainbowed water. Kolt guided her across a bridge of dark opaque crystal. Hearing a splash, Aylyn ran back toward the middle of the bridge and gazed down at the water. She laughed when she spied a sleek creature leaping in and out of the water.

"A slifer. They can live on land and in water."

"Do they bite?" she asked, thinking to pet it.

"No, but you'll not catch it. They are a fearful lot. Come," he said, extending his hand. "We are almost there."

They followed the hard-packed path to an opening and entered Lywl. Aylyn took in everything, the small, thatch-roofed cottages, the stone pathways, and the

Golden Conquest

people, who started to wave and chatter excitedly the moment they saw them.

"You will find most Annanites friendly to strangers," Kolt hedged, hoping she would be unable to understand what they were shouting.

"A fact I am most grateful for." Aylyn smiled at him warmly.

Aylyn, familiar with the language of Annan at her father's insistence, could understand brief snatches of conversation, but the rapidity and dialect of the villagers made it difficult. She did, however, recognize one word that a child had shouted as she ran up to them. A young child who now stood silent under Kolt's dark glare.

"Did she call you Laedan?"

"As you have said, we share the same name. They but tease me." His glower deepened. "I like it not."

Aylyn stooped to retrieve the yellow and green blossoms the child held in her chubby fist. Smiling, she thanked her and the child ran back to her parents.

"You said they love him. If they tease you with his name, it is a sign of affection. One that will not last if you bark at each one who uses it."

"I would rather her upset than you." When her brows raised in question, he said, "You were enjoying yourself. Since I cannot change my name, I sought not to remind you unnecessarily of the laedan."

"It's all right. I know you aren't he and no longer hold your name against you."

And what will you do when you learn I am he? Kolt wondered. *Name me a deceiver?* Not liking the flow of his thoughts, he asked her if she would like nourishment.

She shook her head. "I'd like to send the message to my parents first."

"Of course." He pointed to a gray stone building. "The message service."

"What if your laedan won't send it?" she asked, suddenly worried. "What if he means to take advantage of my presence on Annan?"

Patricia Roenbeck

Kolt winced as her innocent query thrust lethally into the center of his conscience, for he was doing just that.

But before he could reply, Aylyn spoke and plunged the dagger in even further. "I shouldn't have said that. Father has said your Kolt is noble. He will send the message, if only to spare them worry."

Curse Aubin and his kind words! He hadn't wanted to send the message, not yet. Selfishly, he wanted to keep her with him. Not as the laedan and the lord director's daughter. Not as the mind-toucher and his mind's love. But just as Kolt and Aylyn. And now, because Aubin thought him noble and had conveyed such feelings to Aylyn, he was trapped. Truthfully, he had forgotten that Aubin and Eirriel thought her in danger, and he owed them more than their continued worry.

But, as he led Aylyn over to the building and he thought of how he would phrase the message, he realized that the communications center at the keep was not inviolate. Anyone could see what came through or went out. And Rakkad, who Kolt was convinced was somehow privy to all that went on within the keep, could very possibly learn more than Kolt wanted him to. Kolt's silent curses turned to prayers of thanks when he saw the sign on the door.

"The unit is malfunctioning," Kolt translated. "We will have to try another day." When he saw her brow crease, he touched a forefinger to it and smoothed the lines. "Do not worry, Aylyn, I will see the message is sent."

"How?"

"I must report back and will see to it then."

"Report back?"

"I've people who depend on me for information. I must return to my position from time to time."

"Oh." That was something Aylyn hadn't considered. That Kolt had responsibilities and couldn't stay with her. "I'm sorry. I—"

Kolt took her hand and tucked it under his arm. "No

Golden Conquest

pardon is necessary. I have the right to spend my time as I will. I will be gone for a few brief periods at the beginning of each day during the next eight-night." He flashed her a warm smile of hidden promise. "You will find I am not so easily gotten rid of. Now, come, I am greatly hungered from our little jaunt, and we've another to undertake before the sun sets. Let us nourish ourselves."

He directed her into a shoppe that opened up to a garden of yellow shrubs and green and orange flowers and over to an outside table.

"Are you hungry?"

"No, but I would love something cold."

Kolt called over the server and gave her their order.

"Tell me what you like to do," Aylyn said. "For fun I mean."

"I love to walk, although I do not get to do it very often."

Aylyn laughed. "You don't get enough walking in the caverns you search?"

Kolt cursed himself for twenty kinds of a fool. He would have to speak with greater care. "I meant walk out in the open, among the trees, under the sky. I love to swim."

Aylyn waited until the server placed two icy flagons of brew and a large platter of hot food on the table. "Do you have a favorite swimming spot?"

"Yes. You are certain you'll not share this with me?" Kolt asked, and when Aylyn shook her head, Kolt began to eat. After a few mouthfuls, he answered Aylyn's question, catching himself before he told her about the Rainbow Falls in the garden he had created for her in the keep. "There's a pond behind the lodge. I'll take you there tomorrow if you like? You do swim?"

"The only thing I love more than swimming is riding. Especially estalons."

"Estalons?"

"Large-winged stallions. Mother had one of the few on Dianthia. When she bonded with Father, she had Onyx and three others, one male and two females, brought from Dianthia. Under Mother's guidance, they've flourished. I have one of Onyx's descendants."

"Annan cannot offer you stallions that fly, but we have uni-horned phedras. I keep one stabled here." Kolt looked up at the sky. "It is getting late, perhaps we will let Ketti carry us back to the lodge."

Kolt drained his flagon, dropped a few whitestones on the table, and took Aylyn's hand. "We have to hurry. We must reach the lodge before the surprise."

"What surprise?" Aylyn asked as they hurried out of the shoppe. "Kolt!" When Kolt didn't answer, she jerked her hand out of his. "Kolt!" She stamped her foot. "Kolt, you tell me now or I'll—"

Kolt said nothing but continued walking. Laughing, Aylyn ran up to him and punched him playfully in the shoulder.

"Kilgra!" she snapped, unaware that she tagged him with the very name her father had given him long ago. Her lips pushed up into a pout. "Please tell me."

"No. The telling of a surprise will lessen it." He threw her a sidelong glance. "Do you not like surprises?"

"I love surprises! But I also like to try and discover what they are ahead of time." She sighed. "It's the challenge. I can't seem to resist."

Kolt laughed. "And do you always have your surprises spoiled?"

"Not spoiled, enhanced. And, yes, almost always. Alaran was the only one who could resist me. Laaryc . . . never could." The last two words were choked out. Suddenly the joy was gone from the day, replaced by guilt. Not once since the cleansing had she thought of Laaryc.

Kolt swore as he heard the catch in her voice. It was to be expected that she remember and mourn her loss, but he need not like it. They walked silently, Kolt giving her the time, hoping the sight of Ketti would drive Laaryc from her mind.

Chapter Twenty

Kolt stopped in front of a short-walled enclosure and whistled sharply. Aylyn's head swung in the direction of the sudden thundering of hooves. From around the stone housing, a large, six-legged, shaggy-haired phedra galloped. It halted in front of Kolt. Learning its long neck down, it nudged Kolt with its horn.

"Oh, Kolt, he's magnificent," Aylyn breathed. She reached out a hand. "May I?"

"Open your palm, like so." Kolt opened his hand and held it palm up to Ketti. "He needs to learn your scent." Aylyn did as Kolt said and was rewarded by a soft purring from the blue-and-silver phedra. "He likes you. Phelan!" Kolt called.

A young blue-skinned female came running up. "Laedan! I had no idea you were come."

Kolt sighed and risked a quick glance at Aylyn and saw her too involved with Ketti to take notice of Phelan's words. "I wish to take Ketti. You will prepare him?"

"At once, Laedan." Before Kolt could tell her not to address him so, Phelan had already turned to fetch the padded hide seat and guiding strap.

Ketti's purring had moved from his throat to his belly, and the increased sound drew a smile from Kolt. "He likes you well, Aylyn. You have good taste, my handsome one," Kolt said, stroking Ketti's furred snout. "We'll have to mount him from within. This way."

Aylyn followed Kolt through a break in the wall to a set of four steps. By that time, Phelan had Ketti saddled and was leading him over to them. Kolt mounted with ease and extended his hand. Aylyn took it, and Kolt guided her up in front of him. Ketti snuffled once, shook his head, and pawed at the ground.

Kolt told Aylyn to hold onto the extra straps attached to the front center of the seat, took the guiding straps gently in his hands, and gave Ketti a slight nudge with his foot. The phedra turned and trotted from the enclosure. Once they exited the hamlet, Kolt gave Ketti his head, and they raced toward the lodge. Aylyn's laughter washed over Kolt like a wave of sunshine, and he threw back his head, closed his eyes, and warmed his soul in it.

After a while, the terrain forced Ketti to slow his gait to a gentle trot. Aylyn, lulled by the chirping of the winged creatures in Bwyndyne Woods, leaned back against Kolt, closed her eyes, and listened. Gradually, she became aware of a slight pressure and a firmness against her back and legs. She realized Kolt had snaked his arm around her waist and had pulled her close, holding her pressed against his long length. She concentrated on the feel of him and was surprised and pleased that she did not feel threatened by his nearness. Instead, she felt safe and secure, and rather than pull away, as she would have expected herself to, she snuggled against him and smiled.

Kolt clenched his jaw as she innocently wiggled her luscious buttocks further between his legs. He cursed first himself for the need that made him pull her against him and then Aylyn for not realizing the affect her body was having on his. Gritting his teeth, he willed his rapidly awakening manhood to remain dormant and swore some more when it refused to obey. Aylyn moved her head slightly, and tendrils of hair that had loosened from her braid teased his lips. Using it as an excuse, he brought a hand up and smoothed them

Golden Conquest

away, running his hand down the silky rope. Unable to resist any further, he pressed his lips against the top of her head, and breathed in her fresh smell.

Aylyn felt him nuzzling her hair, and a moan of contentment welled within her throat. Kolt heard her, and his whole body answered. He drew in a sharp breath. Gods! But he wanted to bury himself deep within her, wanted to cup her breasts with his hands, wanted to . . . With a will he did not think he possessed, he jerked himself away, and his hand returned to his side. He wanted what he could not have. Not yet. Aylyn, as complacent as she was at this moment, was by no means prepared to answer the passion she evoked in him.

The moment Kolt felt her turning he closed his eyes. He knew he would be unable to resist the silent question in her eyes, as he knew now was not the time to answer it.

Aylyn, confused by the abruptness of his movement, turned her head and risked a glance at Kolt. And saw what she expected to see—his mouth set, his brow furrowed, his eyes shut against her. She should never have given in to her instincts. She should have realized that the arm around her waist was merely to keep her from falling and not because he wanted her close. Nothing he had done since they met had indicated a willingness in him to be anything other than a guide to his world, an avenger, a guard. She had placed her own interpretation into his smiles, his looks, his words. And she had been wrong. Terribly wrong. Color blazed in her cheeks at the thought of her brazenness. She nibbled at her lower lip. Should she offer her apologies, or merely pretend nothing happened? Hiding behind cowardice, she stared at the passing trees, not surprised to note they were no longer beautiful.

Kolt cursed when he felt her stiffen and turn from him. He knew she had misinterpreted his reasons for pulling away, but to say otherwise would be to invite a response from his traitorous body that she was unable to meet. It was better this way. For now.

Ketti, well-trained to Kolt's routine, drew to a halt at the edge of the opening that led to the lodge. Kolt glanced at the sky and saw the sun almost below the horizon. He smiled and breathed a sigh of relief. His Annan was about to provide a most welcome distraction, one that was bound to bring laughter back to Aylyn's eyes.

Gracefully, Kolt dropped from Ketti's back and then reached up for Aylyn. Aylyn looked at his outstretched arms and his beckoning smile and returned one of her own. If Kolt wanted to make no mention of her actions, she was content to follow his lead. She swung her leg over and allowed him to lower her to the ground.

He took her hand. "Come. It is almost time."

"For what?"

"For your surprise." He led her into the center of the glade in front of the lodge and gestured at the trees. "Watch."

Simultaneously, hundreds of thousands of tiny silver blossoms popped out along every tree or brush branch within sight. Awed by the beauty of their glistening petals, Aylyn started to walk toward a nearby shrub, but Kolt called her back.

"Wait here and look up."

Just as she did, the sun dipped below the horizon. In unison, the trees, brush, and brambles released their hold on the fragile flowers and they tumbled to the ground.

Aylyn raised her arms toward the falling petals and twirled round and round, enthralled by the swirling blizzard of silver. Her awed laughter reached out to Kolt, caressing his soul, drawing him to her. His laughter joined hers, and he swept her up into his arms.

"What say you to Annan now?"

Drawn by the intensity of his voice from the dazzling spectacle to Kolt's handsome face, Aylyn's breath caught in her throat at the sight of his eyes flaming with dark promise.

"I think," Aylyn said softly, "I think it is truly wonderful."

Golden Conquest

Kolt groaned and gave into the aching need that had been with him since he first saw her. His head lowered and his mouth touched hers. A kiss of poignant tenderness, of gentle restraint. A kiss altogether too brief for Kolt.

When he raised his head, Aylyn experienced a deep sense of loss that would have pleased Kolt greatly had he known, but it left Aylyn puzzled. No other kiss had left her feeling unsettled and empty, wanting more and yet unsure what more was. As advanced as her schoolings had been, Aylyn was suddenly aware of how little she really knew of what went on between men and women. She remembered her mother's secret smile when she laid out the facts of lovemaking and assured her knowingly that the man Aylyn gave herself to would teach her the emotions. Aylyn touched her fingers to her lips and her blood tingled. She had always assumed that the man her mother spoke of was Laaryc, but she was startled to realize he had never fired her blood the way Kolt just had.

Kolt smiled down on her. "Liked my surprise, did you? Are you not glad I withheld the truth of it?" His smile turned smug when she nodded. "I thought as much."

Ketti's whinny caught their attention. Guiltily, they ran to his side and saw to his needs. Once watered and cooled down, he tossed his head and ran off. When Aylyn expressed dismay, Kolt explained that he let Ketti run free at the lodge. When he needed him, he had merely to whistle and he would come. They were carrying the hide seat and the straps to a bin near the side of the lodge when Aylyn's belly suddenly grumbled. Her cheeks burned as Kolt's shot of laughter told her he had heard.

"Come, I've nourishment inside."

As they entered the lodge, Kolt touched the chief server in the keep's nourishment center. Kolt was taken aback to learn a nourishment awaited his retrieval. He chuckled and shook his head. He should have expected Naydir to see to his needs. Promptly, he snatched the

149

nourishment from the chief server and placed it in the warmer. While Aylyn washed up, Kolt laid out the nourishment. Aylyn joined him just as he was filling the flagons with Melonnian sweet and sour. He raised the cover from the large platter and lowered it quickly. A touch transported hand cloths into the lodge's nourishment center, a needed diversion.

"Aylyn, I seem to have left the hand cloths on the counter inside. While I serve this, will you fetch them?"

As soon as Aylyn starting walking away, Kolt picked up the note that had been resting alongside the gropsa. A quick glance held it firmly in his mind. Even as he slipped it inside his jerkin and away from Aylyn's sight, he read it.

Kolt,
The people have heard of your wounding and fear you are life-ended. My word is no longer enough. However briefly, you must show yourself during the Rainbow Lights. I will see to it that none bother you. I trust your Aylyn is well and that you will go with care.

Naydir

"Are these what you needed?"

Kolt opened his eyes and saw Aylyn, two bright blue cloths in her hands. "Yes, my thanks. I hope you are hungry," he said as he finished serving.

Aylyn nodded and slipped into her seat. She sipped at the sweet and sour and nibbled on the nourishment, a distracted air about her. Finally, when he could wait no longer for her to tell him what troubled her, Kolt asked.

"It's empty," Aylyn said, flinging her hand toward the nourishment center. "The whole center is empty. Where did the nourishment come from?"

Gods, but she was quick! "A woman from the village who lives nearby brings the nourishment whenever I am staying here. I never said I prepared it."

Aylyn shook her head, her lip twisted in a half-smile.

"No, you didn't." The puzzle settled, her appetite improved and in no time at all her plate was empty. "You must tell her it was delicious."

"She would be most pleased to hear it."

Once nourishment was finished and the remains cleaned away, Kolt suggested a game of The Warrior and The Lady, a complex game in which intricately carved warriors moved up and down, back and forth among the three levels of the board, each in an attempt to capture the Lady of the Keep and make her his.

They played long into the night. Kolt won each game, but the ease with which he did so lessened considerably with each game.

"You learn well, my lady," Kolt complimented.

"Well enough, I think, that I will beat you in our next game. With a small change in rules."

Kolt quirked a brow. "Oh?"

"This time I will capture you."

Kolt laughed. He should have expected nothing less from an offspring of Aubin and Eirriel. He placed the Crown of Lights on the head of the Lady of the Keep. "I accept your challenge, my lady warrior."

Ayln lifted the first piece. "Prepare to be conquered, fierce warrior. Your heart will be mine!"

Ayln was puzzled by the soft lights that burned within Kolt's blue eyes as he countered her move, and was still there hours later when she had indeed won.

Chapter Twenty-One

Had he gone into her chamber, the sight of her lying in her sleeper would have greatly strained his already burdened control. Instead, Kolt called himself a coward and sent by thought a note explaining his whereabouts to the table next to Aylyn's sleeper. Not that he expected her to awaken before his return. Their games had not ended till the sun had risen. He had managed a few hours sleep and longed for more, but Naydir's message was most explicit. And the Rainbow Lights were but minutes away.

"Are you sure this is a necessity?"

Naydir jumped and spun on his heels, to see Kolt standing in the doorway to his own sleeping chamber, a wide smile on his face.

"Damn you to Nithrach, Kolt! There was no cause for that!"

"I like it not that my time with Aylyn has been interrupted."

"I was not the one so enthralled with a female that I did not hear an attacker. Nor did I cause my people . . ."

Kolt held up his hand. "I cry peace, my friend. And I extend my pardon."

Naydir's amber eyes burned down Kolt. "You are well?"

Kolt nodded. "More than well. She is come."

"So I surmised." Naydir chuckled. "Your little snatch-

Golden Conquest

ings caused no end of trouble. The poor server who was bringing us the tray yesterday morn woke up from her faint with a stutter. Not at all the thing, I'm afraid."

Kolt shrugged unrepentedly. "We had need of nourishment." His expression grew serious. "We have much to discuss, Naydir. I like not what I've learned from Aylyn. The... Father of Creation!" Kolt shook his head, then bolted across the chamber. He yanked open the door to the passageway and came face to face with Cal holding a struggling Dakkar. Morald was running up the passageway.

"What is it, Kolt?" Naydir asked as he came up behind him.

Kolt ignored Naydir for the moment. "What happens here?" he demanded of Cal and Dakkar.

"Laedan, Councilor, I beg forgiveness. I was told none were to enter," Cal explained. "Dakkar heard Morald giving orders to the guards and surmised that you were to return." Cal's eyes met Naydir's. "I sought to stop him."

Kolt turned to Naydir. "Dakkar is to be kept from me?"

"It was my hope that all but myself were to be kept from you. You did seek to return to Aylyn, did you not?"

Kolt nodded, then addressed Cal, "Release him."

Cal obeyed at once. Dakkar rushed to Kolt. "Laedan! You were so ill, and when I was not permitted to see to you, I feared the worst!"

"Laedan," Morald interrupted. "The Lights are almost upon us."

Kolt nodded. "We will discuss this when I have reassured my people." He turned and strode angrily to the terrace.

Naydir glowered first at Dakkar, who backed away cowering, then at Cal and Morald, then slammed the door, barring all three from Kolt's chambers. Cal and Morald exchanged worried glances, both aware that they were in for a severe tongue-lashing when Naydir was ready.

Naydir approached Kolt who stood by the door to the terrace. "The commotion between Cal and Dakkar did not send you tearing from this chamber. I saw the shock on your face. What happened?"

"I was probed," Kolt said quietly as he stepped out on the terrace.

Immediately shouts began.

"What?" Naydir shook his head; he could not have heard correctly.

People started pointing up at Kolt and cheering.

Kolt waved. "I was probed by a mind-toucher."

"Laedan! Laedan!" The chanting grew.

Naydir remained in the doorway, all color gone from his face. "Did . . . did he succeed?"

"No."

The Lights began and the chanting rose to a fevered pitch, forcing their conversation to a halt. Kolt kept waving and smiling, smiling and waving. When the Lights were gone, and there was still no sign of the chant lessening, Kolt gave one final wave then *actualized* into his chamber. The chanting dissolved into shouts and frenzied shrieks that reached into the chamber, even after Naydir had closed the door.

Without warning, Kolt grabbed Naydir's hand and *actualized* them to Koltrax's cubiculum.

"You might have given me some warning!" Naydir snapped, not liking the spontaneity of Kolt's actions. "Do you never think?"

"How could I with all that noise?"

"All that noise would have died down if you had walked from the terrace."

"I thought they needed a final assurance that I was as I have always been."

Naydir nodded reluctantly. "Perhaps you are right. Now, would you tell me, did he succeed?"

"I have had my shields well in place since I learned that Aylyn was taken from her ship by a mind-toucher. All he can touch is what I let him touch. And until I am ready, he will touch naught at all."

"A mind-toucher?" Naydir repeated. He swore when

Golden Conquest

Kolt nodded and continued swearing as Kolt relayed all he had learned from Aylyn about Rakkad, son of Kedar.

"Gods, Kolt, but I erred! Grievously."

Naydir looked so passionately distraught that, in spite of the seriousness of the discussion, Kolt could not refrain from arching a brow and teasing, "You? Never."

"So you say now, but . . ." Naydir quickly told him of Goron and the manner of his life-ending. "I remember thinking that the life-ender was a mind-toucher, but I dismissed it. Truthfully, I thought another one with the skills you possess an impossibility. And of all we have heard of the one we searched for, this Rakkad, never once was there mention of such skills."

"All that proves is that he has been diligent and that his men are loyal. Would you not be if I had threatened to kill you with an arc of light?" Kolt asked dryly.

"As you say," Naydir concurred, then mentioned his belief that the hijacker and assassin were one and the same.

"It is no more than I suspected," Kolt said. "The assassin knew my movements, the hijacker my ships' movements. I thought we had a traitor within the keep. Now I no longer think it. I know. And it is this Rakkad."

"But if Rakkad is truly a mind-toucher, would he need to be within the keep to learn all he knows?"

"Ere now I've not felt myself probed, yet he knew my movements when none knew but many could have observed. No," Kolt said firmly. "Rakkad bides within the Crystal Keep."

"What you say makes sense. Did his touch tell you aught?"

Kolt shook his head. "It was too brief. There and then gone in less than a breath. My barriers must have frightened him off."

"Your Aylyn said he was well cloaked. You are certain it is a man? Though *he* claims to be Kedar's son, it could be a woman, Kedar's daughter."

Kolt frowned. "A woman?"

"Iilde has access to the Khrystallyn and to the keep."

"It is not Iilde. For all her sly machinations and avaricious behavior, she is no more and no less than what she appears. Her mind is open to me. Too open." Kolt shuddered. "No, Rakkad is a man who claims vengeance against Lady Eirriel for his sire's life-ending. He had plans to use Aylyn, plans I thwarted. And he will keep trying till he has her once again." Kolt's eyes glittered fiercely, and he ground out, "I vow, by all the gods, that as long as there is breath within me, he will never touch her again!"

There was a moment's silence as Naydir waited for Kolt to continue and when he did not, he asked, "What will you do?"

"I will speak with Cal and Dakkar and then I will return to Aylyn." He offered his hand to Naydir. "Are you prepared for a trip?"

Naydir nodded and placed his hand in Kolt's. "All I have ever asked, my friend, is a lit . . ."

" . . . tle warning," Naydir finished in Kolt's antechamber, and then glowered at Kolt.

Kolt chuckled. "I gave you my hand. As I am not in the habit of holding hands with you that should have been warning enough."

"I will remember that next time," Naydir said dryly. "Shall I let them in?"

"Yes."

Cal and Morald strode in. Dakkar scooted around Naydir and headed quickly to Kolt's side.

"Laedan, if I have displeased you . . ."

"No, Dakkar," Kolt said kindly. "You have not."

"But Naydir . . ."

"Is overzealous where my well-being is concerned. Do not trouble yourself." Kolt walked to the table where a carafe of liquid and several beakers were. He picked up the carafe. "My friends, I must beg your indulgence."

With no other warning than that, Kolt reached out and touched the minds of those within the chamber. Each reacted differently to the pain of the probe. Cal's

Golden Conquest

eyes clamped shut, and he threw back his head; Morald's hands clenched into a white-knuckled fist; Dakkar grabbed his head and cried out, and Naydir blinked. But none gave Kolt what he sought.

Kolt finished pouring the drinks, giving the men the chance to collect themselves or to protest. But so deep and binding was their trust in him that none did. And that rocked Kolt to his very soul. Silently, he handed each a beaker, then raised his in the air.

"To loyalty," he said as he tossed down the fiery liquid.

One by one, the beakers were raised, the toast repeated, and the drinks consumed.

Kolt met each man's direct gaze with his own, and vowed, "By the light of the Mother of us all, I give you my pledge. Were it not that a life I hold more dearly than my own is at risk, I would answer all you would ask of me. But until she is well and truly safe, I cannot."

Naydir, who well knew what fears drove Kolt, said nothing. Cal and Morald nodded their support, if not their understanding, and Dakkar smiled. "Does this mean she is come?"

"Yes, Dakkar, she is come."

"When can we meet her?" Dakkar slapped his forehead. "Do not answer. I know it will be when she is safe."

"Is she all you thought her to be, Laedan?"

"All and more, Cal. All and more."

Kolt arched a brow at Morald. "Have you no question?"

"I have many, Laedan. But, apparently, none that I may ask. Yet. As for personal questions, it is not my place to ask. I am here to serve, not to—to socialize."

Kolt gave a shout of laughter and then slapped Naydir on the back. "You have trained him too well, I think."

Morald looked to Naydir. "I should return to my post."

Naydir nodded. "I will give you further orders shortly."

"Unless you have need of me, I will accompany Morald." When Kolt shook his head, Cal and Morald both left.

"And me, Laedan. Do you have need of me?" Dakkar asked hopefully.

Kolt handed Dakkar the coded message he had written before he left the lodge. "See that this is sent at once."

"Yes, Laedan. At once." Dakkar rushed from the chamber.

Kolt held up his hand to stop Naydir's comment. "It was coded, Naydir." Kolt threw himself into the relaxer. "I am not such a fool as you think."

"May I know what it said?"

"Of course." Kolt frowned at the edge in Naydir's voice. "You are displeased?"

"I had hoped that I had earned your trust," Naydir said tightly. "It appears I hoped in vain."

Kolt moved to Naydir and placed a hand on his shoulder, giving it a firm squeeze. He waited until Naydir raised his eyes to his. "You alone do I trust, Naydir. I probed not to learn if you are the mindtoucher, but to learn if he had touched you." Kolt dropped his hand and walked away. "Where once I touched, I can no longer."

"Aylyn?" Naydir asked, stunned.

Kolt turned to face his friend. "He has done something." His hands raked through his hair in frustration. "I know not what, but I know it is because of him that she is blocked to me."

"Gods, Kolt, but I am sorry."

"She has ever been with me, Naydir. Whenever I felt tired or alone, I would reach out and she would be there. Now, I touch only emptiness. I had hoped . . ." Kolt shook his head. "I know not what I had hoped."

Naydir knew nothing he could say would comfort Kolt. Instead, he poured them each a Melonnian sweet and sour and asked, "Does she know where you are?"

Golden Conquest

"She was asleep when I left." Kolt dropped into the relaxer.

"Asleep?" Naydir handed Kolt the flagon. "But the sun had almost reached its zenith!"

"I'm afraid I didn't let her sleep last night. Playing Warriors," Kolt added quickly at Naydir's smirk.

"Of course, Kolt."

"Take your mind from the slime, Councilor, and put it to better use," Kolt chided. "Now come, time grows short. What else has need of my attention."

Naydir took the chair next to Kolt. "All else is under control. Young Cal has held his own these past days."

"That he would was never in doubt."

"As you say. The councilors have voted Luthias stripped of all wealth and holdings and imprisoned for the duration of his life. It but waits your approval."

"I'd not see Cal punished for his sire's crimes."

"Cal has wealth enough in his own right from his growing stations. He has requested his sire's ill-gotten gains returned to the Mayraldans. All of it, even the keep. I have drawn up the necessary forms."

"Leave them and all else that warrants my attention on the table. When I return tonight, I'll see to them."

"Tonight?" Naydir arched a brow. "And sleep? Do you plan to indulge in it?"

"When I finish all you have left me. Does that please you?"

"If you were to rest now, it would."

"I cannot. Aylyn waits for me, and we've yet to come up with a plan to rid Annan of Rakkad."

Naydir stood and walked to the terrace doorway and glanced out. After a moment he turned. "If he wants Aylyn . . ."

Kolt was on his feet. "No!"

"She can bring us Rakkad." Though he liked it no more than Kolt, Naydir felt it was a definite solution. "It is your life that is at risk."

"Aylyn is worth more than my life," Kolt snarled.

"To you, perhaps. To Annan, no."

"In this, Annan must come second." When Naydir

opened his mouth to speak further, Kolt slashed the air with his hand. "I'll hear no more of it, Naydir. Aylyn is not to be a pawn in this."

"As you wish. I would think more on it. Morald and Cal as well."

Kolt nodded. "As will I. If you should . . ." A wave of need hit Kolt forcefully. He turned his head toward the door, just as Morald's shout reached them.

Kolt's stomach roiled. "Iilde comes."

"Iilde? How came she to learn . . ." Naydir shook his head. Kolt was gone.

Chapter Twenty-Two

When Kolt entered the lodge carrying the tray of nourishment he had retrieved from the keep as he had *actualized*, Aylyn was dressed and waiting.

"Yes, I sent the message," he said as he placed the tray on the table.

"Thank you." Aylyn looked at the nourishment.

"I met Hargref on the way over with it," Kolt lied quickly.

"I *can* prepare nourishment, Kolt."

"I did wonder if the daughter of Rhianon's lord director was comfortable in the nourishment center."

"It was an important part of my schooling. Right after the course on how best to shoot and kill Blagdenian invaders." She looked at Kolt pointedly. "And other unsavory types."

Kolt laughed. "I thought to spare you work."

"You thought to spare your belly."

Kolt put up his hands. "I surrender. I will see the center supplied. Does that serve, my lady warrior?"

Aylyn nodded, pleased at the camaraderie. When she had awakened to find a note instead of Kolt, she had worried that Kolt might return from tendering his report stiff and unapproachable, regretting his impulse to act as her guide and host.

"How long will it take for the message to reach my father?" she asked, and realized that she hoped it would not be too soon.

"An eight-night," Kolt replied, stretching the truth. In his message to Aubin he had requested Aylyn be given time to get to know him and had set an eight-night as the limit. That Aubin might refuse, Kolt had not even considered. "What say you to another jaunt?"

"On Ketti?" She couldn't help but ask, afraid he would still be put off by her wanton behavior during yesterday's ride.

"Yes. Hujji is too far to walk to."

Both anxious to spend time with the other, though neither would admit it, they finished consuming the nourishment quickly, and together cleaned up the platters. Aylyn asked if the outfit, similar to the one she wore for yesterday's excursion was appropriate. Kolt nodded and told her to bring the shawl.

As they rode, they passed the time much as they had on the first jaunt, Kolt pointing out anything he could think of that might be of interest to Aylyn. The villagers of Hujji greeted them much as the villagers of Lywl had. Kolt explained away his popularity by another half-truth.

"I located the ryliyne they needed."

"Ryliyne?"

"A rare crystal needed to power safety shields. The harvesting of it brought much wealth to this sektor."

The conversation came to an end when a pair of comely young women ran up to Kolt and instead of flowers, they gave him kisses. Deep, probing kisses. Kisses Aylyn did not see Kolt seem to mind. And try as she could, their rapid and, to Aylyn's way of thinking, simpering speech pattern was beyond her, except for one word—Laedan. With a husky murmur, Kolt finally untangled himself from the buxom pair.

Aylyn arched a brow. "Is it only children you glower at when they call you Laedan?"

Sensing the reason for Aylyn's snide remark, Kolt said nothing and merely pointed the way to the local public nourishment center. They had just seated themselves at a corner table when a breathless voice asked for their order. Aylyn looked up to see a tall, volup-

Golden Conquest

tuously curved server leaning over Kolt, her low-cut jumpsuit falling open, her silver eyes offering more than was on the nourishment listing. Kolt merely shook his head and ordered two large flagons of brew.

During their brief time in the center, Aylyn watched and listened as several other women stopped to talk with Kolt. Far from being annoyed, Kolt seemed to accept their attention, fending off the more suggestive remarks (She did not have to speak their wretched language to know what they wanted!) with an ease that could only have come from familiarity. When she said as much, Kolt just laughed and shrugged his shoulders in helpless resignation which earned him a harsh glower from Aylyn.

During a stop at the nourishment supply shoppe where more of the same occurred, Aylyn was forced to examine her reaction. Why did it bother her that the women of Hujji wanted Kolt? She knew it shouldn't have. After all, they hardly knew each other, and he had a life long before she arrived. And would have one long after she left. That thought brought an instantaneous sinking sensation to the pit of her belly.

Kolt turned to ask her of a particular seasoning and found her staring at her hands, a lost look on her face.

"Have them delivered to my lodge," he said to the supply master. He frowned at the master's slender and seductive daughter. "Send them with your son."

"Yes, Laedan."

Kolt nodded his thanks and offered his hand to Aylyn. "Come."

Aylyn had caught Kolt's glance at the daughter followed by his sharp order to the master, and misinterpreted the discourse. Believing him so uncaring for her feelings as to have arranged a meeting right in front of her, Aylyn refused Kolt's proffered hand, spun on her heels, and stalked from the shoppe.

"Aylyn?" Kolt ran after her. "Aylyn?"

He stopped directly in her path. Each time she tried

to brush past him, he was there.

"Would you please get out of my way!" she snapped.

"Not until you look at me." He placed a forefinger under her chin and gently raised it. "Look at me."

Aylyn knew she was being foolish. She had no ties to him. She kept her eyes tightly closed, fearing to face him, to see him looking down at her with a knowing look, that mocked her unreasonable jealously. And it was jealousy. Plain and simple jealousy. No, she countered, not simple. It was too strong, too present, too soon to be simple.

She jerked away from Kolt and ran.

Villagers had stopped and watched as their laedan tore out of the center after the beautiful Rhianonian.

Kolt caught Aylyn in a few easy strides and swept her up into his arms. The crowd broke into cheers.

"Put me down!"

"Not until you listen to me! Stop that!" he ordered when her twisting almost caused him to drop her.

Kolt and Aylyn both realized they had an audience at the same time. Red heat burned Aylyn's face. Groaning, she buried her face in Kolt's shoulder. Kolt glowered at the crowd, who quickly dispersed, then carried Aylyn away from watching eyes into a nearby shoppe. A short jerk of his head sent everyone outside.

Kolt set Aylyn on her feet. His hands held her firmly but gently by the shoulders. "Aylyn, softling," he said, his voice husky and tender. "Please look at me."

Aylyn did and was captured by eyes dark with an emotion she could not name.

"I'd not have you angered by what I cannot change. I cannot help that the women think me fair game, but, Aylyn, on my honor I vow none have I taken to my sleeper."

Aylyn wanted to run, to hide. His knowing what caused her behavior was almost too much to bear. Her shame increased tenfold. Gods! What he must think of her!

Kolt thought her wonderful. In truth, he greatly liked her possessiveness. It told him much. Though she understood it not, some part of her recognized him as hers. But until she learned to trust what she felt, she would question the feelings he caused in her. And she would continue to fight all that she felt. But in the end her struggles would all be for naught. She would be his, as he was hers.

Confident as he had not been before, Kolt smiled. "Come, if you will not forgive me . . ."

She shook her head. "Forgive you? But you've done nothing. I'm the one who should apologize." She gave him a weak smile. "I'm not always so miserable to be with."

"Shall we forget all this, my lady warrior?"

"Yes," Aylyn said fervently. "I would love to forget all of this." *If only I could*! she moaned inwardly.

You cannot, my love. You cannot, he thought as he nodded. "It is forgotten. Now, I have a surprise for you."

"Another one?"

"You seem to like surprises greatly so I arranged one. It is why we are here in Hujji."

"What is it? Where?"

Like yesterday, Kolt said nothing, but started walking. This time Aylyn knew not to ask and fell in step as they exited the shoppe and crossed the square to a large stone building surrounded by a short stone wall.

There prancing and snorting in the center of the walled area was a silver-and-gold phedra. Kolt gave a sharp whistle. Her head swung around toward them.

"Her name is Seonaid." Kolt extended his hand, palm up and open, and the phedra trotted over and nuzzled him. "She is yours."

"Mine?"

"Yours."

"But . . . Oh, Kolt!" Aylyn put her hand out. Seonaid rubbed her nose into it and began to purr. Aylyn ran her hand down Seonaid's long neck. "She's a beauty."

Kolt, his eyes on Aylyn not Seonaid, murmured, "That she is."

"Thank you."

"It is my pleasure."

Not taking her eyes off the phedra, Aylyn said, "You are keeping a tally of all that I have cost you, aren't you? My father . . ."

Kolt stiffened. "There is no tally."

"But, Kolt, you cannot expect to lay out all . . ."

"These are gifts, Aylyn. Your father owes me nothing." Kolt growled.

"I cannot accept—"

"You can and will, Aylyn."

Aylyn's gaze swung to him, and his set expression registered at once. She had injured his pride. Not at all what she had planned to do. "I did not mean to imply you could not afford all of this and I'm sorry if I have offended you. I accept your gift and the spirit it was given in." *And I will keep the tally*, she added under her breath. Whether he could afford it, she would see him recompensed for all his expenses.

Once Kolt got over his irritation, which he did rather quickly, the return to the lodge was an adventure for Aylyn as she accustomed herself to the subtleties of riding a phedra, though Seonaid needed little guidance.

The next few days passed much the same as the first two. Kolt would wait until Aylyn slept, then return to the keep to complete any work Naydir thought needed his attention, remaining there until after his appearance at the Rainbow Lights. He would arrive at the lodge to find Aylyn dressed and nourishment waiting. They would spend the later part of the day walking and riding, each day in a new direction, and return for the evening's nourishment and a few games of The Warrior and The Lady, the honor of being the Warrior bestowed on the winner. Much to the chagrin of both of them, they were equally matched, and often the chance throw of the crystal cube determined the outcome.

Neither mentioned the domesticity of the pattern nor did they confront the need escalating within them

Golden Conquest

to move their relationship onto another level.

Aylyn set her mind to accepting her unwanted attraction to Kolt. Though she had no plans to act on it, her acceptance rid her of the internal struggle and external reaction, and she was able to see him and the villagers' response to him in an unmuddied light. She soon realized that while the women were always there to greet him, it was always with the same affectionate awe he received from the men. She had no doubt the villagers truly loved and respected Kolt. Something she did not question since she herself had felt the instantaneous pull of his magnetic personality. As for the more aggressive women who flocked to his side, she noticed that Kolt always politely but firmly brushed them aside, his eyes locking with hers as if to reassure her that they held no attraction for him.

Kolt viewed each day as a step forward. A weakening in Aylyn's resistance of him. A step closer to the time when he would confront her with her feelings and then admit all he was to her. However, as much as he looked forward to that day, he dreaded it. He greatly feared that she might name him a deceiver and shut him out of her life forever.

A break in the routine came just before the zenith of Aylyn's fifth day on Annan.

"So, my Aylyn, we meet again."

Aylyn whirled around. Her heart slammed in her chest as she saw Rakkad standing in the doorway of her sleeping chamber. She backed away into a grasping warmth and whirled—right into Rakkad's waiting arms!

"You cannot escape, my Aylyn. I have need of you."

Crying out, she jerked away and ran to the door leading to Kolt's chamber. She snatched it open and found Rakkad, his hands on his hips, laughing.

"Wherever you go, I will be there. You are mine for now and for always!"

"Kolt!" Aylyn screamed, the sound of her own voice jerking her from her sleep. Aylyn sat up, frowning. Why had she been calling for Kolt? She ran her hands through her tangled curls. Had she had a dream? She thought for a moment but could not remember any dream. She stretched and glanced at the timepiece on the dressing table. She still had two hours before Kolt's usual arrival time. She slipped from the sleeper. A leisurely soak in the cleanser would take up some of the time, and after that a walk.

Two hours later found Aylyn sitting on a long branch that extended over the pool of rainbow water behind the lodge, her feet dangling in the cool water. A sudden chattering high in the branches overhead drew her attention. Shielding her eyes against the glare of the sun, Aylyn looked up and saw something green leaping from black branch to black branch. Although Kolt had assured her that the local animals were friendly, Aylyn decided that she was unwilling to take a chance of confronting it while hanging out over the water. Her eyes searching the branches for the creature's location, she started to hoist herself to a crouching position when a green ball of fur landed directly in front of her.

Startled, Aylyn cried out and grabbed the branch to steady herself. As the ball of fur stretched and opened to a small three-hand-high furred animal, Aylyn gave a quick prayer to the gods that Kolt's belief that all within Bwyndyne Woods were harmless was true. When it merely stood there, unmoving, the toes of its two feet wrapped around the branch, Aylyn breathed a sigh of relief. Kolt was apparently correct. Reassured, Aylyn took time to study the intriguing creature.

Its eyes were large, round, and a clear yellow. It had small pointed ears, a scrunched-up snout, smallish mouth, hopefully with very small teeth. Obviously it was bipedal, though it did possess a total of four legs, and a long narrow tail that was looped around the branch. Its head cocked from side to side as it stared at her, and Aylyn got the impression she was being studied, too. She gave it a hesitant smile. It smiled back. Carefully, not wishing to lose her balance, she released her hold on the branch and slowly raised her hand, palm outstretched. The creature followed suit.

Golden Conquest

Aylyn pulled her hand back. So did it. Realizing it was mimicking her, she laughed. It cocked its head and blinked. Then released a long trilling chatter.

"And what are you called?" Aylyn asked.

The trilling increased. Aylyn slowly extended her hand again, thinking to try and pet it, when suddenly, its head jerked around to face the woods. It fell silent and cocked its head again. Aylyn had the distinct impression it was listening to something. It started to tremble.

"What is it?" she asked softly.

Its head swung back to her, and it started chattering again. Its arms extended toward Aylyn. The chattering grew agitated, and it started to jump, rocking the branch.

"No! Please, don't!" Aylyn cried as she grasped onto the swaying branch.

The chattering reached a crescendo. Yellow-feathered wings sprouted from the creature's back. Before Aylyn could react, it lunged at her, its arms, legs, and tail wrapping itself around her. Aylyn screamed as the creature knocked her into the water.

Kolt, who had arrived to an empty lodge for the first time, had experienced a sense of unease that rapidly changed to fear as he heard Aylyn's plea. He realized it came from the direction of the pool and, without thinking, *actualized*. He appeared and looked around. Her scream reached him, and he broke into a run, arriving at the pond just as she plunged beneath the water.

Chapter Twenty-Three

Kolt ran and arced into the air, breaking the surface with nary a splash. A few powerful kicks brought him to the area beneath the branch. Luckily, the water was pristine and clear. He saw Aylyn struggling to unwrap what appeared to be a yiichi from around her torso and push up to the surface. A few strokes and he was under her, shoving her upward.

Aylyn and the yiichi broke the surface, gasping and sputtering, Kolt a moment later. He quickly sent out a wave of reassurance toward the yiichi, and it calmed, making it easier for Kolt to slip his arm around Aylyn's neck and pull her and her burden to shallow water.

"I thought you said you could swim!" Kolt roared as he got to his feet.

On her knees, Aylyn slashed her hair out of her eyes and glowered up at him. "I have a living coat wrapped around me in case you're too blind to see it! Not even your great and powerful laedan would have been able—"

"Do they not teach you anything on Rhianon? These are wild creatures, harmless in truth, but—"

"Harmless! Harmless!" she shrieked as she found her feet and stood. "It damned near drowned me!" She tried to disentangle the creature from her body, but it would have none of it. "Damn you, let me go!"

The yiichi seemed to take offense at her tone and leapt away, the sudden jarring motion sending Aylyn

Golden Conquest

sprawling backwards. Kolt's arm shot out and he grabbed her to her feet. Aylyn glared at the yiichi as it clambered up the nearest tree and sat on one of the overhanging branches. It chattered at Aylyn, as if taking her to task for yelling at it, then opened its wings to the air to dry.

Kolt took advantage of Aylyn's momentary distraction and attempted to calm himself. It didn't work. Over and over he saw the picture of her at the bottom of the pond. If he hadn't returned when he did ... Gods! With an oath, his hands snaked out and he grabbed her to him. His mouth crashed down on hers in a hot, punishing kiss. Just as abruptly, he jerked his head away.

"I could have lost you, curse you!" he ground out.

Aylyn, her blood thrumming from his all-too-quick kiss, looked at him and saw the fear in his eyes. All her rage fled, replaced by a warmth that touched her very soul. Her eyes softened. She placed her hands on either side of Kolt's face and smiled.

Kolt groaned low in his throat and lowered his head. "I could have lost you," he murmured as he recaptured her mouth. "I could have lost you."

His tongue traced her mouth. Aylyn gasped and her hands moved through his hair to pull his head closer. Kolt slipped his tongue between her lips and teased at her sensitive inner lip.

"Open for me." Kolt's voice was hoarse, rough.

Open for you? Open what? Aylyn thought, but when she started to ask, she quickly learned the answer as Kolt's probing tongue slipped inside her mouth. *Oh my!* was her last conscious thought before losing herself in the warmth that was sweeping over her. She heard Kolt groan as she met his seeking tongue with hers and his hands came down to her buttocks to hold her snug against him. At some other level she was aware of a hard length of heat grinding against her lower belly, but she was too lost in the wondrous sensations his tongue and mouth were causing to focus on anything else but that.

Kolt's pleasure-giving mouth moved from her lips to her ear and finally to her neck as his one hand glided along her waist, up her side, to mold the full curves of her breast. Aylyn shivered at the bright heat of his hand as it cupped her breast and when his thumb raked over her nipple, she rolled her head back and leaned into his hand.

And then the heat was gone. Suddenly. Without warning.

Something was wrong. As inexperienced as she was, she knew Kolt had been enjoying her as much as she had been enjoying him. She opened her eyes and was not surprised to see his head cocked, his eyes closed. To her he appeared to be listening.

And he was. The yiichi's persistent chattering and jumping had finally penetrated Kolt's passion.

"Something's not right." Kolt frowned. "Yiichis are extremely sensitive to undercurrents." He took Aylyn's hand. "Let's go back to the lodge."

"He's been—"

"She," Kolt corrected absently, his mind still listening and still hearing nothing. "Females are green with yellow wings, males reversed."

"She's been acting like that all along. It's what prompted my little swim." At Kolt's questioning glance, Aylyn explained the events leading up to his arrival.

"I like it not."

Kolt opened the door to the lodge and was about to close it when the now silent yiichi, whom neither noticed had been following them, scooted in. Kolt's eyes darkened. Aylyn, thinking Kolt meant to evict the yiichi, quickly extended her arms. It leapt into them.

"Sh, little one," Aylyn cooed, running her hand down its back. "I won't let the big bad man hurt you."

"Aylyn, really!" Kolt said, offended. "Think you I was going to toss her out?" Aylyn's carefully schooled expression told him she thought just that. "Have a little faith in me. I but wondered what caused her to come in. Yiichis are not known to bother with any but their own kind, and our experiences with them show they have an aversion to contained spaces. She shouldn't have come in." Kolt walked over and rubbed the yiichi behind her ears. "What is it, little one? What do you fear?" Kolt wished he had the ability to truly touch its mind, but he knew he couldn't. Several times he had tried to touch the mind of an animal and been unable to do aught but soothe its fears.

"She won't sicken if she stays here, will she?"

Kolt shook his head. "No. We've cared for them often enough and while they're recovering, they're fine. But as soon as they are healthy, they want out. And they keep up the trilling until they are released."

"Good, then I shall name her." Aylyn thought a moment, then brightened. "I'll call her Mikki. It's Vargarian for 'little one.'" She looked the yiichi in the eyes. "Does Mikki suit you, little one?"

Mikki trilled softly and wrapped her tail around Aylyn's waist.

Kolt chuckled. "So it would seem." His smile faded, and he walked to the casement and looked out. "I see nothing, but I would check anyway. Stay here."

"But—"

"Stay here."

"Is it Rakkad?"

Kolt's head swung toward Aylyn. "Rakkad? Why would you think it is he?"

Aylyn shook her head. "I don't know. His name just popped into my head."

That it did, Kolt liked not at all. "You think to find him here, on Annan?"

"Yes."

"Why?" he asked. He knew she would not have recognized Rakkad's ship or his supplies as he had, but he was hopeful that Aylyn might have remembered something that might lead him to Rakkad's hideaway on Annan.

"How else would he have known to place me in supposedly unreachable caverns? And then there's the way you talk."

"I talk?"

Aylyn nodded. "Your Hakonese is accented the same way Rakkad's is. You use the same inflections, the same speech patterns."

He had yet to speak Annanite to her, fearing she would recognize him from his touch, but now he had no choice. He had to know more. "Think you he hails from the same place as I?" he asked in the formal speech of Inner Sumal. "Or from one of the hamlets?" he finished in the common local dialect.

"The same place as you."

Kolt nodded, pleased by what she said. Annan, though not as large as many planets, was large enough, and the rough mountainous terrain and many isolated hamlets made for easy hiding spots as Kolt had learned a few years earlier when he had tracked a marauding band of thieves to an abandoned keep secreted within Quixtallyn Heights. Rakkad was proving an even greater adversary. His expression darkened. And a taunting one. More than likely, his hideaway was within easy access to Inner Sumal, something Aylyn's statement seemed to point to as well.

Aylyn watched Kolt's changing expression. She had hoped her information would help him locate Laaryc's life-ender. "You are frowning. What I said didn't help?"

"Yes, it helped," he said in Hakonese. Though she had appeared not to recognize his voice, he thought it more likely that she would should he continue in Annanite. "I was thinking."

"Of what?"

"That I now know where to confine my search."

"Then you've believed all along that he is Annanite?" This she had not expected.

"Yes."

"Why didn't you tell me?" she demanded, her eyes flashing with anger. "He is *my* enemy, Kolt! *My* enemy! He robbed my best friend of his life, of his future!" She stormed away and then whirled back to him. "And what of your vow to help me seek vengeance? Does your word mean nothing?"

Golden Conquest

"Aylyn . . ." Kolt's voice was soft, deadly, as was the glint in his eyes, but Aylyn was too enraged to notice.

"How can you expect to pick him out of a crowd? You don't even know what he looks like." Had her temper not gotten the best of her, she would have realized the foolishness of her words.

A foolishness Kolt was quick to point out as his brow shot up, and he asked blandly, "And you do?"

"Of course, I saw him."

"His face, describe it to me."

"But I told you his face was cloaked. Oh," she said as his question forced her to hear herself.

"Exactly." Kolt saw her anger flee and struggled with his. Finally he raked his hands through his hair and sighed. "You will learn, Aylyn, that I am well known to have little use for bullies and petty tyrants. Annan's link with the Protectorate is weak and leaves us vulnerable. I am no stranger to fighting these invaders. Kedar especially."

"Kedar?" Aylyn repeated, stunned. "But you would have been just a child."

"Even at twelve I had little stomach for injustice, Now that I am a man full grown, I find I can tolerate it even less. Rakkad is thought to be behind thefts that have caused Annan no end of trouble. He will be found." He took her hands in his. "I did not give my vow lightly. Rakkad will be life-ended. I will see to it. I, not you." When Aylyn opened her mouth to protest, Kolt brushed his hand along the side of her face. "I know how much your Laaryc meant to you. But know this, you have come to mean much to me. I cannot let you risk yourself in this act of vengeance. I cannot." Kolt did not wait for Aylyn's response. He walked to the door. Without turning, he said, "Stay here. I will be back as soon as I can."

No sooner had he closed the door, then he cursed loudly and viciously. How could he have given voice to his feelings? How? Was he so besotted that he would place such a weapon in her hands? Would she taunt his feelings? Compare him to her dearly loved Laaryc? He swore once more, then got his emotions under control. He needed to concentrate on Rakkad, not on the young beauty whose mere presence scrambled his thoughts.

Aylyn stared blankly at the closed door. Kolt cared for her! Why did that knowledge fill her with such joy? Other men had said as much and more to her, yet none had evoked such extreme feelings within her. How could this be? She began to pace, the yiichi snuggled in her arms, thrumming softly with contentment as Aylyn stroked behind its ears. How could it mean so much to her that a man she hardly knew cared for her? He was handsome. Beyond handsome if she were truthful. Good and kind. She could see that from the way the villagers responded to him. Fun to be with. He appeared to accept her not because she was the lord director's daughter but because she was Aylyn. He was honorable. He had never once tried to take advantage of her dependence on him. Intelligent. And ... She stopped pacing as it struck her. He was as much of a paragon as his namesake!

Gods, but this was madness! She threw herself onto the relaxer and was startled by the yiichi's sudden shrill chattering. "I'm sorry," she soothed, "I forgot I was holding you."

The yiichi did not appear to think her excuse acceptable. She hopped from Aylyn's lap, scurried to the casement's ledge, leapt up onto it, hunkered down, and went to sleep.

Aylyn leaned her head back against the wall and closed her eyes. She remembered the feel of him. Was this what her mother meant when she said she would know when it was time to share her sleeper with someone? She had always assumed Laaryc would be the one to teach her the wonders of lovemaking, but now ... As painful as it was, she summoned up the memories of the last kiss she shared with Laaryc. And then she knew. As nice as it was, it did not compare to Kolt's. Laaryc was not to have been the one to awaken her passion. Still, some of what she felt when Kolt kissed her was not unfamiliar. Yet she knew none of her suitors had done more than evoke apathy and on one occasion, revulsion. Her eyes shot open. The only other time she had felt anything like what she'd felt with Kolt was the last few times her mind-toucher had touched her. He had wanted her as badly as Kolt did now. She had known it then. And she had been afraid.

So why wasn't she afraid of Kolt?

Having found no sign of Rakkad, not that he truly expected to, Kolt returned to the lodge. He hesitated for a moment before opening the door and wondered what his reception would be.

Aylyn, who had decided that only time would give her answers, looked up when Kolt entered.

"Anything?"

"No."

She motioned to the nourishment she had spread out on the table. "Are you hungry?"

He nodded and sat down.

"Would you like some brew?"

"Please."

Kolt frowned as Aylyn went through the motions of serving him as if nothing out of the ordinary had happened. Was it possible she had not heard him? Had not realized what he meant? He studied her as she ate silently. No, she had heard and obviously did not know how to react to it. He tossed down a mouthful of brew. Could it be she was as confused as he? What if he dragged her from the table, from the chamber and made love to her? Would she respond in love or hate? He reached for another portion of gropsa just as she did and had his answer when she jerked her hand away.

"Aylyn?" Gods, help him he had not meant to question her!

Aylyn raised her eyes. Kolt was staring at her, his eyes dark, intense, seeking an answer she could not give. "Please, Kolt, I . . ." *I what?* she asked herself. *I want you to make love to me? I want more time?* And answered, *I don't know. I just don't know.*

Kolt saw the play of emotions on her face and knew there was nothing to be said.

Silently, they finished eating and silently, they attempted to play one game of Warriors. When it became painfully apparent to both of them that there was no enjoyment in it, Kolt's hand swept the board clean of its pieces.

Mikki, asleep on the casement ledge, was startled awake. Screeching, she ran in to Aylyn's arms. Aylyn, stunned by Kolt's sudden display of temper, clasped the yiichi to her chest and stared at the tall Annanite. "Kolt?" she asked hesitantly.

He glowered at her. "Kolt what?"

Aylyn backed away from the challenge. "Nothing. I—I find myself suddenly tired. I—"

Kolt watched as she fled to her chamber. He crossed to the carafe of sylva, splashed some into a flagon, and drank it down in one long swallow. Another followed. And another. And another. And with each one came the knowledge that nothing helped. He hurled the crystal across the chamber.

Aylyn heard the crystal shatter against the wall and jerked her door open to an empty living chamber. She frowned.

Kolt was gone and she had not even heard him leave.

Chapter Twenty-Four

Iilde looked over her shoulder as the door opened. She smiled when she saw the handsome figure of her lover enter.

"Ah, my love, I have missed you greatly."

"Have you, Iilde?" He gestured at the pink smoke that filled the chamber. "How can you miss aught when you are pleasured by the mist."

Iilde slowly started to unlace her shirt. "The mist is merely to free my inhibitions and set my essence wandering. It sends me on journeys of beauty and swirling visions. I have learned it heightens the senses. Would you like to see how much?"

He waited until her heavy breasts spilled free and then said, "No."

Her eyes widened. "What?"

"You heard me. I have not come for a quick game of thrust and parry. I have come for information."

Her hands trembled as she yanked her shirt together. "Get out!"

He laughed. "I think not."

She stormed over to him. "Think you I do not know you seek news of her." She jammed her fists on her hips. "She is not here."

"Oh, she is come, of that I've no doubt."

"I did not say she is not come. I said she is not here."

"Speak plainly, Iilde, if you can through all this mist."

Iilde shook her head. "No."

"No?"

"No. I like it not that you demand me stay at readiness for whenever you should come. For more than an eight-night I have see little but my chambers. And now you at last are come and what say you? 'No! You would have news.'" She threw back her head and laughed. "To use your words, I think not."

"I think the mist is responsible for the rashness of your words and I will forgive you. But do not push me," he warned, his voice whisper-soft.

"Push you!" she shrieked, his softly spoken words not registering in the heat of her drug-fed rage. "You have not been the one waiting. I care not at all for this treatment!"

"I have given you cause to think I care what you like?"

His anger had at last penetrated hers. She stared at him, stunned. "But we are lovers!"

"For the moment, yes. Think you it gives you rights? It does not," he answered before she could. "What we have goes not beyond the sleeper, Iilde. Not beyond lust. There is naught about you to command aught else. My life and my love are mine alone."

"They are not yours," she spat. "They belong to the mind-witch and her daughter. Which one do you want more? Tell me?" Her gaze raked down him and she laughed. "Which one think you to please? Eirriel of Rhianon has Aubin, a man of some repute, I have heard. And now Aylyn has Kolt. And they say she pleases him greatly."

"They?"

"The villagers within the south region. Kolt and Aylyn are thought to be lovers. You have come in second again."

His lips drew back in a evil sneer of dark promise. "So you think, Iilde."

"Not think. Know."

He, too, had heard the rumors. It was what had

Golden Conquest

brought him to Iilde this day. Her sources were impeachable and he had hoped she would prove the gossip unfounded. Obviously, they were not. And now he had had enough. What her foolish words could not do, the confirmation of Aylyn and Kolt together could. He raised his hand and a bolt of blue-white energy shot out from his palm.

Iilde screamed. "No, please. Rak—"

"Silence," Rakkad bellowed, and reenforced it with a red-hot mind-touch. "You have been warned never to speak my name."

Iilde's hands flew to her head, and she dropped to the floor, screaming in pain. "Please, I am sorry."

Rakkad nodded and smiled. At once, Iilde fell silent and her thrashings ceased. It irked him to need her, but he did. She alone stood a chance of keeping Kolt occupied long enough for him to find Aylyn. A map and rumor placed them in one of two locations. The first had proven empty. Tonight he would try the second. He cursed his foolishness in not realizing the vxanza would keep Aylyn blocked to him as well. If he had realized, he would have compensated for it. Now he was forced to rely on Iilde's blatant sexuality. Few could resist her when she was fully primed.

"You will be waiting for him when he returns and you will keep him from leaving."

"How?" she asked weakly.

"That, my sweet Iilde, I leave up to your skills."

Rakkad did not wait for Iilde's nod of compliance. She had learned her lesson, she would do as he bid. He touched her mind once more before he left, a gentle reenforcing of the undetectable barrier behind which were locked all her memories of him. He stepped into the passageway of the keep without a care, his face was well known to those who resided within its crystal walls.

It was his identity which was not.

"Father, the envoy is here."

Aubin raised his head from the reports he had been

studying and not seeing for the past hours. He pinned Alaran with his demanding gaze. "And?"

"She insisted she speak with only you."

Aubin knew then that the information she carried was not good. It had been almost eight days since Aylyn's capture by Rakkad. Eight days with no communication. Eight days of waiting. Of wondering. Of fearing. Eirriel could sense nothing, and they could not even imagine what that meant. Was their daughter out of danger? Or beyond help?

Four days after the first and only contact, when all his resources had failed to find a clue to his daughter's fate, Aubin had swallowed his pride and gone begging to the Protectorate. As luck would have it, Kliu, the high commander in charge of search and recovery, was the very man Aubin had beaten out for position as captain on the *Celestial*'s maiden voyage. His was also the loudest voice protesting the purely diplomatic relationship between the Protectorate and Aubin's powerful and well-respected Rhianonian Alliance. That Aubin had had to ask the Protectorate, and especially Kliu for assistance, had rankled Aubin and pleased the high commander.

The Protectorate would help, Kliu had informed Aubin, if Aubin would at last agree to undertake a mission for the Protectorate—something they had been trying to inveigle since Aubin had resigned his commission twenty-three years earlier to become lord director of Rhianon. Aubin had agreed, hoping the mission would at least be of some importance, but he had held no true hope for it.

And he was soon proven right.

Kliu had chosen a mission that would have better suited a medic than the director of an alliance of six planets and a former fleetship captain. It seemed Xeril, another "upstart isolationist planet," had specifically requested Aubin's help with a plague that was threatening their people, and Kliu had assured them they would have it.

Aubin had gotten up from the communication's

Golden Conquest

board and gone directly to his work chamber and trashed it. The effects of his rage were still being corrected. And so now, four days later, Aubin awaited the Protectorate's envoy in a small temporary chamber.

"Bring her in," Aubin said grimly.

Alaran left to fetch the envoy, and when the door opened, Aubin expected to see her not Eiriel.

"There is news."

Aubin nodded. His golden eyes took in the strain in his lifebond's dull green eyes and the dark stain of sleeplessness that circled them. He rose and went to her side. Eirriel buried her head in his shoulder.

"I am afraid, Aubin. So afraid."

"I know, little one." He pressed a kiss to the top of her head. "I would give all I possess to have the news be good."

"But it will not be."

"No, it will not."

"Father, this is Envoy Uilini."

Aubin tucked Eirriel under his arm, and they turned to face the petite, dark-skinned envoy. Alaran crossed to stand beside his parents. He gestured to the relaxer, but the envoy shook her head.

"What is your news?"

Uilini's glance swept to Eirriel. "You wish me to speak now, Lord Director?"

Her question struck Aubin like a blow to his belly. Envoys of the Protectorate were notoriously cold. Her hesitantcy told Aubin that the news was worse than they had imagined. His grip tightened on Eirriel and he nodded.

"We have located the remains of the *Star Jumper*."

"Remains?" Eirriel gasped.

Uilini nodded. "Our scanners picked up minute fragments that have been identified as the *Star Jumper*. It is our conclusion that it exploded, killing all aboard."

"No! Aubin—" Eirriel slumped into Aubin's arms.

He swept her up and passed her to his son. "Take her to our chambers. I will be there shortly."

Alaran nodded and left.

"I would not have told her that way." Uilini's glare was accusing.

"My lady is not one to be denied, Envoy. She had a right to hear all your news." Aubin extended his hand. "I would see the report for myself."

"Of course." She handed the tube to him. "And I am to inform you that you have a three-day grace period before your enlistment begins."

"Three whole days. How kind."

Aubin slipped the tube into the computer. The envoy correctly assumed she had been dismissed and left. Aubin waited until the door closed, and even then, it proved little barrier. His anguished roar was heard by all.

Alaran rose when his father entered the chamber.

"How is she?" Aubin's intense gaze swept the prone form of his lifebond.

"As you, I expect," Alaran said quietly. "Father, you will think me crazed but I don't believe the report."

"Why?"

Alaran shrugged his shoulders and shook his head. "I don't know. Perhaps because Mother sensed none of this."

"She knew the *Star Jumper* was in danger."

"True, but as distraught as she was she wasn't terrified. If she sensed Aylyn's death, she would have seen it."

"So she has insisted as well."

"So you believe Aylyn is alive, too."

Aubin turned grief-ravaged eyes on his son. "No, Alaran, gods help me, but I do not. I know the accuracy of the Protectorate. Their scanners are infallible."

"Could they have falsified the report to gain your help?"

"No, as power-hungry as Kliu is, even he would not risk my anger. He is merely content that I have been forced to seek their aid, something I have eschewed for years. He believes that I will become enthralled by their technology, that I will lead the Rhianonian Alliance in a plea for membership. It would be a great coup for him. He would be the first high commander to succeed in drawing in the Rhianonian Alliance. No, Alaran, Aylyn is dead."

"And the mission?"

The mission! Aubin's scowl deepened. Six times during the recent months, the passive agrarians of the planet, Xeril, had spied streaking lights in their night sky, and each time had dispatched an untrained investigative team to analyze the strange activity. And each time, only a few of the Xerilians returned, their normally purple eyes colorless, their flowing white hair gone. And Aubin's orders were to discover why.

"The mission is a farce!" he spat. "But I have given my word and I will see it done." Aubin sighed. "I must send word to Kolt of Aylyn's death. It is his right. You will stay with your mother?"

Alaran nodded.

Aubin's communication with Kolt proved impossible. The laedan was away.

"You will have your laedan contact me as soon as he returns," Aubin demanded. "The matter is urgent."

"As soon as he returns, Lord Director," came a dull-witted reply. "You can count on me."

"Fine. Rhianon out."

A slender hand severed the signal from the Crystal Keep's communications chamber, and its owner laughed triumphantly. It had been pure chance that had placed him near the communications chamber when the call from Rhianon had come in. A gentle touch had rendered the on-duty tech asleep, leaving him free to take the message.

So Aubin had urgent news for Kolt, did he? He sounded distressed. And when Aubin did not hear back from Kolt, one could only hope he would sound enraged.

Pleased by his handiwork, Rakkad laughed and then left.

Kolt looked up as Naydir pushed the door to his sleeping chamber open.

"Kolt?" Naydir whispered, and then felt foolish when he saw Kolt staring at him. "I thought you asleep else I'd have just entered."

"I tried to sleep, but I found my mind too awake to obey my body's urgings. I am ready now so you may remove that look of concern. It mars the beauty of your face."

When Naydir did not respond to his teasings but only crossed the chamber to stand in front of him, Kolt frowned. "What is it?"

"Aylyn's father demands you return his call."

Kolt quirked a brow. "Demands?"

"Yes. He sought to contact you earlier and thinks you ignore him. He is most irate. I assured him that we had not received his message."

"I'll not give Aylyn back."

"Stay your rage. He does not seek her back." Naydir paused, then added solemnly, "He thinks Aylyn life-ended."

"What!"

"Her ship was found destroyed, and it is concluded all on it were life-ended in the explosion."

"But our message?"

"He received it not. Dakkar swears to have given it to the on-duty tech, and it was logged in."

"Aubin would not speak falsely."

"I did not mean such. Rather I but question whether it was sent or intercepted. The tech is life-ended, Kolt."

Kolt swore violently. Gods! But the one thing he had not considered was that his friends would be grieving for their daughter. "I must contact him at once."

"So I thought. The connection is ready; it but lacks your presence."

Kolt raked his hand through his hair. "I will speak with Aubin now. Wait for me."

With those parting words, Kolt *actualized*. The on-duty tech in the keep's communications center looked up startled when Kolt suddenly appeared in front of him.

Golden Conquest

"Get me Rhianon's lord director."

The tech moved away from the seat in front of the comm board. "He awaits, Laedan."

Kolt sat down heavily. He had expected the conversation with Aubin to be strained, considering that he had commandeered Aubin's daughter, but now he knew he would wish for the strain. Aubin was very protective of Eirriel and to hear that she had been mourning without reason! No coward, Kolt found himself very glad that he was not telling Aubin about Aylyn in person.

"Kolt?"

A wave of remorse swept over Kolt at the ragged edge in Aubin's voice. "I am here, Aubin."

"I have grave news for you, my friend."

"No, Aubin, you do not. Aylyn is safe and here with me."

The silence that followed Kolt's statement was deafening. When at last it was broken, Aubin's rage was palpable.

"What in the name of all the gods goes on here, Laedan of Annan!"

Kolt winced at Aubin's use of his title. Tersely, Kolt explained his knowledge of the events that led up to his finding Aylyn in the cavern. Holding nothing back, he told Aubin of his decision to keep Aylyn and the reasons for it, and ended with his apology that the message that would have spared Aubin and his lifebond pain had not been sent.

"Fine. Now, bring her home," Aubin said quietly, his voice edged with steel. "Eirriel needs to see her."

Kolt groaned. This was not going at all well. "I have given you my apology, Aubin."

"And I have accepted it, Laedan. I repeat, bring her home."

"I cannot. Aylyn belongs with me now."

"Don't do this," Aubin warned.

"I have no choice. I cannot let her go."

"Think well on your decision, Laedan of Annan. You will not like the results if I must come and get her."

"I will mourn the loss of our friendship, Aubin, but know this. Aylyn is my life. I will not willingly surrender her nor would she chose to go."

"So be it. Rhianon out."

Kolt stared at the communications board as the indicator light went out, and he couldn't help but wonder if he had lost a friend for naught.

"I will kill him!"

Eirriel watched her lifebond pace about their chambers. "Aubin, you are overreacting."

"Overreacting! He refuses to return my daughter to me after letting us think her dead, and I am overreacting?"

"Kolt explained that to you. Surely you cannot blame him because the message wasn't sent."

"Of course I blame him. He is the laedan. It was his duty to see the message sent."

"It was his duty to see to Aylyn. You heard him, she was frightened and disoriented. She needed him and he was there."

"How do we know Kolt wasn't the intruder aboard the *Star Jumper*? We both heard Aylyn say he was a mind-toucher. Perhaps Kolt decided to force her to go with him."

Eirriel put her hand on Aubin's arm. "You are letting your anger make you irrational, my love. Kolt loves her. You and he have spoken of it before. You had even promised her to him."

"If she agreed. She was given no choice in this."

"True, the circumstances are not to my liking, either, but Kolt only took advantage of the situation laid before him. Laaryc had said Kolt has long been in touch with her. Can you blame him for not giving up the chance to see if she can love him?"

"She doesn't love him, she fears him. Fears him enough to run from him."

Eirriel smiled. "She is your daughter, Aubin. Think back. You were not so ready to admit your love for me. You feared placing yourself in such a vulnerable position. You armed yourself with your anger and mistrust. Ayln had not your background to fall back on. So she ran. But, as we ourselves have learned, destiny cannot be avoided, merely delayed. And Kolt is Aylyn's destiny."

"And if he is not?"

"He is. I know it." Eirriel's eyes darkened. "You worried for me when I heard the Protectorate's report about the ship and shut myself up within our chambers, speaking to no one. Not even you. I was afraid, Aubin. Not because of the loss of Aylyn, but because I could not feel that loss." She touched her chest. "My heart should have been dark with despair and it wasn't. Even with my limited skills, I should have sensed her death and I didn't. I thought myself an unnatural mother when I could give no tears for Aylyn. I thought that I had no warning of it because, in the deepest part of my soul, I didn't care whether she lived or died. That was the pain you heard in my voice, the despair you saw on my face. That my daughter was dead, and I could not grieve."

Aubin was stunned. "You should have shared this with me, little one. I would have helped you see otherwise."

"You were so distraught. How could I add to your burden? I consoled myself with the hope that I was merely in shock. That in time the grief would come. But now I know, Aubin. I did not grieve because I knew she was not dead. That she was not in danger."

"You forget how you were before she left. You forget what you felt when you saw the *Star Jumper*."

"And you forget that one we love did die on the *Star Jumper* and that Aylyn was in danger."

"I forget nothing. And Aylyn is still in danger."

"No, she is not."

"As long as she is with that treacherous Annanite, she is in danger. She will be safe soon enough."

"What are you going to do?"

"I have arranged to have the *Ceallach* prepared for flight. I leave tomorrow to fetch our daughter home."

Since her pleas for reason were not working, Eirriel changed tactics. "And your pledge to the Protectorate?"

"The Protectorate be damned! When Aylyn is here on Rhianon, I will go to Xeril. Not before."

Eirriel looked at Aubin, taken aback by the rage she was suddenly sensing and the cause of it. "That's what this is all about, isn't it? That you gave your bond to the Protectorate and now know that it was unnecessary? You will let your pride ruin your daughter's chance for happiness?"

"And that chance is with Kolt?"

"Yes, so I believe."

"Well, I no longer do." He looked down on Eirriel, his eyes dark. "You have chosen Kolt over me, Eirriel."

"Chosen Kolt over . . . Aubin, what are you saying?"

"What? Don't your powers tell you?" he sneered. "It is obvious to me, though I am mind-blind, that you have sided with your kind. So much for the strength of the love you have given me."

Eirriel gasped. "You cannot believe that! Aubin?"

But Aubin refused to look at Eirriel. He turned and stormed from the chamber, ignoring Eirriel's frantic pleas for him to come back.

When Kolt entered his antechamber, Naydir looked up and arched a brow. "You walked," he commented, surprised.

"I'd not wanted to risk *actualizing*."

Naydir looked closer at his friend and noted the whiteness around his mouth and the shadows under his eyes. "You are weary."

Kolt dropped into the relaxer across from Naydir. "Gods, but weary seems such a paltry statement for what I feel," he admitted candidly.

Dividing his time between Aylyn and Annan left little opportunity for sleep, and what little he did get was plagued by conflicting visions of Aylyn. He saw her naked and loving, clothed and distant, or worst of all, storming from his life in hatred. And now. . . .

Golden Conquest

"Aubin demands that I surrender Aylyn to him when he arrives or else he will take her."

"Will she go?"

"I know not, Naydir. All I know is that I cannot let her go without a fight."

There was naught Naydir could say that would rid his friend of his concern. Kolt's belief that Aylyn was his had always been with him. Naydir could only hope that when Lord Aubin arrived Aylyn would stand by Kolt. His gaze swung to the chrono-keeper. "Dare I hope you will forego the Lights?"

Kolt shook his head. "My people expect to see me."

Naydir rose. "Then go and rest. You've two hours till the Lights. Take advantage of them." Naydir moved to the door and opened it. "I will return later."

Kolt quickly stripped, then dragged himself to his sleeper, and thunked down on it. Two hours of sleep would be better then none, he thought as he pulled the covering up over him.

It was in the middle of one of his more explicit dreams of Aylyn, just as he was thrusting inside her, when Kolt realized the lips he was kissing were suddenly kissing back. Even before he came fully awake, he understood why the dream had felt so real, so intense. He shuddered and threw up his shields to block out Iilde's overactive imaginings—at least he hoped they were imaginings. If he opened his eyes to see that he had actually . . . *No!* he thought firmly. He couldn't have been so tired, so lost within his dreams that he had taken Iilde. Muttering a prayer to the Mother of the Universe, he opened his eyes and met Iilde's passion-glazed pink eyes. Gods, but they were too close to his face! When his hands reached up to push her off him, relief rushed through him. The gods be praised, she was clothed!

"Kolt! What is wrong?"

Kolt leapt to his feet. Snatching his clothing up as he went, he crossed to the opposite end of the chamber. "What is wrong? Not even you could be so misguided as to not know the answer." He swiped his hand across his mouth, not caring that his action caused Iilde to flinch.

"You wipe my taste from your mouth. Why?"

Kolt paused in the middle of pulling on his leggings and stared at her, stunned by her question. "You would hear the truth?"

Iilde rose and walked slowly toward him, confident that the sheer caftan displayed her charms to their best advantage. "Yes."

"Because I find the taste of you repulsive."

She laughed. "So you say, but your body said otherwise. Think you that was our first kiss?" She ran her hands up her body and cupped her breasts. "Or that you did not touch?"

"Gods, Iilde, I was asleep!"

"And dreaming. Obviously, your little pet cannot satisfy you if you respond to my offerings."

"My little pet?"

"Your Aylyn."

Kolt grabbed her arms. "What know you of Aylyn?"

"That she does not please you in spite of what they say."

"Who says?" he demanded.

"The ignorant villagers. They think you are lovers." She placed her hands on his chest, and Kolt, needing the information from her, gritted his teeth and fought the urge to thrust her from him. "I know better. Your response to me was not that of a man well satisfied."

"And where do these ignorant villagers claim to have seen me with my lover?"

"Think you your treks to the hamlets have gone unnoticed? All know you have been spending time in the south region."

Kolt swore. He had never considered the gossips when he sought to share Annan with Aylyn. He should have, for his every move had been fodder for them since he first came of age. Disgusted by his stupidity, he dropped his hands from Iilde. "Leave me and do not come back. As I have said before, you have naught that I want."

"Not even the Khrystallyn?"

He was bending down to retrieve his clothing and raised his head to her. "Have you no pride that you would sell yourself for such a minor price?"

"I have long wanted you. If it takes the Khrystallyn to bring you to my sleeper, then so be it. Once you are there, you will never leave. You see, I have great pride."

"I will never come to you, Iilde. Somehow I will free myself from the pledge of the charter I gave to your lifebond. Somehow, I will find a way around it and wrest the mines from your control."

Iilde laughed. "You are too honorable, Kolt. You will never break faith with my poor life-ended Nnels. Never." Iilde was smart enough to know when to retreat. She turned and sauntered toward the door to the antechamber. "When you realize that I alone can give you all you need, send for me. I will not make you pay too highly for keeping me waiting."

"Get out, Iilde," he ground out. "Now!"

She bowed. "As you wish, Laedan."

Kolt heard the outer door to the passageway open, and Morald's startled demand, "How came you here?"

Kolt joined them in time to see Iilde's secret smile. "Answer him, Iilde."

She shrugged her shoulders. "Your captain of the guards was asleep and—"

Even before Morald could deny her accusation, Kolt snapped, "Try again. The truth this time." His eyes narrowed. "Do not force me to take it, Iilde. You would not like the feel of it."

Iilde's panicked gaze flew to Kolt. "You would not?"

"You are so sure?" Iilde nodded. "Then speak a further mistruth and see what I would or would not do."

"The passageway from the cubiculum, of course."

Morald swore. "Laedan, forgive me I did not think—"

"Neither did I nor Naydir, Morald. We believed it unknown. Obviously, we were wrong. Iilde, how came you to learn of the passageway?"

"On one occasion I thought to speak with you while

you were within the cubiculum and I arrived to find the hidden door closing behind you. I knew I would have only one chance to use the passageway to get to your chamber so I waited until my need was the greatest." She sighed. "I suppose I will have to seek out another way to come to you now."

"Do not, Iilde," Kolt growled. "Else you will find yourself banished from the keep."

"You cannot!" Iilde gasped. "I have the right as owner—"

Kolt put up his hand. "Enough, Iilde. You have my warning. Do with it as you like."

"It will not happen again, Laedan. I will see it guarded."

"My thanks, Morald. Iilde." Kolt bowed his good-bye and shut the door in her face. Her shriek of outrage followed by Morald's hearty chuckle and her departing footsteps told Kolt that she understood that for this day, at least, she would be kept from him.

Kolt pulled his shirt over his head as he walked back into his sleeping chamber. The Rainbow Lights would be in a few minutes and then he could return to Aylyn—an Aylyn who would hopefully be more receptive to him today than yesterday. She had to be. Her sire would be on Annan in four days, demanding her return, a return Kolt wanted desperately for her to protest. He swept his hair out from underneath the shirt and slipped on the jerkin. He was just pulling on his boots when the realization of what Iilde had said earlier sent a jolt of fear through him.

If Iilde could link him to the south region through gossip, surely Rakkad, who was far from a fool, could as well. And from the south region. . . .

Kolt raced over to his desk and yanked out a map of the south region. It was well known that he had been appearing at the Rainbow Lights every day. Known as well, apparently, was the time he and Aylyn spent in each hamlet and how they traveled there, by foot or phedra. Kolt's brow furrowed as he tried to remember the mode of transportation for each trip, then he ran his finger from each hamlet backwards to the lodge. His motion cut true and deadly paths across the map. Lywl, by foot, midafternoon, half it for the return by phedra. Hujji, by phedra both ways. Smpo, by foot. With each precise and unvaried motion of his hand, the evidence became indisputable.

His need to show Aylyn Annan had led Rakkad right to her!

Chapter Twenty-Five

Rakkad hovered above her. He reached out for her. "You are mine, Aylyn. Mine. None can prevent me from having you."

Shouting her name, Laaryc rushed Rakkad. Aylyn screamed as a jagged white bolt of glowing energy arced from Rakkad's palm and struck Laaryc in the chest. The force of the impact picked him up and hurled him against the wall.

"Aylyn! Help me!" Larryc pleaded. "Make him stop."

Rakkad laughed. "Do you come to me, Aylyn?"

Her eyes never leaving Laaryc, she shook her head. "Please, Laaryc, understand. I cannot."

"So be it."

Aylyn jumped. Rakkad was suddenly right behind her. His laughter deepened and echoed off the walls which shook and shuddered. Suddenly, the wall Laaryc was pinned against started to dissolve, revealing the black void of open space.

"Gods! No!" Aylyn screamed. She started to run forward, but Rakkad's hand clamped down on her shoulder. Helplessly, she watched as Laaryc was sucked out and away, her name on his lips.

As suddenly as they had dissolved, the walls returned.

Sobbing, she jerked away from Rakkad and sank to her knees, her head in her hands.

"Will you come to me?" he repeated.

She shook her head.

Golden Conquest

Aylyn?

Aylyn's head shot up at the tender strength of the voice that spoke within her mind. "You're back!"

Then it was gone and emptiness remained. Aylyn started to shake. A hand touched her cheek, and she wrenched from it.

"Do not cry, my lady warrior."

Kolt was kneeling in front of her. "Kolt! Oh, Kolt!" Aylyn threw herself into his arms. "Please take me from here."

"He cannot. You are mine."

Rakkad waved his hand, and Kolt vanished to reappear a distance away. Aylyn watched as Kolt struggled against unseen arms that held him from her.

"Come to me, Aylyn." Rakkad held out his hand. "Come to me."

Aylyn looked once more at Kolt and knew that she would die if she cost Kolt his life. She raised herself on unsteady legs and crossed slowly to Rakkad.

"Aylyn! No!" Kolt fought frantically, the cords on his neck straining, the muscles on his arms knotted. Finally he was free.

Aylyn placed her hand in Rakkad's.

"No!" Kolt roared. "Take your filthy hands off her!"

He flung himself at Rakkad. Aylyn saw Rakkad raise his hand and knew what was coming next. She screamed as the bolt shot out from Rakkad's palm and with that scream a shrill trilling sound.

"Kolt! No! Watch out!" Aylyn cried out as she bolted up in her sleeper. Her chest heaving, tears streaming from her eyes, it took a moment for her to realize that she was still in her sleeper, in her chamber within the lodge she shared with Kolt, the yiichi sitting on the sleeper next to her highly agitated. It had all been a dream.

"Sh, Mikki, it's all right," she murmured as she reached over and lit the flame light, and the soft glow illuminated the chamber. "I'm sorry if I scared you. I was scared, too."

She lay back on the sleeper, her trembling fingers running reassuringly down Mikki's back, and waited for her heart to stop its pounding and her hands to stop shaking. But her body refused to cooperate.

"It's just a dream." She spoke the words aloud as she had done so often as a child, the mere act reenforcing her knowledge that it was but a dark dream. But it did not work. And that it did not terrified her.

What if her Mother's Kiiryan blood, which had never evinced itself before, was now? What if it was no dream, but a warning of what would happen? But Laaryc was dead, and in this vision over and over she had seen Laaryc dying, felt the voice of her mind-toucher silenced, and knew that she had awakened an instant before Rakkad had destroyed Kolt.

She gasped. Did that mean she could still prevent Kolt's life-ending?

Frantically, she tore from the sleeper and raced to Kolt's chamber. She cared little that her sudden flight had set Mikki to chattering again or that she was garbed only in a short thin sleeper gown or that her eyes must be red and swollen from crying. She just knew she had to reach Kolt. Had to warn him that Rakkad was coming.

"Kolt," she called as she opened the door, surprised by the raspiness of her voice and the sharp pain in her throat. If she didn't know better, she would have thought it was strained from screaming. But that couldn't be. Surely Kolt would have heard and come to her?

Then she saw why he hadn't. Not because she hadn't screamed, but because he wasn't there. His sleeper was empty and undisturbed, as if it hadn't been slept in. She tried to remember. Had he returned last night? She wasn't certain. She had fallen asleep waiting for him.

She went into the living chamber and stopped suddenly, Mikki bumping into her legs. It, too, was empty. She shivered. Had her unwillingness to confront the emotions he evoked within her driven him away?

Golden Conquest

Would he come back? He had to. If he didn't, she couldn't warn him about Rakkad. Couldn't tell him that Rakkad now looked at him as a threat. But . . . A faint hope glimmered within her. Perhaps his leaving would keep him safe. Yes. That was why she had not seen his death in her dream. Somehow, her unconscious mind had registered that Kolt was no longer around and therefore safe. But even as she experienced the relief that swept through her from her conclusion, she shook her head. Kolt would be back. He would never desert her. His honor would not let him.

Her hands clenched at her side. Gods protect him! His honor would lead to his death.

She had to warn him. She started for the door and then stopped. But how? The phedras. Yes. She opened the door to unyielding blackness and a fierce wind her mind had heard but not identified. Mikki raced about her legs, her trilling loud and strident.

"Yes, Mikki, I know." She shut the door. "It would be madness to ride now. We will wait until the sun rises."

She reached down and the yiichi jumped into her arms. Absently, she stroked behind Mikki's ears as she began to pace. Where would she go? Kolt had never said where he went, merely that he had to render reports. She hadn't wanted to ask. She had been afraid it would add to the intimacy of their daily life to know exactly where he was and what he was doing. And now her cowardice would prevent her from warning him away. Her fear of the mind-toucher had led to Laaryc's death, and her fear of what she could have with Kolt would lead to his.

She sank to the floor, sobbing. Mikki, her head cocked, her confusion obvious in her high, choppy chatterings, sat near Aylyn's head and listened to the harsh soul-wrenching sounds coming from Aylyn. When at last they stopped, and Aylyn drifted off into a fitful sleep, Mikki turned to face the door and waited.

Kolt, who had forgotten about the Rainbow Lights in his need to see Aylyn safe, *actualized* just outside the lodge. His heart slammed into his throat as he pushed open the door and saw her lying on the floor in the middle of the living chamber.

Mikki, softly trilling, watched carefully as Kolt quickly ascertained that Aylyn was merely sleeping. But why on the cold flooring? Had she fallen? Was she ill? Shucking off the gauntlet he had grabbed before *actualizing* from the keep, he slipped his arms under her and lifted her into his arms.

"Kolt?" Aylyn murmured sleepily.

"Yes, softling."

"I was so afraid when I woke and you weren't here. I thought you were angry and wouldn't come back."

He pressed a kiss on her forehead. "I'll always come back, Aylyn. You're not to fear otherwise. Is that why you were on the floor?"

She nodded. "That and the dream."

"What dream?"

"Later. Right now I just want you to hold me."

"With the greatest pleasure, softling."

He carried her to the large chair and lowered himself into it. Mikki, as usual, was not far behind and scrambled onto the back of the relaxer, curled up into a ball, and went to sleep. Aylyn snuggled into Kolt, her arm snaking up his shoulder, her fingers threading through his hair. Sighing contentedly, she nuzzled her nose into his neck, then screwed it up as it twitched. She rubbed at her nose, trying to relieve it from the tingling sensation caused by the strong cloying scent that clung to his skin. Frowning, she followed the smell up his corded neck, over his beard, to his lips.

Kolt pleased at Aylyn's unusual aggressive behavior, waited patiently for her kiss and was stunned when her hand cracked him sharply across his cheek. The sound sent a startled Mikki darting for cover.

"What in the name of Nithrach?" He saw her swing her hand back for another slap and grabbed her wrist. "Do not, Aylyn," he growled.

"Let go of me!" she cried.

Kolt shook his head. "Tell me why?"

Golden Conquest

"Why?" Her eyes blazed with fury. "Because you reek!"

Her answer stunned him as much as her slap, and he released her wrist. Aylyn scrambled from his lap.

"Bastard!" she hissed. "I cried myself to sleep fearing for you, and you were romping in a sleeper with some smelly servicer!"

Smelly servicer? It was then that he remembered Iilde and the heavy spicy fragrance she always wore. Thinking of Iilde's reaction to being named a smelly servicer, he foolishly chuckled.

The sound of his laugh sent Aylyn's temper spiraling out of control. Gone was her concern about Rakkad, about Kolt's life, about anything. All she knew was a need to be far from where she was. She spun on her heels and crossed to the door.

"Aylyn? You can't mean to go out there! We're in the middle of a flash storm." When she pulled the door open, he tried a different approach. "You're not clothed."

Aylyn looked down, saw that she wasn't, turned, and went into her chamber. She returned from throwing on a long-sleeved jumpsuit, a woven covering, and boots to see Kolt standing in front of the door.

"Let me pass."

"No."

"Let me pass," she repeated through clenched teeth.

Kolt shook his head. "Not until you tell me what has brought about this mood." He put his hand up. "And don't tell me it is the smell."

"I won't."

"Good."

"Because I'm not telling you anything!" She shrieked the last words. "Now, let me pass!"

"No!" Kolt roared.

"Fine!" Aylyn spun on her heels and stormed to her chamber, hurling the door closed before Mikki could follow her in, and slapping the bolt shut.

Kolt frowned. She had given up too easily. He ran to the door. "Aylyn?" When she refused to answer, he repeated her name, accompanying the shout with a punch to the hardwood. Mikki, who was already chattering demandingly, starting jumping up and down as Kolt hit the door again.

"Aylyn, stop this and open up! Aylyn!" Realizing his tactics weren't working, he reached down and lifted the irate yiichi into his arms. "Aylyn, you've upset Mikki," he chided. "It isn't good for her. Won't you please open up?"

Irritated to find himself pleading with her, Kolt decided he had had enough. He lowered Mikki to the floor, took a few steps back, and delivered a flying jumpkick to the door. In the time it took him to remove the splintered pieces from his path, Mikki had already scooted into the chamber and was jumping up and down, chattering shrilly, on the ledge of the open casement. He was not surprised when a quick check showed no sign of Aylyn.

"Damn her!" he swore as he turned and ran to the front door. He opened just as Aylyn, on Seonaid, raced passed. "Aylyn, you little fool, get back here!"

He was halfway to the animal shelter when a shrieking Mikki, her wings extended and fluttering wildly, leapt into his arms, and wrapped herself around him.

"Mikki, not—" Kolt bit back the rest of the words as he felt the telltale tingle of a mind-probe.

Chapter Twenty-Six

Kolt spared a brief touch to soothe the agitated yiichi, then concentrated on the man who again sought to gain entrance into his mind.

Rakkad! Show yourself! Oblivious to the sudden downpour and the fierce gusting wind, Kolt stood in the middle of the yard, a trembling yiichi wrapped around him, and closed his eyes, focused his mind, and listened.

Greetings, usurper. Kolt's eyes shot open at the malevolence he felt in Rakkad's touch. *You are well. A pity.*

It will take more than the cowardly attack of stabbing me in the back to be rid of me, Rakkad. Come. Show yourself. Kolt challenged, though he did not expect the cunning mind-toucher to do so. *Are you too fearful to confront me to my face?*

Not too fearful, too preoccupied! As much it pains me to say it, it would seem I must give you my thanks.

Thanks? For the hijacked Khrystallyn that has no doubt made you rich?

Well, yes, there is that. But I meant for your care of my Aylyn. She is more beautiful than ever.

It was then that Kolt realized the import of Rakkad's comment that he was too preoccupied. He was near Aylyn! And watching her! Kolt thrust Mikki from him and ran toward the animal shelter.

Yes, I am near my Aylyn.

Patricia Roenbeck

Not your Aylyn, Rakkad. Never yours. Mine!
We shall see.

Kolt suddenly realized that Rakkad had answered his thought that he was near Aylyn. Though confident that his mental shields were well in place and impenetrable and Rakkad could only touch what Kolt permitted him to touch, Kolt decided that voicing his doubts about his barriers might force Rakkad's attention on him and away from Aylyn. The tone of Rakkad's touch revealed an arrogant confidence in his abilities. If Rakkad thought Kolt believed it as well . . . Kolt led Ketti out of the animal shelter and down the only path Aylyn could have taken. Putting his plan in motion, he questioned Rakkad, making sure his touch had the right amount of insecurity to feed Rakkad's enormous ego. *You answered my thought! How can that be? My shields—*

I need not touch you to know your fears, your vulnerabilities, usurper.

A sudden swirl of wind threw Kolt's hair in his face, and Kolt tossed his head, flinging the sodden strands from his eyes. Usurper, Kolt thought behind his shield, he has used that word before. *That is twice now you have called me usurper. Why?*

Twice?

Kolt lost Rakkad's answer as a loudly screeching Mikki landed behind him, her arms, legs, and tail snaking around Kolt, seeking an anchor against the gusting wind and the phedra's jarring movements.

How twice?

Kolt smiled at the impatience of Rakkad's touch. So, Rakkad did not like to be ignored. Kolt's smile deepened. Rakkad would like Kolt's answer less than his silence. *When you attacked me, it was in the forefront of your mind, I but took it from you.* Kolt felt Rakkad's rage. *You like it not that I can touch you and you cannot touch me.*

Rakkad laughed. *You think me such a fool that I let you touch all of me?*

Golden Conquest

When Rakkad's gloating laugh ended suddenly, dread shot through Kolt, driving any questions about Rakkad's statement from his mind replacing them with one. Did Rakkad have Aylyn? Rakkad's next words proved Kolt's fear a certainty.

Ah, sweet Aylyn, how nice of you to join me.
Leave her alone!
I think not, usurper. I think not.

Kolt felt Rakkad break contact and swore. He look around, but the blinding rain made it difficult to see. Where in Nithrach was Aylyn?

Aylyn cursed as a fierce gust of wind slapped the icy rain on her face. Why, she demanded, if she had to give into her rage and run, could she have not at least had the sense to take her wide-brimmed hat? She held on as Seonaid again slipped on the muddy ground. This was ridiculous! If Seonaid broke one of her legs, Aylyn would never forgive herself!

Aylyn leaned forward and stroked Seonaid's long neck. "I'm sorry, pretty girl. Let's go back, shall we?" Seonaid snorted and bobbed her head up and down in apparent answer. Aylyn smiled, then grunted as Seonaid stumbled again, and she slammed into the bony protrusion at the base of the phedra's neck. Seonaid swung her head around. "Don't worry about me, Seonaid. Just get us home."

The phedra's answering whinny changed to a shrill screech, and she reared. Aylyn, caught unprepared, barely managed to maintain her seat.

"What the—Gods! No!" she cried when she saw what had caused the phedra's reaction.

There, hovering in the air several hand-spans in front of them, was Rakkad!

Aylyn yanked back on the riding strap. Seonaid responded and whirled, rearing again when a bolt of energy sparked into the ground near her forefeet. This time, Aylyn was unable to keep her seat. She slid backwards and landed on her back in the mud, the force of her landing driving the breath from her. As

Aylyn lay gasping, another energy blast sent Seonaid bolting away.

"My poor Aylyn. Would you like a hand up?"

The pain from her landing vanished as Aylyn looked up to see Rakkad hovering next to her, his hand extended.

"Don't touch me!" she cried as she scrambled to her feet and retreated.

Rakkad moved forward and found himself the victim of a sudden assault from the air as a shrieking Mikki dropped onto him.

"Aylyn! Here!" Kolt shouted as he and Ketti burst out of the trees behind the flying yiichi, and he saw the enshrouded form hovering uncomfortably close to Aylyn.

Aylyn, shouting Kolt's name, raced toward him as best as she could. Though the rain had abruptly stopped, as was usual in a flash storm, the heavy precipitation had already done its damage and Aylyn had to struggle against the thick gripping mud. Rakkad, momentarily stunned by the yiichi's attack and Kolt's sudden appearance, recovered. He tossed Mikki aside.

No! You'll not have her! Rakkad vowed, and hurled a jagged energy dagger at Aylyn's back.

Kolt, however, had been expecting just such a cowardly feat and even before he had called Aylyn's name had shielded her back. Rakkad roared his frustration when the dagger was absorbed by the translucent shimmering shield he had not noticed. He threw out both his hands, and blue-white energy arced outward, joining and expanding into a huge ball of pulsating light. Kolt, reaching down to grab Aylyn's outstretched hand and hoisting her up in front of him, barely had time to enlarge and to reenforce the shielding so that it withstood the impact of the energy ball. He thought of the neutralizer he had hidden from Aylyn's curious eyes in the waistband of his leggings and cursed. He had no free hand to grab it. They would have to run. He could not risk Aylyn's life.

Golden Conquest

"Hold on to me and keep your head down," Kolt ordered.

Aylyn was quick to comply. Her arms snaked around Kolt's waist, and she buried her head in his shoulder as Mikki settled onto her lap. Kolt, once Aylyn was secure, whirled Ketti around. The phedra needed no encouragement and thundered back the way they had come.

Aylyn safe and Ketti well able to carry them to the lodge without guidance, Kolt turned his mind to the man who would take the woman he loved. Rakkad's need for vengeance was strong, stronger than anything Kolt had ever felt. Strong enough to demand action.

You are not as I, Rakkad. I have learned as much this day. It is why you chose to attack from the back, is it not? You fear me. What I am. What I can do.

I fear no one.

Think you you do not? Then behold.

Before Rakkad could create another energy weapon, Kolt conjured up one of his own. A pulsating spear of fire streaked forward and froze ten hand-spans from Rakkad.

Do not think to contact your ship, Rakkad. You will find they cannot hear you.

Rakkad tried anyway as his vile curse told Kolt.

Perhaps it is better that you try. Care you to try again? He paused a moment, then added, *Once more, Rakkad?* Kolt laughed. *It is not my plan that they whisk you to safety, Rakkad, for I have much to say to you.* Kolt's touch turned as cold as the pulsating fire was hot. *Be warned, Rakkad. Aylyn is mine!*

The spear shot forward and whizzed between Rakkad's legs and back again. It spiraled around him in an ever-decreasing circle until Rakkad could not help but feel its heat. Then it darted away only to zip back and freeze a hand-span from Rakkad's face.

Doubt it not, Rakkad. What is mine, I guard with my life.

Kolt could feel Rakkad's fear as he stared at the fiery projectile and his frustration at his impotence to thrust

207

it away or to flee. Kolt knew Rakkad was wondering why Kolt hesitated to use the weapon when Rakkad would have driven the bolt home with great pleasure. Kolt wondered as well, and the spear quivered as he wrestled with the almost overwhelming urge to end Rakkad's life here and now. Had Rakkad wanted someone life-ended the manner of weapon would matter not at all to him so long as it accomplished its purpose. But Kolt was not Rakkad. His honor held the spear motionless. His need for vengeance freed it. For every thought of honor came the counter one that Rakkad had almost taken Aylyn. That if it were not for the yiichi's remarkable link to Aylyn, Kolt would have been too late.

Within a few breaths, Kolt had the answer, an answer which did not sit well in Kolt's present mood. Kolt's honor demanded that his enemy have an equal advantage. Rakkad's mind-touching skills were lacking. He could not *actualize*, penetrate Kolt's mental shielding, or create a thought-weapon stronger than Kolt's. Neutralizers would put them on even ground, but seemed to Kolt a coward's way out. A quick shot when his opponent was unprepared or unknowing was not for him. Kolt discarded method by method and weapon by weapon until all that remained were the hand-held kinds. And it was no wonder the choice came down to them, for they were Kolt's favorite, putting those who used them at equal risk. Kolt's mouth twisted wryly as he realized he need go no further. Rakkad himself had already made the selection of the specific weapon. Had he not proven his skill in daggers? Of course, he had yet to confront Kolt face-to-face. . . .

So be it. Kolt sent the spear whizzing skyward and released his interference with Rakkad's communicator.

Rakkad could have watched the fiery trail, to see how long and how far Kolt could maintain the thought-weapon. But quickly realizing that he had been granted his freedom, he instead barked an order to his ship. Hearing this, Kolt knew his display was unwatched and unneeded. The spear there one instant was gone the next. Much sooner than Rakkad, who had to wait for his men to activate the T-M unit.

Before Rakkad dematerialized, Kolt heard his laugh. *You are a fool, usurper. A weak fool. You should have life-ended me while you had the chance. I will be back, you know.*

If you come back, it is you who will be proven the fool, Rakkad. My honor and Aylyn's presence held my hand this day. They will not again. Should you come near Aylyn, you will find me merciless.

Rakkad snorted. *Your honor will hold your hand then as it held it today. It is ever the way with noble fools. You will be life-ended and Aylyn will be mine.*

Never!

Rakkad laughed confidently. *So we shall see.*

Kolt did not need his mind-touching skills to know that they would soon meet again, and when they did, only one would survive.

Chapter Twenty-Seven

The confrontation with Rakkad had happened within the space of a few moments. In that time Aylyn had gathered her wits and was ready to face Kolt. Turning, she looked up at him, not surprised to see the dark scowl that marred his handsome face.

"I'm sorry, Kolt," she said quietly, placing her hand on his cheek. "You've a right to be angry. Since you found me, I have been nothing but trouble."

Aylyn's gentle touch was all that was needed to drag Kolt from his dark thoughts. And once that happened, he allowed himself to give into relief. Ignoring her words, he voiced his concern. "You are unhurt?"

"Yes. Thanks to you. Again."

"Mikki helped."

"Mikki?"

Kolt nodded. "The accursed weather kept me from seeing your path once you crossed into the meadow. Precious moments were wasted as I searched for your trail. Mikki, it seemed, had no problem. One minute she was gripping my back, the next she was flying. I followed her."

Aylyn rubbed the sleeping yiichi behind her ears. "It is strange, isn't it, that she could find me?"

"It is not that she found you that is strange, her hypersensitivity to strong emotions was more than likely what led her to you. But that she has linked somehow with you. It is unknown."

Golden Conquest

There was nothing to be said to that, and they rode in silence for a few moments, each realizing that they owed much to a tiny and very unique creature, until Aylyn noticed the changes in the woods. "We aren't going back to the lodge, are we?"

"No." Instinctively, Kolt's grip around Aylyn tightened. "It is no longer safe."

Safe, he thought bitterly. She would have been safe if his desire to keep her on Annan had not gotten the best of him. To make her see Annan for what it was, and for her to love it and him and to want to stay, had been his arrogant plan. And while doing that reveal her location to the life-ending bastard who sought her. Rage tore through him at his stupidity. Why had he not realized? And now that he had, where could he take her? Where would she be safe from prying eyes?

As much as he hated the thought of it, Rhianon seemed the obvious answer. But Aubin was not due to arrive for a few more days, and he'd not risk sending her on one of Annan's antiquated ships. They would be no better equipped to handle Rakkad than Laaryc's vessel had been. Rhianon's fleet, he was confident, could withstand any attack he could think of. And should an attack come, Aubin's training would serve him well.

But until then, where would she be safe?

"We go to Chaslydon," he replied, suddenly knowing it was the best choice. Chaslydon, Annan's newest city, had been built with a specially constructed dome that prevented random T-M beams. With guards posted at each T-M unit and at the entrances to the city, any who would enter would be monitored.

Aylyn shivered as a gust of wind plastered her wet clothes to her. Till now her emotions had been in too much of an upheaval for her to take note of the cold. She looked up at the sky and saw clouds rolling in again. "Is it far?" she asked as another shiver ran down her spine.

"Yes." Kolt frowned as he felt her shudder. "You are chilled."

"I was too afraid to feel anything before and now I can feel nothing but the cold."

Kolt looked around and got his bearings. "There is a cottage nearby where an elderly couple resides. They will give us shelter, nourishment, and a change of clothing."

"We can't risk involving them, Kolt. If Rakkad follows—"

"He does not."

"How do you know?"

"I know."

Aylyn heard the certainty in his voice and suddenly felt reassured. "If you are sure..."

"I am."

"... then I would be most grateful of dry clothing."

"And will your gratitude lead you to explain why you ran from me?"

Aylyn looked at Kolt in dismay. "I had hoped you had forgotten."

"I have not."

"So I noticed."

"You will tell me?" he asked again.

Aylyn met his unyielding stare. He had sheltered her within his home, seen that she had clothing, nourishment, companionship, and had risked his life for her. She owed him his explanation. "Yes," she said quietly.

"Good." He pulled her closer against him before she could react. "Lean back against me and I will see to the problem of the wind."

She was too startled by his smug statement to comment on her new position, especially when it placed her snugly against his lean hardness. "See to the problem of the wind?" She giggled. "You will tell it to stop no doubt."

"If I did, it would obey me."

"Of course, it would. Just as I do."

Kolt gave a shout of laughter. "I think, softling, the wind would obey me easier."

Grateful that he had thought to slip the gauntlet back on before rushing to confront Rakkad, Kolt pressed a

Golden Conquest

switch on the gauntlet, activating the shielding. As he had predicted, the wind proved no longer a problem.

Aylyn snuggled into Kolt. "You are so clever, my warrior."

"Am I?"

"Clever? Of course, this"—Aylyn flicked a hand at the shielding—"proves it. I don't think its creator had a wind-buffer in mind when he designed it."

Kolt chuckled. "No, *she* would have been in awe at my cleverness." Humor fled his voice, replaced by a husky intensity. "I would know not if I am clever, but if I am your warrior?"

Aylyn did not hesitate. She met his questioning gaze with her own firm surety. "Yes."

Kolt's eyes darkened to an almost black. "Once spoken you cannot say otherwise."

"I do not want to." From the moment she had agreed, all confusion was gone from her mind. He was hers. For whatever reason, the gods had seen fit to bestow Kolt on her. She would question it no longer. She twisted around so that she could place both her hands on his chiseled cheeks. "Gods help me, Kolt, but I find I do not want to."

Kolt felt as if he would burst with his need for her. But trapped on the back of a phedra, his one hand holding the riding strap, the other the shielding, he could no more than kiss her. And so his mouth swooped down and captured hers. Aylyn, free from all doubts, all questions, kissed him without restraint, pouring all her feelings into her kiss.

It was moments before either one of them realized that the rain had started again. A fierce gust of wind had carried the icy liquid up over the top of the shielding and slapped it down on the unsuspecting couple, driving them apart. Kolt swore, then laughed when he heard Aylyn's muttered remark mirror his.

"Hold on," he said as he spurred Ketti into a section of woods. "The cottage is just at the end of this path."

Aylyn did and minutes later, he swept Aylyn down from the phedra's back and into his arms. Mikki leapt onto Kolt's other shoulder and secured herself by snaking her tail up and around Aylyn's arms which were encircling Kolt's neck.

"Lorgra, are you within?" Kolt shouted as he moved toward the cottage.

"Kolt, put me down. I can walk."

"I'll not have your feet wet," he said dryly.

Aylyn wriggled her muddied feet. "You're right. I wouldn't want to ruin my boots."

They laughed, both knowing that Kolt no more wanted to release Aylyn than Aylyn wanted to be released.

"Lorgra! Open up!"

A wizened gnomish man opened the door. "Yes. Yes. What is it?" His impatience quickly changed to surprise as he recognized the tall form of his laedan. "Father of Creation!"

"Greetings, Lorgra. We've need of nourishment and a change of clothing."

"Enter! Enter! Serline!" He yelled over his shoulder as he swept the door wide. "Look who is come!"

A small, buxomy, white-haired woman came bustling out from a back chamber as Kolt reluctantly lowered Aylyn to her feet. Serline's hands flew to her cheeks when she saw Kolt. Her amazement quickly changed as her bright eyes took in Aylyn's wet chilled form. She shook her head. "Shame on you! Taking your lady out in a flash storm!" She snatched up a woven covering from the large corner chair and hurried to Aylyn. Chattering, Mikki took herself off to the casement, and spread her wings to dry as Serline tucked the covering around Aylyn. "I'd expect better from you," she remarked, wagging a finger up at Kolt.

Aylyn tried to hold back her laughter, but the sight of the tiny woman chiding Kolt, who was more than twice her height and weight, was too much for her. Her merriment spilled over onto Kolt, and his hearty laugh joined hers.

"Do you tell them, my lady warrior, or do I whose idea this little jaunt was?"

Golden Conquest

"I will tell them, Kolt." Catching the impish gleam in her eyes, Kolt wished he could swallow back his words. He raised his eyes to the ceiling as she turned to the couple and lied baldly, "It was his idea."

She squealed when Kolt's hand came up and caught her gently behind the neck. "A mistruth you will have to pay for, softling."

As Kolt snatched Aylyn to him and kissed her soundly, Lorgra and Serling exchanged knowing glances. All they had heard was true. The laedan was in love.

Kolt at last raised his head and pushed Aylyn toward Serline. "You have something that will fit?" he asked hopefully. When he had remembered this cottage, he had forgotten the slight stature of its inhabitants.

Serline nodded. "I have just completed an outfit for our son's lifebond. I believe it will fit."

"Oh, no," Aylyn protested quickly. "I couldn't possibly take it."

"You will honor us by wearing it, lady," Serline said gravely.

"Honor you?" She turned to Kolt sensing the honor was to him.

He shrugged nonchalantly. "You are not the only one who has fallen prey to my charms," he teased. "Now cease your protests. You are chilled to the bone."

Aylyn could not deny that she was. She and Mikki followed Serline into the other chamber. Kolt took advantage of her absence and *snatched* an identical outfit for himself from the lodge. Lorgra smiled widely at Kolt's feat and indicated another chamber in which he could change, then went into the nourishment center, and started ladling out heaping bowls of a steaming soup.

"This weather always sets Serline bustling about in here," Lorgra explained when Kolt rejoined him. "She seems to think it will bring company. And this time it has." He placed bowls, flagons, and a carafe of a dark brew on the table.

Kolt frowned when he noted that there were only two of each. "You will join us," he told the older man.

215

Patricia Roenbeck

Lorgra bowed, his gray eyes twinkling with pleasure. "You do us honor, Laedan."

"It is you who honor me by caring for my lady." He took a hearty swallow of the spicy brew. "Lorgra, it would please me greatly if you did not address me as Laedan or mention my gifts."

Lorgra was so startled by Kolt's request that he forgot himself and asked, "But why?"

"Aylyn does not yet know who I am. I would keep that from her a little longer."

"But you love her!"

"Is it so plain then?"

Lorgra nodded. "As white crystal." He frowned and tugged at his pointed ear. "Lae—Kolt, if you will take some advice from one who has seen much, be truthful with your lady. To be anything else will bring pain."

To Kolt, who greatly feared Aylyn's reaction to the truth, Lorgra's words had all the ominous overtones of a prophecy. He took another swallow. His eyes went to the door of the chamber where Aylyn was. "You are indeed wise, Lorgra, but as much as I wish it otherwise, in this I have no choice. Until she is ready, I am only Kolt."

"As you wish. I will speak to Serline."

"And you will join us?"

"And we will join you." Lorgra nodded and went to fetch two other servings.

Kolt used the time alone to touch Naydir. He smiled. From the feel of Naydir, it seemed he had woken him from a nap. Kolt gave him a moment to rouse himself fully, then told him of the latest events.

Aylyn is safe?

Yes, my friend. As am I, Kolt added before Naydir could inquire. *I am, however, in need of transportation. Chaslydon is too far for the phedra.*

You want a conveyor? Would it not be quicker . . . He paused, then continued, and Kolt could hear his dismay. *You have not told her yet? This delay, is it wise?*

Kolt did not like having a decision he was unhappy with questioned twice and snapped, *You question me?*

My pardon, Laedan.

Kolt shook his head. As always, Naydir was able to put him in his place with a few words. *That bad, was I?*

I doubt not Lord Aubin could have done better. I can have a conveyor at your location within the hour. I will send word to have the residence in Chaslydon stocked. Your people within the keep would find another bout of snatchings most disconcerting.

My thanks, Naydir. Is there anything that requires my attention?

Naught that cannot wait until tomorrow.

Till tomorrow, then, Kolt said before withdrawing his touch.

Kolt looked up to see Aylyn approaching and noted that the high-necked, knee-length tunic and leggings fit Aylyn's curves nicely. He smiled when he saw that Serline had managed to rid her boots of most of the mud, but waited until Lorgra had finished talking with Serline and the two of them joined them to tell her.

"You've done well, Serline. My thanks."

Serline flushed with pride. "We've room for you to rest, Lae—Kolt"—Serline caught herself quickly, aided by her lifebond's foot on her toe—"should you wish it."

"Our thanks, Serline, but . . ." Kolt's voice drifted off. Serline may have very well given him an answer. It was obvious to him that it had been his movements which Rakkad had tracked. His movements that had led Rakkad to Aylyn. Now it was time to let his movements lead Rakkad away from Aylyn and to him.

"Yes, Serline, I would be pleased to accept your offer."

"You honor us greatly," Lorgra said as Serline beamed in pleasure.

"But . . ." He turned to Aylyn. "It will be Aylyn alone. I must leave. I have been called to duty." At Aylyn's puzzled stare, he dissembled. "This cottage is a distance from the village. Lorgra has a signaler. I used it to check in. There is a lost mine-searcher. I am needed. I am sorry, softling," he added when he saw her disappointment.

"When do you leave?"

"There is time yet before the conveyor arrives."

"And when do you return?"

"I know not," Kolt said truthfully. "I know only that I will return as quickly as I can. Now come." Kolt took Aylyn's hand. "Let us see to the nourishment Serline has prepared. Lorgra insists that it is the best you will ever taste." When she was seated, Kolt bent and his lips brushed hers. "I am sorry, softling, and as disappointed as you."

Aylyn managed a weak smile. She *was* disappointed. Greatly. She had grown accustomed to Kolt's presence and the thought of his absence caused an ache deep within her. She watched him as he laughed at some story Lorgra was relaying. Gods, she would miss him!

Lorgra and Serline aware of the undercurrents passing between the laedan and his lady sought to keep them amused, and nourishment passed quickly and pleasantly. When they were done, Aylyn and Serline cleaned up, and Kolt took advantage of their involvement with their chores to speak with Lorgra.

"Your offer is most kind and you have my thanks, but you may wish to rescind it when you hear that it may bring danger to your cottage."

"I will not, Laedan," Lorgra said firmly. "Your arrival, wet and alone, told me that more had happened than a misreading of the weather."

"Still, I would have you hear all of it." Succinctly, Kolt explained all he felt Lorgra needed to know.

"My offer still stands, Laedan. You honor me in placing your chosen in my old hands. I'll not let you down."

Kolt gripped Lorgra's small hand in his. "You have my deepest gratitude."

"What are you two so serious about?" Aylyn asked as she and Serline entered the living chamber.

"We were but being two worrisome fools," Kolt said, pulling her into his arms. "What say you to a walk in

Golden Conquest

Serline's beautiful garden." He had decided he could wait no longer. Aylyn had given him her word, and in the time before he left, he would hold her to it. Her extreme reaction to him needed to be addressed else they would never move on to where he knew they both wanted to be—naked and joined. The garden was walled and secluded and would give them the privacy they needed without the danger.

Aylyn, who was already missing Kolt, readily agreed, and a few moments later found herself being led to a bench under a large willowy, red-blossomed cheybry tree.

"We have time, Aylyn, and I would have my answers now."

Chapter Twenty-Eight

"Answers? To what?" Aylyn stalled. Gods, help her! Kolt's determination was evident in his face. Could she speak the truth?

Kolt's eyes danced with amusement. "Think deeply, my lady warrior, I am certain it will come to you." He touched the cheek Aylyn had slapped earlier. "I well remember your previous response."

Aylyn flushed and lowered her eyes to her hands. "Please, Kolt."

"Aylyn, think you I will beat you should I not like what you say?"

As Kolt had known it would, Aylyn's head shot up. "Of course you will not beat . . . Oh." She stopped when she saw Kolt's knowing smirk. "You will not let me forget my actions, will you?"

"It is important and needs to be addressed."

"It is hard, Kolt. I am not used to any of this. I don't know what to do."

Taking pity on her dejected look and yet unwilling to drop the subject, Kolt took her hands in his, his thumbs caressing the tops of them. "Just speak to me of what lies within your heart, Aylyn. Trust me. I'd not throw your words back at you.

"I know. From the first I've trusted you. Even when I didn't know you, I knew you'd never hurt me. And you haven't. You've never been anything but gentle and caring. That's part of the problem."

Kolt quirked a brow. "That is a problem? You'd rather I be demanding and rude?"

She gave him a weak smile. "It would make it easier if you weren't such a paragon."

"Paragon? Think you to mistake me with the laedan?"

Aylyn shrugged. "From all my father has said of him, I think you are much alike."

Kolt's heart thudded in his chest. "And if I were the laedan?"

Aylyn giggled. "You aren't. You're much too . . . relaxed. Your eyes are always sparkling, as if you love life enough to laugh at it. If you were laedan, you'd be burdened by your title." She remembered the leaders who had come to visit Rhianon in an attempt to court her father and win his favor and Rhianon's support, and her nose screwed up in distaste. "Stuffy and pompous, too, I think."

"And your father, the lord director? He is stuffy and pompous?"

"Never could my father be described as stuffy and pompous. Arrogant, yes. And at times, demanding. But like you, he enjoys life." She frowned.

He touched a finger to her brow. "You frown. Why?"

"I was just thinking that my mother is responsible for all my father's smiles."

"All?"

"Well, most. Alaran and I provide him with a few."

"Think you only a few? More like many. But tell me why the thought of your mother helping your father to enjoy life brought such a dark look?"

"Because I realized that she did it out of love for him. By bringing a smile to his face and love into his life, she has eased the weight of his position. I have heard how serious and driven he was in his youth. He is not like that now."

"That does not explain . . ."

"I knew someone once, who offered love, and I ran from him. I thought he would control me, not set me free. My mother does not control my father, she sets him free. And my father does the same for her."

"And this man who once loved you, does he have a name?" Kolt asked, then cursed himself for a fool. He thought Aylyn referred to him, but what if she mentioned Laaryc's name instead?

"He is gone from my life. I should not have mentioned him."

That answer was far from sufficient for Kolt since it might still mean Laaryc. But he could think of no way to force her to clarify what she meant. So he waited silently to see what she would say next.

"I was jealous," she blurted out suddenly. "That's why I raged at you. I know I have no right, Kolt, but I have promised you the truth. And the thought of someone else holding you fills me with rage. And pain."

"There is no need for jealousy, softling. Why would I take another to my sleeper, when you, of all women, are the only one I want."

Aylyn searched Kolt's face. "You mean that, don't you?"

"As I have never meant anything else." Kolt took a deep breath. Now was the time to tell her. "Aylyn, there is much of me you know not. Much I thought to keep from you until you were ready to hear of it." His blue eyes burned into hers. "Do you think you are ready now?"

Aylyn answered his question with one of her own. "Are you life-bonded?"

"No." *Not in fact but in spirit*, he finished to himself, and wished for the time when he could say such words aloud.

"Nothing you say could make me change how I feel, Kolt."

"So you say now, but I'd not hold you to your words."

Aylyn chewed on her lower lip. "Would you mind if we put it off till you return? You've convinced me that even though I'm not going to change what's in my heart, I'm not going to like whatever it is you have to say. So much has happened today I don't know how much more I can absorb. My mind and my body are exhausted. And now you're leaving and it tears at my heart that you are."

Kolt at once felt guilty. He had been so intent on revealing the truth that he had forgotten where he had found her when he had arrived and the confrontation with Rakkad. A lesser woman would have succumbed to all that had happened long before now. He cupped her chin and placed a tender kiss on her lips. "As you wish, softling. Always."

"Thank you."

"But," he added gravely, turning away from her, "know this. I am not a man of great patience. You have until I return and no longer."

"Kolt?"

Kolt turned to Aylyn and was surprised to see her smiling impishly up at him.

"Did you mean it when you said as I wish always?"

Kolt had no idea what she was after but did not hesitate. "Yes."

"Then may I have another kiss?"

And so it was, that when Lorgra came to tell Kolt the conveyor was approaching, he was met with the heartwarming sight of their laedan soundly kissing his beautiful Rhianonian lady.

Kolt and Aylyn arrived in front of the cottage in time to see the wings slide into a slot under the belly of the conveyor and then drop vertically down and come to a rest in the open yard thirty hand-spans from the cottage.

"It is much like the mini-cruisers on Rhianon," Aylyn noted. "Except our wings are permanently affixed."

"The terrain on Rhianon is not as severe as on Annan," Kolt explained. "We've need to drop into woods or tight spaces within the monts."

Lorgra and Serline joined them as the canopy rose and a tall handsome man extracted himself from the navigation seat.

Kolt blinked. "I'd not expected you."

Naydir smiled. "And I'd not send anyone else." He

pushed passed Kolt to Aylyn. He bowed. "My lady."

Naydir was please to note the tender lights that glowed in Kolt's blue eyes as he looked down at Aylyn and the gentle huskiness in his voice as he introduced her.

"Softling, may I present Naydir."

Aylyn smiled. "Greetings, Naydir."

"And these," Kolt continued in his usual pleasant voice, "are our gracious hosts, Serline and Lorgra."

Lorgra and Serline gasped at the identity of the tall handsome stranger. Unlike Kolt, Naydir's name and reputation were well-known, but his face was not.

Naydir bowed to each of them. "My thanks for seeing to my friend."

Serline glowed. "It was our pleasure," she said before she and Lorgra excused themselves and returned to the cottage.

Aylyn gestured to the conveyor. "We could have used you to rescue us a short while ago."

Naydir took Aylyn's hand and raised it to his lips. "Had I but known you required one, I would have brought it sooner."

Kolt found that Naydir's lips on Aylyn's hand was not at all to his liking, but unless he wished to be churlish he could say nothing. Instead, he managed an affronted, "I thought it I who did the rescuing."

Naydir, noticing the storm brewing inside his friend's eyes and well knowing the reason why, blithely tucked Aylyn's hand in the crook of his arm.

Aylyn, unaware of the cause of the tension she heard in Kolt's voice, chided him softly, "You are being most unpleasant, Kolt. After all, we did have to ride all the way here on Ketti. In the rain and wind."

"I blocked the wind," Kolt muttered.

"And so you did. But what else should I expect from a paragon like yourself?"

"Think you I am not a paragon?" Naydir asked, feigning hurt. Obviously, the word paragon held a special meaning for Aylyn and Kolt.

"Is your name Kolt?" the laedan demanded. When

Golden Conquest

Naydir just looked at him blankly, he snapped, "Well, is it?"

"You know well that it is not."

"Then you cannot be a paragon. Only one named Kolt can be. And unless one named Naydir would like to be handless, he should place his elsewhere," Kolt growled, no longer caring how he acted.

Naydir laughed, but did not remove his hand. When Aylyn, who was startled by Kolt's possessiveness, tried to pull her hand away, he would not let her.

"Naydir." Kolt's voice had such an edge of steel to it that Naydir dared not push his friend any further. He took his hand away and shook his head. "Aylyn, think you it proper for a paragon to threaten a friend?"

Aylyn looked from one to the other and laughed. "When the friend is teasing him, I do." She crossed to Kolt, stood on her tiptoes, and placed a quick kiss on his lips. "I will fetch your friend a cool drink."

She turned and entered the chamber and missed the startled look on Kolt's face. She did, however, hear Naydir.

"Think you a paragon should stand with his mouth op . . . ooph!" Naydir grunted as Kolt's elbow connected with his side, then smiled. "I like your Aylyn, my friend. You have chosen well."

"Think you I do not know this?"

"I think you know it well. Now, do you tell me what happens here? I do not need to have your abilities to touch another's mind to know something troubles you."

"There has been a change of plans."

Kolt explained his reasons for leaving Aylyn and choosing Chaslydon. By the time he finished, Naydir's eyes were dark with worry.

"I like it not that you set yourself up."

Kolt shot a wary glance at the cottage. "Keep your voice down. Should she know I go in search of Rakkad, she will insist on joining me. And if I refuse, she will follow."

At another time Naydir would have been happy to

learn that Kolt's chosen lady was not one to just accept Kolt's orders without question. No passive wisp of a woman would do for his intensely alive friend. But for now he was too concerned with Kolt's reckless scheme. He opened his mouth to protest, but Kolt's worried sigh stopped him.

"And when I return, it will be the day of truth between Aylyn and me and I can't help but wonder how it will turn out."

"Can you not see it?"

Kolt shook his head. "All I've ever been able to see is her coming. And not the whole of it." His eyes darkened. "Never did I see Rakkad." Kolt drew his hand through his hair. "I cannot fight the belief that I am missing something of great import. That Rakkad has given me a clue to the face behind his mask and I am too much of a fool to see it."

"You are many things, my friend. A fool is not one of them."

"He could have taken her today, Naydir."

"Could have but did not. You will keep her safe."

"I wish I had your confidence."

"Ah, but for all my confidence I am not a paragon."

"Anyone can be named a paragon, Naydir. Few can be named friend."

"Ah, my lady," Naydir said when he noticed Aylyn standing in the doorway, a flagon in her hand and a questioning frown on her face. He took the flagon from her and quickly drained it. "It was most refreshing. You have my thanks."

"Mine as well, softling, for seeing to my friend's needs." He moved to her side and was thus facing Naydir when he lowered the flagon and passed it back to Aylyn. He looked to Naydir for a clue as to how long she had been standing there, and cursed when he received a slight shrug.

Aylyn had heard enough to know that more was happening than Kolt was letting on. She had questioned the legitimacy of his story about the lost mine-searcher, but she also knew Kolt would not answer her questions. She could only hope that whatever he said before he left would give her a clue to what was truly going on.

"Has your friend brought you more ill news?"

"No. I was but explaining my plans," Kolt admitted candidly, thinking to stay as close to the truth as possible in hopes of waylaying her suspicious mind. "He likes them not and thinks I take unnecessary risks."

"Then you will be in danger," she stated.

"None that I cannot handle."

For the first time in her life, Aylyn could relate to the worry she saw on her mother's face when her father's position placed him in danger and Eirriel knew there was nothing she could do but wait for his return. And worry. "You will be careful?"

"Knowing you await my return how could I not?"

Mikki suddenly came chattering from the cottage. Aylyn laughed and opened her arms. Mikki flew into them. "You needn't carry on so, little one. I'm not leaving." *Though I wish I were*, she added silently.

Naydir arched a brow. "A yiichi?" When Kolt nodded, Naydir chuckled, and whispered softly so only Kolt could hear. "It would seem your lady has a skill with wild and untamed creatures. In a short time she has managed to capture both a yiichi and a kilgra."

"So she has, my friend. So she has. I will be with you shortly."

Naydir nodded and left to prepare the conveyor for flight. Kolt entered the cottage to bid good-bye to Lorgra and Serline.

"I will send the conveyor back. If you think she is in danger, flee. All of you."

"I will guard her with my life, Laedan," Lorgra vowed solemnly.

Kolt's eyes darkened. "I go to Chaslydon so that you will not have to."

Her eyes bleak and Mikki clutched to her chest, Aylyn stood near the conveyor, waiting for Kolt to finish his good-bye. She smiled weakly when he exited the cottage and strode over to her.

"I will miss you, softling," Kolt murmured an instant before his mouth crashed down on hers.

And when he at last raised his head, Aylyn was very certain that he was as unwilling to leave her as she was to have him go. "Hurry back, Kolt."

Kolt nodded, then jumped into the conveyor's riding compartment. The canopy closed, and the conveyor slowly moved upward in a straight vertical line. Aylyn watched as it reached its flying height and flashed forward. And she continued to watch long after it had disappeared from sight.

Twenty-Nine

Tall buildings of black crystal spiraled to the sky. Moving walkways at three or more levels wound their way from building to building. Everywhere there were gardens of vibrant flowers and trees of almost every color and throughout the gardens pools of sparking rainbow water. Beautifully and unusually clad men, women, and children walked, talked, and played on streets of green verdanthium crystal.

Chaslydon was Kolt's city, his prototype for an Annan of the future, when the Protectorate granted it member status and its revenues could be used to bring this way of life to the entire planet. He himself had designed Chaslydon, and the master craftsman of Annan had brought it to life.

And because of Rakkad, Aylyn was locked away from all that Chaslydon and Kolt could offer and he was spending his time being visible—walking the streets, talking to his people and now, playing with the children—under the watchful eyes of Naydir, Morald, and ten of his best men. Should Rakkad make an attempt at him, and Kolt prayed that he would, one of them would see.

"Throw it now, Laedan," one of the children shouted, jerking Kolt's attention back to them.

"Are you ready?" Kolt asked, and when the children nodded, he drew his hand back. "Start to run! Go!" When he saw them running, he threw the soft oval high into the air in a spiraling arch. He laughed when it landed at the feet of the littlest girl among them. She picked it up, hugged it to her chest, and toddled toward him. He waited, knowing half her pleasure would be in bringing it back to him.

"I got it, Laedan. See." Klory held the llab out to him.

Kolt took it and bowed. "My lady is the best llab player in Chaslydon."

He handed Klory the llab. "Can you bring this to Tryio, little one?"

"Of course. Am I not the bestest?"

Kolt chuckled as Klory ran off to her join her friends. As he watched her, he couldn't help think how much Aylyn would have enjoyed seeing her at play. As she would have enjoyed Chaslydon's beauty.

"Laedan! Laedan!" Klory ran into Kolt's leg, drawing his attention. "Laedan!"

Kolt knelt down. "Little one, what is it?"

Klory pointed a shaking finger to the railing of the elevated walkway high above their heads. "He's falling!"

Kolt's head swung up to see a small dark shape that seemed draped over the railings. "What the . . ." Even before he finished, he had sought an answer with his touch. He blanched. "Gods! No! It's a child!"

Kolt *actualized* at the spot he thought the child would fall to. Reaching out, he just managed to touch the child reassuringly as the boy fell. Immediately, Kolt raised his arms up to the child. His mind focused, he kept his touch with the lad, constantly telling him not to be afraid, that he would be safe, even as he used all his skills to cushion the child's fall.

The boy's plummet slowed to a gentle drift, his shrieks of fear turned to giggles, and the laughing child drifted slowly into Kolt's waiting arms. As Kolt gathered the little one to his breast in a fierce hug, the chant began.

"Laedan! Laedan! Laedan!"

Golden Conquest

Kolt turned to face the crowd.

And met Aylyn's bewildered golden eyes.

"What in the name of Nithrach!" he shouted above the crowd, his eyes dark with rage. "How came you here?"

Aylyn, her mind already reeling from what she had seen, backed away from the fury clearly revealed on Kolt's handsome face.

"Aylyn! Curse you! Answer me!"

Aylyn continued to retreat. Right into Naydir's arms.

Kolt's burning gaze flicked to his councilor. "Take her to my quarters and hold her there. Once I have seen to this"—he jerked his head at the walkway—"I will relieve you."

With one last fierce glower at Aylyn, Kolt turned and waited for the boy's parents, who were frantically making their way through the crowd, using the few moments to tamp down his anger. And his fear. How dare she be here? How dare she risk herself?

"Rhie! Rhie!" the boy's dam shouted.

"You have an inquisitive son, dam, one who bears closer watching," he chided her as he placed the boy in his dam's trembling arms.

Rhie's sire dropped to his knees. He took Kolt's hand and pressed his forehead to it in a sign of respect and gratitude. "All that I possess, Laedan, I now give to you."

Kolt gestured for the man to rise. "My thanks, good sire, but it is unnecessary. I did what had to be done. I am well pleased that little Rhie is safe. That he stays so is payment enough."

"We but took our eyes off him for a moment, Laedan." Hyit had stopped crying now that she held her son safely within her arms. "I knew not the danger."

Kolt's eyes darkened. "There should have been no danger, Hyit. That he was able to climb up is bad enough, but that he could fall! The walkway was supposed to be shielded." Kolt's eyes swung out over the crowd. "Izar, I know you are here. Show yourself."

231

Patricia Roenbeck

A tall, very thin, pinched-face man approached and bowed to Kolt. "I am here, Laedan."

"How did this happen?" Kolt demanded of the director of the walkway project.

"A malfunction in the main circuitry shut down the safety barriers, Laedan."

"A malfunction?" Kolt roared. "Did I not question the possibility of just such an occurrence? And did you not assure me it could not happen?"

"Yes, Laedan. I know not how—"

"Your duty is to know. You have failed in that duty!

"Laedan, I—"

Kolt's irate blue gaze pinned Izar's purple ones. "Make no excuses! Had I not been in Chaslydon this day, Rhie would have been life-ended!" Kolt jerked his hand toward the walkway. "Destroy it! I'd not have my people risk their lives to spare their feet!"

"Laedan!" A petite, dark-skinned female pushed her way through the crowd. "Laedan! I am Chiela, assistant to Izar," she said as she stopped before an expectant Kolt. Her gaze flickered from Kolt to Izar, who had moved next to her and was glowering fiercely, and back to Kolt. "There is no need to tear the walkway down."

Kolt arched a brow, his expression enraged. "No need! You think the life of a child is no need?"

"You misunderstand, Laedan," Chiela's voice trembled, and it was obvious that she did not relish contradicting her laedan. However, it was also as obvious from her unwavering black stare that she was not to be put off. "It need not have happened. An inferior crystal was used as a power source. I spoke many times of my fear that its strength was insufficient. Izar would not listen."

"Liar!" Izar raged.

He drew his hand back, and the force of his blow would have knocked Chiela to the ground had not Kolt interceded. Thinking to stop the outraged Izar, Kolt's own hand had shot up to block Izar's, but at the last instant Kolt chose to throw up a shield. And so, instead of striking the soft structure of Chiela's face, it was the hard, ungiving wall of energy that Izar's fist struck.

Shrieking in pain, Izar clutched his fist to his chest. "It is broken! You have broken my hand!"

"Be thankful I do not break your neck!" Kolt snarled. "Think you to strike a woman in front of me! Get you out of my sight!" When Izar made no move to obey, Kolt asked softly, "Do your feet need help to walk?"

"No!" Izar said quickly. "No, Laedan! I would but hear what *she* would say. I have not heard it before. I have a right. It is my honor she attacks."

Kolt just stared at the man. Was he so foolish that he thought to mislead Kolt with his lies? Did his panic cause him to forget what Kolt was? Kolt shrugged. If the fool wished to stay and humiliate himself, Kolt saw it as nothing more than he deserved. "So be it. You may stay. It will save me from having to summon you later. Chiela, please continue."

"A pure ryliyne crystal is all that is needed."

"Then what is the problem? They are no longer as rare as they once were."

"You did us a great service by locating the new veins, Laedan, but when you refused to excavate them, you put the cost of excavation on the people," Izar accused. "Think you they can afford to do it now?"

Kolt grabbed Izar's tunic and lifted him from the ground. "Listen well, little man, if you can, for it is not to my liking to explain myself. To be freely given what they could get themselves robs my people of their pride. There was need for more ryliyne, and I sought it out because it was not their inability to locate it that kept it from my people, but the lack of equipment. Something we would have had aplenty had our bid for membership in the Protectorate been approved. But it had not. So *I* sought out the crystal. My Annanites are the best harvesters in the galaxies. It is to their credit that they can harvest anywhere. Had I gone further and removed the ryliyne from the ground because its location proved difficult, it would have cost my harvesters their pride. And to sacrifice that to save your budget I will not do."

Kolt set Izar on his feet with a jarring motion that made him grab his throbbing hand. "Get you gone, Izar. You are removed as director. Do not show yourself within Chaslydon again. You are against all it stands for." Kolt turned to Chiela. "Send for the crystal. If the cost proves great . . ."

"The cost proves great because it robs Izar of his great profit. What is not used in the maintenance of the walkway goes into Izar's account."

Izar's already pale complexion blanched to a deadly white. He started to back away, but Kolt's barked order stopped him.

"Seize him!"

Two burly Annanites grabbed Izar by the shoulders.

"Why have you not spoken of this ere now?" Kolt asked Chiela.

"He threatened me with more than a blow if I spoke of it."

Kolt nodded his understanding. "You need have no more fear, Chiela. My councilors and I will hear formal charges against him, and it is my belief he will find himself locked within the Judgement Hall. Now, go, Chiela, and see to the walkway. Until the crystal is installed, none may make use of it."

Chiela bowed. "I will see it done, Laedan."

"It is only right, is it not, that the new director see to the repairs?" Kolt's eyes twinkled as he waited for her reaction to his words. And he was well pleased by the astonished smile.

"My thanks, Laedan. I will not disappoint you," Chiela vowed fervently.

"Think you I know it not? If you have any problems, you will come to me."

The matter solved to his satisfaction, Kolt was at last free to turn his mind to Aylyn.

Chapter Thirty

"Come with me, my lady," Naydir said as he gently took Aylyn's arm and led her from the crowd and to the five-level building that held Kolt's quarters. "It is not safe."

"Not safe!" Aylyn jerked her arm free and flung it at Kolt who had turned away from them. "Look what he is! How can it not be safe?" Aylyn gave a short self-deprecating laugh. "How could I have not known? Not realized? It is the answer to everything. How my clothes were always there. Nithrach! How I had clothes that fit so well in the first place!

"Sh, Mikki," she soothed when the yiichi she held against her side started chattering shrilly. She stroked her behind the ears and kept up the calming rhythmic motions even as she continued, "How the nourishment came when the server never did!" Aylyn twisted around to look back. Kolt, taller than most, could be seen surrounded by adoring, cheering and chanting Annanites. "Everywhere we went the people flocked to him and called him Laedan. 'More than likely it is because we have the same name,'" she mimicked. "Gods! But how could I have been so blind? So gullible?"

Naydir thought it best to let Aylyn vent her rage and so said nothing. He led her into the conveyor, then keyed in Kolt's special security code. A moment later the doors opened and they stepped out into a small chamber. Two steps brought them to a door. Once

235

again, Naydir keyed in the code and the door to Kolt's upper-level quarters slid open, and they entered. When he closed the door, all outside sounds were closed out. The sudden silence of the chamber penetrated Aylyn's rage long enough for her to look questioningly at Naydir.

"Soundarium crystal is used in the walls and the casements," Naydir explained. "Sound cannot penetrate it. You will find Chaslydon unlike aught you have previously visited. It has all anyone could need and then some. Shall I show you around?" he asked, hoping the distraction would take an edge off her anger.

"Why would I want to look around? I'm not staying."

"But . . ."

"Did you see his face, Naydir? He was enraged. My coming here was a mistake."

"Think you there are not reasons Kolt sought to keep you from Chaslydon? As there are reasons for his silence?"

"What reasons?" Aylyn looked at him, her eyes soft with pleading. "Tell me please. Help me to understand all of this. Please."

Naydir shook his head. "I cannot. It is not my place."

"And it's not Kolt's, either," Aylyn snapped, storming away to stare out the casement. "The laedan of Annan doesn't need to explain himself to anyone." She snorted. "He is as pompous as my father."

Naydir had been about to defend Kolt, but Aylyn's statement stopped him. "Lord Aubin is pompous?" he asked, surprised. "Kolt calls him friend and one who is arrogant and pompous would not be named such. Of course, that does not stop Kolt from being pompous and overbearing at times," he added slyly.

Aylyn whirled on him. "Kolt is not pompous," she said, forgetting that *she* had just said he was. "He is gentle and caring and . . ." She shut her mouth when she saw Naydir's smile and realized she had been defending Kolt.

Golden Conquest

Naydir offered her his arm. "Shall I show you around?" he asked again. "Then perhaps a hot cleansing?" He indicated the carrier she had looped around her back. "You have clothing?"

Aylyn nodded. "I didn't know where I would be staying so I came prepared."

"How came you here?" Naydir asked as he led her through the lavishly decorated large chambers of the ten-chamber quarters.

"I got tired of all the questions. There's a lost minesearcher like there's a lost seventh planet around Rhianon. I asked a few questions and Lorgra, when he finally answered them, was extremely careful in his choice of words. I'm the daughter of the lord director. I can tell when I'm being fed cnuz meant for witless fools!"

"Kolt does not think you a witless fool."

"No? Then why did he keep who and what he is away from me?" Her eyes flickered from taking in the sumptuous sleeper, relaxer, and chairs of one of the guest chambers to Naydir. "And why did he think he should draw out Rakkad?"

Naydir's stunned gaze flew to Aylyn.

"I told you I'm not a witless fool." She slashed the air with her hand. "It all adds up, Naydir. In the lodge when he thought Rakkad near, he went out by himself. And when we did encounter Rakkad, he just rescued me and we fled. He never attempted to confront Rakkad."

"Kolt is no coward," Naydir cut in fiercely.

"I know that. I thought it was because he was unarmed, but now I wonder about the battle I did not see. I know one took place; Kolt would not pass it up. He *is* more powerful than Rakkad, isn't he?" she asked suddenly. And though it was voiced as a question there was a certainty about it that made it more of a statement.

"Why do you say that?" Naydir asked, unwilling to explain Kolt's strength.

Aylyn just looked at Naydir, her lips screwed up in disgust.

Naydir put his hand up in concession. "Yes, it is as you say."

"Then is Rakkad free because you truly don't know where he is?"

Naydir nodded. Gods, but she was quick!

"Tell me where you've searched."

"I cannot."

"Please. Perhaps I can help." At Naydir's doubtful look, she said, "So maybe I can't, but only because I don't know Annan well enough. But at least I'll know what's going on."

Naydir shook his head. "I have said more than I should, Aylyn. Kolt is going to have my heart for all I have said now." He pushed open the last door at the end of the passageway. "Did I not save the finest for the end? Am I not the perfect guide?"

The chamber was indeed splendid. One wall was lined with floor-to-ceiling imagers, the other with shelves and wardrobes. The other two were transparent crystal doors that opened onto the terrace. And in the middle of the chamber, surrounded by sheer gauzy material that draped from a golden hoop that was centered directly over it, was a huge round sleeper.

In spite of herself, Aylyn giggled. "You are cagier than a Drigrian envoy," Aylyn replied, stepping into the luxurious chamber. "You saved the finest for the time when I was pressing the hardest. Had I waited a little longer to ask these questions, we would have toured the nourishment center again before we came here."

Naydir laughed. "As you say, my lady."

Mikki, who had scurried in with them, chattered happily when she saw the large yellow bjoyga trees in the corner between the large door panels, and scampered over to it. She sniffed at the container that held it, prodded the trunk with her paw, and then scrambled to the top and sat down.

"Mikki seems to have found her spot," Naydir commented. "Think you a hot cleansing would make you as content as it has made her?" He tossed his head at the yiichi who was already asleep, her long tail snaked around the tree trunk for security.

"I think it will help," Aylyn said. "But it will not make me content."

Naydir studied the woman his friend loved and saw the mixed emotions in her eyes. "No, I would think not," he said, knowing it would take Kolt's presence to make her content. He pushed one of the imagers, and it sprung open to reveal the cleanser.

Aylyn slipped the carrier from her shoulder and dropped it onto the sleeper as Naydir started from the chamber.

"Should you need anything . . ."

"I'll yell," she said.

Naydir chuckled and closed the door behind him. Aylyn turned on the hot water and quickly stripped. Stepping into the large circular cleanser, she lowered herself into the pulsating water, laid her head back, and closed her eyes, letting the hot swirling water rid her body of its aches. Her heart, she knew, would have to wait a little longer.

Aylyn selected a short tunic dress of bright metallic blue and matching thin, sheer leggings from the carrier. She shook it and was glad to see that the material was wrinkle-free. She drew on the leggings and let the tunic drop over her head, pleased when it fell softly to mid-thigh.

Stepping into matching low-heeled, ankle boots, she moved in front of the imager and began brushing her hair. As she did, she listened for sounds that would tell her whether Kolt had arrived. Kolt had the ability to move very quietly and had often startled her by appearing suddenly behind her. Now she realized he had been merely *actualizing*. Even a Zorgrahagian, reputed to have the best hearing in the galaxies, wouldn't have heard him. She secured her hair by knotting the ribbon and twisting it around until it formed a wide circle and then looped it around her hair near the end of the strands. This kept her hair from her face and, at the same time, allowed it to bunch softly around her neck and shoulders.

With a final glance at the imager, she left in search of Naydir.

Naydir smiled when Aylyn entered the living chamber. It was obvious to him that she had dressed with Kolt in mind. And that pleased him. Perhaps, with a little help from him, their anger with each other would pass quickly.

"You look lovely, my lady." He motioned to the platter of fresh hurga berries and cream on the table. "Would you care for some?"

"No, thank you. Truthfully, I wish Kolt would get here so we could just argue and get it over with."

"You will argue?"

"He will yell because I came when I shouldn't, and I will yell that I couldn't let him face Rakkad alone." Her eyes lit up with a mischievous glow. "And then we will make up."

"And talk?"

"Yes, I suppose we will do that too," she said, and then blushed when she realized, from Naydir's knowing chuckle, what she admitted.

"Do I take it that talking will come later, my lady?"

Her face red with embarrassment, she nonetheless met Naydir's teasing eyes. "Much later, if I have my way," she stated firmly.

Naydir roared. How he wished he could be around for the confrontation.

"May I go outside?" Aylyn asked, pointing to the outside terrace.

"A moment." Naydir stepped outside.

Kolt's quarters were in the center of the building surrounded on all sides by a wide-covered terrace. Naydir frowned as he looked at the opaque woven material several hand-spans above his head. The roof would provide little coverage should a weapon be fired in Aylyn's direction. He scanned the surrounding buildings' rooftops. All were at least two levels lower than

Golden Conquest

them and empty. He walked to the edge of the terrace and studied the crowd five levels below. None seemed to have an inordinate interest in the building. At least not on this side. They were too interested in Kolt. As he reconnoitered the entire perimeter of the terrace, he noted two of the sides had some adult activity going on, the third only children. It would be that side to which he would take Aylyn.

He reentered the chamber through the nourishment center.

"Aylyn?"

Aylyn shrieked and whirled around. Her hand flew to her heart as she saw him. "By all the gods, Naydir, you walk as silently as Kolt!"

"I am sorry I startled you. It was not my intention." He motioned her toward him. "Come. And do not fear that I am a mind-toucher; I am merely well trained."

"So I noticed."

Stepping outside, Aylyn breathed in the air. How fresh the air was for a domed city! She didn't think the undomed hamlets smelled any cleaner or were more reminiscent of a open meadow. The sound of children laughing drew her to the railing. She leaned over and saw five children running through the garden.

Naydir was just about to request that Aylyn move away from the edge when Mikki flew out and settled on the railing next to Aylyn. Naydir watched for a moment and then relaxed. The yiichi showed no sign of agitation.

"Just look at the children, Mikki," Aylyn said. "Doesn't it look like fun?" She scratched Mikki behind her ears, causing the yiichi to thrum softly.

She was about to move away when a movement caught her attention. She leaned further over the railing and saw a young boy of about twelve life cycles, sitting on one of the black crystal benches, in his hand was what appeared to be a study board. She watched, waiting for him to show some sign of wanting to join the other children, but never once did he take his eyes from his reading. *So apart from everyone*, she thought. *So serious. So much like Laaryc.* Did he have no one to help him to have fun?

As if conjured up by Aylyn's wistful wishes, she heard a name called. The young boy's head swung around, and Aylyn saw him smile. A girl, several life cycles younger than he, ran up and took his hand. She pulled on it and pointed to the other children. Aylyn smiled. So this Laaryc had his Aylyn as well. But Aylyn's smile changed to puzzlement as the young boy shook his head and gestured to his reading. The little girl stamped her foot, took the study board from him, and placed it on the bench at his side. He picked it back up. She stared at him hard, then turned and stormed away. He had the open board in his hands, but never took his eyes off the little girl. When she stopped, turned and extended her hand, it appeared to Aylyn that he sighed deeply, then placed the study board down on the bench and walked over to his young friend. Hand in hand, they ran to the other children.

Aylyn knew the little girl would join in with the others as she herself would have, but Aylyn waited to see what the little boy would do. And she was not at all surprised when he merely stood off to the side and watched just as Laaryc had always done. Every once in a while his glance would stray back to the bench and his study board, and it was painfully obvious to Aylyn that that was where he wanted to be.

Gods, Aylyn thought with a jolt, was that what it had been like for Laaryc? Had he wanted to be back at his studies? Had she cajoled him into participating in everything she wanted to do, forcing him to cast aside what he truly wanted? She closed her eyes and called up memories of their times together. She saw herself running and playing, and she saw Laaryc watching. She saw herself diving into the pond in the Garden of Colors, and Laaryc watching. She saw herself riding. And Laaryc watching.

He had never really joined in, never really participated in the activities. The only reason he had even been present was because she had asked him to. But why hadn't he refused? Because she hadn't let him, came the grim answer. Just like the little girl, she had pouted and stormed away, knowing that he would come. And he always had.

Until she had asked him to life bond with her. That was what he had been trying to say when he refused her request. Not only would it have been wrong because of his belief in her mind-toucher, but it would have been wrong for him. Terribly wrong. How could she have been so blind?

She took a closer look at the young boy. He was watching his friend intensely. When she laughed, he laughed. When she smiled, he smiled. He loved her. Enough to do whatever he needed to do to make her happy. Enough to sacrifice what he wanted. That wasn't love; that was control. Mother of the Universe! The very thing she had feared the mind-toucher would do to her, she had been doing all along to Laaryc.

Until the end. Until he realized that he would have to sacrifice all his needs, all his wants to make her happy. And Laaryc had been wise enough to see that, even then, it wouldn't have been enough.

She thought of Kolt. It was because of him that she could see all of this. Because he had taught her the true meaning of love. The need to be with someone, not because life is meaningless without them, but because with them its meaning becomes so much clearer. Her hands trembled as she at last put a name to the feelings and emotions that had been tearing at her the past few days.

She loved him. Desperately and unconditionally. Without question.

When she had told him his words would not change her feelings for him, she had not lied.

She closed her eyes. *This is what you meant, isn't it, Laaryc? This is what you knew we could never have. Yes,* she could almost hear him reply, *and if you don't grab onto it, you're worse than a stupid drogo.*

Aylyn turned to speak with Naydir, to ask him when he thought Kolt might be joining them, but Naydir was gone. To meet Kolt perhaps? She opened her arms to Mikki, and the yiichi jumped into them. She carried her into the sleeping chamber and deposited her back on the tree, then quickly changed.

Wish me luck, Laaryc, she thought as she opened the outer door. Then she laughed. Laaryc would have smiled knowingly and told her she didn't need luck, she needed courage. And then he would have wished her luck anyway.

Determinedly, Aylyn crossed to the large relaxer across from the door to the quarters, sat down, and waited.

Chapter Thirty-One

"She is within," Naydir reported when Kolt *actualized* next to him. "As she has been since she left you." Naydir caught Kolt's arm as he started to brush passed him. "She feared for you."

Kolt's eyes blazed. "*She* feared for *me*! How came she to think I was in danger?"

"She misbelieved your lost mine-searcher story, and when she overheard portions of our conversation, it added to all the questions she had about you. She asked Lorgra about the dangers of mine-searching and the like. Lorgra's answers were justifiably vague and not to Aylyn's liking."

"Think you her actions are to my liking?" Kolt demanded.

"I know they are not, but you were, she pointed out, thrice the target for Rakkad and that was well before he had met her. She loves you, Kolt, and worries for you. My friend, had you but been truthful with her, she would have thought you well able to care for yourself."

"You know why—"

"Yes, *I* know why and now Aylyn must know why. Once you have spoken all the truth, then you can discuss Rakkad. And then you may find your Aylyn, who is no fool, may agree to reside where you feel her safest."

"And should that be with her father on Rhianon?"

Kolt asked harshly. "What then?"

Naydir shook his head. "I know not. All I know is that she is hurt and confused and filled with questions. Go to her, free of rage. Explain your reasons for your deception, your fear that should she learn who and what you are, she would have closed her heart to you. Surely what she witnessed and what she now knows holds the most lasting consequence of what went on today, and not that she was where she should not have been."

"I will keep your counsel in mind," Kolt said. "More than that I cannot promise."

"That is enough." Naydir placed his hand on his friend's shoulder. "I wish you luck, my friend."

"I fear I need more than luck, but I will take it nonetheless." So saying, Kolt took a deep breath, and opened the door.

"You're here."

Kolt blinked. Aylyn was standing before him, a soft white gown clinging to her body, her hair swinging freely about her back, and a brilliant smile on her beautiful face.

"How is the child?"

"Well." Kolt's eyes darkened and he frowned. This was not the Aylyn Naydir had led him to believe awaited him. Where was the confusion, the questions? Did she think to seduce him from his anger? No, he realized quickly, there was no artifice in her eyes. And that disconcerted him. Was it possible, in spite of what Naydir said, that she knew not who he was? "What are you about, Aylyn? Could I have been mistaken? Know you not who I am?"

She took his hands in hers. "You are a mind-toucher. My mind-toucher."

Kolt heard the possessiveness in her voice when she said "my mind-toucher," but was too bewildered to do more than nod.

"I had often wondered what my mind-toucher looked like."

"And?" he could not help ask.

Golden Conquest

"And I am pleased." She looked at him hotly. "Most pleased."

Kolt fought back the urge to forget everything and take what he read in her eyes. Yet he knew if he did, he would forget what he was truly about. "And?" he prodded.

"And you are the laedan."

"Yes."

Aylyn did not understand the edge in Kolt's voice or the wariness in his eyes. "You are beloved by your people. You must be very proud."

"Of course, I am a paragon, am I not?"

Aylyn dropped Kolt's hands and stepped away to study him. "You are angry? Why? Because I came?"

Because she came yes, but more, he admitted, because she seemed to be pleased by who and what he was. Kolt stormed away from her. Gods! But he wished he knew what game she was playing!

"Kolt, please. Talk to me." Aylyn crossed to his side and placed her hand on his shoulder. She flinched when he jerked away from her touch. "I don't understand."

Kolt whirled and the blazing fury in his eyes forced Aylyn to take a step back. "You don't understand? I have awaited this time of revelation with excitement and dread. I feared you would rage at me, but I was certain, given time, I could soothe your anger. But this, this meeting never did I imagine." He jerked his hand at her, and his lips curled in a sneer. "Look at you, smiling, flirtatious, and waiting. Think you I will take you to my sleeper now?"

"You—you do not want me?" Aylyn was crushed. How could she have misread him so?

Kolt grabbed her arms and pulled her close. "Not want you? I have wanted you so long I think I have gone mad with the wanting. But to have you soft and willing because I am great and powerful lies in my belly like rancid gropsa." He dropped his hands. "I'd take your anger over your reverence, Aylyn."

"You misunderstand, Kolt." Aylyn's golden eyes

sought out his and by their very intensity forced him to meet her gaze. Her voice was soft, yet husky with emotion. "I, too, have wanted you almost from the first and that I did sat like rancid gropsa in *my* belly. How could I be so attracted to someone I had just met? What I learned today freed me of my confusion." Aylyn placed her hands on his cheeks. "I didn't just meet you. I've known you for most of my life. You are my mind-toucher. And now that I know, all my fears are gone. All of them. You know my every thought, my every desire, and you used them. Not to control me, but to love me. And that, my Kolt, is why you see reverence. Not because you are great and powerful, but because you are and did not abuse it."

"Gods, softling!" Kolt rasped an instant before his arms enfolded her and his mouth settled on hers.

Aylyn snaked her hands through his hair and pressed his head close to hers. Remembering and wanting the delicious sensations evoked by his demanding mouth, Aylyn opened to him. When his tongue touched hers, a jolt of throbbing warmth coursed through her like a wave rushing a sandy beach, touching every part of her body, leaving her knees weak and her toes curled. She held nothing back, letting her love for him flow from her body into his.

She felt the heat of his hands as they trailed down her back to her buttocks and pressed her against him, molding her to his fiery hardness. Her very being contracted from the feel of him and then opened, reaching out to him. Wanting more. Needing more. Fire and ice merged and curled at the center of her womanhood, sending out currents of pulsating desire.

Kolt was the first to break away. He raised his head, but a breath from her mouth, and stared down on her with eyes blazing. His voice was hoarse, raspy; his breathing heavy, ragged. "And that I am Laedan, Aylyn? That troubles you not at all?"

Aylyn forced her gaze from the fullness of his mouth and met his questing stare. That he still had questions spoke to her of his vulnerability. Her heart swelled with love for the strong, commanding man whose only fault had been to offer to her all that he was. She knew then that she possessed the ability to hurt him as none had ever before. And she also knew she would die before she caused him such pain.

"Know this for now and for all eternity, all that you are pleases me, for you are Kolt of Annan and you and no other are my mind's love."

Kolt smiled, a dazzling smile of promise, of love, of passion. "As you are mine, for now and all eternity."

Kolt branded the words into her skin with a blazing trail of fiery kisses from her mouth to her neck. Anticipation shot through her as she felt his mouth nuzzling her chin, her cheeks, her eyes. She moaned softly. Her mouth was open and waiting even before he moved to capture it once again in a melting kiss that sent her blood thrumming and her heart pounding.

His hands moved up her back to her shoulders. His lean fingers slipped into her gown's closure and slid it open. His hands splayed open. He glided them slowly downward, his fingers working the closure, as his other hand traced the gentle curve of her backbone, then as slowly moved up to thread in her hair and press her head closer to his. Aylyn thought she would die as the kiss deepened, his tongue plundering her mouth, meeting hers in a dance of give and take that left her breathless with need. She moaned when his hands moved from her hair to her shoulders, pushing the gown down, taking her arms with it, trapping them at her sides.

He raised his head to look at her, his eyes glittering with the fierce light of desire. Aylyn felt her breasts swell under his heated stare, and her breath caught in her throat as his eyes dropped to watch the silky material glide down the fullness of her breasts. She heard him groan, and the sound sent a wave of heat slicing through to her very center, as her nipples popped free and her gown dropped to floor. Her eyes closed, and her head rolled back as she let herself concentrate on nothing but the intensity of the feelings he evoked within her. When his hands began to move again, there was a urgency about his movements, a tender roughness as if he sought to penetrate her skin and stroke her very nerves. His hands slid up her arms and then down the sleek curves of her back to her waist.

Aylyn shivered at the flash of heat that coursed through her as his hands moved along the flatness of her belly, thumbs meeting and dipping for a moment into the inviting hollow at its center, before continuing upward to cup the lush fullness of her breasts. She leaned into the caress as his thumbs brushed tantalizingly across her nipples. She moaned as his head bent, and his mouth captured the hardened nub and rolled it between his teeth.

Restless with a need for something she could not put a name to, Aylyn grabbed at the shoulders of Kolt's shirt and inched it up. He lifted his head for the brief moment it took for to her to tug it off him, then eagerly reclaimed the pink-tipped confectionery he had been feasting on. With a quick flip of her wrist, Aylyn sent the shirt spiraling over her shoulders, then let her hands roam freely over his lean powerful back and shoulders. She closed her eyes, allowing her sensitized fingertips to work their magic, and was stunned by the feel of him, the silky softness of a flower's petal over the smooth hardness of crystal.

"By all the gods, how I ached for this," he growled, his mouth once again capturing hers, saving her from a reply she would have been incapable of forming.

His hands kneaded her buttocks, molding her to him, and wildfire shot through her as he ground his iron-hot need against her.

Kolt dragged his mouth from her. "I thought to go slowly, but the gods help me, I cannot!" His hands encircled her waist and he lifted her until their eyes met. "I cannot!"

Aylyn brought her hands to his neck. Her fingers entwined themselves in the long strands of his hair, and she drew his mouth to hers. "Then do not."

Golden Conquest

Kolt groaned, and his fingers came up to press against her lips. He chuckled hoarsely at her confused pout. "A moment, softling, I need to concentrate." He smiled. "Hold on."

"I am," she purred against his neck, her tongue darting out in short little licks. She thought she felt him stumble, and when she heard his curse she raised her head and was surprised to see that they were not where they had been.

"I'd not make you mine in a strange chamber. This is where you belong. Here. In my keep. In my sleeper."

Kolt lowered her to the sumptuous coverings of the sleeper and leaned over her. She watched his eyes as they traveled over her, taking in all she was, all she had to offer, and she was amazed by their brilliance.

"Gods, but you are beautiful!" he rasped as he brought his hands once again to her breasts.

The heat that shot through her as he rolled her nipples between his fingers brought her hands up, and she ran them through the light hair across his chest, loving the feel of it through her fingers. Instinct took over, and she brought her finger first to her mouth and then to his nipple, tracing the soft darkness of it with her moistened fingertip. Kolt's sharp intake of breath told her she had pleased him. It was enough to make her want to do it again. When she saw Kolt's eyes watching her intently, she slowly flicked out her tongue and rolled it around the tip of her finger. But before she could touch it to his nipple, his head jerked down and he grabbed it. Holding it between his teeth, he sucked ever so gently. Aylyn's eyes closed only to open again when she felt his hand between her thighs, his long, lean fingers pressing against her heat. Motionless. Waiting.

His mouth released her finger and moved to suckle her breast. And his fingers remained motionless. Her breath came in gasps. And still his hand remained motionless. His mouth moved to her other breast. Her body tingled. And still his hand remained motionless. Poised. Waiting.

"Kolt, please." Aylyn had no thought to what she wanted, only that she wanted.

When Kolt moved his hand, Aylyn's hips arched as white-hot lightening shot from his fingers to her very center. She felt chilled and flushed. And she wanted more. She moved against his hand and groaned as his fingers slipped inside her to find her hot and wet and ready for him.

"Gods! Kolt!" Aylyn gasped.

"Sh, softling," Kolt rasped as he stroked her honeyed center, his fingers thrusting deeper and deeper within her.

Then suddenly he was gone. Aylyn's eyes shot open, and she saw him rise and tear at his clothing until he stood before her, his manhood jutting proudly from its bed of dark curls and his eyes almost black with wanting. His smoldering gaze burning into hers, he moved over her. Aylyn gasped as she felt his velvety hardness nudge against her, then slowly enter her.

"I'm sorry, softling," Kolt said, and he seized her mouth the very moment he thrust full into her, piercing the barrier of her maidenhood and burying himself in her.

Aylyn felt the momentary discomfort of her initiation into womanhood, but it was nothing compared to the feel of his sleek fullness that throbbed and pulsed within her. She closed her eyes and lost herself in the feel of him. Content, for the moment, with the warmth that was kindling deep inside her, she drew her hands down his back, the tips of her fingers tingling from the heat of his skin, to stroke his lean buttocks in a whisper-soft caress.

"Do not."

The harsh rasp of Kolt's voice brought her hands to her side. She opened her eyes and saw him, his head thrown back as he struggled for control against a hunger fiercer than any he had ever experienced. Sweat beaded on his brow, and he clenched his teeth as he slowly began to move within her. Her fingers dug into the sleeper's covering as he began to roll his hips.

Golden Conquest

Her breaths came in short, shallow gasps, and her head lolled from side to side as liquid fire streaked through her with every thrust of his hips.

Wanting, needing to prolong her pleasure, Kolt kept his thrusts slow and deep, gritting his teeth against the feel of her tight warmth surrounding him, holding him. But Aylyn would have none of it. She arched, her hips meeting his, forcing him to increase his pace.

He raised his head once again, and watched Aylyn's face, waiting for her eyes to glaze and her back to arch. Waiting for her to find the satisfaction she needed so that he could seek his. And when at last she did, he knew it in a way beyond any of his imaginings.

"Kolt!"

Kolt's head jolted back as he realized that he had heard her cry with his ears and his mind. Before he could question how it was possible, he reached out and met her mind touch. Blood thundered in his ears as wave after fiery wave of pulsating release washed over her and therefore over him. The force of the shared experience proved too much for his already-burdened control. Kolt threw back his head and shouted her name as he thrust forward one final time. Even as he poured his seed into her, a part of his mind was stunned by the unimaginable as he heard her cry out again and knew that she had felt his climax as completely as he had felt hers.

Chapter Thirty-Two

Kolt rolled onto his back, taking her with him, afraid to let her go, afraid that he would wake and find that it had been a dream. As he lay there, waiting for his breathing to slow, he remembered the exquisite intensity of their *touch-sharing*, and his arms tightened around his love. Had she have any idea how truly remarkable their experience had been?

Aylyn lay with her head on Kolt's chest, listening to the rapid staccato of his heartbeat that she knew matched her own, and sensed that what they had shared only a few couples had ever been blessed with. And she had almost never had it.

She raised herself up on her elbow and stared down on the man who had come to mean so much to her. Tenderly, she traced his lips with her finger, and when his eyes opened and she saw his love for her naked and unhidden in his brilliant eyes, she couldn't help the tears that sprang to hers.

Kolt frowned as his hand traced the path of her tears. "Regrets?"

She shook her head. "Never."

"Then why?"

"It just struck me how close I came to losing you. If I had gone to Dianthia . . ."

"I would have come after you. You are mine, Aylyn. Never would I have allowed anyone else to have you. Never." Kolt paused. Now was the time to tell her

Golden Conquest

Aubin was coming for her and to ask her if she would stay. Caught up in all they had shared, he forgot, for the moment, that he wanted her to go. He looked at her, saw her eyes soft with love, and gave a quick fervent prayer to every god he believed in that she would choose to stay with him. His uncertainty making his voice harsh and flat, he said, "Your sire comes to take you home."

No! Aylyn cried silently. She didn't want to go back to Rhianon. Not now. Not ever. She started to protest, but she hesitated, hearing Kolt's words again. Her eyes flew to his face. It was closed to her, shuttered. Void of expression. Did he want her to leave? Did he not care for her at all? Did what they had just shared mean nothing to him?

Kolt held his breath as he watched Aylyn's reaction to his statement. His hope that she would want to stay with him died when she did not protest immediately. He closed his eyes against the pain that sliced his heart in two. Mother of the Universe! How was he to live without her?

Aylyn caught the brief flash of ragged pain that shot through Kolt's eyes before he closed them, and her soul smiled. She placed her hand at the side of his face, her thumb teasing at his beard, and said simply, "I am home, Kolt."

Kolt's eyes shot open. His hands came up to tangle in her hair and drag her mouth to his. "I love you, Aylyn," he groaned, and then poured all of that love into a fierce, binding kiss. When at last he released her, he said, in a voice hoarse with emotion, "Bond with me, Aylyn. Promise me you will stay with me always."

Tears pooled in her eyes, and she nodded. "For now and always, my love, my soul, and my life I place in your hands. And nothing my father can do or say will force me from you."

Her impassioned words struck Kolt like the frigid water of a mont stream. Her life! Gods, he had forgotten the threat to her, a threat he seemed unable to obliterate. Pain ravaged his face, and he shook his head. "As long as Rakkad lives, your life is at risk. Though I would have it otherwise, you must go with your sire, softling."

Aylyn pushed herself into a sitting position and looked down at his face with eyes that glittered fiercely. "Yes, Kolt," she agreed, "my life is at risk. But"—her voice grew intense—"it is *my* life. And no one tells me how to live it. Not my parents and not you! Rakkad has already robbed me of someone I loved. I will not let him rob me of another! I will not!" She drew in a ragged breath. "Don't send me away, Kolt. Please."

"And your dam? What of her should he take you and use you to get to Lady Eirriel?"

"That won't happen. You and my father will see to it."

"You ask for more than I can give."

"I ask for a chance, Kolt. A chance to live."

Kolt heard her unspoken words, that life would be meaningless without him. It was no more than he believed. His arms tightened around her, and he took a deep shuddering breath. "I'll keep you safe, Aylyn," he vowed, pulling her down to him. "By all that I am, I will keep you safe."

"I know, my love. I've never doubted that. Never."

Kolt's mouth slashed across hers and he tasted the sweetness he thought only moments before would be forever denied him. Suddenly, Aylyn pushed herself away. Kolt frowned. "What is it?"

"Turn over." Aylyn prodded at his side, trying to push him over. "Please. Turn over now. I have to see."

Puzzled, Kolt rolled over and presented his very muscular, very unmarked back to Aylyn. She ran her hands across it, and Kolt realized that this was no lover's caress. He twisted around to look at her.

"You are looking for something?"

"The scar." She pushed him back down. Her hands touched a spot slightly off to the right. "I remember feeling it about here first."

Golden Conquest

Kolt rolled over and held her hands in his. "You remember feeling what?"

"My mind-toucher was attacked. A knife sliced through his back. Twice. Since you are my mind-toucher, I just wanted to make sure—"

"You felt it?"

"Yes. The pain took my breath away."

"Know you what this means?" Kolt asked in whispered awe. What had happened during their lovemaking had not prepared him for the depth of their connection. "We are linked in a manner beyond my knowledge, my skills. I knew I was bound to you, but I knew not that you were bound to me. It explains how I was able to experience your pleasure."

"Linked?" Aylyn's eyes widened as she realized the implication of his words. "You experienced what?" she cried, then groaned, and fell back onto the sleeper.

Kolt rolled onto his side, his elbow crooked, and his head leaning on his closed fist. He smiled knowingly as she pressed her hands to her burning cheeks.

"Everything you felt, just as you felt it. Somehow." Hopeful that what happened had cleared the block that was preventing him from touching her, he reached out and found nothing changed. "I think it comes from Eirriel's Kiiryan blood, and you must be under great emotional stress to accomplish it. Twice you have called out to me when you were afraid. Both times I heard you but was too weak to respond. And now, though I can no longer touch you, you can and did touch me, again at a time of great emotions."

"But it has never happened before. Ever. When I was a child, I used to pray to every god I knew to give me just one small portion of my mother's skills. And now, when I was convinced that the Kiiryan blood which runs in my veins too weakened by the Dianthian and Rhianonian blood that flows within me as well, this happens. I don't understand."

"It has always been within you, softling, waiting for a catalyst. And until now, you have never been so afraid or so . . . pleasured."

It was all too overwhelming, and heat rushed over her once again. To have forced herself on him! "I—I'm sorry," she stammered, not knowing what else to say.

"For reaching out to me?" Kolt took her hands from her face and pressed them to his lips. "Think you I am upset? It was . . . incredible."

"And what I felt at the end . . ."

"Was what I felt."

"Gods!" she said, a wealth of emotion in that one word.

"Yes, it is a little daunting, is it not? To believe you have pleasured your partner feeds one's pride, but to know it, makes one humble. It leaves you a little worried that you'll not do as well the next time." Kolt's hot gaze seared Aylyn. "Never fear that you'll not please me, softling. As for myself, I will do my best to see you well pleased always."

Kolt moved back onto his back and stretched out his arm. Aylyn quickly took the hint and curled up next to him, her head on his shoulder and her hand on his chest. They lay like that for a few moments, Kolt's hand stroking her hair and Aylyn's finger tracing little patterns on his chest.

"Kolt?"

"Hmmm?"

"Will it happen again?"

Kolt chuckled. "Your pleasure isn't enough," he teased. "You want mine as well?"

"Yes," Aylyn stated unabashedly.

Kolt's hand stilled. "It is my deepest hope that it will, softling."

Aylyn sighed contentedly and snuggled closer into his chest. After a few moments her breathing slowed, and she drifted off to sleep. Kolt, who seemed to live in a constant state of fatigue, quickly followed her.

He was jolted awake a short time later by soft whimpering. It took him but a breath to recognize that the sound was coming from Aylyn. She was curled up next to him, her head on his chest, her knee between his legs, and she was trembling. His alarm grew as he felt

Golden Conquest

her tears against his chest. He ran his hand down her back and called to her softly, "Aylyn, softling, what is it?"

Aylyn's eyes shot open. "Kolt!"

"I'm here." Holding her close, he moved onto his side so that he could see her face. And what he saw shocked him. Her eyes were wide and unfocused, her face colorless and drawn. "Aylyn! Are you in pain? What—"

"I'm afraid, Kolt. So afraid."

"Sh, love, there's no need to be. Tell me, what did you dream?"

"I don't know. All I remember is the fear."

Kolt swore. If he could touch her, he would know what plagued her. "Cast aside your fear. Do you think I would let anyone harm you?"

"No, it's not me. It's you. It's you," she repeated frantically, her eyes closing against whatever it was that she had seen. When she opened them again, they were haunted. "First Laaryc and now . . . Kolt, if I lost you, I would lose my soul."

Kolt's arms tightened around Aylyn. "You'll not lose me."

"Take away my fear, Kolt. Share with me again." Her hands snaked through his hair, pulling his mouth to hers. "Let me feel your life."

Kolt groaned. His mouth covered hers and over the next few hours he did just that—twice.

Aylyn came awake to a thrumming. She opened her eyes and met Mikki's unblinking yellow eyes. Immediately, the yiichi started to chatter.

"Shhh, little one," Aylyn whispered, her hand coming up to stroke behind Mikki's ear. "Our laedan needs his rest."

Aylyn looked over at Kolt, who was sprawled on his belly, snoring gently. She had realized after Kolt had soothed her fears and given of himself to her, that what he had done was nothing more than all he had done since she arrived. And that she could give a little of it back to him in a way that obviously pleased him greatly, pleased her as well. She had also realized that he had been getting very little sleep. She, however, had been getting enough.

"Shall we explore our new home?" she asked Mikki as she slipped from the sleeper. Naked, she moved to the great wardrobe and pulled out one of Kolt's robes. Rolling up the sleeves and tripling the belt around her waist, she took Mikki's hand and quietly left the sleeping chamber.

"Day's passing to you, lady."

"And to you, Naydir," she replied, not a little startled to see him. "I did not expect to see you."

"Neither did I, but you will find when the laedan wants something, he wants it immediately." Naydir gestured to Mikki. "He remembered very early this morning that she had been left behind. And so we are here."

Aylyn's hand went to her mouth. "Oh, no. I'm sorry. I was the one who asked about her."

Naydir chuckled. "From Kolt's touch, he wasn't too pleased at the choice of hour."

Aylyn flushed. It had been shortly after they had shared each other again and Kolt had indeed not liked that her mind had been on anything other than him.

Still chuckling, Naydir pulled out a chair from the table next to the casement—a replacement for the one Kolt had *snatched* from under Cal. "Think you a bit of nourishment would be to your liking?"

Aylyn nodded. "If you will join me."

Naydir remembered Kolt's warning while back at Lorgra and Serline's cottage. "Kolt may not be pleased."

"He was only teasing."

"I'd not thought you heard all he said."

"Well, I didn't think he'd like it if he knew I knew he was jealous." She smiled, her eyes crinkling at the corners. "Truth be told, Naydir, I liked that I knew."

"Well, if you ask me, it was more threat than tease. More than likely he'll toss me out the casement."

Golden Conquest

"Then we won't tell him. At least until he catches up on his sleep. He hasn't been getting much has he?"

"No, he has not. Do not," Naydir said firmly when Aylyn opened her mouth to apologize. "He has long been awaiting your arrival, Aylyn. He would not care if he never slept again."

Aylyn's eyes drifted toward the door behind which the man she loved with a passion she had never believed existed slept. Sometime during their long night together, between the time of sharing and the time of sleeping, Kolt had explained to Aylyn how he had known from the moment he had met her father that she would be coming and when she would arrive, and that she would be his. Her eyes grew soft and dreamy, and her lips curled into a secret smile.

"I understand how he feels. I don't want to miss a moment of him, either." She sighed. "But for now, he needs his sleep more than he needs me."

Naydir knew Kolt would have corrected Aylyn's mistaken belief, but Naydir said nothing. He was too pleased that she cared enough to want what was best for Kolt. He had worried that Kolt's love for Aylyn would be stronger than hers for him, but her words and her expressions laid his fears to rest. "I will see to our nourishment," he said as he moved to the door. "I will not be long."

During Naydir's absence, Aylyn took the time to look about the chamber and was drawn to the large casement. She pushed opened the door, and her breath caught in her throat as she saw the Garden of Colors.

"What think you of *our* garden?" Naydir asked as he joined her.

"It is similar to the one my father made for my mother."

"Except for the Rainbow Falls, it is identical." Naydir chuckled. "Not even Kolt could change the color of Annan's water." He paused then added softly, "All was done for you."

"For me?" she asked, touched once again by the depth of Kolt's love for her.

Unknowingly, he confirmed Aylyn's thoughts. "He loves you well, our laedan."

They fell silent as a server arrived with several platters of nourishment which she quickly placed on the table. Self-consciously, Aylyn raked her hand through her tangled curls and pulled the neck of Kolt's robe together as the server bowed in front of her.

"Thank you."

"I but do my duty, my lady," the server replied.

"And that you do it so well requires my thanks. Your laedan will be told."

The server beamed with pleasure. Naydir knew that within hours all in the keep would hear from the server how beautiful and gentle and thoughtful the laedan's chosen was.

As they ate, Naydir answered Aylyn's questions about Kolt, questions both knew Kolt, by his very nature, would not answer.

"His people love him. I saw it everywhere we went."

"He has done much for Annan."

"But to have had all of this placed on him when he was still a child! He possesses a strength of will beyond anyone I know. Even my father."

"Kolt would be greatly pleased if you told him that. Your sire has long been someone he has admired."

Aylyn's mouth twisted in an amused grin. "And to Kolt's dismay, my father returns that admiration."

"To his dismay?"

"Yes, but I will leave the telling of that to Kolt."

"And he will like not the telling, I've no doubt."

Thinking of Kolt's expression when she called the laedan a paragon, Aylyn giggled. "Not especially."

Naydir poured Aylyn another cup of the steaming orange liquid. "The cleansing chamber is prepared if you want to make use of it."

"Yes, that is very considerate of you."

"Of Kolt. I but relayed the orders."

"Did you perchance pick up my clothing when you picked up Mikki?"

Naydir nodded. "Yes, but you will find a chamber

vent to his anger, his despair. His anguished cries were soon joined by arcs of energy, their dark color an indication of the state of Kolt's soul.

Amidst the flashes of light, the vision that had tormented him through the long hours of sleep replayed itself. Over and over. Unchanging. Unrelenting. Unalterably.

He jerked the sword from Rakkad's body and then he felt it. A pain sharp and breath-stealing. His name rang in his head. He twisted around to see Aylyn take a step toward him. She faltered then fell, struck in the chest by a blade that had flown fast and true. Shouting her name, he ran to her side, his heart stopping as he saw her lifeblood pouring from her wound. With a flick of his finger, he sent the knife from her. Frantically, he stripped off his shirt and tried to staunch the bleeding. Tried and failed. She moaned his name. Gently, tenderly, he gathered her to him. He saw her eyes staring up at him, their golden lights dim. Her beautiful mouth drawn tight against the pain. Her breathing was ragged. Her skin cold and pale. She reached up to touch his face, but the effort proved too much, and her hand fell lifelessly to the ground. Her eyes closed, denying him for all eternity their brilliance, their love, their life.

"Noooo!" he roared, as he clasped her to his chest.

It was a roar that echoed throughout the cubiculum each time he saw her die. A roar carried again and again by violent flashes of energy until he could summon no more.

"Why?" he asked the empty chamber. "Why give her to me only to take her away?"

His knees gave way, and he sank to the floor. His head in his hands, he sobbed.

Golden Conquest

adjoining the cleanser that holds much more."

"More?"

"Did I not say Kolt has long awaited your arrival? You will find all you need within the keep, and all that is here is by Kolt's command."

Naydir escorted her to the door of the cleanser. "The wardrobe chamber is beyond the far door. Morald, our captain of the guard, is without. Should Kolt still be asleep when you are through, he has orders to escort you anywhere you will."

While Aylyn was soaking in the cleanser, Kolt was tossing restlessly in the sleeper, locked in a dark despairing dream that he fought to awaken from. And when at last he did, he wished with all that he possessed that he could return to the land of dreams and never wake up.

Aylyn exited the wardrobe chamber over an hour later, refreshed and anxious to explore the garden Kolt's love for her had created. She crept to the door of the sleeping chamber and peeked in, chiding herself at the disappointment that washed over her when she saw that Kolt was still asleep. He needed his rest and they would have time together when he woke. And every day after that. Quietly, she closed the door. From this day on, they would have all the time they needed.

Kolt, his brow beaded with sweat, his soul torn asunder, slammed his eyes closed as he heard the door to the sleeping chamber open. And he kept them closed as Aylyn's soft sigh of disappointment reached him, and after the door closed again. Desperately, he prayed to all the gods that what he had seen was naught but a dream. And cruelly the gods laughed at him. It was no dream, it was the future. And the darkness of it clawed at him.

With a thought, he was in the cubiculum, the one chamber in the keep constructed out of soundarium crystal. There, safe from prying eyes and ears, he gave

Chapter Thirty-Three

"Naydir? Would you mind if I asked a question about you?" Aylyn asked. She, Naydir, and Mikki had been walking in the garden for the better part of an hour, Naydir continuing to answer her questions about Kolt.

"You may ask anything."

Her eyes twinkled. "But you won't promise to answer."

"Ask and we will see."

"The amulet you wear around your neck. Does it hold significance for you?" Aylyn wished she could withdraw the question when she saw Naydir's eyes darken as if with pain and his hand clutch at the golden image. "I'm sorry, I didn't mean to pry."

"You asked for a reason. Why?"

"The estalon . . ."

"Estalon?"

"The winged stallion that flies cross the golden sky is called a estalon." Aylyn frowned. "You did not know? Then I am sorry again to have called forth painful memories."

"The estalon is familiar to you?"

"Yes. My mother breeds them on Rhianon from four she brought from her home world of Dianthia. And on Dianthia they were rare. My mother believes estalons were bred on one world and traded to others, Dianthia being only one of them. I thought perhaps you came from their home world."

"I know not from where I hail," Naydir said, his voice tight. "I have no memory beyond five years past when Kolt rescued me from my damaged ship." Briefly, Naydir explained how Kolt had found him among the wreckage and had brought him to the keep. How though Kolt had never been able to touch him, he had given Naydir his friendship and his trust. He looked at Aylyn, a spark of hope in his eyes. "Think you I can trace my home world through this?" he asked, the amulet in his hand, his thumb gently caressing the engraving.

"It may take time, but with Kolt's powers and my father's connections, perhaps we may find your home." Aylyn saw the spark of hope in his eyes and was dismayed. "It may mean nothing, Naydir. I would not want you to be disappointed."

"I have longed believed this"—he gestured with the amulet—"was the key to my identity." Naydir took her hand in his and raised it to his lips. "You have given me hope, Aylyn. Think you not I will ever forget it."

Aylyn looked into his fierce, passionate gaze and knew that he would not.

Naydir released the amulet and his gaze swung skywards. It was almost time for the Rainbow Lights. Kolt would be disappointed that he was not there when she saw them for the first time. Though Loridan had Rainbow Lights as well, Kolt often boasted how Aubin had reluctantly admitted the Lights over the Crystal Keep were brighter, the colors more vibrant.

"Pause a moment, Aylyn, and look you around."

Aylyn stopped and followed Naydir's sweeping hand. She gasped as the Lights burst into evidence. Her eyes sparkled with pleasure at the dazzling display, and she could tell from Mikki's contented thrumming that she was pleased as well. When they had passed, Aylyn smiled at Naydir.

"I had no idea. Your Lights are so much more than Rhianon's."

"Kolt will be pleased. He will not like that he was not here to witness—"

Golden Conquest

Mikki suddenly started jumping up and down, chattering shrilly.

"Mikki, little one?" Aylyn reached down for the agitated yiichi. "What is it?"

Mikki's chattering grew shriller. She alternated it with a high-pitched trilling. Her wings sprung open and fluttered rapidly.

Aylyn turned to Naydir. "Something is wrong."

Naydir, remembering what Kolt had told him of the events at the lodge, activated his gauntlet and pulled out his neutralizer. Kolt had believed that at the lodge the yiichi had reacted to Rakkad's presence. He drew Aylyn next to him, holding her behind his shielding.

"What is it, Naydir?"

"I know not, but she senses something."

Just then Mikki took to the sky, flying around and around in little circles, then she darted away toward the keep.

Naydir scanned the garden. "I like this not. Come." He took Aylyn's hand. "Your Mikki has the right idea. We will follow."

"You think it's Rakkad, don't you?" Aylyn asked, fighting against the panic that threatened to choke her. The last time it had been Kolt's timely arrival that had kept her from Rakkad. As much as she trusted Naydir, she wanted Kolt.

"Very possibly. Kolt seems to believe the yiichi can sense him."

A rustling in the bushes drew Naydir's attention. He spun to face the sound and then he heard it from behind him. He spun again, each time keeping Aylyn safely within the gauntlet's protective shielding. *Is there more than one assailant?* he thought. He doubted not his ability to defend Aylyn, with his life if necessary, but if he should find himself overwhelmed, she would be taken. That he could not risk. He opened his mouth to bellow for Morald, when Morald and Cal stepped into the opening.

Both halted as they noted Naydir's shielding, then Morald was running to him, activating his gauntlet and drawing his weapon as he did. Cal followed close behind. No sooner had they drawn up next to Naydir and Aylyn, then the sound to the right of them increased. Two neutralizers swung in that direction.

The instant he exited the brush, Dakkar squawked and dropped to the ground, his trembling hands over his head. "Do not shoot! Do not shoot!"

With a curse, Naydir turned to Morald. "You passed no one."

"No, Councilor. The courtyard was empty."

"Dakkar, did . . . Get up, fool!" Naydir snapped when he saw that Dakkar was still groveling on the ground. He waited impatiently until the young man found his feet. "Did you encounter anyone?"

"N–no, C–councilor."

Naydir deactivated his shielding and reholstered his neutralizer. Morald followed suit. "It seems your Mikki was just reacting to her strange surroundings, my lady."

"Don't look so disgruntled, Naydir. Where Rakkad is concerned, I would rather be overcautious." Aylyn smiled. "I felt quite safe. Thank you."

"I but did my . . ."

"Duty," Aylyn finished, laughing. "But you have my thanks just the same."

"Ahem."

Naydir turned to Cal. "Yes, Councilor?"

"Think you it is time for the introductions?"

"Of course. My lady Aylyn, may I present Cal, Councilor of Mayrald."

"Greetings, Councilor," Aylyn said, extending her hand palm up in friendship.

Cal took Aylyn's hand and turned it. Bowing, he kissed it and raised it to his forehead. "My honor and my service are yours, lady."

Aylyn flushed. "I am honored."

"Morald, captain of the guard," Naydir stated as Morald stepped forward.

"Captain."

Golden Conquest

Morald placed his hand on his gauntlet, his neutralizer, and his heart. "My life is yours, lady," he pledged gravely.

There was something in Morald's serious black eyes that told Aylyn that this man's allegiance was not lightly given. Carefully matching her tone to his, Aylyn replied, "Gratefully I accept it, Captain."

"And me? Do I get to meet her . . . I mean, the lady," Dakkar quickly corrected as Naydir glowered at him. When the tall councilor's eyes darkened even more, Dakkar stammered, "Er . . . Kolt's . . . I mean, the laedan's . . ."

"Naydir, just do it, else he will stammer himself into apoplexy," Cal said disgustedly.

"Come then and greet your lady," Naydir growled impatiently.

Dakkar hurried to Aylyn, stopping in front of her.

"My lady, may I present Dakkar."

"I serve the laedan," Dakkar said hurriedly when Naydir attempted to explain his position. "And you as well."

"Dakkar." Aylyn smiled. She found him charmingly innocent and informal after the formality of the others' greetings.

Dakkar reached for her hand and was just about to grasp it when he jerked his hand away. His eyes glued to a spot beyond Aylyn, he staggered backwards. "I did not think . . . Everyone else . . . Oh, gods!" he groaned. "Laedan, I beg your pardon."

Aylyn, who had been startled by Dakkar's bizarre behavior, heard the name Laedan and instantly forgot about Dakkar and all else.

"Kolt," she breathed, turning to face him.

Kolt watched her as she turned to greet him. Her eyes were as brilliant as golithium, her smile wide and welcoming, the off-the-shoulder gown flowing seductively over her curves as she walked toward him. It was all he had imagined it to be that day not so long ago when he had looked down on the garden he had created just for her and pictured her waiting for him. So beautiful. So perfect. So fleeting.

And it hurt so much he thought his heart was surely dying.

Then he watched her inviting smile fade, and the sparkle leave her eyes as he met her warm and loving gaze with his own cold, unyielding one.

"Leave us," Kolt ordered.

"Kolt, what . . ." Naydir asked, puzzled.

"Leave us! Now!"

"As you wish." Naydir bowed to Aylyn, "Lady," then turned and strode away.

Cal and Morald bowed their good-byes to Aylyn and then left as well. Dakkar, still stammering his apologies, scurried after them.

Aylyn, confused by Kolt's chilling glare, waited until they were alone to move closer to him. She stared into his eyes and saw a glimpse of something dark and terrible. She raised her hand to touch his cheek.

Kolt knew if she touched him he was lost. He would pull her to him and never let her go. And she would die. He backed away.

Aylyn's hand froze halfway to his face. "Kolt, please. What is it?"

"Gather what you will, Aylyn, you leave for Rhianon within the hour."

Aylyn blanched. Dear gods! Something must have happened! "Is it Rakkad? Does he have my mother?"

"No." Kolt, seeing the pained confusion on her face, fought against it and kept his voice polite, impersonal. "She is well. As is your sire."

"Then why are we leaving? My father is on his way here."

"I told him it was no longer necessary."

"Why, Kolt?" She held her breath, waiting for him to tell her it was his way of letting her bid farewell to Rhianon before she began a life with him on Annan, but she knew it was not the reason. As she watched him open his mouth to speak, a small crack began in the center of her soul, and when he at last spoke, his words acted as a hammer and her soul splintered.

"*We* are going nowhere," he said in a voice stripped of emotion. "*You* are. I want you off my world and out of my life."

Then he turned on his heels and left.

Chapter Thirty-Four

Kolt had not expected her to confront him and so had slowed his pace once he was free of the garden. The pain in his heart and the ache in his soul robbed him of the strength to do more than trudge.

She was leaving.

He had sent her away.

"Kolt!"

He stiffened at her voice, but he refused to stop.

"Kolt, please. Tell me what is wrong?"

"Why think you something is wrong? It is not. Merely the time has come for you to leave." Though he had not seen the actual location of Aylyn's life-ending, he *knew* it would happen on Annan. Once she left she would be safe. "Naydir will see you to Rhianon."

"Naydir?"

"Did I not say Naydir?"

"I never thought you were a coward. If you want me to leave, you will have to take me. It's the only way."

He cursed silently. He should have realized she would not make it easy for him. "So be it. One hour, Aylyn. I'll like it not if you keep me waiting."

Aylyn struggled for a calm she did not feel. He was sending her away! She nodded her head. "One hour." Then she brushed past him, but not before Kolt saw the tears in her eyes and a trembling hand pressed to her lips. He had made her cry. Gods, but this was unbearable!

Golden Conquest

"If you ask me you are a fool!" Naydir growled.

He, Cal, Dakkar, and Morald had heard most of what had been said, and now stood surrounding him.

"Yes, I am a fool," Kolt said bitterly. "A fool for thinking to keep her."

"Is it Aubin? Has he forced you to comply?"

"No."

"Then why?"

"You forget yourself, Councilor. I am the laedan of Annan. I need explain myself to no one."

Kolt strode away, leaving the four men to stare after him, their questions unanswered.

After a moment, Naydir turned to Morald. "I want the grounds searched. Order it! Then see you to your lady."

"At once." Morald bowed and left to find Aylyn.

"Cal, see that the laedan's ship is readied and well-stocked."

"What about me?" Dakkar asked. "May I not do something?"

Naydir had forgotten Dakkar's presence. "You have ceased your sniveling?" Naydir was too distracted by the recent events to take note of the darkening of Dakkar's eyes and the tightening of his mouth. "Then your laedan will need nourishment before his journey, fetch it."

"Yes, Councilor."

"And what do you do?" Cal asked when they were alone.

Naydir looked up to his friend's chambers. "There is something amiss. I go to find out what."

"I would be alone," Kolt snarled.

Naydir entered Kolt's chambers unbidden and for his trouble found himself wearing an untasted portion of sylva. The flagon had struck the wall near his head and thumped to the floor. Naydir swiped at his face with a cloth grabbed from a nearby table as he moved into the chamber.

"Then take yourself away, for I am not leaving." When Kolt made no move to *actualize*, Naydir crossed to his side. "What has happened to make you drive her away?"

"You think I am driving her away?"

"Yes."

Kolt's shoulders slumped, and he looked at Naydir with bleak and haunted eyes. "I know not if I can go through with this. I have waited all my life for her and now . . ." His voice drifted off. Kolt's gaze returned to the garden he had once thought to be the site of many joyous happenings and had instead witnessed the darkest of events.

"And now," Naydir prodded.

"And now I have seen her death." Kolt's voice was ragged with emotion. "I have searched all the variations for our future and they all end the same. If she stays, she will be life-ended."

"Mother of the Universe! You are certain?"

Kolt nodded. "Naught I can do will change it."

Silence greeted Kolt's unwavering statement. Naydir walked to the table and poured two flagons of the potent sylva. He handed one to Kolt, who swiftly downed it.

"Does Lord Aubin know you are bringing her?"

"He knows she is to arrive." He laughed, a short bitter snort of self-derision. "I had thought to save myself the pain of seeing her to Rhianon. She would have none of it."

"You cannot share what you know with her?"

"She has her father's warrior blood and her mother's fierce pride. Do you think she would flee to save her life? No, it is better that she leaves in hate and lives, than stay in love and life-end."

"Rakkad?"

Kolt raked a hand through his hair. "He is there in my vision, but it is not he."

"But that he is there is a start. We must find him." Quickly, Naydir relayed the events in the garden. "It may be naught but I ordered the keep searched."

"You did well, though it may have been my dark thoughts the yiichi sensed."

"Perhaps, but should she act as a sensor . . ."

Golden Conquest

"Then we may yet find Rakkad in our grasp. But as for Aylyn, naught will change. She will still be life-ended."

Three days from Annan and only a day's journey to Rhianon a heartsick Aylyn paced the small cubicle that was her chamber aboard Kolt's ship, the *Marcail*, trying to think of a way to make Kolt confront her. Only once, since he had coldly agreed to see her to Rhianon, had he spoken with her. As he had escorted her to his ship, she had again asked for an explanation and again her questions were answered by dark, soul-stealing silences. Until she had accused him of forgetting his vow to see to Laaryc's life-ender. He had told her that the laedan of Annan would see Rakkad punished. Annan's future depended on it. Then he had opened the portal to this cubicle and motioned for her to enter. Then he had walked away, and she had not seen him since.

Nothing she had done had brought him to her. Not even that she was refusing nourishment, though truthfully it was no ploy. She knew anything that reached her stomach would leave it again in an instant. She slumped against the cool metal of the wall. Perhaps he no longer loved her. Perhaps it had all been a game. No! She slammed her fist against the wall. A love as strong and as binding as theirs couldn't just vanish. She shoved herself forward and began to pace. There had to be a way to reach him! There had to be! Suddenly she stopped pacing. Yes! If her rages wouldn't cut through his silence, she would use the one weapon that would.

Determinedly, she strode to the container that held her clothes. He had promised he would accompany her to her mother. She would see him at that time, or, if the gods favored her, he would come before. She drew out an outfit. And he would see her.

Let him refuse her if he could.

Kolt stood in front of the portal to Aylyn's cubicle, a nourishment tray in his hands, and cursed. Till now he had managed to avoid her, knowing that as long as he kept his distance, he could keep the mask of his false disenchantment with her in place. But he had just learned that she had refused nourishment again. Something apparently she had been doing since Annan. Well, he thought grimly, she would eat this if he had to feed her himself.

Steeling himself against the sight of her, he flashed his hand across the portal sensor, and it slid open. Try as he might to do otherwise, he found he could easier hold back molten rock that flowed from a ruptured mont than he could his eyes from seeking her out. And when he did, he wished to all gods that he had not!

She was seated on the sleeper, garbed in one of the outfits he had ordered made for her before her arrival on Annan. A mate to one he was to have worn. He did not think it possible, but the pain in his heart increased. His eyes raked her face and saw it was pale, her eyes shadowed by the hurt he had placed there. She rose as he crossed the cubicle. He kept his back to her as he set the tray on the corner table.

"You have not taken nourishment," he said without turning, and hoped his voice was not as shaky as his hands. "I'd not return you to your father's keep weak from lack of sustenance."

"It is not nourishment I need," Aylyn replied huskily. "It is you."

Kolt stiffened. Surely he misinterpreted her words. Surely her pride would keep her from throwing herself at him. His lips curled derisively. Fool! It was her pride in herself that fortified her belief in their love. A belief that told her it would be a lie if he said he did not love her, did not want her. It was why he had kept away from her. He believed himself incapable of making the lie a truth. And now she was using the one weapon she had left, her knowledge that their lovemaking was more love than lust to make him speak the truth. As painful as it would be for him to witness it, he could not hold back his admiration of her strategy. It was no more than he would have done had she refused him.

He heard her move closer to him and knew that he had to turn, to face her, before she touched him, because if she did, he would be lost.

He turned. And was lost.

Aylyn reached up and slowly began to unbutton the crystal studs at the side of her tunic, then the four on each cuff. She walked away from Kolt, unhooking the crystal-encrusted girdle and letting it slip to the floor. Her hands went to her head, and she removed the harkbone clasps that held her golden mass of curls in a tight ball at the top of her head. A toss and they spilled free. Another toss and her hair settled on her back. Aylyn grabbed the edge of her tunic and very slowly began to lift it over her head. She let it fall to the ground. She paused, leaning up against the sleeper-table, and kicked off her slippers, then hooked her hands in the waistband of her blousy trousers. Leisurely, she drew them down, bending at the waist; then in two small steps she left them in a pool on the floor. A tug at the fastenings and her undergarments were quickly dispensed with.

Aylyn turned—right into Kolt's waiting embrace.

Kolt's mouth swept down and captured hers in a punishing kiss as he gave into the demands of his body. He plundered her mouth, stealing what would have willingly been offered. Roughly, his hands pressed her body against his throbbing groin, forcing her to feel the heat that she had caused. He meant to scare her, to make her think he would take her in rage. But when her hand came down to encircle his pulsing hardness, and she breathed against his mouth, "Share with me, my love," he knew he could not. His love for her was too strong, too potent. With a groan, he shoved her from him and turned away.

Aylyn stared at him, unable to believe, to accept that he had shut her from him again. Forever.

When he started toward the portal, rage took over her pain and hurt. "Don't you walk away from me, damn you!" she spat. "You owe me an explanation!"

Kolt schooled his expression into one of icy disdain. What was left of his heart contracted at the sight of her. Her cheeks were red with a heat fed by anger and diffused passion, her back was held rigid by pride, her breasts heaving with fury and frustrated desire. But though her eyes flashed with rage, he could see the hurt deep within them. Hurt he had placed there. Hurt he would keep there.

"I am the laedan of Annan. I owe an explanation to no one," he sneered.

"And that's it? After all we had, you are the laedan and I am supposed to accept that as an explanation?"

"All we had?" His brow arched, and his lips curled in a smile that did not touch his eyes. "Think you it was more than a pleasant diversion?"

She slapped him then, and the force of her blow jerked his head to the side. "Bladgenian loving scum! You lied to me! You used what I am against me! You controlled me, Kolt, just as I feared you would. But you did it so subtly, I didn't even realized it was happening."

Kolt forced himself to shrug. "I am well skilled, softling. Control, you see, is knowing when to act and when to wait. I did but wait till you came to me."

She struck him again. Though he saw it coming, Kolt made no move to block her blow. It was the least he could do, and it was much less than he deserved. A Zandarian blade in his heart would be more appropriate. But then his heart was already dead, so she would find little satisfaction in that act.

"Why, Kolt? Tell me why? Why did you make me love you? What did it get you?"

Kolt felt his resolve weakening, and he knew he had to end it now, end it for all time. End it before he dropped to his knees and begged her forgiveness. Before he thrust himself inside her and proved the only way he knew how that it had all been an act. He raked his eyes down her naked body. "It got me a willing sleeper-mate."

Her eyes wide with shocked pain, Aylyn watched him leave, and when the portal slid shut, she collapsed on the floor and sobbed. She had tried and failed.

She had lost him.

Chapter Thirty-Five

Eirriel glanced at Aubin as he stood watching the *Marcail's* shuttle set down on the landing platform. She had hoped the knowledge that Kolt was returning Aylyn to them would rid Aubin of his irrational anger, but it had not. Neither had it changed his belief that she had chosen Kolt over him. Eirriel sighed. Maybe the sight of his daughter would help.

The portal slid open, and Aylyn stepped out. Eirriel's worried gaze followed Aubin as he opened his arms to his daughter and she ran into them. A movement near the portal drew her gaze, and her eyes widened in shock.

Koltrax!

Though she knew it could not be him, her mind nonetheless filled with memories of Koltrax: the dashing hawker who had flaunted himself before her in an attempt to make her his, the fierce rebel leader who vowed to rescue his men and her Aubin from within Kedar's sanctuary; and the brave and courageous captive whose intense gaze sought and held hers even as he vanished, a victim of the sonulator's deadly blue light.

As often happened when in pain, Eirriel unwittingly reached out, and her thoughts and memories were seen not only by herself but by Aubin and the man who had triggered them.

He loved you.

Eirriel smiled sadly at the touch of the child, who had befriended her so many years before, the child who had stayed with her and had offered her his comfort when he had to have been just as devastated as she was at the loss of his brother. *I know, Boruk. If only. . . .*

"If only what," Aubin growled, jerking his mind free of Eirriel and her memories. Memories and emotions so strong, so bittersweet they staggered him. "If only I had died at Kedar's hands instead of your beloved Koltrax!"

"Father!" Aylyn and Alaran gasped.

Aubin pushed Aylyn at Alaran. "Take her inside."

Brother and sister exchanged worried glances. Neither knew what caused their father's outburst, but both knew his statement untrue.

"I think it would be better . . ." Alaran began.

"Now!" Aubin roared.

Aylyn looked from her father to her mother, then quickly closed the distance between herself and Eirriel. Let her father rage, she would greet her mother!

"You are well?" Eirriel asked as Aylyn kissed her.

"I am alive," Aylyn replied quietly.

Eirriel studied her daughter's face. "You don't look it. Go and do as your father says. I will come to you shortly and then we will talk."

Aylyn turned to her father, standing afar from them, his hands clenched at his side.

"He has been worried, Aylyn," Eirriel said in an attempt to rid Aylyn of her concern. "Now that you are safe it will be all right. Go."

Aylyn nodded and went with Alaran. In truth, her own troubles weighed too heavily on her mind to deal with her parents'. Later would be soon enough.

Eirriel moved to her lifebond's side and reached for him, but the look in his eyes as he spun to face her stopped her hand.

"All these years you loved another and I never knew," he snarled. "What a fool I have been!" He turned from her. "But no longer."

"Aubin, please listen to me." When he said nothing, but continued to walk away from her, she

Golden Conquest

cried, "Where are you going? Come back!"

"Lost him again, did you?"

Eirriel spun around to face a Kolt much amused by a scene that reminded him of their first meeting in the open marketplace of Inner Sumal. Eirriel had been looking for Aubin then, too.

"Mother of the Universe! Boruk?" Aubin had often chided her for using that name, but to Eirriel Kolt would always be Boruk, the young mind-toucher who had shouldered the burden of a ravaged world.

Kolt bowed his head in greeting. "You had no idea?"

"That you mirrored your brother?" She shook her head. "No."

"Where does Aubin go? We have much to discuss."

Eirriel's eyes darkened. "Now is not a good time."

Kolt, not one to mind-drop, was only beginning to realize that Eirriel had projected her thoughts to more than just him. "He heard?"

"Yes," she said grimly, her eyes returning to Aubin's departing form. "And he believes I loved Koltrax."

"You did," Kolt stated. Well he remembered the look in her eyes as she had watched Koltrax.

"He touched my heart, yes. But I didn't love him. I couldn't. There was always Aubin, you see."

Kolt heard the truth in her voice, but it was obvious that Aubin had not. "Fear not, when Aubin calms, he will see the truth. He loves you well, your lord director."

Eirriel shook her head. "He already believes I chose you over him. And now this. Oh, Boruk, he looked so hurt."

Kolt reached out to Aubin and liked not what he touched. "He means to go to Xeril. Now."

"But he's too angry. He'll . . ."

"Fear not, Eirriel. I will watch him."

Eirriel smiled her relief. "Thank you. Will you bid farewell to Aylyn?"

"There's naught to be said that hasn't been said already," Kolt replied gruffly.

Eirriel did not need her mind-touching skills to sense Kolt's pain; it was so evident in his eyes. "I don't understand. You love her."

"More than my life," came the hoarse reply.

"Then why?"

"It is the way it must be."

Eirriel took Kolt's hand. "Tell me, Boruk. Let me help."

"There's naught you can do, Eirriel. Naught anyone can do." He kissed her cheek. "Your Aubin is about to leave. I must go." He looked, one final glance at the keep that held the woman he loved enough to give up. "Take care of her, Eirriel."

And then he was gone.

The *Ceallach* was the finest, swiftest vessel in Rhianon's fleet as befitted the flagship of the lord director. Her crew was fifty of the best found outside the Protectorate, having been chosen and trained by the lord director himself. Normally, all ten posts in the *Ceallach's* command center would have been manned, but it was a well-known idiosyncrasy of the lord director that he and he alone piloted his ship during the departure from Rhianon.

Skills that kept him alive during his years with the Protectorate screamed at Aubin, and he knew he was no longer alone. Since his computer was sensitized to recognize all variations of the T-M beam, Aubin knew his unwanted visitor had not arrived by the usual method.

"Go back, laedan of Annan," Aubin ordered without turning. "Your presence aboard my ship is not welcome."

"Welcome or not, I am here and here I stay," Kolt replied pleasantly. Years of friendship with Aubin told him how to handle his friend's volatile temper. Kolt approached Aubin and glanced at the viewer. Rhianon was already becoming smaller. "Think you even I can manage to cross that void?"

"You managed a moment ago."

Golden Conquest

"True, but your need to place great distance between yourself and your world has made it impossible. More than likely I would reappear well above Rhianon. I do not think I would like that."

Aubin swung toward Kolt, his golden eyes blazed with fury. "Then use the T-M unit, damn you, but get off my ship!"

Kolt calmly dropped into the seat next to Aubin. "Shout all you want, my friend, but I am pledged to accompany you."

Aubin's lips curled. "Your dead brother's lover?"

Kolt was on his feet, Aubin's shirtfront in his hands, before the lord director even saw him move. He glared down on Aubin, his blue eyes dark. "You would do wise to watch your words, Lord Aubin of Rhianon, else I will see you eat them."

Aubin, amazed both at the younger man's speed and audacity, snarled, "You dare to threaten me?"

"When your tongue outflies your brain, then, yes, I dare." His lips drew back. "And if you think this a mere threat then think again."

"You actually believe you can take me!"

"Yes," replied Kolt without hesitation.

They glowered at each other, neither moving, neither relenting, the silence growing, until Aubin at last lowered his eyes.

"You can release me now, Kolt of Annan. My tongue no longer outflies my brain."

Kolt, relieved for he'd not wanted to make his threat a fact, quickly moved away from Aubin. The tall Rhianonian stood and adjusted his clothing, a reluctant smile on his lips.

"I still can't believe you thought to take me."

"I'd not have wanted to injure you."

Aubin's grin widened at the confidence he saw in Kolt's stance, and he completed Kolt's statement. "But you would have."

"You were speaking foolishly."

"Yes." Aubin drew a hand through his curls. "I know Eirriel loves me, has always loved me. Though at times like this I wonder why. In the past my temper has reared its unthinking head, but this . . ." He shook his head. He had needed his head knocked against the wall to clear it. He threw a sideways glance at Kolt and smiled. Even as a boy, Kolt had been unafraid to speak up against fools and tyrants. Aubin cleared his throat. "I wouldn't have made it easy for you."

"Think you I doubt that? Neither of us would have been much good on this mission we have undertaken." Kolt watched the humor leave Aubin's eyes. "It is this that has you so overwrought?"

"It is not the mission. It is the circumstances," Aubin growled. "Since resigning my commission, the Protectorate has tried their damnedest to embroil me in their schemes, and now they have." Aubin quickly explained the Xerilian mission.

"Gods, Aubin! But I ask your forgiveness. If I had seen the message, none of this would have come to pass." Kolt planted himself in front of Aubin. "Should you wish to strike me, I'll not resist."

Aubin waved Kolt off. "Now you're the one spouting nonsense." Aubin pressed a switch and barked an order. "Plaria will see you to your quarters. Give me a third of an hour and join me in mine. If you smell burning, do not open the door."

"Eirriel is likely waiting for your call."

"I hope you're right," Aubin said grimly. "I hurt her deeply."

Kolt placed his hand on Aubin's shoulder. "She will forgive you. Go and see."

Aubin had just left when a tall, slender Rhianonian female entered the command center followed by ten other crew members. She stopped before Kolt.

"I am Plaria, Laedan. If you will follow me."

As Plaria led Kolt through the ship, he was amazed by all he saw. Rhianon's fleet was reported to be rivaled only by the Protectorate's, but he had always thought the rumor exaggerated. Now he knew it was not. Gods! If Annan but had one of these ships, Rakkad would have had a fight on his hands.

Golden Conquest

Rakkad's name brought Aylyn to Kolt's mind, a place he had been trying to keep her from. And she was still there a short time later when he requested entrance to Aubin's quarters.

Kolt sniffed as he entered. "No smoke. Then your lady is well?"

"Though her tongue may be burning from the words she said, she is well and I am forgiven."

"It is as I thought."

Aubin rose to pour himself a beaker of Melonnian sweet and sour, then one for Kolt when he nodded his desire. Eirriel had said Aylyn was healthy but melancholy and refusing to speak of the reasons for her mood. She had asked him to broach the subject with Kolt, but, as Aubin studied the younger man, he saw that Kolt was not much better. Whatever was bothering Aylyn, was obviously bothering Kolt. He handed Kolt the beaker, then lowered himself into the chair across from the Annanite.

"Why do you want membership in the Protectorate?" Aubin asked suddenly. It wasn't the question Eirriel had wanted him to ask, but he thought it would ease the way.

Kolt looked up from his drink. "I have seen my people starving, and I'll not allow it to happen again. Unless we become members, we will never see the profit we truly deserve."

"Is your colony contract with them binding?"

"They claim it is, but if you ask me, the allotted time has run out. It matters not. Were the Protectorate to disassociate themselves from Annan, which they will never do, Annan has not the ships to trade elsewhere."

Aubin looked at Kolt over the brim of his beaker. "Rhianon does."

Kolt shot him a startled look, then seemed to realize what he was revealing, and replied stiffly, "I'd not ask."

"Nothing's changed," Aubin said, shaking his head. "After Kedar left, you wouldn't ask. Why would you ask now?"

"Annan does not take charity."

"Charity? You misunderstand. An alliance is what I'm offering."

"Alliance?" A shutter slammed down on Kolt's eyes. "It can no longer be between Aylyn and me."

Aubin looked stunned. He had thought the problem a mere a lover's quarrel. "For years you have said my daughter would be yours, and you did not want to return her to me. Yet you have and now that she agrees to be yours you turn her away. Why?"

"It cannot be," Kolt said tightly.

"It is my daughter you dismiss so lightly. I—"

Kolt shot to his feet. "Dismiss lightly!" He laughed, a sharp bitter sound, heavy with loss and not a little self-pity. "I could easier dismiss my heart than I can Aylyn."

Aubin watched Kolt's tortured pacing. Something was very wrong, and he had to find out what, because the one certainty in the situation was that Aylyn was the product of two very determined personalities. If she wanted Kolt, she would do anything to get him. He watched Kolt toss down another draught of brew. Kolt would not take Aubin's prying lightly, but it was his duty as Aylyn's father to determine the cause of Kolt's sudden rejection. He cursed. If Eirriel were here, she could get a sense . . . He cursed again. His preoccupation had caused him to forget what Kolt was. He forced unconnected thoughts into his mind.

Kolt winced and grabbed his head. "You needn't, Aubin," he rasped. "I'll not touch you."

Aubin grinned. "Habit. Eirriel would always 'test the wind.'" He frowned. "If you didn't touch, how . . ."

"You're very loud."

"Ah, then that's how Eirriel knew when I was hiding something. I often wondered."

Kolt smiled. "It *is* very obvious."

"I'll remember that." Aubin gestured to Kolt. "Sit down."

At once, Kolt's smile fled. "I'll not talk of Aylyn."

"It is my daughter's welfare I am concerned about."

"Then keep her with you. She will only have unhappiness on Annan, for I will not take her back."

Kolt's closed expression told Aubin he would get no further this day. "As you wish—for now. Now sit and let us discuss the alliance."

Kolt lowered himself into the chair.

"I would never offer Aylyn. She alone can do that. I meant you need no longer rely on the Protectorate or Iilde. I have ships, harvesters, and equipment, more than Rhianon needs. As a member of the Rhianonian Alliance, you would be entitled to all."

"And the cost?"

"You support the harvesters, maintain the equipment, supply the fuel, and give me one percent."

"One percent. And you would have me believe it not charity? The Protectorate would demand ten percent."

"The Protectorate and I do not agree on many things. This is one of them."

Aubin's plan to send more men would add to Annan's already-burgeoning population, but it would also supply jobs for Annan's own harvesters. The change in the profit margin would also benefit Annan's people. That left Iilde, but Kolt knew greed would bring her to his way of thinking. He smiled widely.

"I accept your offer." He reached for the carafe. "Shall we seal it with a toast?"

When Aubin nodded, Kolt poured the golden liquid. The two men, so different yet so alike, raised their beakers.

"To the Alliance," Kolt said, and wished with everything he was and would be that Aylyn was part of the Rhianonian Alliance.

"To the Alliance," Aubin repeated, then qualified silently, *to more than one alliance*.

"How can this help you?" Kolt asked when both had taken long swallows.

"Prosperity is not always without problems. We have striven to see that our offspring have everything they want, including the education and training to be anything they want. But what they need the most, we cannot provide. New fields in which to use their skills. Rhianon and it allies are too well established. By giving work to those Rhianonians who would test their skills elsewhere, you are giving them the chance to do more than follow the well-treaded path. You are giving them the freedom to soar where they will. And once that happens, the gods alone know what they can accomplish."

"You are very wise, Lord Aubin," Kolt said sincerely. "It is little wonder Rhianon prospers."

Aubin laughed. "I know. I am a paragon."

The beaker that was halfway to Kolt's mouth paused. "No," he said quietly. "You are wise. I am the paragon." He forced himself to smile. "As you yourself have said."

"I have said?"

Kolt took a swallow, then set the beaker down. "Aylyn spoke much of what you thought of me. Because of you, she thought me perfect." He paused then added, "A perfect bore."

"And when she found out you were not?"

Kolt's eyes clouded and he turned away. "Then she thought me her love."

Chapter Thirty-Six

The *Ceallach*'s mini-cruiser dropped from the dark purple sky and headed toward Xeril's West Cavern Landing site.

Aubin shot a glance at Kolt, who was in silent communication with their Xerilian contact, Mayryn, the lone survivor of the last Xerilian investigative team. Two days had passed since Kolt's acceptance of Aubin's offer. Two days of planning this mission, of settling the terms for the alliance, of discussion of the weather conditions on both Rhianon and Annan. Of everything, but the one thing uppermost in the minds of both men—Aylyn.

Nothing Aubin had said or done had loosened Kolt's tongue or changed his mind.

During those two days, Kolt had come to believe that his missing shipments of Khrystallyn would be found on Xeril. When Kolt continued to insist, Aubin wondered if the Annanite's belief was founded in his mind-touching skills or the growing coincidences. From Kolt, he had learned that the Xerilian sightings of the streaking lights in their night sky had all occurred on the dates of the Khrystallyn hijackings; that a map of the shipping lanes and knowledge of Annanite vessels made the brief hop to Xeril a possibility; and both had to admit that Xeril's refusal to allow outworlders on their planet made discovery of the hijackers less of a possibility.

And now Kolt was getting what he claimed would be absolute proof.

"It is as I thought. The surviving members of the Xerilian investigative team spoke of a group swathed in blue aboard the ship," Kolt said as he broke contact with Mayryn. "It is the hijackers." Kolt kept a tight lid on his emotions, not wanting to give anything away to Aubin. For Kolt, knowing full well Aubin's reaction, had lied and denied knowledge of the leader's name. Aubin would want Rakkad and that was something Kolt could not allow. Rakkad's presence in Kolt's life had robbed him of Aylyn, and for that, Rakkad would pay. "They also made mention of a non-Xerilian prisoner being held. One of Naydir's investigators disappeared. It may be him."

"Are the Xerilians ready for us?"

"It will only be Mayryn, but, yes, she is ready."

"Then let's get this over with. Eirriel promised to make me work off my apology, and I find myself anxious to do so."

The landing was effortless, the Rhianonian vessel's shielding keeping her hidden from watchful eyes. Armed, Kolt and Aubin carefully exited the ship and waited a moment before they were joined by Mayryn.

Aubin swore as she approached, seeing firsthand the tragic results of the plague. Xerilians were tall, ethereal humanoids whose every movement was fluidly graceful. Their pride was their long flowing white hair, and large, slanted, purple eyes. Mayryn's steps were choppy, her hair was gone, and her eyes were as clear as white crystal.

Mayryn smiled into Aubin's eyes. "We have learned, Lord Director, that the effects are temporary. Already, the two survivors of the first team have regained their grace and their hair is starting to come back."

"And their eyes?"

Mayryn shrugged. "We don't know."

Aubin was relieved that he did not have to act as a medic, but his curiosity compelled him to ask the cause of the plague.

"We overreacted, Lord Director, by naming it such. It seems a reaction to the powder the ships carried."

"Where is the prisoner?" Kolt asked.

She pointed to a tall building cut into the mountainside. "Below ground level there. I have seen no sign this day of any of the intruders."

"How many guards are usually within?" Aubin asked.

"Two hands' worth."

"And the shipment?" This from Kolt.

Mayryn's hand swung to a large opening at the other side of the building. "It is stored within the cavern. You will find one ship within as well. The others have been removed over the last few days."

"Guards?"

"Not many, Lord Director. A hand count, no more."

The trio entered the cavern. Aubin and Kolt quickly dispatched the handful of false Guberians with a few well-aimed blasts from their neutralizers. All too easily the Rhianonian, the Annanite, and the Xerilian stood before the shipment.

"It went too smoothly," Aubin commented as he stepped over the stunned body of one of the impostor Guberian guards.

"Agreed." Kolt cocked his head and *listened*. "But for the three of us and the fallen guards, the area is void of life. I like it not."

"Neither do I," Aubin said grimly. He nodded to the four large white containers emblazoned with a black kilgra that stood before the ship. "The Khrystallyn?"

Kolt nodded. "Yes. Not all of the shipments, but this will satisfy the Protectorate's quota. For now."

"We must hurry if we are to . . ." Aubin fell silent as a batch of the powder vanished. "Gods! But your power has grown!" he exclaimed, looking in astonishment at Kolt.

"Not enough," Kolt said cryptically. "Not nearly enough. Think you the cruiser can hold all of this?" he questioned after he *sent* another batch into the rear of the cruiser.

"If you can fit it in, she can lift it," Aubin replied confidently.

When Kolt had it all loaded, Aubin turned to Mayryn. "I will keep Xerilian airspace patrolled. Not many will risk a confrontation with a fully armed Rhianon warship."

"That is the reason we sought help from the lord director of Rhianon and not the Protectorate," Mayryn explained. "Quayra knew what you would offer. She bade me give you her thanks."

Kolt frowned suddenly. Something had changed. He swung around, his eyes and mind seeking the change.

"What is it?" Aubin asked.

"I know not. Let us go, before we find ourselves trapped within this cavern."

The three ran to the cavern's opening. Kolt motioned them out. "Go and prepare to leave. I will join you shortly."

Aubin, who had known from the start, though Kolt had made no mention of it, that the Annanite leader would not leave without freeing the prisoner, reached out and grabbed Kolt's arm. "I'm going with you."

"And I," Mayryn said. "He was wounded helping me escape from the intruders."

"No. There will likely be trouble. I have not the strength to carry all of us. We would then have to fight and should you, Aubin, take a hit, Eirriel would have my head. No, I go alone. Get the ship off the ground. I will get him aboard."

"I would see him safe," Mayryn pleaded, her colorless eyes anxious. "He means much to me."

When Kolt remained firm in his stance, Mayryn quickly gave him directions to the chamber that housed the prisoner.

Kolt nodded and ran toward the building. Aubin watched a moment, then he and Mayryn headed for the ship.

Kolt slowly pushed open the door and stuck his head in. A quick glance showed the corridor was empty. Stealthily, he moved down the dimly lit passage to the second door from the end. He paused and *reached* out and felt only the pain of the wounded man. Kolt frowned. Why had he been left unguarded? Certain he was walking into a trap, but knowing he had no choice, Kolt slipped down the stairs to the last door.

He pushed it open and came to a shocked halt as the prisoner turned to face him.

"You!"

The prisoner squinted his swollen eyes. "Do I know you?"

Kolt shook his head. "No, but well I know you, Laaryc of Dianthia." Kolt laughed at the irony of rescuing Laaryc. "I am Kolt, laedan of Annan."

"I don't understand."

"There is not the time to explain, Dianthian. Come."

"I cannot. My leg is broken"—he pulled off the thin cloth that covered his legs—"and shackled.

Kolt crossed to Laaryc's side. "You think that is a problem?"

Laaryc looked at the neutralizer. "Oh, of course."

"No. Though the building appears empty, I'll not risk alerting them to our presence. There is another way." He slipped his arms around the slim Dianthian and lifted him into his arms.

Laaryc gritted his teeth in anticipation of the wrenching of his legs by the shackle, and then stared at the ground, stunned, when it did not happen. He frowned, raising his eyes to Kolt. "How did you . . . What the . . ." Laaryc gasped as he caught a glimpse of the *Ceallach* over Kolt's shoulder. It hovered two lengths above them, a short distance away. He blinked. His head twisted around to see the building in which he had been imprisoned. "How? You!"

"Do you think it is your way with words that draws Aylyn to you?" Kolt asked dryly.

Larryc was too stunned by the realization of just who Kolt was to react to his sarcasm. "You are Aylyn's mind-toucher!"

Kolt was too preoccupied with getting them to safety to answer. He had wanted to *actualize* them inside the mini-cruiser, but a brief touch told him it was an impossibility. The Khrystallyn did not leave enough room for Kolt to *actualize* while holding Laaryc. They would have to go separately.

"Do you think you can stand, Dianthian?"

"Yes," Laaryc said bravely.

Kolt set Laaryc on his feet. He prepared to *actualize* him, when a mocking touch reached Kolt.

So, usurper, we meet again.

Kolt's head jerked around. *Show yourself, Rakkad.*

I think not. It is more amusing this way. His words were highlighted by a flash of light that landed between the two men.

Cursing violently, Kolt slipped the gauntlet off his arm and onto Laaryc's.

"You can't!" Laaryc protested.

Kolt activated the shielding. "I am not without resources. Now go. Tell Aubin not to wait. He'll understand."

Painfully, Laaryc started toward the hovering mini-cruiser. The ramp was lowered, and Mayryn stood waiting to help Laaryc aboard. Kolt knew Aubin would be unhappy about not participating in the confrontation with Rakkad. But Kolt was also confident that Aubin would realize that should Kolt and Laaryc be taken, Aubin would be the only one who knew where they were. Should Aubin interfere and find himself captive, they would all be lost.

Another bolt of energy landed in front of Laaryc. It was what Kolt was waiting for. He spun to the left and watched a cloaked Rakkad dart behind a group of boulders. He sent a fiery arc of energy slamming into the rocks and Rakkad's protection was no more.

Did I not warn you, Rakkad, that I would not hold back, Kolt growled as he sent another flaming spear at him.

Rakkad staggered backwards as it impacted on his gauntlet shielding. He whipped up a fireball and hurled it at Kolt, but Kolt was easily able to *actualize* out of the way and lob another one in Rakkad's direction. He glanced over his shoulder and saw that Laaryc was almost to the ramp. A few steps more and. . . .

Kolt cried out as a flaming white light struck the Dianthian's shielding. Weakened from the beatings and unwieldy because of his broken leg, Laaryc fell. Kolt spun on his heels and saw another one heading toward the downed Laaryc. Just in time, Kolt threw a shield of energy around the fallen Dianthian.

So you would protect the little Dianthian even though he would take her from you? Rakkad sneered as he continued the assault on Laaryc. *This honor of yours is a weakness, usurper. It will be the end of you.*

Kolt gnashed his teeth. Until Rakkad tired, he was trapped. He could not release the shielding from around Laaryc long enough to *actualize* him to safety. Neither could he launch anything of significance at Rakkad.

Suddenly, a burst of orange smoke shot from the mini-cruiser and surrounded Rakkad. Kolt knew it was a harmless diversion since the mini-cruiser was weaponless, but it was enough and he would thank Aubin for it when he next saw him. Instantly, Kolt dropped the energy shielding even as he touched Laaryc and ordered him to deactivate the gauntlet. Kolt was pleased to note that Laaryc did so without hesitation. A moment later, he had Laaryc safely aboard the cruiser.

But as fast as it had all happened, it had not been fast enough. The shield Kolt threw around himself formed a breath too late. The white-hot energy of Rakkad's assault struck him full force. Blinding pain swept over him, made worse by Rakkad's gloating laugh. His mind spinning, he lost his concentration and the shield dissolved. Before he could summon it again, he felt a blow to his side. And another. He forced his eyes open and saw the foot of one of Rakkad's men slicing the air to deliver yet another blow to his side. Grunting in pain, he fought against the blackness that threatened to overcome him. When the fourth blow came, Kolt knew he would not be able to fight much longer.

This is how you end it, Rakkad? Sending your men to finish what you started. Fear you I might win if it was just you and me?

As Kolt had hoped, Rakkad did not take kindly to his taunting.

"Hold! He is mine!"

Kolt looked up to see Rakkad approaching, surrounded by ten of his men. Father of Creation, but where had they come from?

Rakkad stopped next to Kolt, an energy dagger poised and ready to deliver the final blow.

"It is over, usurper. I have won," Rakkad snarled. "Admit defeat."

Kolt, however, was not ready to concede. Forcing the pain from his mind, he pictured the one clear spot within the mini-cruiser. That set in his mind, he looked up at Rakkad.

"As you will never have Aylyn, Rakkad, you will never have me," Kolt said with a confident smile, knowing the smile and words would infuriate Rakkad enough to make him blind with rage. Blind enough that he would not see Kolt's hand move and grasp his weapon.

"Damn you!" Rakkad roared, then sent the dagger flying down.

Kolt made his move the moment the dagger shuddered. He rolled, his neutralizer firing as he did. He waited until the blue wave hit Rakkad's chest and then he *actualized*, offering a prayer to the gods that he had the strength to complete the act.

"So you are awake."

"I wish I was not," Kolt groaned, then wished he could withdraw the words when he realized his visitor was Laaryc.

"I imagine not," Laaryc replied. "You don't look much better than I."

Kolt pushed himself into a sitting position, not without pain, but it was not in him to lie around in the presence of the Dianthian.

Golden Conquest

Laaryc slowly got to his feet, careful not to dislodge the temporary binding around his leg. Aubin's medic had wanted to fix it, but Laaryc had refused. He wanted to be alert when he again met the mind-toucher he had heard so much about. He bowed. "Laedan, I am La—"

"Well I know who you are, Dianthian," Kolt snarled. "Leave me."

Laaryc was taken aback by Kolt's hostility. Then he remembered the kiss. "Surely by now you realize she was only trying to deny what was in her heart."

"It matters little what she was trying to do. Aylyn is no longer my concern. She is waiting for you on Rhianon."

"I'm not going to Rhianon."

"Aylyn is there and she needs you. You will go."

"She needs you, mind-toucher. She has always needed you."

"I care not what she needs. She cannot have me."

Laaryc was stunned. "You mean that?"

"Yes."

"Why, damn you! After all she has—"

"I owe you no explanation. Now get out of here!"

Laaryc staggered a step closer to Kolt. "Did you take her?"

"Think you I will answer that?"

"So you did! And now you will leave her!" Laaryc raised his hand to strike Kolt, then realized what he was doing. His hand clenched into a white-knuckled fist, and he jerked it down to his side. "You bastard," he hissed. "You have been with her since she was thirteen. A whisper always there she said. Always. And now you would leave her?" Laaryc stepped away, his expression one of disgust. "You are worse than Rakkad. At least his evil is for all to see and feel, not hidden in a pretty package and gentler touch."

Having said his piece, Laaryc threw one last look at Kolt and slowly made his way to the door. It slid open just as he reached it.

"Laaryc!" Aubin said in surprise. "What are you doing here?"

"I thought to meet the man who would love Aylyn as she deserves." His lip curled in derision. "Instead, I met a conscienceless kriekor in the form of a man."

Aubin turned to Kolt once Laaryc left. "What did you say? I have never witnessed such rage in him."

"I told him he was bound for Rhianon. That Aylyn awaited him there."

Aubin shook his head. "I don't think so." Aubin sat in the chair next to Kolt. "Whatever has gone wrong between you and my daughter, Laaryc is not the solution. He has pledged himself to Mayryn."

"Mayryn? He would take the pale flower? More fool he. Aylyn would . . ."

"Aylyn would consume him," Aubin finished. "And at last Laaryc has seen this."

"You speak nonsense. Aylyn is light. And laughter. And song. She is all in life."

"Then why are you throwing her away?" Aubin asked quietly.

As before, Kolt said nothing.

Aubin sighed. "Laaryc said Rakkad kept him alive to use against Aylyn. Yet he never did. I wonder why?"

"Because I rescued her."

"Perhaps. But maybe it was because he knew enough to know that she was no longer all to Laaryc. Is that what this is all about, Kolt?" Aubin demanded, his eyes dark. "Has he threatened my daughter?"

"No."

"But he will?"

Kolt leaned his head back against the wall. "Gods, Aubin, can you not let it rest?" he asked wearily.

"I could help you fight him."

"There is naught you can do," Kolt replied, unconsciously repeating the words he spoke days earlier to Eirriel. "There is naught anyone can do."

Aubin rose slowly. "I will keep her on Rhianon." He crossed to the door, and as it slid open, he said, "You should have told me you sought Rakkad."

"I'd not have you interfere. He is mine."

"He is still free."

"And so he thinks as well." Kolt smiled, a deadly chilling smile. "But know this, Aubin of Rhianon: I know who he is."

Chapter Thirty-Seven

"Come walk with me," Eirriel said to Aylyn.

"I'm really not up to it, Mother."

"You have not been up to anything since you have returned. You need air. Come, the garden is beautiful this time of day."

"No! Not the garden!" Aylyn cried. Since her return, she had avoided it. It only served as a reminder of Kolt. She laughed bitterly. Not that she needed something to remind her of him. Breathing alone seemed enough to call him to mind.

Eirriel took her daughter's hand and led her to the relaxer. "What is it about the garden, sweet one?"

Aylyn closed her eyes against the pain that threatened to choke her. "He made one for me, Mother. Just for me. He didn't want me to miss the one here. Why? Why did he go to all that trouble just to send me away?"

Eirriel pulled Aylyn into her arms and rocked her much as she had when she was a little girl, one hand rubbing her arm, the other gently stroking her hair. When Aylyn's sobs had calmed to an occasional tear, Eirriel said, "Now, tell me."

And Aylyn did.

"Why didn't you come to me. I could have helped you with your fears?"

"I should have, but I think I was afraid that you would tell me there was nothing to fear. That he was my destiny and I should accept him."

"I would have counseled you to withhold judgement until you met him. Boruk has always been wise, Aylyn, even as a child." Eirriel smiled sadly and shook her head. "I don't think he ever was a child. But, as I was saying, he has always been wise. To give you time to get to know him was showing wisdom not deceit."

"I never thought him deceitful. Not until he told me he had used what he knew of me against me. That I was nothing more than a . . . a . . ."

"Yes, well, I believe I can imagine what he said. When did he say it?"

Aylyn flushed as she remembered. "It was after I tried to seduce him."

"Tried?"

"He refused." Tears threatened to spill over. Aylyn swiped at her eyes.

"He would have had to. I think he loved you, still loves you very much. If he had touched you again, he never would have been able to send you away."

They sat quietly a few moments as Aylyn thought of all that had happened on Annan, all Naydir had said, and all Kolt had said. A sudden fear shot through her and she sat up. The knife! By all the gods! How had she forgotten the knife? And the other attempts.

"I have to go back!"

"What is it?"

"Someone has been trying to life-end him. That's what this is all about. He feared for me." Aylyn got to her feet. "Father didn't expect to be back from the mission for at least an eight-night. If I leave now, I can be on Annan before Kolt returns." Her eyes narrowed with rage. "Who does he think he is, sending me away, to hide like some frightened child?"

"The man who loves you, perhaps?" Eirriel said quietly.

Anger fled. "Yes, the man who loves me. I'm going, Mother. You can't stop me."

Eirriel moved to Aylyn's side and held her hands. Her green eyes glimmered with tears. "The mother in me fears for what will happen when you go and cries out for me to force you to stay. The woman in me rejoices in the love you have found and urges you to go. Both of them shout caution. However," Eirriel added, effectively stopping Aylyn's hurried rush from the chamber, "the consort of the lord director commands that Alaran go with you."

"Alaran? But—"

Eirriel put up her hand. "Or I'll see you confined until your father comes home and we both know he will never permit you to go."

Aylyn knew what her mother said was true and nodded.

"Good. You'll find Alaran waiting for you at the old ship."

"Your mother's ship? The one you were sent from Dianthia in?"

"Yes. I asked your father to have it refitted long ago. He agreed without asking why."

"You knew I would be going?"

"I knew someone would need it. And since you don't want Kolt warned of your presence on Annan, you cannot take the *Marcail*."

Aylyn flung herself into her mother's arms. "I love you!"

"And I love you, my littlest one. Go with care."

"I will, Mother, I will. I have everything to live for."

Two days later, Aubin contacted Eirriel. He told her he was on his way to Hakon to report on the Xerilian mission and deliver Kolt's Khrystallyn, with a brief stopover at Dianthia. After speaking with Laaryc, a joyous Eirriel cut the communication short, claiming a minor emergency involving her estalons and thereby avoiding Aubin's questions about Aylyn. She hoped all would be settled before Aubin returned to Rhianon.

Two days from Rhianon found Aylyn trying to teach Alaran the game of The Warrior and The Lady.

"No," she said impatiently. "You cannot proceed up a level until you have been adequately armed. Gods, but you are as slow-witted as a droga!"

"I may be a droga, but you're nastier than an energy-starved kriekor!" Alaran stared hard at his sister. "Are you nervous about Kolt's reaction?"

"No. Yes, I'm nervous about Kolt's reaction, but no, that's not what's wrong."

"Then what is?"

She shoved herself away from the table. "I don't know. I feel edgy." She stood. "Like something's going to happen. Like . . ."

Suddenly, she gasped and fell forward, grasping the edge of the table.

"Aylyn!" Alaran jumped to his feet and rushed to her side. "Mother of the Universe! What is it?"

Aylyn grunted and felt the breath knocked from her. Struggling for air, she reached for her brother and tried to tell him the attack wasn't meant for her. But before she could, she again felt the pain to her side and what little breath she had gushed out.

Alaran swept her into his arms and carried her to the sleeper. His heart pounding, he lowered his sister to the coverings. Frantically, he loosened the studs at her collar. He watched helplessly as she doubled up, her arms grasping her stomach, looking very much like someone who had been belly-punched.

"What is it? What can I do?" he asked, his voice harsh with concern. He saw her shaking her head. "No? No, what? Aylyn!" he shouted when he saw her suddenly go still. "Aylyn!"

Aylyn sucked in air and opened her eyes to meet her brother's worried gaze. "I'm all right," she said weakly. "Give me a moment."

Alaran suddenly realized he was shaking and sat down heavily next to his sister as she closed her eyes.

Aylyn concentrated on her feelings. She drew in another breath and found it came easy to her. No pain. She opened her eyes. Alaran started to protest when she pushed herself up into a sitting position.

"I'm fine. Really."

"Yes, well, you sure as Nithrach didn't look fine a few moments ago!" he snapped. "What in the name of all the gods happened?"

"Kolt's been hurt." She smiled tremulously. "But he's all right. He's all right," she repeated, needing to hear the words again.

"Kolt?"

"We're linked. I can feel his pain." *And his love*, she added silently.

"You're sure he's okay?"

Aylyn nodded. "This time it wasn't nearly as bad. The first time it happened was when Kolt was almost life-ended from a knife to his back. I became unconscious when he did and stayed that way long enough to frighten Laaryc."

Alaran paled at her words. "What would have happened if he had life-ended?" he asked tightly.

"I would wish I had, also," she said quietly.

And Alaran, although he hadn't meant that, saw the look in her eyes and knew she meant it. He shook his head. "I didn't know this was possible. Mother and Father aren't linked."

"I think they are, though not as strongly as Kolt and me. Remember when Mother saw Kolt. She told me she thought he was his brother, Koltrax, and it triggered memories. She didn't say as much, but I gather they were fond memories, too fond for Father's liking."

"But how did he know? She didn't say . . . Oh. She shared them with him?"

"I believe so."

"And this is why you are returning? Because you need him to live?"

"I don't need him to live, but because of him life is so much more complete. I love him." Tears crept unbiddingly into her eyes. "He's hurt, Alaran. He's hurt."

Alaran took her in his arms. "Sh, little one. You said yourself it wasn't as bad as last time. We'll be in Annan in two days and then you can see for yourself."

Golden Conquest

Aylyn prayed not only that Kolt was all right, but that he would let her stay.

"What do you mean we can't land?" Alaran roared into the communicator.

"I am under orders from the laedan," came the on-duty tech in the Crystal Keeps's communications chamber. "You must leave."

"This is Alaran of Rhianon, heir to the lord directorship, and you dare to turn me away?"

"Yes."

"Why you—"

Aylyn flipped off the com system. "Alaran, please! If you continue shouting, we'll never get permission—"

"Since when does Rhianon ask of Annan? Of anyone?"

"Since it is my life that you'll destroy by getting us escorted out of Annan air space. Do you think I'll ever be able to come back?" When Alaran closed his mouth, Aylyn continued, "I have an idea. Perhaps they'll let me use the T-M unit. At least that way they won't actually be disobeying Kolt."

"And what am I supposed to do? Hang around space, waiting for you to complete your seduction!"

"Alaran!"

Her brother ran his hand through his hair. "Sorry. I don't much like being turned away like an enemy."

"I know. And I'm sorry. I had no idea Kolt left that order."

"So, what are we going to do about it?"

"You're going to try to set down in Chaslydon. I don't think Kolt would have left orders there. He wouldn't want everyone to know his business."

Aláran nodded.

Aylyn hit the switch. "This is Aylyn of Rhianon. I would like to speak to Naydir?"

"Lady? Is that you?"

"Dakkar?"

"Yes."

"Oh, Dakkar, please help me? I've got to come down.

305

I need to see Kolt. Please?"

"Think you they will listen to me?"

"Yes. They will. You are the server to the laedan. You know him as well as Naydir. Please, help me?"

There was silence for a few moments and then Dakkar sighed. "Like as not he will see me in the Judgement Hall for this."

"I give you my pledge. If he tosses you in, I will take you out. Will you do it now?"

"Yes. I must set the coordinates. A moment."

While she waited, she hugged her brother. "Thank you, Alaran. If you hadn't been willing to come with me, Mother would never have let me come. I'll repay you, I swear it."

Alaran put his finger on her lips. "There is no need. Go. See your Kolt."

Aylyn kissed him and then stepped away. "I'll send a conveyor for you."

"Until then?"

"You might want to look up a woman named Chiela. From the sound of her, she's someone you would like."

Alaran was promising her he'd do just that when she dematerialized.

Chapter Thirty-Eight

"Dakkar! What do you in here?" Naydir demanded as he spied the young Annanite at the controls of the T-M unit.

"I . . . I . . ."

"Well?" Naydir demanded.

"He was helping me," Aylyn said, stepping from the materialization platform.

Naydir spun around. "Aylyn!"

"Are you going to arrest me?"

Naydir scowled. "More than likely I'm going to have to protect you. Kolt will . . ."

"Be very pleased when I finish with him," she said confidently. "You have heard from him?"

"Yes."

"He is recovered?"

"Recovered?" Naydir frowned; then his brow cleared as what she said registered. "Again?"

Aylyn nodded. "Two days past."

"It is truly amazing, this bond you have." Naydir thought of the lost Khrystallyn found on Xeril and wondered if she or Kolt realized that they seemed to be linked by more than just minds. It took no fool to see that their destinies were linked as well. If Aylyn had not come to Annan, Kolt would not have returned her to Rhianon, and not have gone with Aubin to Xeril. And the Khrystallyn would have remained lost to Annan forever.

"Kolt told you?" she squeaked, embarrassed. Surely Kolt did not tell him about the touch-sharing!

"That you felt his wounding, yes."

"And that is all that he told you?"

"Is it not enough?"

"Yes. Yes. It most definitely is enough. He is all right?"

"He is a little sore, but otherwise well. He is due to arrive this day, Aylyn."

"Is my father bringing him?"

"No. He uses your father's mini-cruiser."

Aylyn was relieved that she would not have to confront her father, too. "I'd like to be ready for Kolt."

"Of course. Come."

Aylyn turned to thank Dakkar, but he was nowhere to be found.

"He feared I would punish him," Naydir explained.

"But I asked him to help me! You cannot . . ." Aylyn stopped when she saw Naydir smiling. "You weren't going to."

"If you ask me, for once he has acted as he should. Kolt needs you, Aylyn of Rhianon. And I am glad you are here."

Naydir escorted Aylyn to Kolt's chamber.

"As before, Aylyn, Morald will be close at hand."

Aylyn stood on her tiptoes and placed a kiss on Naydir's cheek. "Thank you for being a friend," she said softly.

Naydir, his cheeks red, merely nodded, and watched her close the door. He turned to Morald, who managed to conceal his smirk at Naydir's discomfort. "Do not leave her."

"I will guard her with my life."

"None are permitted within those chambers, Morald." Naydir glanced around the passageway, noting a guard standing at readiness at either end.

"Orym watches the stairway, Gion below the casement," Morald reported. "She is safe."

"Naydir."

Naydir spun to see Cal approaching. "I was passing the landing site. Kolt has arrived."

Naydir watched as Kolt alighted from the *Ceallach*'s mini-cruiser. His movements were stiff and slow, but Naydir was relieved that his injury appeared almost nonexistent.

"How fare you?" he asked, hoping to gauge Kolt's mood.

"I've been better," Kolt growled.

"Eadoine awaits."

"There is no need. Aubin's medic saw to me. I am but stiff. Where's Morald?"

Guarding your Aylyn, Naydir thought, but would not ruin what he hoped would be a surprise. He hedged, "He has completed his shift, but should you need him, I will have him summoned."

Kolt shook his head. "Come."

"Are you going to tell me where we are going at such a fast pace?" Naydir asked as they crossed to one of the rear lower entrances to the keep. "Or am I to guess?"

"My preoccupation with Aylyn has kept me from seeing much. Three times now Rakkad has called me usurper. Usurper of what? Rakkad is Kedar's son. Kedar ruled Annan as laedan. I am laedan. But usurper? Kedar willingly left Annan with Eirriel. How then am I a usurper to Rakkad?" Kolt stopped walking. "Do you not see, Naydir? It is not the Khrystallyn Rakkad sought, but Annan itself. His birthright. The profits from the stolen cargo would aid him in his plan for the future, even as it ruined mine."

Kolt continued to walk. " 'Fool you think you touch all of me,' he said. I knew not then what he meant and now I do. He is shielded, blocked to me."

"Blocked to . . ." Naydir halted, his face white. "I am blocked to you." He wondered if now was the time to make mention of the councilors' grumblings because of his own block. When he heard Kolt's firm reply, he decided to wait. It was obvious to Naydir that his friend had enough to contend with. He would handle the councilors himself.

"And so you are, but never did I believe it was you."

"Then who?"

Kolt grabbed Naydir as he walked passed the doorway to the third stairway. "This way. Think a moment, who was unaccounted for when I was attacked? When Aylyn was captured? When the Khrystallyn was hijacked? Who was within the garden when Mikki became distressed? And who was born but months after Kedar left Annan?"

Naydir was stunned. "Surely you cannot mean . . . But he is ever a fool."

"Do you not think it is clever to hide brilliance with ineptness?"

"Gods, but I should have seen this!"

"There is a reason for that as well. I will explain another time. We are here."

"You think him within?"

"I know not, but Sameria will know of her son."

"You are certain, Kolt, of your conclusions, and not just desperate to see Aylyn free to come to you?" Naydir asked, thanking the gods that he had left her well guarded and that Kolt still had no idea she was so close at hand.

"It has been a niggling doubt in the back of my mind, that I was missing something. And well did I know I would have to present proof before the councilors. Real proof. Not what I have touched."

"But you said he was shielded?"

"And he is, but I have had a sense each time he attacked that it was someone close." Kolt laughed bitterly. "But I'd not thought him quite so close."

"And you have proof?"

"Yes. On Xeril, I heard him speak, and it was a voice I knew well." Kolt pounded on the door. "Should I not know the voice of my server? Should I not know Dakkar?"

Golden Conquest

* * *

Dakkar raised his hand to call to Kolt as he and Naydir crossed to the stairway, then dropped it. Something was wrong. Kolt was much too controlled, too tightly coiled. He pulled back into the shadows of the adjoining passageway and waited to see what Kolt would do. He took a few deep breaths. Perhaps he was overreacting. Perhaps it was the run-in with Kolt on Xeril, the one place he'd never thought to see him, that caused him concern?

But when Kolt turned into the passageway that led only to the chambers he shared with his mother, Dakkar was forced to admit that Kolt knew. How? How had Kolt learned it was him?

He shook himself. Now was not the time for questions; now was the time for action.

He turned and walked calmly and easily through the passageways and stairways of the Crystal Keep. It was obvious from the absence of a guarded escort that Kolt had said naught to anyone but Naydir. Why, he wondered, had he kept it a secret? Dakkar smiled as the answer came to him. Kolt feared his mind-touching skills! Feared that he would touch the minds of Kolt's escort and therefore be warned. He laughed at the irony of it. It was Kolt's actions that alerted him and told him Kolt knew who he was. He would have to remember to tell him so, right before he life-ended him.

Yes, he thought, suddenly pleased by the turn of events. That Kolt knew added challenge and satisfaction, even more than watching him pace and worry about the missing shipments. Dakkar exited the keep through the side entrance and crossed the courtyard. Years of hiding, of pretending, of playing the fool were almost over.

His birthright would soon be his!

He had been six when he realized that he was smarter, more coordinated than others his age. His dam, in a rare moment of lucidity, had reluctantly explained that his father was a Blagdenian, and their rate of developing was faster. Though physically he was six, mentally he was twelve. At first he thought to boast and brag of this, but when Sameria told him his sire's name, he knew he could not. Kedar-Lamd's ways were remembered by all, and hated. As he continued to grow, he soon learned that his odd heritage gave him an advantage. He was treated as he looked, and that except for his coloring, he did not resemble his notorious sire helped as well.

When he was ten, he decided that he would one day reclaim all that his sire had lost. His dam was the daughter of the old laedan, Tiala, and deserved to rule in his place. That she and his sire had been the ones to life-end Tiala mattered little. The blood that flowed in his veins gave him the right to rule Annan. Nothing would stop him. Except lack of funds.

That lack was easily seen to when he formed a band of thieves. Knowing they would never accept him as he was, he called himself Rakkad and swathed himself in blue, impersonating a Guberian. Promises of riches drew many men, but only the best were allowed to join. Any challengers to his leadership, and there had been many, had been quickly laid to rest by a few demonstrations of his skill with weapons—a skill he believed he'd inherited from his diabolical sire.

He moved his band to a remote and abandoned keep, carved into the highest peaks of Quixtallyn Heights, a keep that could be reached by one and only one treacherously winding and very visible route. Dakkar knew he need never fear a sneak attack as long as his guards were vigilant. And all were, for any who were not faced a most gruesome death. As for the usurper, Dakkar knew his precious honor would keep him from *taking* the location of their keep and he took perverse delight in the knowledge that Kolt and his guards, who searched diligently for Rakkad and his marauding band of thieves, could view them every day from the terraces of the Crystal Keep.

By the time Dakkar was twelve, he had enough wealth to seek out the woman who was ultimately responsible for robbing him of his heritage and his dam of her sanity. Sameria had greatly loved Kedar and to learn

Golden Conquest

that he loved another was more than she could handle. Dakkar's quest for vengeance led him to the second most important discovery of his life. Balthasar. And Tri-III.

He left Annan without a word. His mother was too lost within her madness to notice, and his small band had served its purpose. By leaving them uncontrolled, he was certain their recklessness and greed would soon see them all captured and destroyed. And he cared not at all.

He remained on Tri-III for one year. Armed with powers beyond any he thought possible, Dakkar started over, setting up a base on a once-thriving, now desolate planetoid a day's journey from Annan and on the edge of the shipping lanes. Scanning the minds of the captains, Dakkar learned which shipments were lucrative and which were not and which ships held passengers who would bring a high ransom.

In keeping with his planned future, he returned home often, assuming the role of the youthful and often inept Dakkar. At age sixteen, a summons came from the Crystal Keep. When he looked to his dam for answers, she had shrugged and mumbled that the laedan knew she was Tiala's daughter and had taken an interest in her son. It was then that he learned he owed his very existence to Kolt.

To honor the fallen Tiala, Kolt had seen to it that Sameria was well cared for. Dakkar had assumed their funds had come from Tiala, but Sameria had ranted that Kedar had stolen them along with her heart. Kolt's generosity added to Dakkar's hatred of the usurper. After all, he thought, Kolt was only giving them part of what should have been his by birth.

So he and Sameria had moved into the Crystal Keep, and Dakkar, his shields well in place in the presence of a mind-toucher more powerful than he, became Kolt's personal server.

And soon, he would become Kolt's life-ender and Annan's new laedan.

"Look you where you are going!" Gion barked.

Dakkar looked up startled. He had been so lost within his thoughts that he had not noticed the guard in front of him. "Your pardon, I did not see you." He looked around and saw another of Naydir's elite force standing at ready beneath Kolt's casement. "What do you here? Has something happened?"

"I have orders to guard and guard I do. I have no orders to explain myself to anyone. Now get you gone."

Dakkar no longer needed the answer, he had *taken* it. And he, who thought the gods had forsaken him when he could not reach his men in time to intercept Kolt and Aylyn's ship when they had departed Annan, smiled at the further proof that Kolt feared him. Five guards had been assigned to Aylyn. Five! He bowed to Gion and hurried on his way.

A few moments later, Dakkar pushed open the door to Iilde's sleeping chamber.

"Day's passing to you, my beauty."

Iilde, sitting at the dressing table, spun around. "Da . . . My love," she corrected instantly. "You are returned. I had not expected you so soon."

"Have you not learned by now that I am the unexpected?"

Iilde laughed nervously. "It is as you say."

"Yes," Dakkar declared intensely, "yes, it is as I say. And soon all will be as it should."

"What mean you?"

"Our quest's end is upon us."

"I've been thinking . . ."

"Do not," Dakkar growled. "Do you think I have come this far to lose it to your thoughts?" He crossed to her like a myorg stalking its prey. He stopped before her, his finger reaching out, tracing the side of her face. "Do you?" he asked silkily. When she did not answer fast enough, his hand snaked to the back of her neck and he squeezed. "Do you?"

Iilde winced. "N–no. Please. You're hurting me."

Dakkar's thin lips pulled back in a feral grin, and his black eyes gleamed. "Yes, I know. It would be my pleasure should you want more."

She shook her head.

"A pity." He released his hand with a force that jerked her head back. "So be it." He started for the relaxer. "Come, we've plans to make."

Her hand rubbing the back of her neck, Iilde slowly followed Dakkar.

Naydir took a deep breath and hoped Aylyn would forgive him, but Dakkar was not within his chambers and he must alert Kolt of the danger to Aylyn.

"Kolt?"

Kolt's blue eyes swung from the compartment he was searching. "Did you find something?" They were looking through Dakkar's belongings for a clue to Rakkad's hideaway.

"No. But you must listen."

Kolt slammed the drawer shut and opened the next one. "I'm listening."

"Aylyn is here."

Kolt froze. He couldn't have heard right.

"On Annan."

Kolt straightened.

"In your cleansing chamber."

He turned to Naydir.

"Dakkar knows."

Kolt vanished.

Chapter Thirty-Nine

Kolt reappeared in his chambers. A quick touch and he knew the placement of all the guards. He crossed to the table and poured himself a beaker of sylva which he quickly tossed down.

Aylyn was here.

A knock on his door was followed by Morald's bid for entrance.

"What is it?" Kolt barked.

Morald pushed the door open to reveal Iilde. Kolt saw at once that she had come with seduction in her mind. He was about to send her away when he realized she would be the key to driving Aylyn away for good.

Kolt motioned Iilde inside.

She glided in and stopped before Kolt. He tightened his shieldings against her lust and waited.

She ran her hands up his chest.

He waited.

She encircled his neck, her fingers threading through his hair.

He waited still.

She lowered her head and kissed him.

He heard the door to the cleansing chamber open. And he waited no more.

His hands shot out and drew Iilde closer, his mouth grinding against her.

"You bastard!"

Golden Conquest

Startled, Iilde tried to push herself away from Kolt, but he would not let her. Instead, he opened his eyes and met Aylyn's condemning glare. His eyes stayed locked with hers, and his lips locked with Iilde's until he thought Aylyn had seen enough. Only then did he raise his head.

"What do you here?" Kolt asked Aylyn as calmly and with as little interest as he would inquire of a casual acquaintance.

She just stared at him, unable to speak. In all her imagined reunions with Kolt, she had not thought to walk in on him kissing another woman.

Kolt used the time to turn Iilde so that she stood at his side, still within his embrace. Iilde for once did the expected and leaned her head against his.

Aylyn found her tongue. "I thought you were wounded."

His eyes, warm and inviting, touched Iilde. "Think you I am wounded?"

Iilde's eyes burned into Kolt's and she smiled, a small secret smile. "I think you wonderfully fit."

"I see I was mistaken." Aylyn looked at Iilde and shook her head. "I thought your taste more discriminating. I was mistaken in that as well."

Kolt's arms tightened on Iilde's waist, warning her to remain silent.

"Go home, Aylyn. Your Laaryc awaits you," he lied. He knew Laaryc and his Mayryn were on their way to a life of happiness on Dianthia, but he hoped his news would divert Aylyn.

"Laaryc!" Aylyn gasped. "Oh, Kolt! Is it true?"

Kolt nodded. Tears sprang to Aylyn's eyes. Laaryc was alive! She hadn't caused him to be life-ended. "How?"

Although Kolt had mentioned Laaryc for just such a reaction, watching it sent his belly roiling. He scowled. "He seems to believe Rakkad meant to save him for bargaining."

"Is he well?"

"No, he is greviously wounded." Her whitening face was more than Kolt could stand. "He will be well,

Aylyn, fear not. He but needs you to care for him."

"My mother will see to him. My place is here." She paused and her unrelenting stare met his. "With you."

"No, it is not. Now, get you from my chambers, my world, and my life." Deliberately, Kolt ran his hand down the side of Iilde's full breast, cupped it a moment, then continued to move his hand across her chest to her shirt's veed neckline. His eyes never leaving Aylyn's, he slipped his hand inside Iilde's shirt and cupped her breast, his thumb absently caressing her nipple. "As you can see, I have much that I must do."

Aylyn hurled an epithet at him, then spun on her heels. She yanked open the door just as Naydir, who had run all the way from Dakkar's chambers, reached it. She shoved passed him. Kolt waited until she was down the passageway before disentangling himself from Iilde.

"Go after her," Kolt ordered Naydir.

"Morald is with her."

"I would have you see to her."

"Will you tell her?" Naydir demanded. "Or will you let her leave?"

"Tell her what?"

Naydir looked at Iilde as if seeing her for the first time, then continued to address Kolt. "If you think this will work, think again, my friend. She is no fool to think you would take this one over her."

"She does not think, Naydir. She was told."

"Told what?"

"Iilde, go. Now. When I want you, I will send for you. Do not come unbidden again."

Iilde's hand came up to strike Kolt, but she found her wrist locked in Kolt's firm grasp. "Do not." He shoved her into Naydir's waiting arms. "I but used you as you would use me, Iilde. Now get you from my sight."

Wisely, she did. Naydir started to follow.

"Naydir?"

He turned, and the naked pain on his friend's face tore at him.

"See her safe."

Golden Conquest

"With my life."

Kolt moved to the casement and caught Aylyn's flight across the courtyard. His fears for her safety lessened when he saw Gion follow her. And then Morald. And at last Naydir. He was turning from the sight of her when the Rainbow Lights began.

In his mind's eye, he saw her as she had been a few days past when from this very casement he had watched her experience the Lights for the first time. Her eyes aglow with pleasure, her lips curled in a bright smile. And then he saw her moments later void of all joy.

He could not bear the memory or the Lights.

From the depths of his soul, he roared his pain and threw his hands out and up toward the dome. Jagged bolts of black light flew from his palms and impacted against the dome. Again and again. At each strike, the dome darkened, and the darkness spread until the dome above the keep was as black as the despair within Kolt.

Until the Lights dimmed and then were no more.

"Aylyn! A moment please!" Naydir's hand shot out and he pulled her to a halt. "Do not cry, little one."

"Cry!" Aylyn spun on her heels. "Cry!" she spat, her eyes ablaze. "I don't want to cry. I want to scream! I want to tear her heart out of her overdeveloped chest and feed it to him until he chokes on it!"

Naydir began to laugh. Never had he expected such fury. Gods! But she was unlike anyone he had ever known. A fit mate for a kilgra. He sobered. A kilgra who believed he could not have her.

Her fist struck Naydir in the chest. "Laugh will you!" She drew back her hand to strike him again, but she froze in mid-motion as the Rainbow Lights began.

And ceased.

She flung her raised hand at the dome. "And he wants me to believe he doesn't love me! By all that is holy, how can someone so brilliant be such a fool?"

"Love, Aylyn," Naydir said quietly. "Love makes you vulnerable as you have never been before."

Naydir's words sliced through Aylyn's rage. "Will you tell me what he fears?"

The tall councilor thought a moment, then nodded. "Yes. Come. What say you to a ride?"

"Seonaid is here?"

"They arrived just after you left." He waved Morald and Gion over to him. "Have the phedras made ready, Gion."

"At once, Councilor."

"You ride? Think you it is safe?" Morald asked.

"I'm going, Morald," Aylyn answered. "Either with Naydir or alone, I am going."

Morald frowned as Aylyn stormed after Gion. A chattering above her brought Aylyn's arms up, and Mikki dropped into them.

"We will stay within the keep's range. Think you I am such a fool that I would risk her? And as you can see the yiichi goes with us." When the captain continued to scowl, Naydir explained Kolt's belief regarding Mikki's unique relationship with Aylyn. "Lay your fears to rest, Morald, I wear the signaler. Should we see trouble, I will call."

"And if you cannot?"

"Then monitor us at all times. Have the tech at the T-M unit stand at ready and return us. And, should the unforseen happen, do not hesitate. Have him take Aylyn first. Does that please you?"

The fierce captain's gaze swung to Aylyn striding determinely across the courtyard. "He'll not be happy."

"As long as she stays on Annan, he'll not be happy. She needs this, Morald."

After a moment Morald nodded his agreement.

"Now, there is one other matter I would have you see to before we leave."

Naydir quickly outlined his wishes and reasons for them. And when he finished, Morald laughed, a true hearty laugh free of most of his worry.

Golden Conquest

* * *

In the lowest level of the Judgement Hall, Dakkar stepped over the guard's body. He peered into the containment chamber. "Luthias, once of Mayrald, are you within?"

"Think you they have let me out?" came the snide reply. "You are ever the fool."

Dakkar stiffened. "This fool warns you to step back."

"Why?"

In answer, Dakkar hurled a fireball at the door, bursting the locking mechanism. His jaw aslack, Luthias stepped from the chamber.

"Dakkar?" Luthias said, stunned. "Does the laedan know . . ."

"No."

"Then why would you help me?" He continued to gape at Dakkar.

"It suits my purpose."

"Suits? How?"

"There is something I would have you do. Something your laedan will not be pleased with."

"Since he is pleased with me not at all, I will help." He paused, then qualified, "If it suits my purpose."

Dakkar's eyes darkened, and he said silkily, "Would your life-ending suit you better?"

Luthias's gaze swung to the young man. "You would life-end me? But you just gave me my freedom!"

"And I can take it away as easily." Dakkar's hand swung to the bodies of the fallen guards, still smoldering from his fireballs. He snickered silently. The old fool could not know the method of their life-ending, but the usurper would. It had been why he had chosen to use his skills to end their lives. He wanted Kolt to know beyond question that it was he who had freed Luthias. And he wanted him to wonder why. His intense gaze moved back to Luthias. "Well, old man? What say you? Do you help me or no?"

Any resistance Luthias may have had to his savior's plans fled at the sight of the three guards. "You did this alone?"

"Fool! See you anyone else?"

"How?"

"If you wish to be caught, then keep asking your foolish questions. I am gone." Dakkar stormed away, certain Luthias would follow.

"I am from this moment on your server," Luthias vowed solemnly.

Dakkar smiled darkly. He knew Luthias for the scheming self-serving slime he was, and knew he could not trust him. But he did not have to. Luthias would do what he requested, he had no choice.

"Then, server mine, here is what I want."

As they walked through the passageway, calmly stepping over the last fallen guard, Dakkar laid out his plan, reenforcing it with a not-too-gentle touch. When Luthias left to do as Dakkar had commanded, Dakkar's smile broadened, and he gave into the intense feeling of triumph that was swelling within him. It was a plan of great cunning, one worthy of the heir to the power and glory of the house Kedaria and the son of the infamous Kedar. Victory was almost at hand.

Kolt cursed. Naught! Once again he was in Dakkar's chambers seeking clues with as much luck as before. That the search was proving futile did not help his mood. Or that Naydir and Aylyn were riding. It mattered not that they were within the grounds of the keep. The dome was a hindrance to T-M beams. Cursing Naydir to the darkest reaches of Nithrach for risking Aylyn's safety, Kolt yanked open another compartment and dumped the contents out on the floor.

Dakkar's dam, Sameria, had been very talkative, but very little of what she had said had made sense. She had rambled on and on about Dakkar's devotion to her long dead sister. Kolt sighed. Why had he expected otherwise. Few within the keep remembered Sameria before the mind-sickness descended. More than likely it was that very sickness that had made the Blagdenian invader so appealing to her.

Golden Conquest

"Laedan!" Cal rushed into the chamber followed by Morald. "Luthias has been freed. Rakkad . . . we think."

"Three guards are dead, a large burn to their chests," Morald reported. "It was not caused by any weapon I have seen."

"But the fourth guard was still alive when we arrived. He said it was Dakkar, but . . ." Cal shook his head, unable to give credence to the wounded man's words.

"Dakkar is Rakkad," Kolt said matter-of-factly.

"Never say it is so! Dakkar! He is but a child!" Cal gasped.

"In appearance and affectation, yes, but Sameria has explained that his life cycle is twice his twenty-two years. And I, arrogant, all-seeing fool that I am, saw only what I, and he, wanted me to see—an overly naive, young man ever anxious to please and a consistently devoted protector to his dam and her sister."

"You knew and informed me not!" Morald blurted out, at last, then blanched. "Laedan! I beg your forgiveness."

Kolt put up his hand. "None needed. You've a right to your anger. I feared Dakkar would touch you and learn that I knew. It appears he is aware."

"How?"

"I know not, Cal. Dakkar has long been able to move about freely. More than likely he saw Naydir and I enter his chambers."

"I sent my men after Luthias, but—"

"Rakkad now Dakkar has long since seen the clues well covered," Kolt finished.

"As you say, Laedan," Morald agreed.

"What do you here?" Cal asked, gesturing to the spilled drawers and scattered papers.

"If you ask me, I am wasting my time, but I seek the location of Dakkar's hideaway."

"May I aid you?"

"And I?"

Kolt nodded his thanks. "Extra eyes would be most welcome."

Chapter Forty

Her back to Naydir, Aylyn sat on a large slab of dull brown crystal that extended over the river that flowed gently through the keep's riding range on its way to the Rainbow Falls. Her eyes closed, she listened to the sound of the water as it lapped against the crystal. Rhythmically, she stroked Mikki's back, taking comfort in her reassuring thrumming.

Kolt had seen her life-ending.

Her heart ached for him, but her mind wanted to rage at him. After all they shared, how dare he keep this from her. Did he think her so weak-willed that she would run from this danger? He wouldn't have. And neither would she.

She set Mikki down and rose. Naydir watched her as she approached, but when she met his questioning gaze with eyes bright with determination, he knew he had been right to speak.

"Thank you for telling me and for giving me the time to decide."

"Do you return to Rhianon?"

"What do you think?"

"You stay and fight."

She nodded. "I stay and fight. And the first one I fight is Kolt."

Naydir shook his head. "No, the first one you fight is me."

Golden Conquest

Aylyn blinked. "But I thought . . ." her voice drifted off as she watched Naydir remove two objects from the bag attached to his phedra's riding hide.

"Here," he said, holding out a gauntlet, "slip this on."

"The wind-blocker!" Aylyn laughed at Naydir's startled expression. "I know it is an energy shield, Naydir, you don't have to look at me as if I changed into a Melrvian gill breather." As she slid her hand into the gauntlet, she explained, "When we were fleeing Rakkad, we were caught in a flashstorm. Once the rain finished, the wind picked up again. Kolt activated the shielding to block the wind." She smiled in remembrance. "Clever man, your laedan." Her smile faded, and the laughter fled her voice. "So clever and yet he would send me away rather then let me fight this with him."

"He has lived by his visions all his life, Aylyn." Naydir's yellow eyes burned into hers. "He cannot help but believe in what he sees."

"My mother sensed no danger. Surely . . ."

"Kolt has said the Lady Eirriel does not see true visions, but strongly senses."

"Yes, and she felt nothing. My mother loves me. Do you think she would have allowed me to come to Annan if she truly believed I would be in danger?"

Naydir sighed. "I know not what to think. And so I would see you protected as long as you are here." He straightened as he finished adjusting the gauntlet. "How does that feel?"

Aylyn wiggled her wrist and her fingers. "A little awkward but otherwise fine."

"Good, now jerk down swiftly, like so." Naydir jerked down on his wrist and the gauntlet activated. "Try it."

Aylyn did, and the energy shielding sprang to life.

"It protects only the front and sides. Your back is still vulnerable, but since you'll not be alone, this will work." He handed her a neutralizer. "You know what this is?"

"Yes, of course. We have them on Rhianon. Along with hot water to wash and sleepers to rest in and . . ."

Naydir would have liked to have grabbed Aylyn and shaken her, but the shielding prevented him and so he had to be content with a fierce scowl and a growl. "Think you this is all for fun?"

Aylyn sobered at once. "I know how serious it is, Naydir. It is my life that I seek to protect. And I do not mean to do so with these." She gestured with the gauntlet and neutralizer. "Without Kolt, my life will never be more than just survival." She nodded. "Yes, I know how to use this. Would you care to see?"

"Yes." He pointed to a large branch that had fallen from one of the tall ioploi trees. "Strike only the middle offshoot near the end."

Naydir watched and was pleased as Aylyn first checked the setting on the weapon and then raised it. He nodded. Her form was perfect. As was her aim, he thought a few breaths later as he knelt and inspected the broken branch. For the next hour, Naydir pointed out targets, and Aylyn struck them rapidly and with as much skill as anyone who had not been formally trained as a warrior.

Aylyn lowered the neutralizer after striking the third crystal outcropping forty hand-spans away. She looked around at Naydir, her voice as smug as her expression. "Well?"

Naydir shrugged. "It will do."

"Will do! I hit it every . . . Oh!" Aylyn giggled. "Was that for the hot water or the sleeper?"

"Both." He stood up. "Kolt will be pleased at your skill."

Aylyn's eyes shadowed. "Enough to let me stay?"

Naydir gestured helplessly. "Perhaps, but do you ask me truly, naught we can do will change his mind."

"If you believe that, why help me?"

"Should you convince him, I would have you well able to defend yourself should the need arise." He fastened the weapon carrier around Aylyn's slender waist and watched the ease in which she holstered the hand weapon.

"Then Kolt must agree!"

Naydir's hands grasped Aylyn's waist and he lifted her onto Seonaid's back. "But he sees the attack that you do

Golden Conquest

not see and fears for your life. Truthfully so, for Rakkad is ever one to attack without warning. It would not . . ."

As he spoke, Naydir had moved toward his phedra, but before he reached it, he found his words cut off by the weight of three men, garbed in blue, tackling him to the ground.

"Now, damn you! Take her now!" Naydir bellowed to the unseen guard monitoring them back at the keep.

Trusting in Morald's man to see Aylyn safe as they had planned, Naydir concentrated on freeing himself. His elbow came up and struck one attacker in the nose, the force driving it up into his brain and he fell over dead. Naydir rolled and kicked out, his foot connecting with the second attackers groin, but not before he felt the attacker's own fist against the side of his face. As his head jerked back, he saw the third attacker enveloped by the neutralizer's blue beam and fall backwards. Naydir's heart lodged in his throat, something was wrong back at the keep and Aylyn was still here!

"Ride, Aylyn!" he roared as he easily tossed what he thought was his last attacker over his shoulder and found his feet.

Aylyn ignored Naydir's order, not wasting time on answering him. She could see what he could not. Rakkad's men were utilizing the T-M beam and appearing at what appeared to be carefully timed increments. She fired two rapid bursts of her neutralizer, and two of the newly arrived men slumped to the ground, unconscious, even before they had a chance to breathe Annan's air.

Naydir twirled to see Aylyn fire once again and heard the grunt from the beam's impact just behind him. He did not spare a glance over his shoulder. Instead, he started toward Aylyn, activating his gauntlet and reaching for his neutralizer as he did.

His hand found nothing.

"Ride, Aylyn!" He yelled again as he heard thudding footsteps behind him and spun around. "Ride!"

"I will not leave you!" came her reply, followed by a quick dispatch of one of the five who now faced Naydir.

Naydir saw one of the attackers raise his weapon and aim it at Aylyn. "No!" he roared, and leapt at him, only to find himself tackled to the ground by two others. As his head struck the ground, he saw a red beam pass over him and heard Aylyn's gasp and the phedra's shrill pained cry.

Aylyn cried out as Seonaid buckled under the impact of the beam and collapsed. She pushed away from the falling phedra and rolled, fearful of the unconscious beast trapping her underneath it. She gnashed her teeth in frustration. Her neutralizer had fallen from her hand and was lost beneath the phedra.

She jumped to her feet with the intention of throwing herself on the men who were pummeling Naydir, but found herself grabbed from behind by a large hand. She twisted her head and saw the evil smirk of her captor, who jerked her wrist upward, deactivating the shielding. A portion of her registered the fact that they were unmasked and the reason for it was filed away for a safer time. Knowing she had to reactivate her gauntlet, she spun, raising her knee. She delighted in the stunned look of the false Guberian as he groaned in pain and grabbed his groin. Free, she flicked her wrist and held the shielding in front of her and started for Naydir once again. She had gone a few steps when she found herself snatched up against a brawny chest. She kicked backwards with her feet and struck only air. Her futile efforts were rewarded by a breath-stealing squeeze to her chest, but it was the sight of Naydir, enveloped by a red beam that left him twitching on the ground and surrounded by ten men, that caused Aylyn's feet to still. She knew only one person had to ability to rescue them now.

She closed her eyes and called to Kolt.

"What think you of this?" Cal asked as he handed Kolt a strange vial.

Kolt took it from him and raised the transluscent container to the light. "A liquid? One of Eadoine's potions for Sameria?"

Golden Conquest

Cal shook his head. "She recognized it naught." He snorted. "Not that that means aught."

Kolt started to twist off the top, then stopped. *Aylyn?* He freed his mind and listened. When he heard nothing else, he refastened the top. "I'll have Eadoine test this later," he said, slipping it into his jerkin pocket and continuing with his search.

"Strip her of the gauntlet and put her down."

Aylyn's eyes shot open to see a portly green-skinned man standing in front of her. She stretched out her arm in an attempt to keep her wrist from the man holding her, but his reach was several hands longer than hers and he easily divested her of the gauntlet. She scanned her surroundings, hoping for a sign of Kolt, and when she saw none, felt her hope of rescue dwindle. She wanted to cry out, to protest the inconsistency of their link, but knew it would do no good. Instead, she focused her attention on the man before her.

"I said, set her down!" he snapped.

Aylyn found herself roughly set on her feet.

"Now go."

"As you wish," came a raspy coarse voice from behind her.

She twisted slightly, and out of the corner of her eye, caught the sparkling dissolution of her captor as the T-M beam took him to his destination.

"Permit me to introduce myself, Aylyn of Rhianon. I am Luthias, Councilor of Mayrald."

Aylyn's eyes flicked to a too-still Naydir, who was now guarded by only two false Guberians. "What did you do to Naydir?" Aylyn demanded.

"You need have no fear, the councilor is but stunned. A necessity I'm afraid. He would not have permitted me to approach you. You may leave," Luthias said to the two false Guberians. "Tell him all has gone as planned."

The smaller of the two shook his head. "Think you we did this for free?"

Luthias pointed to Naydir. "You will find an amulet around his neck. Take it."

"No, you cannot!" Aylyn cried. She rushed to Naydir's side only to be roughly shoved aside.

The smaller man jerked the chain from Naydir, leaving an angry red mark on the side of his neck. He looked over his shoulder at his accomplice. "Now for her."

Before the heavier man could take a step toward her, Luthias held his weapon and fired. The man screamed in pain and then collapsed, dead. The smaller man slowly backed away.

"Go," Luthias ordered. "If you return, you will join your friend."

Naydir's amulet clenched in his fist, the man quickly left.

Luthias dropped the weapon on the ground. He took a step toward Aylyn. She backed away. He slipped a large dagger out from the pocket of his caftan and took another step toward her. Her eyes flew to his discarded weapon.

"You'll not make it in time, Aylyn of Rhianon," Luthias stated as he slowly advanced on her.

She knew fear then, breath-stealing, soul-rending fear. *This is it. This is what Kolt saw*. She shouted in protest. *No, don't take me from him yet*!

Luthias took another step forward. Aylyn turned to run, but stumbled over the life-ended Guberian. Luthias's free hand shot out and caught her. She struggled to free herself, but his grip was firm. Her panicked gaze flew to the hand which held the dagger. The hand that was moving toward her.

Kolt, good-bye!

Chapter Forty-One

Kolt stood upright, the contents of a carrier that he had found near Dakkar's sleeper spilling from his hands. "Aylyn!"

Cal and Morald came rushing in from the chambers they were each searching.

"Laedan! What is it?" Cal asked.

Morald, however, was not captain of Naydir's elite force for naught. He knew that Aylyn was in danger. "The T-M unit!" he said quickly. "The monitor will notify the tech."

Kolt *actualized* to the T-M chamber.

The tech jumped to her feet. "Laedan!"

"Activate Naydir's tracer and bring him here!"

Aylyn closed her eyes and waited for the first thrust of the deadly blade.

It never came.

Instead, she heard a gurgled gasp. Her eyes flew open, and she cried out as Luthias continued to draw the deadly blade across his own neck.

Screaming in horror, Aylyn pushed herself from him. As blood spurted from the gaping wound, Luthias took one more step toward Aylyn then pitched forward, dead.

Kolt's heart thudded violently within his chest as Aylyn's shrill scream filled his head.

"Now!" he shouted at the tech. "Do it now!

Aylyn was still screaming when she and Naydir materialized on the platform.

Kolt swept Aylyn up into his arms. "Sh, softling," he breathed against her hair.

"Kolt! Oh, Kolt!" Aylyn encircled his neck and clung to him. "You heard me! I knew you would. I knew it." Her words came out in shuddering gasps. "It was awful. I thought this was it, what you saw. But then he . . . The dagger . . . Gods! Kolt, he slit his throat! Right in front of me!" Suddenly, she pushed away. "Naydir! I must see . . ."

Aylyn twisted to look down at Naydir's prone form. "Oh, gods, please don't let him be life-ended."

Kolt gently placed Aylyn on her feet, and the two of them knelt beside the fallen councilor. Kolt searched for Naydir's pulse and found it.

"He's only stunned, Aylyn. More than likely he will wake with an ache within his head and a rage within his heart." He turned to the tech who was standing off to the side. "Send for Eadoine."

The tech nodded and moved to the comm board.

At that moment, Morald and Cal rushed in. "The monitor is life-ended," Morald reported, his calm tone belied by the iciness of his gaze.

"Who?"

"Hjklo."

"Mother of the Universe, he was but nineteen." A tic began in Kolt's cheek. "Dakkar?" he asked, though he was in little doubt of the answer.

Cal nodded. "Much the same as the guards found within the Judgement Hall."

"Aylyn!"

Four pair of eyes swung to Naydir. Kolt's hand shot out to press the struggling councilor back to the floor.

"Naydir!" Kolt barked his name, but it did not seem to penetrate the mind of the semiconscious Naydir.

"Run, Aylyn!"

"Naydir, it is all right," Aylyn soothed, stroking his brow. "I'm safe."

Golden Conquest

Naydir's eyes shot open, and he ceased his struggles. "My lady?" he rasped.

"Yes, Naydir. I am here and well thanks to you."

Naydir tried to push himself up.

"Lie still, my friend. Eadoine is on her way."

Naydir's amber eyes darkened. "Kolt, I failed you. I should have—"

"You did not fail," Aylyn cut in. "They used the T-M beam. You fought like a Rhianonian, Naydir, but not even a Rhianonian could have fought against all of them."

"I should have—"

"They just kept coming and coming. For every one you knocked out, two or three more appeared."

"You dispatched a fare share yourself, my lady."

"Dispatched? Dispatched how?" Kolt demanded, his eyes burning into Aylyn's, but it was Naydir who answered.

"Your chosen lady is highly skilled with a neutralizer."

"And what, in the name of all the gods, was she doing with a neutralizer?" Kolt roared.

"Fighting off attackers," Aylyn said, knowing full well that was not what Kolt meant.

"Quite skillfully," Nadir added. "She missed naught whom she aimed for."

"Think you I care that she hit what she aimed at!" Kolt snarled. "I would know what she was doing with it at all!"

"As daughter of the lord director . . ."

"Aylyn, if you push me, you will not like my response."

"It is a long story. Very long."

"I have time."

"Oh, is this Eadoine?" Aylyn asked as the healer entered, grateful for the distraction. She would rather be alone with Kolt when she explained.

"Yes, I am Eadoine, my lady," the healer introduced herself as she moved next to the group. She smiled down on Naydir. "Did you forget to duck, my friend?"

"So it would seem, Healer."

Efficiently, she scanned Naydir with the mediscan, then turned to Kolt. "I would like to see him in my chambers, Laedan."

"Eadoine, I . . ." Naydir began to protest, but Kolt interrupted.

"It is serious?"

"A broken rib, some bruises, a concussion, naught that I cannot repair."

Naydir tried again. "Then why must I . . ."

"Because you need it and unless you are ordered, you'll not come."

"Yes, he will," Aylyn said determinedly.

"I will?"

"He will?" Four voices asked as one.

Aylyn nodded. "He will because I ask him to," she said simply.

Kolt gave a shout of laughter. "If you ask me, she has the way of it, my friend."

Naydir groaned, both at Aylyn's rationale and Kolt's teasing, then nodded begrudgingly. "You do not fight fairly, my lady."

"With stubborn men, I find I do what I must," she replied, and Naydir knew her answer was for Kolt as well as himself.

"May I at least walk?" Naydir asked, not wanting to be carried through the corridors of the keep like a babe.

"No," Kolt answered, and, before Naydir could reply, *actualized* him to Eadoine's chambers. Kolt smiled at the healer. "You will find him awaiting your pleasure, Eadoine. Though he will be less than pleased by the method of transportation. He likes it not when I catch him unaware," he explained. "You are ready for a like trip?"

Eadoine nodded.

"Keep me informed and him rested for the remainder of the night," Kolt ordered. Then the healer was gone, and he turned to Aylyn. "Can you tell us what happened?"

Golden Conquest

"As you surmised, we were attacked. But I believe their purpose was to frighten us. Well, me actually, because the leader ordered the men away once Naydir was down. And when one of the men disobeyed, he shot him. Oh, Kolt, I forgot. Naydir's amulet! He let one of them take it. How will he ever get home?"

"We will worry about the amulet another time, softling. For now I need to know more of the men who attacked you."

Aylyn looked over at Cal. "The leader called himself Councilor of Mayrald, but I thought . . ."

"He was my sire, my lady," Cal said tightly.

"Your father," Aylyn gasped. How was she to tell Cal his sire life-ended himself?

Cal misinterpreted the cause of Aylyn's concern. "I am greatly grieved for the pain he has caused you, my lady. Somehow, I will make up for it." His lips drew back in a fierce snarl. "At the very least, I vow to life-end him for threatening you."

Aylyn was so stunned by the vehemence of Cal's hatred for his father that she blurted out, "But he is already life-ended. And should he not be, you don't have to apologize for what he did."

"Was it Luthias who sliced his throat?" Kolt asked.

Aylyn shuddered and nodded. "He . . . he seemed to be in a trance. As if he had been ordered to do it."

"And perhaps he was. As a diversion," Kolt surmised. He turned to Morald. "See to a tripling of the guard. Though I think Dakkar well and truly gone from the keep, I'll not be caught unprepared again."

Morald nodded and left.

Kolt reached into his jerkin and retrieved the vial Cal had located in Dakkar's chambers. "Take this to Eadoine and ask her of it when she has finished with Naydir."

Call took the vial. "At once, Laedan."

"Now, softling," he said as he scooped her up into his arms and *actualized* them into his sleeping chamber. "You owe me an answer."

He lowered her to her feet. She looked around. "Did

I tell you I am very impressed by your abilities, Kolt? I feel nothing when you take us from there to here. It just—"

"Aylyn," Kolt growled ominously.

Aylyn backed away. "But I don't. How do you . . ."

"You are rambling, Aylyn, and it will not work. I will have my answers."

Aylyn continued to back away, her mind frantically working for a way to explain away the neutralizer incident without increasing Kolt's anger. There was none, so she planted her hands on her hips and glared at him.

"You sent me away because you saw me life-ended. When Naydir learned I wasn't going to leave, he thought I should at least know how to defend myself. I showed him I could."

"How did you . . . Naydir told you why I would have you away from Annan? It was not his place."

"No, it was your place." Aylyn moved close to Kolt. She placed her hands on the sides of his face. "You should have told me, Kolt. I thought you no longer loved me."

"I could sooner stop breathing than stop loving you, Aylyn," Kolt said hoarsely, then pulled her to him as he was at last able to give into the need Naydir's wounding had made impossible. "I'd thought I lost you," he rasped.

"Hold me, Kolt. For now and always."

His mouth swooped down to slant across hers, but he froze a breath above her lips as she begged, "Don't send me away again."

Kolt jerked away. How could he have forgotten?

"Please, Kolt. I cannot bear it."

"Think you it does not tear at me?" he growled, his voice raw with pain and longing. "As I saw your arrival, I now see your life-ending."

"So you send me away?"

"What would you have me do?"

"Fight for me," she said softly. "Don't throw me away."

Golden Conquest

"You will life-end," he said through teeth clenched against the pain. "Naught will change that."

"But there is no longer anything to fear. Naydir said you saw me life-ended with a knife. Luthias had one and used it on himself, not me. The danger is passed."

"No. In my vision Dakkar is present. He was not today. Naught has changed."

"Dakkar? That is twice that you have mentioned Dakkar. I thought it was Rakkad . . ."

"Dakkar is Rakkad."

"Surely not?"

"I find it as unbelievable as you, but it is so." Kolt crossed to the table and splashed some Melonnian sweet and sour into a flagon and drank it. "I always knew it was someone close, but, gods, this close!"

Aylyn moved to his side. When he turned from her, she followed. "You saw that I was coming and that you would meet me. But your illness altered the time of our meeting. Reality was not as you saw it. It was changed. It could change again," she offered hopefully.

Kolt shook his head. "I cannot risk it."

"You have no choice. Each time you send me away, I will come back." She watched him through her tears. "Don't you understand, Kolt. I love you. With all that I am, I love you. Life without you is no life at all. I would rather life-end."

Kolt jerked her to him. "I cannot risk you. I will not!" When she just kept looking at him, her heart ragged and bleeding and there in her eyes for him to see, he ground out, "What would you have of me?"

Aylyn said the words she had used once before. "I ask for a chance, Kolt. A chance to live."

Kolt felt his resolve weakening. Perhaps what she said was true. Perhaps their knowledge of her fate could alter it. His arms tightened around her. But could he bear it if they were wrong? If he gave into her pleas and she was life-ended? No, came the instantaneous answer, he could not. But neither could he continue to fight her. He would let her stay. Let them have one last time with each other and then he would send her home. He took a deep shuddering breath. "Share with me, softling. Make me believe." *If only for tonight*, he added silently. *If only for tonight*.

Chapter Forty-Two

Kolt suddenly came awake a few hours later. Something was wrong. He gently disentangled Aylyn from his arms and slipped from the sleeper.

"Kolt?" Aylyn asked sleepily.

"Sleep, softling. I will return soon."

Quickly, he drew on his leggings and shirt. He reached the door to his sleeping chamber just as Cal pushed it open.

"Tell me," he said as he stepped into the antechamber, pulling the door shut behind him.

Urgently and fiercely, Cal told Kolt his councilors had arrested Naydir and locked him within the Judgement Hall.

"They took him from Eadoine's chambers," Cal spat. "Two of them followed as we ran from Dakkar's chambers to the communications center to the T-M unit. They overheard the danger Aylyn was placed in because of Luthias. They already knew he was freed by Rakkad, so it followed in their warped minds that Rakkad and Naydir are one."

"Why am I only learning of this now?" Kolt demanded.

"Naydir would have you spend time with Aylyn. Well he knew how you would have reacted to her danger. He hoped the time would see an end to your sending her away. He said the day's beginning would be soon enough to disturb you. He made me swear I would wait," Cal growled. "But now! They have barred me from the hall. I did not leave willingly, and I'll not apologize for any harm I may have caused!"

"And Morald?"

"He lies within Eaodine's chambers, struck in the back by a hidden hand. He was near life-ended! It is what brought me here."

"Gods! But this is madness! Which chamber is Naydir within?"

"The one that held my . . . Luthias." Since learning of Luthias's crimes, Cal had ceased to recognize him as sire.

"I can't imagine Naydir going calmly."

"He did. This has long been coming."

"What?"

"There has been talk of Naydir and that you cannot touch him. It grew worse when you left suddenly for Rhianon. All knew you were sending Aylyn away."

"Dakkar told them?"

"So I believe."

"I knew not of Naydir's troubles."

"Naydir thought he could see to it himself," Cal offered.

"Is he well?"

"Eaodine says she was finished with him when they arrived, but"—Cal splayed his hands—"I know not."

"Then we shall learn," Kolt ground out.

And then he was gone. To return a moment later with Naydir.

"Do not!" Kolt growled when Naydir began to protest. "I care not at all what my *trusted* councilors would say. I am laedan! I will not have you so treated!"

Cal smiled at his friend. "You are well?"

Naydir nodded, then scowled at Kolt. "At least I have not lost my mind. You cannot just set me free. There are laws—"

"The laws are mine to make and mine to break."

"Laws you have striven hard to see followed," Naydir continued. "Should you cast them aside, you will be little better than Kedar."

Golden Conquest

"Laedan, he meant it not!" Cal defended Naydir quickly.

"You think I did not?" Naydir said.

Kolt sliced the air with his hand. "If I must be as Kedar to see you free, then so be it!"

"I would be free because I am innocent, not because I hide behind my friendship with the laedan!"

"You do not hide, Naydir. Never have you hidden."

"Then who am I?"

"My friend."

"That is no longer enough of an answer. They say I am Rakkad. That I have used my skills to manipulate you."

Kolt's eyes widened. "They think me so weak—"

"They know naught but what they hear," Cal cut in.

"They hear? And who claims that I am weak?"

Cal and Naydir exchanged glances. "Dakkar."

"Summon the councilors, Cal," Kolt ordered.

"Hold." Naydir turned to Kolt. "You cannot speak of what you touch, and well your councilors know it. So why do they force you to take from me what I cannot give? Even if I was Rakkad, it would be meaningless. Why all of this?"

Kolt's head swung up. "A diversion."

The next moment he was in his sleeping chamber, bending over Aylyn.

"Softling?" he called gently.

Aylyn's eyes fluttered open. One look at Kolt's worried countenance and she was awake. "Rakkad?"

"So it seems." He handed her an outfit. "You must clothe yourself quickly."

As Aylyn dressed, Kolt explained all that had happened. When they entered the antechamber together, she released Kolt's hand and crossed to Naydir.

"I'm sorry Rakkad's hatred for us has led to this."

"You need not apologize for what is not your fault. Dakkar is mad. None can be blamed for that." Naydir looked to Kolt. "It will not be long before they realize I am gone and only a little longer before they realize how. Will you probe me now?"

Kolt nodded grimly. "It seems I no longer have a choice." He pointed to a chair. "If you would, Naydir? And, Cal, see to the guards. We are not to be disturbed, by anyone, for any reason."

As Naydir dragged the large chair into the center of the chamber, and Cal relayed Kolt's orders to Morald's second-in-command, Kolt drew Aylyn aside.

"It was my plan to send you home . . . Sh . . ." He placed his finger on Aylyn's lips. "For good or evil, it is no longer an option. I would have your promise that you will obey me in all I ask. That you will go nowhere unless I tell you you may. Please do not fight me on this, Aylyn. I cannot do what I must if I am worried about you. Now, do I have your word?"

"I am not a silly child, Kolt. All I have ever wanted was the whole truth. If you ask me to stay within these chambers, I will. But you must explain what you are doing and why. If you do not, I will not promise."

"Then I will hold you under guard," Kolt growled.

"You may try, Kolt. But I will have my questions answered, and if not from you, then I will seek the answers on my own."

"So be it. I will tell you what I can."

And what you don't, I will find on my own, Aylyn vowed silently.

"Naydir, you are ready?"

"Yes."

Kolt looked to Cal and the Mayraldan seemed to understand, for he moved to Aylyn's side. Kolt then stood in front of Naydir. He locked eyes with his friend and *reached* out.

Naydir's teeth clamped together at the first onslaught of Kolt's touch. As the pressure of the probe increased from a gentle nudge to a constant battering, his fingers dug into the hide-bound arms of the chair until his knuckles were white. Suddenly the pressure gave way to a sharp pain and the pain to a blinding white light that seemed to leap from Kolt's eyes into his. Sweat beaded on Naydir's brow as he fought against crying out, against begging Kolt to stop. A stinging began

Golden Conquest

behind his eyes, rapidly spreading until it encompassed his whole head. A groan tore from his throat when the stinging instantly changed, replaced by a searing point of fire that shot straight to the center of his being and exploded.

And then there was only darkness.

The first barrier fell quickly with a little added pressure. Kolt found the second barrier not so easy to penetrate. Knowing that his friend needed his identity back, Kolt kept deepening the probe as layer after layer of the second barrier fell until the last of it vanished. Fragmented slivers of emotions, sensations, and memories leapt from Naydir's mind into Kolt's.

Kolt gently pulled out of Naydir's mind, his own mind reeling from all he had learned. Aylyn reached for him as he stumbled.

"Kolt!"

"I am fine, softling. Just a little drained. Cal, place him on the relaxer."

"Is it done?" Cal asked as he gently lifted Naydir's limp form.

"Yes."

Aylyn had watched with not a little apprehension as Naydir, robbed of all color, was slumped in his chair, and Kolt, his eyes blazing, stood unmoving and rigid. She gave Kolt a quick once over. "You are sure you are all right?"

Kolt nodded. "A drink would help. And one for Naydir."

Aylyn's gaze flew to Naydir. "You are awake?"

"Am I?" he asked weakly. "Gods, but I'm not sure."

"Do not try to sit up just yet," Kolt instructed. "Give yourself a moment or two to get back your strength."

Both men quickly drained the Melonnian sweet and sour that Aylyn had handed them.

"It did not work, Kolt," Naydir said after a moment. "I am no closer to knowing who I was than before."

Kolt shook his head. "It worked, Naydir. You'll remember it all when you're ready."

"You think that is an answer?"

"It is the only answer I can give you. I have released the barrier. Your memory will slowly return. To do more than that will damage you forever."

"I like it not," Naydir growled.

"I would imagine not. I can tell you only that Dakkar is the one responsible for your barrier."

"Dakkar? But how?"

"In time, Naydir, in time. For now, rest and recoup your..." Kolt's voice trailed off. Naydir was already asleep.

"Think you this weakness will last long, Laedan? He will not like it."

"Only a few hours at most, Cal," Kolt replied. "But enough for us to make plans." Kolt motioned to the table at the other side of the chamber. Briefly, he explained that during a trip back to his home planet, Naydir's ship was hijacked by Dakkar. The two men fought and Naydir saw Dakkar's face during their confrontation. As a result, Dakkar double-shielded Naydir's mind, and held him for ransom. But Naydir's brother refused to pay it as he wanted Naydir's position and wife. Dakkar held Naydir for a month, with the intention of killing him, but Naydir thwarted the attempt and escaped. Kolt found him shortly after.

"Then you are no closer to finding Rakkad, I mean Dakkar, than you were?" Aylyn asked.

"No, however, in passing through Naydir's memories to get to the second barrier, I found the memory of our raid against the hijackers."

"The ones in Quixtallyn Heights?" Cal asked.

"Yes. Did not Sameria say her sister resided within Klopireria?" Cal nodded. "It is my guess that it lies within the same T-M zone as the thieves' hideaway. And that, Aylyn, is above the hole in the cavern where I found you."

"The one with the falls?"

"Yes. Which is why Dakkar chose it." Kolt moved to the door and opened it. He spoke to Gion, then returned. "We will know shortly."

"And if it proves so?"

"Then I will go there."

"I cannot let you, Laedan!" Cal protested. "Dakkar could be there."

"True, but there is a way I can go so none can see me."

"You can part from your body?" Aylyn asked.

"Yes."

"And Rak . . . Dakkar cannot?"

"I think not. Else he would have done it ere now."

There was a knock on the door followed by Gion's request to enter.

"Come," Kolt called out.

"It is as you said, Laedan. The records show many such T-Ms in the past month."

"Thank you, Gion." Kolt waited until Gion left. "It will take but a moment."

"If he is there, what will you do?" asked Cal.

"I can do nothing but locate him."

"Do you have the strength? Mother said it takes much energy to do it and after what you have just gone through with Naydir, are you sure you can do it?"

"I have enough, softling. I will *actualize* to the cavern of the falls and then part. The distance will not be so great."

"Naydir will have my head when he learns of this," Cal growled.

"And mine." Kolt kissed Aylyn. "You will remember your promise?"

Aylyn nodded. "You will be careful?"

"Always."

"Then kiss me once more before you go," Aylyn said, as her arms encircled his neck.

"Willingly," Kolt murmured.

He pressed his mouth to hers in a powerful, absorbing kiss. Aylyn leaned into him, tightening her grip on him. She thought she heard him chuckle an instant before she was left holding air. Her eyes shot open. "Curse him, I was supposed to go with him!"

"More than likely he knew what you were about." Cal chuckled. Then the humor left him as his gaze swung to the chronokeeper. "How long is a moment to a mind-toucher?"

Kolt looked down on his body lying on the cold ground of the cavern, ironically in the exact same spot that he had first found Aylyn. Next to the words "SHE IS MINE!" he had carved into the hard crystal ground. He spared a moment to study his handiwork and noticed that Dakkar had obviously tried to obliterate it. And had failed. As he would continue to fail if he had aught to do with it, Kolt vowed. He turned and concentrated on ascending toward the hole in the ceiling. In the space of a heartbeat he was out of the hole and staring triumphantly at the ruins.

Anxiously, he pressed on. Floating in through a shattered window, he entered the hideaway and found it deserted. As it had been for quite some time, he realized as he studied the dust that had settled everywhere. Could he have been wrong?

No, he thought as he moved easily from one chamber to another, one level to another, until he entered a chamber on the top level. It had been carved well into the crystal wall, with only a small door. And it was clean.

And cluttered with clothing, blue Guberian clothing.

And it had a T-M unit.

Chapter Forty-Three

"Was that fast enough?" Kolt asked.

Cal and Aylyn both jumped and whirled.

Aylyn threw herself into Kolt's arms and kissed him. Then she punched him in the chest.

"What was that for?"

"You were supposed to take me with you!"

"That was your plan, not mine."

"And your plan, Laedan? Was it successful?"

"Yes."

"Father of Creation! At last. Was he there?"

"Unfortunately, no. But he will know I was."

"How?" Aylyn asked.

Kolt smiled in anticipation. "I left him a message."

Dakkar stepped out of the T-M unit and crossed to the small table that held the few items that had special meaning to him. A holograph of his dam, in a period of lucidity, smiling and laughing at him when he was but a child; a sack of Drimian currency he had received from his first life-ending; and a tattered and worn jumpsuit and silver cape that had once belonged to his sire. He had much to do and when he had finished, the large chambers on the top level of the Crystal Keep would be the new home for his mementos. Quickly, he tossed them into the carrier. He was about to turn away when the flame light he carried reflected strangely on the wall behind his sleeper.

Patricia Roenbeck

He raised it and shrieked.

"TO THE VICTOR GOES ALL."

He stared at the rear wall of the one place he thought safe and felt rage burn within him. How dare the usurper contaminate his refuge? How dare he!

He hurled a flaming ball of energy at the words, and his rage deepened to a blinding mist when it merely impacted and fizzled out, changing nothing.

"TO THE VICTOR GOES ALL."

Curse him! "All?" What meant he by that? Annan? Aylyn? All?

Another ball of flames spewed from his hand to the wall with even less effect. He drew his shaking hands together and clasped them tightly. He had to get himself under control. He had to.

He paced the chamber. What did it mean? What?

He was still pacing, still wondering a few hours later when the T-M unit suddenly activated. He jumped and spun on his heels in time to see a message materialize. He waited for more. A person. Something. And when nothing or no one else appeared, he ran to the unit and snatched up the communication.

It was from the usurper!

Dakkar also known as Rakkad:

I, Kolt, Laedan of Annan, do hereby offer you a final chance to have once and for all time, all that you would have.

Come to the Crystal Keep when the sun reaches its zenith. One on one, before my councilors, we will fight. In fairness to you, I offer blades as our weapons. The choice of which kind falls to you.

My honor will hold you safe from all but me during and after our meeting.

Send your answer as I sent the challenge.

Kolt, once and always, Laedan of Annan.

A challenge! With blades! Dakkar began to smile. At last, all would be his!

Golden Conquest

* * *

Aylyn's hand slowly traveled from Kolt's lightly haired chest passed his belly to his velvety hard length.

"Share with me, Kolt," she murmured huskily. "Let me feel your life."

Kolt rolled her onto her back. "Ere I do, I will have your word. You will stay within my these chambers during the challenge."

Aylyn's head rolled from side to side. "Do not ask of me what I cannot give."

Kolt drew her hands over her head. He stared down at her, his eyes demanding, intense. "I must focus all I am on this fight, Aylyn. Should I have to worry about your safety, I will be unable to concentrate."

Aylyn looked up into Kolt's beloved face and shuddered. By all the gods, she feared what was about to take place. Feared that Dakkar would prove as dishonorable as ever. "How can I stand and watch, Kolt? Dakkar has no honor, he will—"

"Think you I am such a fool as to not question Dakkar's honor?"

"No, I think you such a man of honor that you will fall victim to treachery."

"I have taken measures against such treachery, softling. Think you, when all I hold dear lies at stake, I will leave aught to chance?"

Silence lay as heavy within the chamber as the feeling of doom within Aylyn's heart. After a few moments, she broke it. "Will you still send me away?"

"I know not," Kolt admitted. "For now, naught has changed. Once Dakkar is life-ended, the future may once again hold all we want it to. Do I have your word?" he asked again.

"Though I give it with great reluctance, yes, you have my word."

"Then, softling," Kolt said as he moved over her. "Feel my life." He thrust forward, entering her in one sleek motion. "Feel me." He buried himself deep within her. "And know that by all that I am, I will see this done and you safe."

Fed by the fear they both had for each other, their lovemaking took on an urgency and a desperation that neither had felt before and when the sharing at last came, it was total and complete. And it lasted.

Once again, Kolt's touch was where it belonged, within Aylyn's mind.

"Kolt?" Naydir called.

Kolt looked to Aylyn, who placed the brush down on the table. *Softling?* Kolt had a need to feel the gentle familiarity of her mind.

I am ready, she replied, smiling at the strength and the love she felt in his touch.

Hand in hand, they entered the antechamber.

Naydir stepped away from the door. "All is in readiness."

"Has Eadoine arrived?"

"She has sent word. She requires a few minutes more," Cal replied.

Kolt's gaze swung to the casement and the sun creeping toward its zenith. He felt Aylyn's hand tighten within his and knew she was afraid. *Do not be, softling. Naught will happen to keep me from you. Naught.*

The door to the chamber opened, and Eadoine rushed in. She handed Kolt a cruet of liquid. "It is prepared, Laedan. As are the two flagons."

Naydir frowned. He had awakened from his sleep to learn of the plans Kolt had made and naught he had been able to say to his friend had altered them. "How do you know Dakkar will drink from the tainted flagon?"

Kolt raised the one that held the vxanza, the precious and unexpected find that Eadoine had identified. "He will suspect a trap and so there will be one. But it is the flagon with the seal of the House of Keda that will be safe. Dakkar will reach for that one, but he will not drink of it."

"You are sure it will work?" Cal asked from his place by the terrace door.

"Yes, Councilor," Eadoine answered. "The sylva contains enough of that drug to render ten men mind-blind for generations."

"And if he sees through the switch? If he drinks the one meant for you?" Naydir persisted.

Kolt rolled his shoulders. "Then so be it."

"But you will be . . ."

"I will be as any other, Naydir."

"Dakkar will be unstoppable then."

"Dakkar will be life-ended, my friend. And all the mind-touching skills in the universe will not help him."

"He is here," Cal reported.

Aylyn threw herself into Kolt's arms. "Oh, Kolt."

Kolt held her close. He pressed a kiss on the top of her head. "Do you hold to your word?"

She nodded.

"Good." He moved his head away so that he could look down into her face. He tipped her chin up. "Do not waste tears for me, softling."

"I'm so afraid," she said through her tears. "He is without honor."

Naydir drew Aylyn from Kolt's arms. "None but Dakkar will be allowed within the shielding, my lady. It will be safe."

Aylyn pulled away from Naydir and flung herself at Kolt. She kissed him fiercely, desperately. "I love you, Kolt. Come back to me."

"Always."

Aylyn released Kolt who clasped Naydir's arm firmly. "Guard her well."

"With my life," Naydir replied.

Aylyn, stood with her hands clenched at her side, as Kolt, Cal, and Eadoine left the chamber.

"Come, my lady." Naydir extended his arm and guided her to him. He jerked his free wrist activating the gauntlet's energy shielding and kept it raised in front of them. "We will watch from here."

Kolt exited the keep and was at once surrounded by Morald and his guards. Their shieldings activated, silently, they walked to the center of the courtyard and Dakkar.

You fear me so, Dakkar taunted, *that you do not come unshielded.*

Rather say I trust you not, Kolt replied.

But I am here in honor.

Kolt stopped a man's length in front of Dakkar, Cal and Eadoine behind him. Morald and his guards moved to form a circle, their shieldings touching and forming an impenetrable barrier. Kolt took the two flagons and held them side by side.

"A toast, Dakkar known to many as Rakkad . . ." Kolt paused so that his councilors could take note of the full import of his words and what Dakkar would admit to by not refuting his words. When he heard the stunned murmurings of the crowd, he continued, "To victory with honor."

Dakkar looked at the flagons, one emblazoned with Kolt's signature kilgra, the other with the flaming spear of the House of Keda.

"A toast?"

"Yes, to the dark god of Nithrach that all that follows follows with honor."

Dakkar reached for the flagon with his sire's shield. His eyes shot to Aylyn, standing pale and frightened on the upper level terrace. He *reached* out. Poisoned. He jerked his hand away. His eyes flew to Kolt, and he nodded his head ever so slightly in acknowledgment of a feat worthy of himself. And reached for the flagon with the kilgra. He raised it to his lips and waited until Kolt raised his. Together they drained the flagons.

Once they lowered the flagons and tossed them aside, Aylyn allowed herself to breathe again. It had worked! She had merely held the notion of poison and the picture of the flaming spear in the forefront of her mind, and Dakkar had taken her thought as she had known he would. She smiled, at least she felt she had given Kolt a chance.

Kolt waited until Cal and Eadoine walked through the opening Morald created and the gap was once again sealed. Then slowly he drew his dagger.

Dakkar followed suit.

The two of them slowly circled each other.

She will be mine, usurper, Dakkar gloated, *when we are finished and you are life-ended*. He summoned an image of Aylyn, naked and pleasured, and hurled it up in the air above their heads.

Shock mutterings swept the crowd.

The vision shattered.

Dakkar tried again. This time all saw Aylyn crying over Kolt's mortally wounded body.

The mutterings grew louder.

And again the image was shattered.

Dakkar tried once more. He evoked an image he snatched from Kolt's mind. Aylyn lying in a pool of lifeblood, a dagger embedded in her chest.

Kolt gritted his teeth as the vision that haunted him blazed to full life for all to see.

"Enough!" Kolt roared, and with a blinding arc of light splintered the illusion.

Enough, usurper? Dakkar laughed, pleased that he had at last broken through Kolt's cool demeanor. *You will find I have just begun.* Dakkar called back the vision that pierced Kolt's control and tried to hurl it upward.

Tried and failed.

He tried again. And failed again.

Something was wrong! He reached out and touched nothingness.

"No!" he shrieked. "What have you done?"

"How like you the taste of your own vileness? How like you vxanza?"

"How—"

"You were careless, Dakkar. I was thorough. And now I have seen to it that your misuse of powers you should never have had will cease."

"You are foresworn, usurper, and thus unfit to rule. By your own word you vouchsafed my safety."

"From all but myself, Dakkar. From all save myself."

Enraged, Dakkar rushed at Kolt, his dagger slicing upward in deadly arc. Unhindered by emotion, Kolt easily sidestepped him.

"Is that the best you can do?" Kolt taunted. He tossed his blade from one hand to the other. "Do you find it less easy to strike a man when his back is not turned?"

Dakkar lunged again, this time his hand swinging across him in an effort to slice Kolt's chest. And the results were the same.

Kolt knew that Dakkar's emotions were controlling the fight and knew that he should end it quickly, but too long Dakkar had plagued him, his world, and the woman he loved. No, he would let Dakkar dance around him a little longer, let him experience a portion of the impotence, the fear that Dakkar's captives and victims had felt.

Dakkar looked into Kolt's smiling eyes and saw his life-ending.

Chapter Forty-Four

Aylyn gasped when Dakkar rushed Kolt, then breathed easily as Kolt remained untouched.

"He is well trained, my lady," Naydir said. "You've no need to fear for him."

"And will he fight with as much dishonor as Dakkar?"

Before Naydir could answer, a movement behind him drew his attention. He spun around, thrusting Aylyn behind him and the shielding.

"Iilde!" Naydir scowled. "How came you here?"

"I used the passageway from the cubiculum."

"It is guarded."

Iilde gestured with the sonulator. "Was guarded."

"What are you about?" Naydir demanded, not liking the wild look in her pink eyes or the weapon in her trembling hands.

"I have come for Aylyn."

"You cannot have her."

"You must come with me, Aylyn," Iilde cried desperately. "There are men within the keep. Men who seek to insure Dakkar's victory. They will kill Kolt."

"Kolt is well protected from treachery, Aylyn," Naydir said. "This is but a trap."

"No! Please, my lady, you must listen to me!"

"Why, Iilde?" Aylyn asked. "Why should I listen to someone who sought to take Kolt from me?"

"I have loved the laedan from the first time I saw him. I only sought to make him mine. I never wanted to hurt him. Dakkar..." Iilde's free hand rubbed at her forehead. "Dakkar did something to me. I tried to disobey him, but I couldn't." Her voice caught in her throat. "He hurt me."

Aylyn studied the tall woman before her. A woman she had no reason to believe, but nonetheless did. "Naydir, let me pass."

"No."

"Naydir, please. I must see to the attackers."

"I cannot let you go."

"Then you go."

"I cannot. I have sworn to Kolt that neither you nor I will leave this chamber."

"And if what she says is true?"

Naydir shook his head. "I do not believe her."

Aylyn drew the neutralizer that she always carried since Naydir had given it to her, and aimed it at Naydir's unprotected back.

"Forgive me," she said, and then fired.

Naydir slumped to the ground.

Aylyn drew off Naydir's gauntlet, slipped it on, and activated it. "Let's go, and as you can see, I am not afraid to use this. Keep that in mind should you play me false."

Iilde nodded, then led Aylyn through the passageway down to the cubiculum. The stunned guardsman still lay as she had left him.

"Where are the ambushers?" Aylyn demanded.

"There are four of them. They are spread out in the windows of the second level."

"How are they garbed?"

"As servers. But they will be the only servers armed with Blagdenian sonulators."

"Lead the way."

The first server was found with no problem and easily dispatched by Aylyn. The second by Iilde, who frowned down on him.

"This is a new face." She looked up at Aylyn. "There are still..." Whatever she was going to say was cut off by a blast from a sonulator. Aylyn didn't even wait

Golden Conquest

to see Iilde fall. She dropped to the ground, rolled, and fired. The assailant fell back into the passageway.

Fearing his body would alert his fellow ambushers, Aylyn raced to him and dragged him into the chamber. She shoved the door shut with her foot then ran to Iilde. It was then that she saw that the sonulator had not been set on stun. A large blackened area cornered most of Iilde's chest.

"Iilde," Aylyn called gently as she gathered the mortally wounded woman onto her lap.

Pink eyes flicked open. "Tell Kolt I am sorry," Iilde gasped weakly. "Tell him the Khry... Khrystallyn is his."

Aylyn's eyes blurred with tears. "Iilde, hold on, I will get help."

"No, find the others. It is too late for me."

Aylyn realized that what Iilde said was true. She gently lowered her to the ground and rose to her feet. "I will tell Kolt."

Iilde nodded, and before Aylyn closed the door to the chamber, Iilde knew no more.

Aylyn slowly crept down the passageway, her neutralizer held at ready. She tried to fight against the memory of Iilde and to concentrate on finding the other two attackers. Stealthily, she pushed open the doors to the next three chambers and found each of them empty. Her heart thudded louder with each empty chamber. Where were they? She gripped the neutralizer until her fingers were white-knuckled.

Only two more chambers lined this side of the keep. They had to be in one of these.

Her hand flat against the door, she eased it open.

And saw him leaning out the window with his weapon trained on some point below. She must have gasped, for he whirled.

"You!" Aylyn cried, recognizing Naydir's amulet. "Throw it across the flooring to me."

"Come and take it," he taunted.

"You were warned," Aylyn replied, and fired.

Patricia Roenbeck

The small thief never knew what hit him. His weapon clattered to the floor. Aylyn cautiously approached him. She nudged him with her toe, then jerked her wrist and deactivated the gauntlet's shielding so that she could remove the amulet without putting down her weapon. She had just slipped it from his neck when she heard the sound of chuckling.

"What have we here?"

Aylyn spun and fired. But she was not quick enough. The dagger hurled by the ambusher before he fell victim to her weapon's blast flew true. She cried out in pain as it buried itself deep within her chest.

Kolt's arm shot out and he grasped Dakkar's wrist, stopping its deadly plunge.

Kolt!

Kolt jerked away as Aylyn's pained cry reached him. Blindly, he shoved Dakkar from him as he saw what Aylyn saw—the dagger handle sticking out of her chest. And then blackness.

"You killed her!" Kolt roared. He arched with his dagger just as Dakkar rushed him. Kolt's blade ripped through Dakkar's shirt, tore through skin and muscle, and lodged in his heart all in one smooth motion. Kolt watched dispassionately as Dakkar staggered backwards, his hands working desperately to free the blade. Desperately but futilely. He took two last steps, then fell backwards, dead.

Aylyn! Kolt *actualized* to the chamber he had seen through Aylyn's eyes. Though he had seen the sight a thousand times since it had first come to him, nothing had prepared him for the reality. His heart slammed in his chest as he saw her sprawled on the ground, her lifeblood pouring from her.

"Aylyn!" *Aylyn, my love, can you hear me?* He ran to her. Gently, he cradled her head in his lap. He flicked a finger at the knife, and it flew from its deadly resting place. Tearing a long piece from his tunic, he made a wad of the soft material. Pressing it to the gaping wound, he was able to slow the gushing blood.

Golden Conquest

"Aylyn, my mind's love," he rasped, his voice ragged with unshed tears.

Her breath coming in short shallow gasps, Aylyn's eyes fluttered open. "Kolt?"

"I'm here, softling."

"You are well?"

She worried for him? Not trusting his voice, he only nodded.

"That is good." She tried to move her arm, but found that she could not. But she did succeed in opening her hand. Kolt's anguished gaze moved to her hand and the glistening amulet within it. "Take it."

He closed her hand around it. "You give it to him."

"I think not." She drew in a ragged breath, then grimaced. "By all the gods, this dying does not come easy."

Kolt's heart contracted. "No. Do not speak so."

"It is the truth. You must see . . ." Aylyn closed her eyes as another spasm tore through her.

Kolt gritted his teeth as her pain became his, and he wished with every unencumbered breath he took that he was the one wounded. The one . . . No! Not even now would he say it. But he knew! Gods! He knew! And he cursed the fates that were about to take his love from him.

"Don't want to leave you." Desperately wanting to touch his face one last time, Aylyn struggled to lift her arm, but the effort proved too much, and her hand dropped limply to the ground.

Kolt blinked at the unfamiliar moisture in his eyes and shook his head. "Don't leave me, softling," he pleaded.

"I love you." Golden eyes closed and Aylyn's head sagged to the side.

"Nooo! Do not leave me! Do not!"

His face twisted in anguish and his eyes alight with dark fires, Kolt leaned over Aylyn and extended his arms, open palms down a hand-span from her chest. His eyes closed, he left the physical world and entered the inner plane of life energy.

Patricia Roenbeck

He saw the life strands that held Aylyn's essence to her body rapidly dissolving. He reached out and grasped the edges just as they sundered completely.

A warm blue-white radiance flowed through him, out through his hands to the sundered strands. Slowly, they began to grow and weave together. The thin strands knitted until they were thicker and stronger than before.

Satisfied that Aylyn would live a long life, Kolt started to withdraw, but stopped when a warm glow pulsating in her lower belly caught his attention.

He drew in a sharp breath as the realization of what it meant struck him. A child. Their child! That it pulsed so strongly told him all was well. The babe had not been affected by the blow that had almost destroyed its mother. Kolt shuddered. In one stroke, he was almost robbed of his love and his child. But fate had been with him, and, the gods willing, the three of them would share a long life of love and peace.

Resisting the urge to take a closer look at his child, Kolt returned to the physical world. Aylyn's weary eyes opened. Kolt smiled, pleased with his handiwork, for her chest was as unmarked and beautiful as ever. Gently, he gathered her to him and pressed a tender kiss to her forehead. In that moment he decided he would keep his knowledge of their babe a secret. He would not rob her of her right to tell him. It was the way of things.

"My love." Aylyn was staring up at him in wonder. She knew she should not be alive.

"I could not permit you to leave me," Kolt said huskily. His eyes darkened, and his voice grew rough with emotion. "You are my mind's love. Life without you would be no life at all."

Chapter Forty-Five

Aylyn paced. Kolt paced. Naydir watched, puzzled.

Aylyn walked to the terrace door and looked down at the garden. Kolt walked to the terrace door and looked down at the garden. Naydir watched, still puzzled.

He thought their pacing and waiting had something to do with the mission Kolt had chosen Cal for. A mission Naydir should have gone on. Not for the first time, he wondered if Kolt was as disappointed and distressed with him as he was with himself. He had failed Aylyn. Again, he thought and believed, though both Kolt and Aylyn tried to convince him otherwise. Aylyn insisted that he could not have expected her to shoot him, and Kolt insisted that naught Naydir could have done would have prevented what had happened. More than likely, he had said, Aylyn's stunning him had saved his life. Yet, why had Cal gone and not him? And why were they surreptitiously sending glances at him and refusing to telling him aught?

"Do you tell me what this is all about?" Naydir finally asked.

"No," Aylyn and Kolt replied together as they had replied before.

Naydir shook his head. For the last two hours he had watched them pace and look and pace and look. The only break had been when he had reminded them of the time and they had gone into the sleeping chamber to dress.

And now they stood, hand in hand, waiting. Ah, but what a sight they made, he thought. Clothed in a delicate irridescent material that caught and reflected the light, the lovers looked as if they were veiled in a rainbow. Kolt had replaced his usual leggings and jerkin with loose, ankle-length pants worn over his boots and a sleeveless loose shirt that fastened over his right shoulder, leaving his left shoulder and both arms bare. His dark hair hung unbound to his back. It was the traditional garb of the Annanite Bonding Ceremony, but it made Kolt look like the warrior god of Varyr. Naydir smiled. And Aylyn was a fit mate. Her long flowing gown clung to her full breasts and narrow waist and was fastened over her left shoulder. Like Kolt, her other shoulder and arms were bare.

Perhaps, Naydir thought with not a small amount of hope, perhaps they were experiencing pre-bonding jitters and a reaction to Aylyn's near life-ending but a few days before. And they were thinking of the reunion with her parents and brother. And Laaryc. Or the glimpses of his past that had been haunting his dreams since Kolt had freed the barrier. Naydir cursed. All his conjecturing amounted to naught. He would have to bide his time and wait for Kolt to explain.

Aylyn caught a glimpse of Laaryc in the garden, off to the side, his arm around the lovely beauty he had life-bonded with. He laughed at something Mayryn said, and Aylyn smiled. It had been a tearful but joyous meeting of friends when Laaryc and Mayryn arrived from Dianthia. Aylyn had quickly found the short-haired Mayryn a charming match for her best friend.

"You don't mind?" Kolt asked, as he saw the object of Aylyn's gaze.

"How could I mind when it has always been only you. You knew it. He knew it. And I knew it, only it took me a little longer than the rest of you to catch on." She leaned on tiptoe and kissed him. "I love you, Kolt. Only you."

Kolt was just about to kiss her back when he caught sight of the prearranged signal. Cal was here.

"Naydir, it is time."

"It pleases me that you do this," Aylyn whispered to Kolt. "Naydir has done so much for you, for us." Then she moved away from Kolt to Naydir. She studied him, making sure all was perfect. And as always it was. His tall form was garbed in the black tunic shirt and pants Aylyn had requested that he wear. And around his neck hung the amulet that had almost cost her her life. She kissed his cheek, then turned to see Kolt standing in the open terrace doorway. She took Naydir's hand and led him to Kolt. Then she slipped her arm through Kolt's, and the three of them walked out onto the terrace.

"My friends," Kolt's deep rich voice reached out to the small group of friends and family gathered below in the garden. As one, all eyes raised to Kolt. "May I present to you Naydir, Cyning of Aingeal."

Naydir turned to Kolt, stunned. "Then it is true? What I have been seeing these past days?" he asked hoarsely.

Kolt smiled at Naydir. "Did I not tell you you would remember?"

"Yes. But do you tell me now how was it that I forgot?"

"Dakkar feared you would reveal his identity and since he could not life-end you, though he tried, he saw you double-shielded. I broke the shields the other day, but I could do or say no more. Forcing your memory to return may have sent you into a true memory block."

Naydir and Kolt locked forearms in a firm grip of friendship. "All I have is yours, Kolt."

"All?" Kolt asked, his eyes twinkling.

Naydir nodded. "For giving me back my identity, all you ask of me will be naught compared to what you have given me."

Kolt's smile deepened. "Then what will you give me for this?" he teased, and swept his hand toward the center of the crowd.

Naydir turned slowly, and before he finished the turn, he was standing on the ground. Behind him stood a beaming Aylyn and Kolt, and twenty hand-spans in front of him a petite and fragile beauty.

Naydir's heart slammed into his chest. "Cayri?" he rasped, unable to believe it was she.

She nodded, her black oval eyes glistening with tears.

"Cayri!" Naydir roared her name, and then he was holding her, lifting her to him. His mouth crushed down on hers and he felt all that he remembered. When he finally raised his head, his amber eyes were moist, and his voice was rough with emotion. "Cayri, how I have missed you. I was always so empty inside and I knew not why." He pressed her close to him, his hand brushing her ear-length black hair. "How came you here?"

Through watery eyes, she smiled up at him and tried to speak but found her throat too clogged with emotion to allow words.

"Cal brought her," Kolt explained.

"I saw your face, Naydir," Cayri said softly, her voice at last free of her tears. "And I heard a voice that told me you needed me and wondered if I needed you." She gave a short, choked laugh. "As I needed air I told the voice. And then I saw Cal's face. The voice said he would come and bring me to you."

Naydir searched for Cal and found him standing off to the side. In his large furred hand, he held the hand of a small boy with hair of black and eyes of amber. His throat tight with emotion, Naydir knelt and slowly stretched out his arms. And the son he never knew he had ran into them.

A short time later, they were all gathered beneath the sun, amid the lushness of the Garden of Colors, cooled by a soft breeze that carried the spicy fragrance of the vyarli blossom and serenaded by the gentle thunder of

Golden Conquest

the Rainbow Falls and Mikki's excited thrumming.

"Kolt, Laedan of Annan, and his chosen Lady," Morald announced as Kolt and Aylyn appeared at the entrance to the garden.

"I cannot believe you will at last be mine," Kolt said as he looked down on the woman he had loved for so long.

"I have always been yours, my laedan," Aylyn replied truthfully. "Always."

They walked down an aisle created by the elite guard, preceded by Morald and flanked by Naydir, as best friend to Kolt, and Laaryc, as best friend to Aylyn.

"Oh, Aubin." Eirriel sighed as her daughter and her chosen mate glided past her.

Aubin enfolded Eirriel in his arms, pulling her against his chest. "She is a beauty, this daughter of ours."

Eirriel leaned her head back. "That she is, my love."

"Almost as much as Kolt is," Alaran quipped.

"Behave, cubling!" Aubin growled, the lights in his eyes belying his fierce glower.

"And if I do not, will you exile me to Chaslydon?" Alaran asked, gathering a flustered Chiela to him.

Alaran had only returned three days before, retrieved by an embarrassed Aylyn, who admitted to forgetting about him. He had snarled and growled and promised to make her pay, until Chiela had stepped out from behind him. Then Aylyn had laughed and told Alaran that she had known he would enjoy Chaslydon.

All chatter ceased as Aylyn and Kolt stopped near the water's edge and turned and faced each other. Naydir and Laaryc moved around them and stood facing the crowd. In their hands they held the flat circular prism crystals on which the three bonding symbols rested.

From Naydir, Kolt picked up the armlet—a black crystal kilgra leaping across a band of faceted diamond crystal, its eyes and uni-horn brilliant safirium.

"Know you this, Aylyn of Rhianon," he said, his eyes dark with love, his voice intense. "For now and for all eternity, you and no other shall be the love of my body"—he clipped the armlet on her right upper arm—"of my heart"—he fastened a teardrop safirium crystal around her neck—"and of my soul"—he placed the circlet of safirium around her forehead—"so do I pledge."

From Laaryc, Aylyn picked up the mate of the armlet Kolt had just given her, with one exception. As with all the symbols Aylyn would present to Kolt, the safirium would be replaced with golithium.

Her golden eyes bright, her voice husky, she said proudly, "Know you this, Kolt, Laedan of Annan and my own mind's love, for now and for all eternity, you and no other shall be the love of my body"—she clipped the armlet on his upper left arm—"of my heart"—she fastened the choker of golithium around his neck—"and of my soul"—and slipped the circlet into place—"so I do pledge."

Led by Morald and his men, the small group of family and friends broke into cheers as Kolt's hand shot out and he drew Aylyn to him and kissed her.

When at last he raised his head, he murmured, in a voice ragged with emotion, "The gods have truly given me their blessing, softling. They have given me you."

And he kissed her then, with his lips and his mind. A strong gentle caress of passion. Of possession. Of love.

Of a promised destiny fulfilled.

Futuristic Romance

Love in Another Time, Another Place...

Golden Temptress

PATRICIA ROENBECK

The moment his men bring the mysterious green-eyed woman from an enemy transport, Aubin wants to make the provocative stranger his own. And Eirriel longs to lose herself in his hard, muscled embrace. But she has vowed to stop the invaders who threaten her world—even if it means leaving the virile rescuer whose mere touch arouses a burning desire like none she has ever felt.

_3111-6 $3.95 US/$4.95 CAN

LEISURE BOOKS
ATTN: Order Department
276 5th Avenue, New York, NY 10001

Please add $1.50 for shipping and handling for the first book and $.35 for each book thereafter. N.Y.S. and N.Y.C. residents, please add appropriate sales tax. No cash, stamps, or C.O.D.s. All orders shipped within 6 weeks via postal service book rate. Canadian orders require $2.00 extra postage. It must also be paid in U.S. dollars through a U.S. banking facility.

Name _____
Address _____
City _____ State _____ Zip _____
I have enclosed $_____in payment for the checked book(s).
Payment <u>must</u> accompany all orders. ☐ Please send a free catalog.

SPEND YOUR LEISURE MOMENTS WITH US.

Hundreds of exciting titles to choose from—something for everyone's taste in fine books: breathtaking historical romance, chilling horror, spine-tingling suspense, taut medical thrillers, involving mysteries, action-packed men's adventure and wild Westerns.

SEND FOR A FREE CATALOGUE TODAY!

Leisure Books
Attn: Customer Service Department
276 5th Avenue, New York, NY 10001